FLOWERS AND GEMSTONES

What Reviewers Say About Alaina Erdell's Work

All Things Beautiful

"There's so much to love about this story. The characters are vibrant and well-developed, the story beautifully crafted and multi-layered, and the backdrop of the art world depicted so skillfully it drew me into its beauty and depth. …If you like a romance with depth that reflects how falling in love weaves into the fabric of our lives, this book is for you."
—*Lesbian Review*

"Every time Leighton and Casey are on page together, magic happens."
—*Jude in the Stars*

"[I] could not put this book down. …With a plot that moves from educational and emotional to suspenseful and steamy, *All Things Beautiful* is a heartfelt journey of finding and following the path that truly makes you happy."—*Queer Aussie Reviews*

"The book's smartly-crafted prose and well-developed characters lend themselves to an enjoyable and captivating read, one that hooks readers from beginning to end. …Filled with the complexities of life, the beauty of art, and the joy of finding true love, this heartwarming love story is an absorbing and enjoyable read"—*Women Using Words*

"From the art details to the MCs chemistry to the suspense, it was absolutely incredible."—*lesbereading*

"I was beyond invested in these characters and seeing how this story played out. …Erdell has a way of truly pulling you into all elements of the story with her descriptive writing. I absolutely cannot wait to read more of Erdell's books!"—*Queer AFictionado*

"Erdell is amazing at writing books about what she knows, and it shows so well with her knowledge of painting and art. I know nothing about the art world, and Erdell made it easy to follow and I even learned some things."—*Jess Reads With Pride*

Two Women, Two Weddings, *novella in* **Hot Hires**

"[Alaina Erdell] never misses with her work. One of the things that readers appreciate about Erdell is the way she weaves her unique passions into her storytelling. She has a real knack for captivating readers with the details. …Erdell demonstrates that she knows how to create believable tension while keeping the romance fun. Her vivid descriptions and fluid prose add so much life to the storytelling. Erdell may have just recently cut her teeth in this business, but she's proven she's quite comfortable on the page. Whether it's a full-length novel or a short story, she always provides a pleasurable read."—*Women Using Words*

"All the stories were fantastic and I enjoyed them thoroughly. They took me through a range of emotions, and have left me hoping these wonderful characters are going to turn up in future stories."—*LesBIreviewed*

"This was my first taste of Erdell's writing & will undoubtedly come back for more. With family expectations & drama, this novella gave me everything I didn't know I was craving."—*Station12reads*

"Alaina writes such wonderful chemistry between the characters in her books and this read was no different!"—*BlossomBookish*

"It is a delightful read, and I particularly appreciated the portrayal of the Indian wedding ceremony. The vivid descriptions painted a beautiful picture in my mind."—*Lez.be.readin.ya*

Off the Menu

"In terms of the actual writing, Erdell has an easy-to-read writing style. She excels at creating chemistry between the main characters and she is not afraid to have the characters do things that are not necessarily in line with expectations around romance novels. …I like the way Erdell writes chemistry. I loved the restaurant setting and how awesome it was to have such a realistic feel for it. …Erdell's books explore genuine character flaws rather than romanticised ones and I am here for it."
—*Lesbian Review*

"The frying pan isn't the only thing sizzling in the kitchen—the heat between Taylor and Erin is palpable in this contemporary romance, brimming with drama and effervescent characters. ...One of the best books I've read in some time—five gleaming stars!"—*Reader Views*

"Erdell's writing style is engaging and thought-provoking, leaving the readers with a lasting impression of the power of understanding and collaboration in both the kitchen and in relationships."—*Literary Titan*

Fire, Water, and Rock

"Erdell's love for the desert flowed out of the story like a love poem. One of my highlights of the book was getting to discover the setting through the author's words."—*Lesbian Review*

"When I read a book with themes that I know next to nothing about and the narrative makes me want to go investigate. ...Well, credit must go to that writer. This is Erdell's first published novel and one can easily see the passion she has for storytelling. Using colorful language and vivid detail, she immerses her readers in an impressive story world. Erdell's debut is a compelling and read-worthy tale; it's definitely a sign of exciting things to come."—*Women Loving Words*

Visit us at www.boldstrokesbooks.com

By the Author

Fire, Water, and Rock

Off the Menu

All Things Beautiful

Flowers and Gemstones

Two Women, Two Weddings novella in Hot Hires

FLOWERS AND GEMSTONES

by
Alaina Erdell

2025

FLOWERS AND GEMSTONES
© 2025 BY ALAINA ERDELL. ALL RIGHTS RESERVED.

ISBN 13: 978-1-63679-745-8

THIS TRADE PAPERBACK ORIGINAL IS PUBLISHED BY
BOLD STROKES BOOKS, INC.
P.O. BOX 249
VALLEY FALLS, NY 12185

FIRST EDITION: FEBRUARY 2025

THIS IS A WORK OF FICTION. NAMES, CHARACTERS, PLACES, AND INCIDENTS ARE THE PRODUCT OF THE AUTHOR'S IMAGINATION OR ARE USED FICTITIOUSLY. ANY RESEMBLANCE TO ACTUAL PERSONS, LIVING OR DEAD, BUSINESS ESTABLISHMENTS, EVENTS, OR LOCALES IS ENTIRELY COINCIDENTAL.

THIS BOOK, OR PARTS THEREOF, MAY NOT BE REPRODUCED IN ANY FORM WITHOUT PERMISSION.

CREDITS
EDITOR: CINDY CRESAP
PRODUCTION DESIGN: SUSAN RAMUNDO
COVER DESIGN BY INKSPIRAL DESIGN

Acknowledgments

I'd like to thank Radclyffe for the initial chance and the continued opportunities to do my dream job; Sandy Lowe for the helpful insights and the good sense simply to say no to me once in a while; my editor, Cindy Cresap, for her keen eye and ability to catch mistakes for which I should know better and yet still make; and Ruth Sternglantz for all her help with my various questions and attempts at marketing. I'd also like to thank Toni Whitaker, Susan Ramundo, Stacia Seaman, Gina Miller, and all the folks with Bold Strokes Books who make our words into beautiful books and ebooks and get them out into the world. Thanks to Inkspiral Design for the gorgeous cover, my favorite to date.

My writing group is a continued source of inspiration and assistance I couldn't do without. Thank you. I'd like to thank BC for her support and for joining me at events and making them even more fun. I'm so grateful for the reader friends and writer friends I've made—too many to list—who have supported me, alpha or beta read, been my emergency website servicer, or who have enjoyed my books and told their friends about them. Special shout-outs to WW, MH, RA, JE, JL, DSL, AG, BC, ASM, KM, JH, SM, DS, and JG.

My heartfelt thanks to the readers who have read my books, and especially those who have reached out to tell me they enjoyed my writing or that one of my stories meant something to them. As a writer, there's not much better than that. Thank you all for your support. And I'm so grateful that I've been able to meet so many of you at events. It's been my honor.

And lastly, thanks to Callie for encouraging me to write and reminding me to take breaks. I couldn't do it without you.

Dedication

For A, with love

Part One

Part One

Chapter One

Like the rain often did in Seattle, it sprinkled over the city and trickled down Hannah's windshield. As she slowed to a stop for a red light, she unclenched her fingers from the steering wheel and fumbled in her purse for the sheet of paper. The rhythmic whooshing of the wiper blades quickened her pulse. She only had time for one more glance at her notes. By now, Bren would be home from her conference in San Francisco.

Hannah had rehearsed what she wanted to say throughout the day, but seeing the words on the page helped calm her racing heart. Only a few more blocks. She silently mouthed each line and smiled. Everything would be different after tonight.

The driver behind her honked, and Hannah jumped. A green light. She dropped the paper onto the passenger's seat and pulled into the intersection. Sweat covered her palms. She was doing this. Today was the day.

When she turned the corner, the back of her neck prickled. Bren's car wasn't there, and a Washington State Patrol SUV stood at the curb. Its lights weren't flashing, but two troopers in rain jackets waited on the sidewalk.

Hannah's neck prickled. Whatever was happening, she wouldn't be breaking up with Bren this evening.

She pulled into the driveway, and in the seconds it took to kill the engine and release her seat belt, they'd crossed the yard and met her as she climbed out of her car.

"Good afternoon, ma'am. Do you live here?" The woman came slightly closer than the mustached young man.

"Yes." Hannah looked between them. "What's wrong?"

"May we see your identification?"

She dug in her purse for her wallet, then presented her ID.

The trooper glanced at it, nodded, and handed it back.

"What's your relationship with Brenda McAvoy?"

"She's my girlfriend. Why?" Hannah swayed and grabbed the top of the car door to steady herself. Too many scenarios flooded her mind.

The woman shifted her weight to her other foot. "I'm afraid there was a pileup on I-5 this afternoon. I'm sorry to inform you Ms. McAvoy died in the accident."

Hannah's vision blurred, and their voices seemed to fade in and out.

"Here, I'll put the stuff back in your bag. Just sit."

Her knees weakening, Hannah eased into the driver's seat. When had she dropped her purse? It'd stopped raining. Why that stood out to her, she didn't know.

"Ms. Baros, did she have any other family?"

Hannah shook her head. "No, no one." It was uncomfortable sitting sideways behind the steering wheel. When she tried to stand again and pitched forward, strong arms caught her.

"Let's get you inside."

Only vaguely aware of the troopers on either side of her as they all made their way up the walk, Hannah succumbed to the images that invaded her mind. The digital marketing conference three years ago when she'd met Bren. Their late-night dinner dates due to their mutually busy work schedules. The day Bren had shown her the house she'd picked out for them, the one into which Hannah was now being led. Warm fingers slipped the keys from her hand. Bren's suitcase had been missing from the hall closet so often that Hannah had wondered if she was having an affair. Why had Hannah waited so long? She should've broken up with Bren two years ago.

Now it was too late. *Now* it didn't matter.

"Ma'am, you need to turn off the alarm."

Hannah blinked. She hadn't heard the shrill blare until the woman squeezed her forearm. She autonomically entered the code.

Silence fell like an anvil. Her life that should've been so different after today, so much brighter after she walked away from this withered relationship, was now changed forever. Her traumatized mind couldn't fathom it.

"Ma'am, can you hear me?"

Hannah looked up from where she slumped on the couch. How had she gotten there? Where had the glass of water in her hand come from? She straightened. "Yes."

"Who can we call for you?"

She looked around. "My phone. I think it's in my purse in the car."

The man stepped into the entryway and retrieved it. "It's right here. We brought it in. If you'll just unlock it, we'll do it for you."

The woman kneeled before her. "Ms. Baros, look at me. Who should we call?"

Hannah lifted the glass she held, the spots from the dishwasher capturing her attention. Bren never would've used it in this condition.

"Ms. Baros. Who?"

Hannah raised her gaze, bringing the woman's dark features slowly into focus. "Zara," she whispered. She needed her best friend.

❖

Hannah pulled another glass from the dishwasher and buffed it with a towel so hard it squeaked. After she held it up to the light to ensure its surface gleamed, she slid it into the open cupboard.

Nothing made sense. She stood in her kitchen in a suit and heels on a Friday night cleaning spots from glassware her girlfriend would never drink from again. She'd been told Bren died at the scene, her death likely instantaneous. That's all Hannah had needed from the troopers, the knowledge that Bren hadn't suffered.

A key scraped in the lock, then the front door slammed, but Hannah didn't turn.

"Han? Where are you?" Zara's heels rapidly click-clacked across the tiled floor.

"Kitchen." She pulled out another glass.

Zara rushed in. "I got here as fast as I could." She wrapped her in a hug, trapping a drink tumbler between them. "You poor thing. I can't imagine what you're going through."

No, she couldn't, because while Hannah cared about Bren and certainly never wished her harm, she wasn't devastated like she should be. The thought made her chest ache in an entirely new way. Bren was—had been—her girlfriend, even if their relationship had been tumultuous and run its course long ago. Hannah wished she felt more, but she'd already given up on their relationship. Hannah had grieved the loss of Bren back then. Unfortunately, she'd been too wrapped up in her work and stupidly hadn't taken care of the situation when she should've.

Zara held her at arm's length. "Have you cried?"

Like Hannah, Zara still wore what she'd worn to the office that day, her violet dress and chartreuse scarf only slightly wrinkled. The fact that she'd clearly rushed over straight from work touched Hannah. Zara was more than her VP of marketing. They'd met in college and had been friends ever since. Zara must've run inside without an umbrella. The rain and humidity had frizzed her ebony hair that had been sleek and straight earlier.

Hannah shook her head and stepped from Zara's embrace. "No." Afraid Zara might see the truth in her eyes, sorrow but not heartbreak, she returned to her task. Disclosing her embarrassing secret to her best friend, her plan to break up with Bren the same day she'd been killed, sounded so heartless. No, she'd keep it to herself. No good would come from sharing the awful fact, and the result was the same. She'd wanted out of the relationship, and now she was free to move on with her life.

Zara pulled her by the hand down the hallway toward her bedroom. "First things first. We're going to change into something more comfortable. Where would I find sweats or pajamas?"

"Third drawer. If you want leggings, top shelf, left side of the closet." The right held Bren's clothing, items Hannah would eventually have to address. She sat, too numb to figure out what to do next.

"Take that off." Zara wiggled a finger at her before pulling open the drawer. "Here's a top, and oh, even matching bottoms." She threw both on the bed beside Hannah and disappeared into the closet.

Hannah undressed, ignoring Bren's navy robe hanging on the back of the door. By the time she'd put on her pajamas, Zara had emerged wearing leggings that didn't quite make it to her ankles and a faded, decades-old sweatshirt from their days at the University of Washington.

Zara draped their work clothes over the upholstered chair near the window. She pulled Hannah to her feet and thrust a pair of socks at her. "You're going to sit, and I'm going to scrounge up something for us to eat."

"No." Hannah shook her head but followed Zara downstairs. "No food."

Zara searched her face with evident concern. "Is your stomach upset? It's perfectly normal in this kind of situation."

Situation. That was certainly a name for whatever this was. No, she didn't recoil at the thought of food. Her eleven o'clock meeting had run long, so she'd only had time for a power bar for lunch. If she thought about it too much, her belly might even rumble. "I'd just rather not eat."

Zara scrunched her forehead. "Why? You should. Life's going to be emotionally draining for a bit, hon. You can't let yourself get physically run down, too." She opened the refrigerator like the argument had been settled.

Hannah slid onto a stool on the other side of the island. "You'll think it's stupid."

With a glance over her shoulder, Zara raised an eyebrow. "Doubtful. Remember, I was there when you vomited off the second-floor balcony of that frat house and hit all those poor ducks below." When Hannah didn't answer, Zara closed the refrigerator and leaned on her forearms across from her. "You can tell me anything. You know I love you no matter what, and if I didn't hold your incident involving your atrocious treatment of our feathered friends against you, you're probably safe from my judgment on anything."

Hannah wished she *could* tell her everything. That's what you're supposed to be able to do with your best friend. The only thing she'd really kept from Zara in all their years of friendship was how empty her relationship with Bren had become. Although, Zara had always been perceptive and probably had an inkling of her discontent. But this—*My girlfriend was killed before I could break up with her today, so I'm not heartbroken*—made her sound certifiable.

Zara squeezed her hand, still waiting.

Hannah avoided eye contact and studied her pale skin against Zara's tanned fingers. "I don't want to remember this day every time I eat whatever food you're going to make." Past painful experiences had linked everyday innocuous things, like food, to times of great sorrow. To this day, she couldn't look at a bag of barbecue-flavored potato chips without recalling the day they'd buried her grandmother. It had been the one thing she'd been able to eat at the reception when everything else had turned her stomach.

"Okay, then. Fair enough." Zara straightened. "That's easy. You need to eat, so I'll make something you don't like. Then you won't have that issue in the future." She slapped her hand on the counter. "And no arguing. I saw what you ate for lunch."

Hannah zoned out, lost in her thoughts, while Zara tried to determine what unlikable dish to cook.

"When's the last time either of you bought groceries?" Zara turned from the open refrigerator with a look of horror on her face. "Sorry."

Behind Zara, Hannah spotted the photo of her and Bren in Port Orchard on the freezer's door. They looked happy, but Hannah remembered feeling Bren's distance and secrecy even then. The trip had been almost two years ago come Memorial Day, an effort to reconnect. It hadn't helped.

"Hannah."

She snapped her attention to Zara.

"Should I take the picture down?" Zara touched it.

Hannah inhaled. "No, but you could help me when it comes time to pack up her things." This morning, she'd been wondering if it'd be her or Bren putting their belongings into boxes come the weekend. She'd assumed her. Bren had been the one to push for them moving in together and picked out the place. Hannah, being so busy at work, hadn't had time for house hunting. She'd never felt at home here, and now she'd be the one left having to deal with breaking their lease as well as cleaning everything out.

Thirty minutes later, Zara set a bowl of something unrecognizable in front of her. "Sorry." Her grimace didn't bode well for Hannah getting much of the food into her.

"What exactly is it?" Hannah pushed it around with her fork. It smelled nasty.

Zara gave her a pained expression. "It doesn't really have a name. I found a bag of spaetzle in the back of your pantry, and I've never known you to eat it in all the years we've been friends, so I thought it'd be safe. There was a tin of anchovies next to it, and a bag of frozen peas hiding behind the plant-based meatballs."

The mushy green dots stared up at Hannah from the beige mass. She forced down a gag. "Bren bought them."

Zara sailed past the mention of Bren without apologizing for the twentieth time. "I figured. I know you like them fresh. So, you get veggies, carbs, and a little protein. A balanced meal."

Hannah took a bite and rested her head against Zara's shoulder.

"How is it?" Zara's fork hovered above her bowl.

With more force than necessary, Hannah swallowed the salty mouthful. "It's truly awful. Thank you. I'll definitely never eat this again."

Zara put an arm around her. "You're welcome. I'm staying the night, and I'll be here for you as long as you need me, okay?"

Hannah straightened. "Thank you. I don't know if I could get through this without you." She meant it. No value could be put on Zara's friendship. The coming weeks and months wouldn't be easy, especially developing the new line at work. With Bren having no family, Hannah would have to write an obituary, plan a funeral, pack up Bren's things as well as her own, and move. God, she didn't even know if Bren wanted a burial or cremation. Important things like that certainly hadn't been discussed when Bren disclosed next to nothing about normal things like her family or her prior relationships. Procrastination had bitten Hannah in the ass before, but she'd outdone herself this time. It left her with an overwhelming feeling of sadness. Sadness that someone had been taken from this world so young, at the failed state of their relationship, and the regret she hadn't let Bren go sooner.

Chapter Two

Vanessa glanced up as Chloe entered the cold room. Like Vanessa, she wore an emerald shirt with the Late Bloomer Florist & Gifts logo.

Chloe stopped short, as if surprised to see her. "What're you doing?" She planted her fists on her hips.

Vanessa waved her gloved hand at the buckets before her. "Stripping roses, obviously."

"Nah, girl. It's Friday, my day." Chloe tied up her straight, dark hair and nudged Vanessa aside with a shoulder bump. "You're on funerals. The folder's on your desk along with doughnuts fresh out of the oil at five forty-five."

With a glance at the large wall calendar that held all their big orders, Vanessa pulled off her gloves. Beside it, the pinkish hues through the window gave evidence of the rising sun. She hoped it'd be one of those special clear days that Seattle didn't get enough of, where if she had time to look, she'd spot the Cascades in the distance in one direction and the Olympics in the other. Not to mention majestic Mount Rainier to the south. "Well, score one for me today. Two, if you count bringing me breakfast. Thanks, Clo." Too bad Vanessa's shoes were already soaked through from when she'd knocked over a bucket. She stifled a yawn as she entered her office, her Converses squelching with every step.

With a cruller in one hand, Vanessa flipped through the funeral orders. Chloe had already found the obituaries and printed them. Vanessa liked to have a little background on the deceased, so no potential faux pas occurred. Only three this weekend. Nothing they couldn't manage. Three people, that was. The tiny sprays needed for the funeral they'd done last month for the family of four killed in an accident still haunted her. Adults she could handle. A ninety-two-year-old pastor, a woman who died in a house fire, and—

The letters blurred on the page, and the doughnut bounced off her thigh and onto the floor. The sweet mouthful threatened to choke her, so she spit it into a tissue. With one hand flat on the desk to steady herself, she grabbed her glasses and read it again. No. It couldn't be. It had to be someone else with the same name, of the same age. But Vanessa already knew it was her.

Brenda McAvoy, her ex-girlfriend, had died.

Chloe burst in, the door banging against the stopper. She glanced at the floor, then at Vanessa. "If you didn't like it, you could've just thrown it away. Hey, why are you so pale?" When she didn't respond, Chloe stepped beside her to look at the piece of paper. "What?"

It was shaking. *Vanessa* was shaking. She dropped it onto the folder. "I know her—knew her."

"I'm so sorry." Chloe gave her shoulder a reassuring squeeze. "Were you close?"

Close? As close as she'd ever been to anyone. "We used to date." When she'd hired Chloe as the store's manager three years ago, Bren had already exited Vanessa's life.

Chloe picked up the doughnut and threw it away. "Hey, why don't you let me do funerals? We can finish the roses together. Cai gets here at seven, and he can help before he washes the buckets."

"No." Vanessa stared at the obituary. *Preceded in death by her parents, Jonah and Adelaide McAvoy. Survived by her partner, Hannah Baros.* She'd had a girlfriend. "I need to do this one."

Chloe huffed, whether out of irritation or acceptance, Vanessa wasn't sure. "Okay, but I'm getting you some water, and you're going to drink it. Your coloring is translucent on a good day, and you're scaring me right now."

Vanessa nodded, still staring at the printout. Bren was dead. And Vanessa was doing the flowers for her funeral. What strange, coincidental tricks life played on people.

Chloe brought her a glass of water and silently stood watching until apparently satisfied with Vanessa's intake. "Try to eat a few bites." She pointed to the box of pastries. "We need you on your feet today. Dorothy's off for her daughter's graduation. It's going to be busy, and you still look like you might keel over."

Vanessa had no words. She could only nod again as Chloe left, though she had no intention of putting anything in her churning stomach. Memories rushed in, one after another. She'd tried to forget them, work through them, push them from her daily existence. The pain Bren had left her with. The paralyzing grief and devastating betrayal that had spiraled until they'd consumed her. The questions never answered. And her mother, making everything worse. She'd been there that day with her cutting remarks, and her voice continued to be in Vanessa's head.

You can't hide from the truth. Ran away as soon as you could and got your fancy college degree. Think you're better than all of us back here. But there's no escaping it, is there? Even your girlfriend doesn't want you. What happened? Did she find out you're trash after all?

Vanessa closed her eyes and clenched her jaw. One deep breath, two, then three. At ten, when the voice had quieted, she looked at the paper again.

With sudden clarity, Vanessa decided she'd attend Bren's funeral and face her demons head-on. No one would recognize her. All their friends had remained hers after their breakup, and she'd only met one of Bren's colleagues, an officer of the company who'd since moved on. And Bren had no family. If this wasn't the perfect way to get closure, Vanessa wasn't sure what was.

CHAPTER THREE

Hannah shivered as the swirling wind seeped through her thin jacket, but at least the rain had stopped. It'd left the ground waterlogged, though, and the cemetery crew had laid rolls of artificial grass on which the mourners could stand. The smell of fresh-turned earth and the perfume of the flowers on the casket and nearby standing sprays filled the air. Beside her, Zara gripped her hand.

As the minister spoke words Hannah only half heard, she stared at the closed walnut coffin with what remained of Bren inside. How had it all ended here? It seemed not so long ago when Hannah attended the conference at Bell Harbor and caught the attractive brunette in the third row looking at her every time she'd glanced over. Bren had approached her after the seminar, and through her steady flirtation the remainder of the weekend, finally convinced Hannah to have dinner with her.

Now here Hannah stood, more emotional than she'd expected as she stared at the hole in the ground that would be Bren's final resting place. But even her sadness didn't assuage the guilt she'd felt as her friends and Bren's coworkers showered her with support. They treated her like a true grieving widow who'd been madly in love with Bren, which only intensified her self-rebuke. And rightly so. The longer it went on, the worse Hannah felt about misleading everyone, but by now, it was too late to say anything. It gnawed at her, though, and she hadn't been able to stomach food in two days. Did they think it strange she hadn't cried? Hadn't needed the tissues she'd stuffed in her purse? They had to wonder.

Worse than being dishonest with the attendees she really didn't know all that well, she'd lied to Zara, even if by omission. Hannah couldn't tell her, not now. In retrospect, she should've told her the night Bren died.

Now she'd coupled the awkward truth about her failed relationship with being duplicitous. As much as she tried, she couldn't imagine a suitable time to come clean, and the longer she waited, the more hurtful her deceit would be if ever found out. No, she'd have to just live with it. And right or wrong, it would all be over soon, and hopefully she could heal and get on with her life.

Movement caught her eye. A woman stood on the opposite side of the casket in the back row. She appeared to be looking at Zara, but she shifted her focus to Hannah, and their gazes locked. One beat, two, three. Then she stepped behind the broad shoulders of one of Bren's former colleagues. Hannah could no longer see her, only her arm and one high-heeled shoe, but the image of her flaxen-blond hair and conservative dress under her black trench coat was clear in her mind's eye. Who was she? And when did she arrive?

Hannah thought she knew everyone in attendance, mostly members of the softball team Bren had quit two summers ago when she'd started traveling more, and executives from her company. Some Hannah knew from one function or another. Others she was introduced to in a whirlwind of names earlier. One thing was certain. She'd never seen this mystery woman. She would've remembered.

A funerary worker in a worn gray suit pushed a button and set the casket-lowering mechanism into action. When prompted, Hannah took a few steps forward, grasped a handful of dirt, and tossed it into the grave. Numbness overtook her. Zara led her away and wiped her dirty palm with tissues. The mourners began to disperse. A few bid their farewells, clasping Hannah's fingers too hard and saying how sorry they were, but most quietly moved toward their cars parked along the narrow paved path that wound through the grounds.

That's when Hannah saw her again.

The mystery woman hurried away in the opposite direction of everyone else, toward a sedan parked on an adjacent road.

"I'll be right back," she told Zara, and followed her. The woman had a head start, but a small incline separating the grassy area from the pavement seemed to slow her pace. Hannah broke into a jog, no easy task in heels. "Excuse me."

The woman didn't hear her, or simply didn't acknowledge that she had. She was about halfway up the small hill when Hannah reached the bottom.

"Excuse me," Hannah called, this time more loudly.

FLOWERS AND GEMSTONES

Near the top, with Hannah only a few yards behind her, the woman's heel sank into the soaked ground and stuck. Her momentum pulled her foot from her shoe and sent her stumbling, but she managed not to fall. She stopped and turned, her bare foot planted in the wet grass.

Hannah bent and retrieved the shoe, pulling it from the sodden earth with a sucking sound. It held the warmth of the woman's foot, though the bottom was now half-covered in mud. "I don't think we've met."

"No, we haven't." Her voice, low but lilting, surprised Hannah. "I'm so sorry for your loss, but I really must be going."

With a few steps, Hannah put them on equal ground. The woman was almost her height. This close, her hair was even paler than Hannah had initially realized, the shade that often allowed a woman to transition from blond to white with little notice as she aged. "How'd you know Bren?"

For a split second, the woman hesitated, her expression shuttered. "I did the flowers."

Hannah studied her with skepticism. "Do you attend all the funerals you do arrangements for?"

"No." The woman sighed and looked away for a moment. When her eyes met Hannah's again, she'd clearly made a decision. Her composure regained, she straightened her spine. "I'm Vanessa Holland. Bren and I used to date. When I saw her name on the order, I wanted to pay my respects."

Used to date? Was *she* one of the women Bren would never discuss? Hannah swallowed. She desperately hoped her utter shock wasn't plastered all over her face. "Hannah Baros. Nice to meet you. It was kind of you to attend." Curious as to what Vanessa might be able to tell her, she wanted to keep her talking. She held up the shoe. "Sorry about your heel." She glanced down. "And your foot. I have some tissues."

Vanessa reached for her dirty footwear. "I'll be fine. I shouldn't keep you."

Hannah was already opening her purse. "It won't take but a minute. It'll be easier if you sit."

With a beep, Vanessa unlocked her car, gingerly walked across the asphalt, and perched on the edge of the seat.

"Here." Hannah pulled out half a dozen tissues for Vanessa, then grabbed some for herself and went to work on the shoe.

Vanessa inched her dress higher so she could prop her foot on her knee and wiped away the mud and grass. Scarlet nail polish appeared.

• 29 •

When she'd finished, Hannah handed her shoe back. "Good as new."

Vanessa slipped it on. "Thank you, but you should be getting back. Someone's waiting for you." She gestured toward the gravesite where Zara conversed with a man, but watched them over his shoulder.

Hannah turned back to Vanessa. "Yes, soon. She's my ride." But she didn't want to leave when answers she might never have access to again could be standing right in front of her. Bren had always been so closed lipped about the women in her past, but Bren had been important enough to *this* woman for her to attend Bren's funeral, and after how long? Hannah *assumed* their relationship had been in the past, but had it? Bren's strange behavior and the possibility of an affair still niggled at her. She shifted nervously. "How long ago did you and Bren date?"

"Years. Over half a decade." Vanessa's answer came without hesitation. She swiveled into the driver's seat.

Though Vanessa's response seemed genuine, the realization that the question might not receive a truthful answer made Hannah bring the conversation to a close. "Thank you for doing such an impressive job with the flowers. They're beautiful."

Vanessa's small smile seemed tinged with sadness. "It's what I do. Good-bye, Hannah."

Hannah watched Vanessa's car curve around the headstones and monuments as she walked back to Zara.

When Hannah reached her, she realized Zara was speaking with Miguel, Bren's boss. His crisp white dress shirt complemented his light-brown skin and thick dark hair.

He took Hannah's hand between both of his. "It was a beautiful service. Bren would've thought it was top-notch." He gestured to the white flower wreaths on the easel stands beside him, including the one containing an oval portrait of Bren.

"Yes." Hannah couldn't help recalling how Bren detested the smell of flowers and wouldn't even order a cocktail if it contained rose water. And yet, she'd dated a florist. Did that have something to do with *why* she disliked flowers?

"I hate to talk business on a day like today," he said, clearly intending to do just that, "but did Bren leave a will?"

Hannah shook her head. "She died intestate. The court will determine if she has any living relatives, but I don't believe she does."

"I see." He stroked his chin. "So, will you be the one dealing with the court concerning her belongings?"

Behind him, Zara rolled her eyes.

"Yes, I suppose so," Hannah said quietly.

He nodded. "Why don't you stop by in a week or so, and we'll have Bren's things from her office as well as any outstanding paperwork ready for you."

"Of course." Hannah hoped her answer would accelerate his leave. He handed her his business card. "Lovely service. We're going to miss our girl."

As he stalked away, Zara came to stand beside her. "You seem to be holding up well. I'm proud of you."

Hannah shrugged.

"What was that about?"

Hannah showed her the embossed card with the familiar logo. "Loose ends, I guess?"

"No, her." Zara motioned to where Vanessa had been parked.

They walked toward Zara's car. "An ex of Bren's."

Zara's eyebrows shot up. "No way. Have you ever met one?"

She made it sound like they were talking about leprechauns. They might as well have been. Hannah shook her head. "Never."

"Well, that was nice of her to come, especially since they probably didn't keep in touch."

The last thing Hannah wanted to do today was speculate about how many women might be lingering on Bren's contact list. Too many unanswered questions had plagued their relationship. But a small thought comforted her. If she had more questions, she knew where Vanessa worked.

❖

A week later, Hannah found herself following a thin administrative assistant wearing a tie so skinny it recalled a style of dress from decades past. He ushered her into a conference room in the high-rise building where Bren used to work.

"Miguel and Cam will be in momentarily. Can I get you anything? Water? Coffee?"

"Water, please." She chose a seat on the long side of the table. Seattle's waterfront stretched out before her, and in the middle of Elliot Bay, a white wake streamed behind a ferry chugging its way toward Bainbridge Island.

The slight shift in air current and a reflection in the window told Hannah someone had entered the room. She rose.

"Ms. Baros. Here you go." Miguel placed a bottle on the table, the kind that cost more than a gallon of gas. "It's good to see you." He offered her a handshake. "This is Cameron Everstrom. He does our HR stuff."

The tall, dark-skinned man extended his hand. "You can call me Cam. I'm the chief human resources officer."

"It's a pleasure." Hannah didn't recall him being at the funeral, but maybe he didn't know Bren. She wasn't sure why he was here now though.

Both men sat across from her.

"Let's get down to business." Miguel opened the folder Cam slid his way. He glanced up when his assistant entered again. "Thanks. Just put it here." He tapped the table beside him, and the young man deposited a banker's box with a thud. Someone had written *Brenda McAvoy Personal Effects* on the end in black marker.

Miguel looked at Hannah. "So, with Bren apparently having no will or family, and since you've been in a personal relationship with her for..." He squinted at the top sheet inside the folder.

"Three years," Cam said quietly.

"Yes, three years, and resided at the same address, we're releasing her belongings to you. It's not much, really. Some toiletries, a change of clothing, an award, and a few personal papers. We just need you to sign this statement confirming that we've turned them over to you, and you'll then need to include them with the rest of her property and cooperate with the court to find their rightful inheritor."

She couldn't read the itemized list from where she sat, but it didn't matter. "That's fine." She inked her signature at the bottom.

"Oh, and there's this." Miguel pulled a photograph from the folder and slid it toward her.

A woman with a sunset behind her, her hair backlit and flaming, laughed in obvious delight for whomever held the camera. She was unmistakably gorgeous.

"The custodian found this behind the credenza in Bren's office. He's not sure if it belonged to Bren or the prior occupant. Do you recognize her?"

Hannah stared, transfixed, then nodded.

"Okay, then." Miguel slipped it into the box. "Unfortunately, Bren didn't have any vacation or sick time payout for whomever turns out to be the beneficiary of her estate because, well, you know Bren." He tilted his head. "She used her vacation days as fast as she earned them and always maxed out her sick days."

Hannah blinked. She did? Bren was never ill and certainly hadn't been using any time off with *her*. "I'm sorry. I think you must have her records mixed up with someone else's."

Miguel frowned and turned to Cam, who pulled the folder in front of him and ran his long finger down the page.

"There's no mistake." Cam looked up. "Why do you say that?"

Where had Bren been going? Her unwillingness to even agree to a mini vacation had been a frequent argument between them. "She was the healthiest person I know. I can't even remember a time she was ill. And we haven't taken a trip in two years. The only place she travels is to the San Francisco office for work."

The men exchanged glances as though determining who'd speak.

"Ma'am," Cam's dark eyes softened with clear compassion, "the San Francisco branch has been closed for years."

Hannah shivered. Closed? She didn't know how to respond. Bren traveled there for work nearly every month, and almost always needed to stay the weekend to finish whatever they'd tasked her to do. "That can't be."

Both men seemed as uncomfortable as she was with the turn the conversation had taken.

"I'm afraid it's true." Cam glanced at Miguel, then back to Hannah. "If she was traveling to San Francisco, it wasn't for her job. She often signed in remotely, but we assumed she was working from home."

Bren never worked at home.

Hannah pulled at her collar, suddenly needing air. She cracked open the water and gulped some down.

"What can we do for you?" Cam extended his hand across the table, not close enough to touch her, but still reassuring.

"Nothing." Hannah lowered her gaze. "That's what she told me, and I believed her. I guess the joke's on me."

Miguel cleared his throat. "I'm sorry you found out this way. I'm afraid I need to run to my next meeting, but Cam here will take care of you. We can arrange a ride home for you or—"

"That's unnecessary." Her voice came out more confident and controlled than she expected. She inhaled and hoped her cheeks and neck weren't pinking, revealing her embarrassment. Christ, why hadn't she broken up with Bren sooner?

She stood and picked up the box.

"Let me have Enrique carry that down for you," Cam said, holding the door for her.

Like the skinny assistant could carry a lightweight box better than she could. "I've got it. Thank you both for everything."

As Hannah rode down to the parking garage, her neck and shoulders tensed, not from the weight of her load, but from her apprehension about what other bombshells she might find in it. She considered ditching it on the floor of the elevator. And then there was the photo.

The beautiful woman, though slightly younger, was Vanessa.

By the time Hannah got home, her adrenaline had dissipated, leaving her numb. After setting the box on the coffee table, she poured a glass of wine and collapsed onto the couch. Part of her wanted to know what was inside, and part of her didn't. She was tired of surprises and wasn't sure she could deal with any more on her own.

She hefted her purse onto the couch and pulled out her phone to call Zara. "Fuck." The meditation retreat Zara had been looking forward to for months started this weekend, and Zara had left early to drive to Aberdeen. Hannah called anyway.

Zara answered on the first ring. "What's wrong?"

"Why do you assume the worst?" Hannah kicked off her shoes.

"Because I left an hour ago, and you're already calling me. Do I need to come back?"

Hannah sighed into the phone, hoping Zara could hear. "I'm calling because…well, I'm not sure exactly. I went to Bren's work today and picked up her belongings."

"Anything interesting?"

Hannah pulled her legs onto the sofa. "I don't know."

"Okay, hon, start at the beginning. I know you wouldn't be calling me if it wasn't important. I offered to cancel and stay with you if you needed me, and I'll come back if you do. Just say the word."

It was tempting. With Zara beside her, she could face whatever the box had to offer. "No, you've been so excited, and isn't Derrick leading it?" Zara had been drooling over her meditation facilitator since last fall. She'd shown Hannah a photo of him. With his muscular physique and bright smile, no wonder Zara was interested.

"Yes, but I'll survive if I don't get to ogle Derrick for a week. Tell me what's wrong. Should I pull over?"

"Don't you dare. I just wanted someone to talk to. I haven't opened it because I don't have the courage to do it by myself." Hannah rubbed her temple. "That's only part of it. They told me Bren had no sick time or vacation payout because she'd used it all."

"What? Bren?" The incredulity in Zara's voice came through the speaker.

"Right?" Hannah rested her head on a pillow and closed her eyes. "And when I said there must be some mistake, that the only place Bren ever went was to San Francisco for work, they told me that branch closed years ago."

Silence.

"Hey, come on. Don't leave me with crickets," Hannah said with levity. "Are you still there?"

Zara sighed. "I'm so sorry, hon. You sure you don't want me to turn around?"

"No, I really don't. I want you to have an amazing vacation and meditate your ass off whenever you're not objectifying Derrick. I'll survive. It's just been a day, you know?"

Zara let out a short laugh. "It's a respectful objectification. As for the box, do you think you'll dig into it?"

Hannah opened her eyes and stared at Bren's full name written on it. "Honestly, I don't know. I want to. I have so many questions. But it scares me, too. If there's one more instance of something turning out to be the opposite of what I thought it to be, I just might crack."

"Perhaps you should wait then. This week will fly by. We'll get some champagne and see what other fucking secrets Bren was keeping, the lying bitch. I'm really sorry, Han."

Could she wait that long? It'd been in her home for twenty minutes and seemed to consume more space than all her furniture combined. Shoving it into a closet wouldn't make it any better. She'd know it was there. What if there was a will inside? Since Bren had never mentioned it, Hannah had assumed she'd never drafted one, but it was becoming clear there were several things Bren hadn't mentioned. She *might've* kept it at work. Miguel had referred to personal papers. Hannah really should open the box. It would simplify things with the court. And she already knew Bren lied to her. A need to know why was already smoldering within her, a burning desperation to know more.

"I have to open it, and I'm not sure I can wait for you to get back. I just need a bit of moral support."

As Zara rambled on about sneaking away and FaceTiming with her while she did it, Hannah thought of Vanessa, not that Vanessa hadn't entered her mind more than a few times since their meeting. She sat up and lifted the lid enough to slide her hand inside and pull out the photo resting on top of everything. Now that she had more time to study it, Vanessa's eyes drew her in. Even slightly silhouetted, the vibrant green mesmerized her. But the photo lacked the tiny lines that had crinkled at their corners when Vanessa had smiled and said, "It's what I do."

"You're going to think this is weird, but I'm going to ask the woman from the funeral if she'll be here with me when I open it."

There was a pause. "Okay." Zara teased the word into three syllables. "Do you think she'll go for it? It's not like you know her. You only talked for a few minutes."

Hannah thought about it. "I have no idea, but she dated Bren, too. Maybe opening the box will provide some answers for *her*."

"How do you know she has questions?"

Zara had a good point. "I don't, but Bren's proven herself to be a chronic liar. I doubt that started when she began dating me."

Zara made a frustrated sound. "Hon, I'm so sorry you're going through this on top of grieving."

The guilt hit Hannah like a loose shutter in a hurricane. "I'm okay. I just need to deal with this box. I can't have it sitting around here haunting me for a week. It's already bothering me."

"Then call that woman. What's her name?"

"Vanessa." Would she sit with Hannah while she went through it? She came to the funeral, so she was obviously there for some sort of remembrance and to pay her respects. And maybe closure? Plus, she'd dated Bren, too. They had that connection. Or would Vanessa think Hannah was crazy for calling? She hoped not. For some reason, she wanted Vanessa to view her in a positive light.

She let Zara go with wishes for a successful retreat and poured herself a glass of wine.

As she sat on the couch in front of the box again, snippets of Bren's strange behavior came back to her. Vague explanations, always too tired to discuss the details of any trip, and prolonged periods of no communication during which her phone always seemed to be on silent. Instances like those, and the knowledge Bren had lied about her whereabouts, almost guaranteed an affair. But with whom? Had Vanessa been truthful about how long ago she'd dated Bren?

Hannah sipped her wine and stared at the photo. Strangely, she didn't want Vanessa to be the other woman.

Chapter Four

Vanessa inhaled, long and deep. Finally, she'd been granted a few minutes of calm. The shop had been filled with customers since she'd opened. If she hurried, she'd have time to put a bandage on the particularly nasty puncture from a thorn on her index finger before anyone else came in. She reached for the first-aid kit under the counter.

Salmon-colored dahlias, golden sunflowers, and bluish-purple hydrangeas flanked the register area, but her sense of smell had long ago acclimated to the barrage of floral scents. Without burying her nose in a bloom, she could hardly detect its fragrance after so many years doing this job. Thank goodness this phenomenon didn't apply to other favorite scents, like almond lotion and fresh laundry. Still, the pre-arranged bouquets on the counter and around the store were gorgeous, and she couldn't imagine not being surrounded by such beauty every day.

She also enjoyed the customer service aspect of her business and worked the front more than anyone on her staff, but sometimes she craved the laid-back conversations with coworkers or the ability to pop in ear buds while creating flower arrangements in the back. It gave her time to think. So far this morning, she'd been too busy to have many meandering thoughts, but they seemed to sneak back whenever they could. Like now, when snippets of last weekend's cemetery visit filled her mind.

At times, it didn't seem real that Bren was gone. While she hadn't been in Vanessa's life for years, somehow knowing she no longer breathed hit differently. Vanessa *had* loved her once. Oddly, that era seemed so long ago and yet not distant enough. And the fresh memories from the service conjured older ones of Bren that Vanessa had no intention of revisiting. Whether attending the funeral had been wise, it'd been her decision to go.

Vanessa had hoped to disappear after the service without speaking to anyone. She'd been right about not knowing any of the other attendees, so Hannah chasing after her had been a surprise. She should've known Bren's girlfriend would be stunning, even while mourning.

At first, Vanessa hadn't been sure which of the two women holding hands had been the partner named in the obituary. The brunette had paid her no interest, but Hannah had noticed her and zeroed in. God, how awful she must've looked. Why hadn't she bought something new to wear instead of throwing on a dress she'd had for a decade that wasn't even in style anymore? It did nothing for her figure, and the humidity had flattened her hair. What had Hannah thought? She probably wondered what Bren had ever seen in her.

For a split second, Vanessa had debated lying, saying she'd worked with Bren a long time ago, but something about Hannah's quiet questions made her tell the truth. At least an abbreviated version of it. It didn't matter. Bren was gone, Vanessa had paid her respects, and now she could close that chapter of her life for good.

Her phone buzzed, and she tensed at the "Cruella de Vil" ringtone. She tossed the bandage wrapper in the garbage, then steeled herself and answered the call. "Is it an emergency?"

"How dare you? I didn't raise you to be so rude."

Ten in the morning, and Vanessa could tell by her mother's tone she was already drinking. "Mom," Vanessa lowered her voice, "I've told you, you can't call me at work unless it's an emergency."

"Always bragging that you're some bigwig who owns her own business. Must be a lie, or you could talk whenever you wanted."

Vanessa *could* talk to her; she just didn't want to. But she couldn't say that. The trepidation from her childhood of losing the only person she had still lingered deep within her. It was irrational, but fear was a bitch that held on tight. "I'm not doing this now. If nothing's wrong, I'll call you when I get off work."

"When they *let* you off work. You've always been a terrible liar. You think you can pull one over on me, but mothers know."

"I'm hanging up now." And she did. Her tolerance for her mom's harassment was low today. She slid the phone into a drawer, then squatted behind the counter to return the first aid kit to its place. In the quiet solitude, she took a moment to recover, gently massaging the pressure points at the back of her neck.

When the bell above the door dinged, Vanessa rose quickly with a smile, ready to greet her next customer, but she found herself completely dumbstruck by who it was.

Hannah Baros looked different than she had graveside. Instead of the somber black dress, she wore a burgundy skirt and blazer, complemented by a champagne shell and gold jewelry. Her honey-colored hair fell in glossy waves, a sharp contrast to the tight bun that'd imprisoned it at the funeral, and a healthy glow replaced the pallor that had made her look tired and frail. She radiated an energy she'd been missing when they'd met, despite having sprinted after Vanessa.

Hannah glanced around the small gift area until her gaze fell on Vanessa. She smiled, her expression a little tight.

"Good morning, Ms. Baros." Vanessa moved from behind the counter. "What can I do for you?" She was primed to direct Hannah toward individual blooms that could be fashioned into a quick bouquet or the pre-prepared vases on display in the refrigerated cases. The succulents in handmade ceramic pots also made great gifts.

"Oh. You remember me," Hannah said, her surprise obvious.

Venessa laughed softly. "Of course." How could she forget a woman who'd run her down in a cemetery and insisted on cleaning her shoe, a woman with whom she shared an ex?

"Oh, well, please call me Hannah." She took in a breath. "God, it smells good in here." She bent to sniff a bunch of lilies, then faced Vanessa again. "Actually, I have something I want to talk to you about."

Was she nervous? Should Vanessa be nervous? They had only one thing in common.

"I'm sorry to bother you at work," Hannah rushed on before Vanessa could respond, "but I wanted to speak with you in person. Do they give you a break around here? I noticed a café around the corner."

They? Vanessa blinked and silenced her mother's voice in her head. Hannah didn't mean it that way. Looking back, she'd told Hannah she did the flowers for Bren's funeral, not that she owned Late Bloomer. "Uh..."

"Could you get away for ten to fifteen minutes? I know it's short notice."

Hannah sounded so serious, Vanessa couldn't decline. Besides, she was intrigued. What could Hannah want? "I don't think it'll be a problem."

With perfect timing, Chloe came out from the back, carrying an arrangement of carnations. She headed for the rolls of ribbon behind the counter.

"Hey, do you mind if I take a quick break at Seismic?" Vanessa untied the apron she wore over her polo.

Chloe looked around with a who-me expression. "Um." She glanced back and forth between them with wide eyes. "No?"

"Great. Thanks." Vanessa gave her a wink, then followed Hannah out of the store, leaving Chloe open-mouthed.

The coffee shop smelled of freshly roasted beans and Lou's cinnamon rolls. Hannah insisted on paying even though Vanessa had an open tab with Lou and Lottie, but this was Hannah's show, so Vanessa let her.

When they'd settled at a corner table with their lattes, Hannah danced her fingers along the edge as though nervous. She didn't touch her drink.

Vanessa decided to rescue her for time's sake. "How are you doing? You know…"

Hannah hesitated. "I'm doing well. Thanks for asking."

"I'm sure it's a lot." Vanessa wasn't certain what else to say. How strange. She'd had plenty of experience talking with people grieving the loss of a loved one, but this seemed different somehow. Perhaps because Bren had also once been *her* loved one? In the silence, she sipped her coffee. Lou had made a foam orchid on the surface like he always did. She glanced at Hannah's and noted he'd given her a sun. He could be perceptive about what his customers needed.

"It is a lot," Hannah said finally, in response to Vanessa's comment. She picked up her latte and tried it. "That's why I'm here. I have a favor to ask."

A favor? They barely knew one another. Counting today, they'd probably spoken for no more than ten minutes. But for some reason, Vanessa was willing to listen. "What kind?"

"You'll think it's strange." Hannah gave her a sheepish, tight smile. "*I* think it's strange."

Vanessa considered her. "All right. I make no promises, but let's hear it."

Hannah pursed her lips, then cleared her throat. "Well, I picked up Bren's belongings from her work a few days ago," she said, obviously uncomfortable.

Vanessa wrapped her fingers around the warm mug. "I imagine that's difficult, going through her things." She tried to sound encouraging.

"That's just it." Hannah stared at the tabletop. "I can't bring myself to open the box." Her gaze still lowered, she let out a deep, slow sigh. "I found out Bren had been lying to me." She looked up, her eyes clouded with sadness.

The frailty from the funeral was back, and Vanessa considered giving her a comforting hug, but they weren't friends. They didn't even know one another. "About what?" She wasn't sure she wanted to know. It felt too personal, asking a stranger questions like this, but clearly, Hannah didn't feel that way. There was something down-to-earth about her, and every aspect of her appeared genuine, as if what you saw was what you got.

"Her boss told me the branch she's been traveling to for work almost every month has been closed for years." Hannah's shoulders slumped. "I don't know where she went. The why, I can guess. I knew something was off because she was often evasive and secretive, but I took her at her word." She looked away, her cheeks reddening. "I'm such a fool."

Lies. Deceit. Secrets. Vanessa should've been shocked, but when it came to Bren, she no longer was. "You loved her." She reached over and gave Hannah's hand a gentle squeeze. "Of course, you wanted to believe her." She admired Hannah's fingers, long and tipped in polish that matched her suit. Her skin was cool and soft. When Vanessa looked up, Hannah's brow had furrowed. Had Vanessa been presumptuous about Hannah's feelings for Bren?

"Anyway," Hannah said, "I'm sure they expect you back soon, so I'll come right out and ask. I was hoping you might be willing to be there when I open the box. Normally, I'd ask my best friend, Zara—you saw her at the funeral—but she's out of town, and I'm not sure I can manage more surprises on my own." She paused, biting her lower lip. "And you knew Bren. So, would you be willing to come over some night this week? I'll provide dinner as payment for your troubles."

Again, those large intelligent eyes took Vanessa in. Blue, she realized. The same vibrant shade as the sky on a summer day when she lifted her face to the warmth of the sun. But a prickly sensation crawled up her spine. A warning. While Hannah's revelation about Bren's dishonesty piqued her curiosity, Vanessa had worked too hard to put Bren and the pain she'd caused behind her. Diving back in was a terrible idea.

She leaned back in her chair. "I'm sorry, but I can't. Bren's a part of my past, and I can't go there again."

Hannah's eyebrows rose. Clearly, she'd been expecting a different reaction. "Oh. Of course. I shouldn't have asked." She straightened and gathered her purse. "I'm sorry to have wasted your time. Should I walk you back and apologize to your boss for keeping you so long?" She stood, her nearly full coffee abandoned.

Vanessa rose. "That's unnecessary." She hadn't meant to make Hannah uncomfortable or feel bad, but nor did she owe her an apology for taking care of herself. Hannah had asked a favor, and Vanessa had simply declined. She waved good-bye to Lou and ushered Hannah toward the door.

Outside, they turned the corner in silence. At what point would they part? Was Hannah parked this way?

Vanessa slowed in front of her shop. She searched for something to say so as not to leave things between them so awkward. There was one thing she could clear up. "Before you go, I feel like I should come clean." She pointed up at the Late Bloomer sign. "I started this company almost twenty-five years ago." She smiled. "I don't have a boss."

Hannah's cheeks pinked. "I'm sorry. I assumed when you said you did the flowers that you were the person who arranged them."

"I was, but I also own the business." With renewed ease, Vanessa leaned against the building, her hands in her pockets. "It's hard to believe I've been doing this half my life."

Hannah blinked a few times. "I could say the same, though with my company being family-owned, I can't remember a time when I wasn't wandering its halls annoying my parents' staff."

It didn't appear Hannah was in a hurry. Or had she relaxed now that she knew Vanessa had more than a ten-minute break? Vanessa turned and glanced inside. Chloe dusted the shelf displaying the mini herb garden kits and packets of local wildflower seeds. No customers were in sight.

She returned her attention to Hannah. "So, what do you do?" With her crisp tailored suit, Hannah had to be a professional of some sort. She had a couple of inches on Vanessa in her heels.

"I'm in the jewelry business. My family owns a chain along the West Coast." She said it matter-of-factly, not in a boastful manner, but in a way that exuded comfort in her role and, if they had multiple stores, likely success.

"Oh, Hannah Baros. Baros Family Jewelers." It clicked in her brain. That's why Hannah's surname had sounded familiar. "I know it. I bought my cousin's daughter a gold chain there for her tenth birthday." She softened, remembering how Sasha had squealed and danced around the room after she'd opened it. "It was a big hit."

"I'm glad." Hannah smiled, and for the first time since they'd met, it seemed to be natural. She stepped closer to allow a bike messenger to pass.

"And what do you do there?" It was easier to ask another question than try to find a way to end the conversation without reigniting the earlier tension between them.

Hannah fingered the links on the strap of her purse, drawing Vanessa's attention. She wore a stunning ring on her index finger. Gold filigree surrounded an oval of sparkling clear stones that were probably diamonds. In the center, an emerald caught the light. "Like you, I'm the boss, although I've worked in every department within the company at some point. My parents took an early retirement last year, so I've taken over." She glanced at her phone. "Which means I have to get back."

"I should, too." Vanessa pushed herself off the wall. "Thanks for the coffee."

Hannah grimaced. "Did you even get to drink it?"

"Some." They stood close now, only a foot between them. Vanessa glanced up. She'd been right. Hannah's eyes mirrored the color of the sky.

"Sorry." Hannah shifted her gaze to the sidewalk. "And I apologize for asking what I did and making things awkward. You don't know me, and I should've given the idea more thought."

And here they were again. "It's not that." Vanessa still didn't owe Hannah an explanation, but this time one formed on her tongue before she could stop it. "Without going into detail, and if you'll pardon a metaphor, I've worked hard to roll my stone to the top of that hill, and I can't allow it to gain any downward momentum, not after all I've done to get where I am."

Hannah nodded, as though she understood. "I see." She smiled, but it wasn't the genuine smile of moments ago. "So, okay then. Enjoy the rest of your day."

There really wasn't anything else to say. Vanessa gave a little wave. "You, too." She watched Hannah walk down the block, her steps authoritative and sure, her posture confident. She'd be fine confronting whatever was in that box.

Vanessa took a deep breath, trying to assuage that little twinge of guilt that still niggled at her, and pushed open the door to her store. It was only midmorning, and, like Hannah, she had things to do.

❖

"Chloe, I'm going for a run." Vanessa tightened the laces on her shoes.

She didn't necessarily need to let Chloe know. It was three o'clock, the time she usually left when she opened. It still made for a long day when her alarm chimed at five in the morning, but running a small business was a commitment. Vanessa didn't mind. It gave her less time to ruminate on the state of her personal life.

In the hallway, she almost ran into Chloe carrying a stack of buckets.

"Watch out for cars."

"Always." It was their usual back and forth whenever Vanessa started her run from work rather than home. There was something about jogging through downtown that appealed to her. The rush of workers, the meandering of tourists, the tall buildings, the waterfront. She'd always loved Seattle. The only considerable time she'd been away was when she'd gone to Oregon for college. And she'd missed it. The city at least, not living with her mother and dealing with her constant criticism.

Outside, the sky had turned overcast, which was far from unusual. It didn't look like it would rain though, and it rarely bothered her when it did. She'd be soaked after her five-mile route one way or another. After starting the app and tucking her phone into her armband, she headed south.

As her soles slapped the pavement in a moderate cadence, Vanessa reflected on her morning. Hannah showing up had been a surprise, though not an unpleasant one. She'd enjoyed hearing Hannah's raspy voice again, so different from anyone else's she knew.

The metaphor Vanessa had used as an explanation had been silly, but it'd seemed to satisfy Hannah. She'd left off the part about how if the stone got rolling, she wasn't sure she'd be able to stop it. It'd taken five years, but she'd finally gotten past having Bren or anything Bren-related in her life. Vanessa had thought she'd put all of that behind her.

In spite of that, whatever Bren had been up to intrigued her. Lies of that magnitude had to mean an affair. How could they not? If they did, had Bren cheated on Vanessa, too? She prided herself at her response, one of interest rather than emotion. Her work in therapy had given her distance from what had happened between her and Bren. At one point in time, even the possibility would've crushed her. Now she approached it with a, *Huh. I wonder who it might've been with?* mentality. Bless the wonders of psychotherapy and the brilliant cognitive and behavioral techniques Dr. Martinez had taught her.

Nevertheless, she tried to imagine lying to a partner for years regarding her whereabouts. How much mental and physical effort had it taken for Bren to pull off such a stunt? And had it been worth it? If it had, she wondered who'd been so important for Bren to go to such lengths. Hannah was right. The box probably held more information that might shed light on all these questions. If she were in Hannah's shoes, she'd want someone with her, too. Her stride faltered. Did Hannah really have no other friends?

Vanessa huffed out a short laugh. Like *she* had a wide circle. For some reason, the older she got, the more difficult it seemed to make close ones as old ones drifted away. She still had Sonja though. God, they'd been best friends for thirty years come fall. She'd have to remind Sonja of that. College seemed so long ago. Three decades of friendship required a bottle of champagne next time they were together.

Was Zara Hannah's Sonja, the person she relied on for anything important? She'd said Zara was out of town. At work, Vanessa was friendly with everyone, but she tried to maintain a certain level of professionalism. She didn't socialize with her staff and certainly didn't share many personal details, other than occasionally with Chloe. Since Hannah was in a leadership role, too, the same might be true for her.

Vanessa stopped at a red light but jogged in place and checked her time.

Hannah surely wouldn't have asked a virtual stranger unless she had no one else. Vanessa's heart ached for her. Hannah had just lost her lover, found out devastating news, and was afraid of whatever might come next. It's possible Vanessa had been too quick, too selfish with her answer. Maybe she should rethink it.

With a lift in her strides, she ran past the aquarium and the Great Wheel, dodging meandering tourists. A light drizzle mingled with the scents of salt air, seafood, and sourdough bread. She turned back toward the shop, and when she arrived, a sense of clarity accompanied her.

Vanessa entered the store. Near the refrigerated case, Cai helped a customer with a bouquet of gerbera daisies, and Chloe swept behind the counter.

"Good run?" Chloe leaned on the broom.

Vanessa nodded. "Need some water." She pushed through the swinging door into the back and, after downing half a bottle, woke her computer. Chloe had scanned last week's orders, and she quickly found the one for Bren's service that contained Hannah's phone number. She tilted back in her chair and took another sip. Being out of breath when she called wasn't the impression she was going for, so she waited a bit. Then, she picked up the office phone, knowing the business name would appear on Hannah's screen, increasing her chances of Hannah accepting the call.

It rang twice.

"Hello?"

"Hannah, it's Vanessa Holland. I'm sorry to bother you. Do you have a minute?"

"I do." She sounded cautious.

Vanessa leaned forward. "I've been thinking. Would you let me consider your request overnight and give you an answer tomorrow?" It occurred to her then that Hannah might've already opened the box. But she'd said she was headed to work, hadn't she?

"I would."

So, she hadn't opened it. "Okay." Vanessa straightened. "I'll give you a call in the morning. Or would you prefer a text?"

"Call or text me anytime tomorrow afternoon. I'm in meetings until lunch, so I might not be able to pick up or respond right away. And you'd have more time to decide."

Vanessa wouldn't mind the additional few hours to mull it over. "Sure."

"Would you mind shooting me a text right now so I have your personal number? That way I'll know it's you."

"I'll do that."

"And even if you decide you can't do it, thank you for giving it more thought."

"You're welcome." Would she change her mind? A night of sleep might bring considerations she hadn't thought about.

"Talk to you soon."

Vanessa entered Hannah's number into her phone. What should she text? Her name? That seemed a bit impersonal. Instead, she typed, *Have a good evening*, and signed it with Vanessa.

A thumbs up immediately appeared.

That wasn't so hard. But making the decision she needed to make, now having a better sense of what Hannah was dealing with, would be.

Chapter Five

At promptly one o'clock, Hannah's phone vibrated on her desk. Her hopes soared as soon as she saw the name on the screen, and she tried to subdue them before answering. She pushed her green goddess salad aside, then swiped to connect the call. "Hi, Vanessa."

"Hi." She sounded a bit breathless. "I'll do it."

Hannah couldn't hold back a grin. "I can't thank you enough." The magnitude of her relief surprised her.

A soft laugh came through the line. "I made you wait."

"That's okay. You said yes in the end." Hannah found herself smiling.

Vanessa exhaled. "So, from what you said, you probably want to get this over as soon as possible. I'm free tomorrow evening. Unfortunately, I'm closing tonight, so I'll be here late."

"That's okay. I'll probably be *here* even later." Hannah's meetings had eaten up her entire morning, and now she had to play catch-up. And she preferred working in her well-lit office rather than dragging her full briefcase home to her dark, depressing house. "How's seven?"

"It's great. Text me your address."

Hannah looked at her lunch. "And don't forget, I'm providing dinner."

Another laugh. "That's unnecessary."

"Eating? I completely disagree, so bring your appetite." She jotted down *address* and *dinner* on a sticky note. "I'll see you tomorrow then."

"Yes."

Hannah ended the call. She'd been dreading opening that wretched box so much, she'd had to stash it in her garage to avoid looking at it, and now she was looking forward to it. Almost. Did the pleasant anticipation come from knowing she'd be seeing Vanessa again? Or was having

Vanessa beside her when she discovered whatever awaited her in the box simply a perk?

Hannah rubbed her chin. What made Vanessa change her mind? She'd been so adamant with her answer at the coffee shop. Whatever the reason, Hannah was grateful.

The afternoon and the following day sped by, keeping her mind occupied with agendas and business decisions. It wasn't until she was on her way home that it occurred to her she hadn't spoken to Vanessa since their call. Hannah had sent a text with her address, and Vanessa hadn't responded, something Hannah tried not to read much into now. Instead, she spent the rest of the drive worrying whether Vanessa would actually show, but when she answered the doorbell after putting the takeout in the oven to warm, Vanessa stood on her porch with two bottles of wine.

She held them up. "Hopefully, you drink. I brought a red and white."

Hannah had seen her twice before, once dressed for a funeral and the other time in jeans and a polo shirt at work. Vanessa had found a happy medium with the casual pants and blouse she wore tonight. Her hair was down, the delicate strands curling at the ends. Hannah assumed the humidity helped create her beautiful ringlets. "I do. Please come in."

She ushered Vanessa past the box in the living room and into the kitchen, then peeked at the food. "Don't get too excited. I'm only reheating. I picked up chicken Florentine from Ernesto's on my way home. Have you had it?"

"I haven't." Vanessa put the bottles on the counter. "Sounds delicious."

Hannah reached for them. "Let's chill this one. I already have a bottle of white open if you'd like a glass now." She glanced over her shoulder at Vanessa. "Depending on how this box thing goes, we might need the red, too."

That earned her a smile.

"I'd love one." Vanessa looked around. "Your home is unique."

Hannah didn't turn from pouring their drinks. "Yes." She returned the wine to the refrigerator, then handed Vanessa a glass. "Honestly, it's not really my style. Cheers," she said, hoping to move past her disclosure.

Vanessa didn't seem to notice as she surveyed the dark walls and cabinetry. "I get that. It has Bren written all over it."

Hannah motioned to the living room. "Let's go relax. The food needs another ten minutes." She settled into an armchair, and Vanessa chose the couch. "You found the place all right?"

Vanessa nodded, then set her drink on a coaster. "I know Fremont quite well."

"Do you live in this neighborhood, too?" Hannah had made a mistake bringing the box in so early. Even the sight of it made it difficult to focus on the conversation.

"No." Vanessa adjusted, turning more toward her. "I live in Queen Anne, but I'm a lifelong Seattle resident." She raised a finger. "Other than college."

"Same here, though I didn't even get to escape for that. Where'd you go?"

"Southern Oregon University in Ashland. You?"

"Seattle University, then UDub." Hannah was interested in Vanessa, but she wanted to know more than could be found on a CV. "What made you change your mind? About this?"

Vanessa picked up her glass and stared at the swirling liquid before answering. "I thought about what it must be like for you right now."

Caught off guard, Hannah couldn't find words. She'd expected something superficial like curiosity, or perhaps selfish, like Vanessa wanting to find out whether Bren had been cheating on her, too. "That was kind," she said finally, then stood. "I should check the food."

She didn't know what to do with Vanessa's response. Behind her surprise came a wave of nausea. Vanessa probably imagined, in addition to Hannah reeling from finding out she'd been lied to for years, how she grieved the loss of her soulmate when Hannah had known for some time that Bren was wrong for her and certainly not her forever person. Jesus. Now she felt like she'd lured Vanessa here under false pretenses. It was her own damned fault. But she still didn't want to be alone opening that damned box. Talk about selfishness.

The sauce around the food bubbled, and that seemed a good indicator. She'd never been the most experienced cook. "It's ready," Hannah called, leaving the other thoughts behind. The evening was already in play. "We can eat in here."

Vanessa appeared carrying both their glasses. "Need topping off?"

"Sure."

They sat at the two-person table near the windows, the one Bren never liked to use because of the glare on her screen. It was nice tonight to be able to look out on the setting sun and the long shadows being cast across the backyard without a device in sight.

"Oh, you have a Golden Ruby." Vanessa pointed out the window with her fork.

"I have what?" Hannah craned her neck to see whatever might be out there.

"The low bush over there." This time Vanessa leaned in and used her finger to show her. "I bet it gets bright red and orange in the fall."

Hannah had no idea what the plants—bushes?—in her yard were, but she *had* noticed that one. "Oh, right. My gardener wanted to remove it because it had thorns, but I like the splash of color."

Vanessa smiled, delicate lines appearing around the corners of her mouth and eyes. "Good call."

In the waning light, her eyes appeared even more green than the foliage outside. Hannah went back to her food.

Eating took far too little time, and Hannah could no longer avoid the thing she'd been dreading. Armed with their wine, they returned to the living room. Vanessa sat on the sofa, while Hannah pushed the coffee table aside and settled on the floor with the box between them.

"How do you want to do this?"

The soft and careful note in Vanessa's tone made Hannah look up. "What do you mean?"

Vanessa tilted her head. "I'm happy to be here as moral support, if that's all you need, or I can look at things first and give you a bit of warning before I pass them to you."

Vanessa would do that for her? Some of the weight that had settled on Hannah's shoulders eased. "I'd appreciate a heads up on anything… you know. So, the latter would be great."

Vanessa tugged the box closer, spreading her legs so it nestled between her feet. She took off the lid and placed it beside her. "Oh."

Shit. Hannah had forgotten she'd put the photo in the box. It would've been thoughtful to have given Vanessa a bit of warning, too. "I'm sorry. I should've told you that was in there. Bren's boss asked me if I recognized you before he included it. Apparently, it'd fallen behind something in her office."

"It's fine." Vanessa stared at the picture for a moment. "I haven't seen this one in a long time. Makes me realize how much better I looked back then."

"Let me see." Hannah took it. She held it up, making a display of glancing back and forth between it and Vanessa. Finally, she set it on the coffee table. "Nope. You're wrong."

FLOWERS AND GEMSTONES

Vanessa laughed, the delightful, melodic sound echoing off the walls and giving Hannah's home a cheerfulness it hadn't possessed in ages, if ever. "Okay, let's get started." But even as Vanessa moved on, the pink in her cheeks didn't.

She passed Hannah inconsequential items like lip gloss, breath mints, too many promotional items with Bren's work logo to count, a softball trophy for most-improved player, protein bars, Bren's business cards, tampons, a change of clothing, and a mini umbrella. At length, she paused and said, "All the remaining items are paper."

"Okay, I'm ready." Hannah wasn't sure that was true, but she tried to paste on a brave face.

"This seems innocuous." Vanessa handed her a birthday card signed by coworkers.

Hannah found nothing unusual about it, none of the well-wishes any more significant than the others, at least not to her eye. She added it to the pile she'd made on the floor beside her.

"As does this." Vanessa passed her a certificate Bren had received for completing a sexual harassment training. "Hmm. Not sure about this though." She leafed through an envelope labeled Receipts. "Do you want to go through them now? They seem to be from multiple cities, including many from San Francisco." She didn't offer them to Hannah.

"Let's leave them for last." Hannah wasn't sure what they could tell her unless the items purchased held some significance.

Vanessa pulled out a manila folder. "This seems to be copies of her time sheets and pay stubs. I'm kind of shocked a company of that size hasn't gone digital, or at least offered a paperless option." She flipped through it, then stopped. "There's a greeting card in here." She pulled it free and looked up. "Should I read it first?"

Hannah hugged her knees to her chest and nodded.

Vanessa set the folder aside and scanned the front of the envelope. "The return address is a Georgina Kaplan in Daly City, California. Ring a bell?"

A woman. Hannah didn't recognize the name. With Vanessa watching her so intently, Hannah couldn't meet her gaze. "No." She rested her head on her arms.

She listened to the sound of the card being pulled from the envelope. Then a quick intake of breath told Hannah all she needed to know. It was exactly what she'd feared, the entire reason she hadn't been able to face opening the box on her own. When Vanessa didn't speak, Hannah looked up.

Vanessa's expression held compassion and something else. "How much do you want to know?"

"You can just sum it up for me." Her voice cracked midway through.

"Well." Vanessa scanned it again. "It's a birthday card dated last year. It's signed Georgie." She got quiet again.

"What else?" Was Vanessa's reluctance for Hannah's benefit or another reason?

Vanessa blinked a few times. "Um, she wishes Bren a happy birthday and laments being apart." She looked up. "I'm sorry. She also suggests not-so-subtly that the next time they're together, she'll be the present."

Hannah had wondered many times if Bren could be having an affair, but having it so blatantly spelled out rattled her. What a mess she would've been if she'd had to face this alone. "Anything else in the box?"

Vanessa hesitated. "Do you want to take a break, or talk, or something?"

Hannah shook her head. She wanted this finished.

Vanessa riffled through a few sheets of paper. "Nothing of consequence, but there are the receipts."

"I think the card told me all I need to know."

Vanessa pushed Hannah's wine closer to her. "You did it. Here's to making it through." She lifted hers and waited for Hannah.

Granted, Hannah was a bit numb, but she was in one piece. And she had Vanessa to thank for that. She clinked glasses with her and sipped. "Who the fuck is Georgina Kaplan?"

Vanessa choked and covered her mouth with her hand. When she'd recovered, she softly laughed. "You can't do that when I'm drinking. Do you want me to google her?" At Hannah's nod, she pulled her phone from her purse. "Let's see. There's a woman by that name in California, age thirty-five." Vanessa moved to sit beside Hannah on the floor.

Hannah leaned in and looked at her screen. "The same age as Bren." Vanessa smelled like flowers. Was that perfume or the scent that lingered from her being at work? It *was* the same amazing smell Hannah remembered from the shop.

"It appears she resides at the same residence in Daly City with a Jamal Kaplan, age thirty-six, and a Noah Kaplan, age thirteen." Vanessa turned to her. "What do you think? Husband and son?"

"Looks that way."

"Daly City is…" Vanessa typed.

Hannah placed a hand on her arm to save her the trouble. "It's just south of San Francisco."

"Ah." Her tone said volumes. Vanessa scrolled. "There's a phone number."

Hannah laughed, though she found none of this humorous. "I can't call. What am I supposed to say? 'Hi, I'm Hannah. Were you screwing my girlfriend?'"

"Something like that," Vanessa muttered. She held up her phone. "I'll call, and on the off chance she answers, I'll ask her if she knew Bren McAvoy."

"We already know they were intimate." Hannah motioned toward the card.

"Yes, but if she lies about it, it'll tell us whether we can trust her regarding other things."

Hannah pushed herself up. "We need to open the red for this."

Vanessa uncorked it while Hannah rummaged in her cupboards for something sweet. Good Lord, if there was ever an evening not to care about calories, this was it. Armed with more wine, cookies, and dark chocolate, they sat on the couch.

Vanessa touched Hannah's leg. "How are you holding up?"

"You know, I'd suspected she was having an affair." Hannah looked at Vanessa, expecting to see surprise in her expression, but she appeared unmoved by the information. "Still, it's shocking, you know, to have it confirmed."

"Mm." Vanessa got a faraway look in her eyes, then seemed to realize she'd wandered. "Okay, any idea how to block a number?"

"For what?"

Vanessa shifted a bit. "She may know my name. We don't know how long ago their affair started."

"Oh, God. I've been so self-absorbed, I didn't consider this might affect you."

Vanessa waved her off. "Infidelity during your relationship has been all but confirmed." The look was back. "With mine, only suspected."

Hannah cringed. She'd completely forgotten that the entire reason she'd asked Vanessa to come over tonight was their shared connection with Bren. Of course, some of this might apply to her, too. "Good God, she might've cheated on both of us with the same woman." She squeezed Vanessa's hand. "I'm an ass and so sorry. Is that why you broke up? Your suspicions?"

Vanessa gently tugged her hand free. She opened her mouth but closed it again.

"Sorry, that's none of my business." Hannah picked up her wine, hoping to signal that she was ready to move on.

"I never suspected anything." Vanessa's voice had become so low that Hannah almost missed her speaking. "So, I was devastated when she left me at the altar."

"Vanessa." Hannah didn't even know where to begin.

Vanessa waved her off. "It was a long time ago. I've struggled to get over it, so you can see why being involved in this frightens me a bit."

"Understandably." Hannah's stomach clenched at the knowledge she'd put her through this. "I can't thank you enough."

"You already did." Vanessa smiled. "Dinner was delicious."

Hannah wasn't ready to move past it. "Do you think she'd been having an affair with this woman, and that caused your breakup?"

"Breakup is a tactful way to phrase it." Vanessa set her glass on a coaster. "It crossed my mind, but it doesn't make sense. If she'd left me for Georgina, wouldn't she have been with her, not you?"

Hannah gave a half shrug. "Honestly, none of it makes sense to me."

"Well, shall I call the infamous Georgina?" Vanessa playfully growled her name.

With a bit of online help to figure out how to block a number, they soon stared at Vanessa's cell on speaker between them. It rang and rang, finally going to a generic voicemail. Vanessa didn't leave a message.

"I kind of wanted her to answer."

Vanessa stared thoughtfully at the screen. "Me, too. I'm trying it unblocked." She did, with the same result.

Hannah studied her. "You know, I feel bad I asked you to do this for me, and I can't do anything about that now, but I have to say, it's nice being here with perhaps the only other person who might understand the situation."

"True." Vanessa shot her a rueful look. "And while I won't go so far as to say I had fun this evening, I did enjoy dinner and the company."

Yes, Hannah had relished Vanessa's presence, too. "Did you drive?"

"No, I took an Uber."

"Perfect." Hannah held up the bottle. "More wine?"

Vanessa smiled and held out her glass.

As Hannah poured, she appreciated that she'd already grieved the loss of Bren long before tonight. Even so, facing she'd been cheated on stung.

But wow. Being left at the altar? *That* would hurt like hell.

Chapter Six

At the counter, Vanessa slipped a pair of ladybug gardening gloves into Bette Mason's bag as a spontaneous thank you for her loyal patronage over the years. The iPad used to ring up sales said it was almost two o'clock. "Will that be all?"

"And these." Bette pushed a couple of miniature pots containing marigolds toward her. "My granddaughters will love them."

When Vanessa finished the sale, she smiled as Bette bustled out of the store with her arms full. She glanced around. Only one customer remained, Moshe, who came in every Friday to buy his husband a bouquet he insisted on choosing himself. Based on her experience, he'd be awhile. "Dorothy, can you manage the front for a few minutes?"

"Of course. As long as you need."

Like many of her staff who weren't delivery drivers, Dorothy was in her sixties and had been arranging flowers for decades. The in-store employees who weren't Dorothy's age tended to be young and bursting with creativity and innovative ideas, like Cai. It made for a great balance, the young infusing the place with needed youthful energy and the veterans providing hands-on education and tutelage. Vanessa had little turnover, and her benefits package was partly why. She still couldn't believe she got to wake up every day to do what she loved. It'd made all the difference after Bren had left her. Yet, at times, she longed for someone with whom she could share her success.

She checked on the cold room and everyone seemed fine, so she ducked out to the garage where Reyna worked on one of the vans. "How bad is it?"

Reyna, face up on the creeper, rolled out from under the vehicle, her undercut somehow still perfectly coiffed. "Just a broken gasket. She'll be ready to go out tomorrow."

"Fantastic." The day continued to move right along. "Thanks." Vanessa headed inside.

As she heated water for tea, her phone vibrated. She eyed the screen. Hannah Baros? She hadn't expected to hear from her again. Hannah had seemed relatively unsurprised at the confirmation of Bren's infidelity two nights ago, and her good-bye had sounded more like *take care and have a good life* rather than *see you later*. "Hello?"

"Hi, sorry to bother you at work. Do you have a minute?"

"I do." More than a little curious, Vanessa leaned against the break room counter.

"I have something I'd like to talk to you about. Would you be able to meet for dinner tonight, that is, if you don't have to work late or already have plans?"

Vanessa grinned at Hannah's rambling. "I'm free."

"Perfect. Text me your address. No takeout this time. How's six forty-five?"

That would give Vanessa an opportunity to go home and change. "That's great."

"All right. See you then."

Vanessa swore she could hear Hannah smile.

"Okay. Bye."

"Did you just get asked out on a date?"

Vanessa startled. She'd forgotten Chloe lounged at the table nibbling the last bite of her chocolate chip cookie. "Not at all."

"You look like you were," Chloe said, with far too much delight in her tone.

"Well, I wasn't." Was she? How ridiculous. Hannah had just lost her partner and then found out she'd been cheated on. Hardly a time to start dating. Vanessa went back to making her tea.

Chloe threw away her garbage. "So, what was it then?"

Vanessa glanced at her. "When did I start paying you to grill me?"

"Fine." Chloe grinned. "But if you're taking personal calls in public spaces, you can't blame me for being nosy."

Vanessa gave in. It was Chloe, after all. "Remember that woman I told you about? The one I met at my ex's funeral? She wants to ask me something." Chloe didn't know about the box or her going over to Hannah's.

"Awkward, don't you think? Current girlfriend wants to ask ex-girlfriend questions?" Chloe's eyebrows performed gymnastics.

And yet it hadn't been. They'd interacted with ease. "I'm sure it's nothing." Vanessa grabbed her mug and escaped before any further interrogation could take place.

By six thirty, Vanessa had made it home, changed, and even had a few minutes to touch up her hair and makeup. Hannah hadn't mentioned where they were going, so Vanessa didn't know how formally she needed to dress. She erred on the side of safety and wore gray pants and a crisp Oxford shirt. With the top two buttons left undone, the sleeves rolled once, and a few jangly bracelets, she'd be presentable in most restaurants. With her attire complete, she did things she normally didn't do, like pace, fuss, and fret for reasons unclear. What was wrong with her?

By seven, Hannah hadn't arrived, and Vanessa's annoyance at herself for glancing out the window every thirty seconds had reached a high. She forced herself to sit. Her nerves must be due to the unknown nature of the meeting. And how inconsiderate of Hannah to leave her hanging like this with no word. Vanessa didn't know if this was typical behavior on Hannah's part, with them having so little interaction. Could something have happened to her?

Her phone buzzed.

Running late. Sorry. Be there soon.

Vanessa sent a short response, then returned to perseverating. What did Hannah want to talk about? If she had come across more of Bren's belongings she found disturbing, Vanessa assumed she would've said something over the phone. Besides, if she were upset about more discoveries, she probably wouldn't want to talk in public. This must be about something else.

The doorbell's chime made her jump. *Finally.* She grabbed her coat and stepped outside.

"A Victorian. Nice." Hannah glanced around the porch. "It suits you."

"Thank you. I did a lot of the renovations myself." She locked the house, and they descended the steps.

"Impressive. And the gardening is all you, I assume." Hannah touched a branch of the honeysuckle Vanessa had planted along the sidewalk.

Her angst easing, Vanessa chuckled. "How'd you know?" She'd expected Hannah to be dressed in a jacket and skirt like when she'd shown up at the shop, but she wore a simple blouse and black pants.

Hannah smiled. "Lucky guess."

Hannah had parked her midnight blue Lexus LS behind Vanessa's Honda in the driveway. The sophisticated model suited her.

"Sorry I'm late. I got hung up at work." She held the door open for Vanessa. "The restaurant's holding our table."

As Hannah made her way to the driver's side, Vanessa wondered if that was a normal courtesy or if the Baros name held some sway. They might be a family-owned business, but based on how many billboards and advertisements Vanessa had noticed recently, they weren't small by any standard. Vanessa hadn't realized it, but that'd probably played a part in her earlier anxiety.

"Hungry?" Hannah put the car in reverse.

Vanessa took a deep breath and allowed herself to relax. "I am."

Thankfully, they didn't have far to go. Hannah quickly found parking in the Mount Baker neighborhood near Lake Washington, and they soon sat at a window table overlooking downtown Seattle that had already begun to sparkle with lights. The restaurant was unknown to Vanessa, and to her surprise, its menu mostly featured burgers.

"You needed a reservation?"

Hannah turned away from the skyline. "No. The chef is a friend of mine, and I wanted this table. Isn't the view spectacular?"

Vanessa appreciated it a few more moments. "It really is." Was the vista something Hannah enjoyed whenever she ate here, or had she been trying to impress?

"It only gets better as darkness falls." Hannah picked up the cocktail list. "Drinks?"

When the server brought their beverages, Hannah clinked her glass. "To the view." They both sipped, and then Hannah laced her fingers together and leaned closer. "So, why Late Bloomer?"

A flash image of herself as a teen made Vanessa's cheeks warm. "Why the name, you mean?" At Hannah's nod, she continued with her usual answer. "We're open and deliver later than most florists. It's a fun play on words."

"Is that all? You're blushing."

Hannah appeared delighted, which probably made it worse, and Vanessa couldn't refrain from returning her smile. "I've always been a bit behind on milestones. The name pokes fun at myself, as well."

"Milestones? Such as?"

"I'm regretting the name choice at the moment."

Hannah laughed. "Now I really have to know."

Vanessa considered what to say, then rolled her eyes. "I can't believe I'm going to tell you this." She sighed and pointed to her breasts. "These, for one." She'd made up for her slow start, but still.

To her credit, Hannah didn't lower her gaze. "And for another?"

Now even the tips of Vanessa's ears were hot. Oh, well. In for a penny… "I didn't have sex until I went to college. I gave my virginity to my roommate my first year." She paused to take a much-needed drink. "We're still friends. I just realized the other day it's been thirty years."

"Wow." Hannah swirled her drink. "But you don't sleep together anymore?"

"God, no. We only lasted two months as a couple. Sonja's married now."

"Any other late-blooming anecdotes for me?" Hannah nudged Vanessa's foot with her own.

"None as juicy as those two."

Hannah bit her lower lip as if holding back a retort.

Vanessa didn't want to know. She pulled a menu closer. "What's good here?"

"Have you decided?" The server held his pen over a small notebook, its edges curled from wear.

Hannah motioned for her to go first.

"I'll have the black bean burger and a side salad with ranch." Vanessa looked up just in time to see Hannah blanch. Whatever was wrong with her, she managed to control it until she'd placed her order and the server left.

"Oh, my gosh." Her words came out in a rush. "I served you chicken the other night. I didn't know you were a vegetarian. I should've asked. I'm *so* sorry."

Vanessa laughed gently. "I promise you, I'm not. But I enjoy a plant-based meal occasionally."

"Are you sure?"

Vanessa reached across the table and gave her hand a quick squeeze. "Yes. The chicken was delicious."

The frown on Hannah's face softened with obvious relief.

By the time their meals arrived, they'd almost finished their drinks and the poutine appetizer Hannah had suggested. While Vanessa savored the delicious food, she kept expecting Hannah to ask whatever questions she had. Instead, she inquired about Vanessa's day, her music tastes, and whether she'd had any childhood pets.

When they finished eating, the waiter cleared their plates.

Hannah caught his attention before he moved away. "Could we have a few minutes before looking at the dessert menu?"

"Of course. Just let me know when you're ready."

Apparently, the time had come.

With her cocktail cradled in her hands, Hannah looked at Vanessa. "So, your bravery inspired me. I called Georgina Kaplan again."

"Oh." Vanessa couldn't hide her shock. After Hannah's reluctance to open the box on her own, this news stunned her.

"Yeah, I know. It surprised me, too." Hannah studied her drink. "It occurred to me that I never really knew Bren. She kept so much of herself locked away, and then the lies..."

Vanessa understood all too well. "Did Georgina answer?"

Hannah looked up. "Not at first, but the second time, a woman, presumably her, said hello, then hung up when I told her who I was."

"Interesting. Right after you said your name?"

"I'd barely gotten it out." Hannah gave a short laugh but turned serious. "I suppose we could play this telephone game ad infinitum, but I have a better idea." She drummed her fingertips lightly on the table. "I think we should go on a road trip." She sat back and folded her arms across her chest, looking almost smug.

"To California? Both of us?"

Hannah nodded. "We have a better chance of getting to talk to her if we're face to face. Aren't you curious who she is? I don't know about you, but I must have a hundred questions."

"Why not fly? It's faster." Vanessa took a gulp of her Paloma. She hadn't expected this. A tingle of excitement flared in her, but the idea was also a bit unhinged.

Hannah shrugged. "I have to pick up some lab-grown diamonds in San Francisco anyway, and sometimes the airlines are strict. They've been known to confiscate precious stones, even if everything is legitimate.

It's not worth the risk. Plus, it'd be fun. When's the last time you did something like this?"

When *had* she? Vanessa used to love getting away. And she liked being around Hannah and wanted to support her when she encountered Georgina. There was something about Hannah's vivaciousness, her outgoing personality that Vanessa enjoyed. She'd probably be a fun travel companion. "It's been a while, but what would we do when we get there? Just knock on her door?"

"We absolutely knock on her damned door. She won't talk to us on the phone." Hannah drank the last of her Moscow Mule and set the copper mug aside. "Listen, I know you like to think things over, so you don't have to dec—"

"I'll go."

Hannah blinked. Twice. "What?"

"I said I'll go, but under one condition. It's June, and summer's the busiest time of year for me with all the weddings. I can't go until September, at the earliest."

"Three months." Hannah pursed her lips. "Okay, then. That's when we'll do it."

"What about your gemstones?"

Hannah shrugged. "I guess I'm picking them up in September. If Baros Family Jewelers has a diamond shortage, it's on you."

Vanessa playfully batted away the finger Hannah pointed at her.

As Hannah drove her home after dessert and a short walk along Lake Washington to burn off some calories, Vanessa let her mind wander back to their dinner conversation. What had she agreed to? Or, perhaps more importantly, *why* had she agreed to it?

It *would* be advantageous for both of them to meet and assess Georgina—and hopefully obtain answers that'd allow them to move forward with their lives. Vanessa couldn't lie to herself. Bren's betrayal on their planned wedding day had wrecked Vanessa, as evidenced by her inability to make it through a single first date since. She'd concluded a year ago that she'd had enough of dating and relationships, and most definitely with love, because no matter how much she wanted it to be different, it was impossible to believe what people said.

And even if Bren had been cheating on Vanessa, she probably still would've been with Georgina and not dating Hannah. Still, Vanessa couldn't help but wonder. Was Georgina the reason Bren pulled her runaway-bride stunt?

Secretly, she wanted to spend time with Hannah. Should that concern her? Could she keep her feelings toward Hannah strictly in the friend column?

She stole a glimpse of her in the driver's seat. Hannah was stunning, but being attracted to someone grieving was so utterly wrong.

"You're awfully quiet."

Hannah's voice resonated softly, seemingly in mockery of Vanessa's thoughts. *Friend column.*

"Just thinking."

Hannah glanced sideways. "About what? Georgina?"

"Mostly."

The slight shift of Hannah turning onto Vanessa's street caused Vanessa's phone to drop between the seats.

"Can you reach it?" Hannah switched on the interior light.

"I think so." Vanessa squeezed her hand into the narrow space and her fingertips touched her phone and something else. A piece of paper. She pulled them both out. "Got it."

"Sorry if there's crap down there." Hannah maneuvered into the driveway and shifted into park.

Vanessa stared at the lined sheet that had *Reasons for Breaking Up* written across the top and a bulleted list below. What was she reading? Her stomach churned, and nausea rose in her throat. What had she just been reminding herself of? *It was impossible to believe what people said. Why would Hannah be different?*

"Oh, God." Hannah swiped it from her grasp and crumpled it. "Let me explain."

Vanessa got out of the car, and Hannah leaped from the driver's side.

"Vanessa, wait." She ran around the front.

Vanessa turned to face her. "You don't owe me an explanation. We barely know each other, and it's none of my business. Thank you for dinner." She walked up her steps and into the house.

Once inside though, her emotions weren't so easily dismissed. Even as she readied herself for bed, she kept visualizing Hannah's note. She hadn't meant to read it, but it hadn't been lengthy, and it'd only taken her a moment to scan. Hannah clearly had been planning to break up with Bren.

A text alert brought Vanessa to a standstill with her toothbrush hanging out of her mouth. Hannah.

Please call me. I need to talk to you.

The gall. Seriously? Hannah wasn't going to let this go? She'd led Vanessa to believe she'd lost the person she loved and used Vanessa's empathy to make her go through Bren's belongings with her.

Vanessa finished in the bathroom and sat on the edge of her bed, the text still displayed on her phone.

Had Hannah misled her? What exactly had she said, and how much had Vanessa assumed? Her decision to support Hannah while going through the box had been hers. She could've stayed firm and said no. But Hannah must've been feeling *some* kind of emotion or been going through *something* for her to ask Vanessa, a virtual stranger, to be there. Perhaps Vanessa had been too hasty in her assessment.

She pressed call, and Hannah answered right away.

"I'll tell you anything you want to know. I know how it looks."

"I'm not even sure where to begin." Vanessa rubbed her forehead to ease her tension.

Hannah sighed. "You could start by letting me in. I'm still out front. I want to look you in the eyes and apologize for not being transparent with you."

Vanessa stood and parted the blinds. Hannah's car hadn't moved, although she'd turned off the interior light. "I'll be right down." She ended the call and put on her robe.

By the time she opened the front door, Hannah stood on her porch. It'd begun to rain, and tiny droplets dotted Hannah's hair and face.

Vanessa moved aside and allowed her to pass. "I guess we can sit in here." She motioned to the formal living room she rarely used.

"This is fine." Hannah turned and faced her in the entryway. "I won't keep you long. As you quickly deduced, I planned to break up with Bren."

"So, why didn't you?" Vanessa crossed her arms, suddenly self-conscious about not being fully dressed.

"I should've." Hannah slowly shook her head. "Way before I wrote my list. But taking over the business from my parents had its issues, and I prioritized a new project at work over my personal life. I knew things were bad between Bren and me. They had been for two years. She'd been distant and traveled more and more. Being busy helped me avoid dealing with it, I suppose."

"But you must've thought about it at one point if you wrote that note." Vanessa eyed her.

"I did." Hannah's chin trembled. "But I never got the chance. When I got home the day I finally decided to do it, state troopers were there to inform me of her death."

Vanessa gripped the banister to steady herself. "You mean—"

Hannah nodded. "The day she died. That's the goddamned day I chose to break up with her." She pressed her lips together, and her eyes shone with tears.

"What are the chances?" Vanessa tried to wrap her mind around it all.

"Apparently, very good." Hannah took a step closer. "I haven't told anyone else besides you. Not my mother, not Zara, no one. How could I? Bren had just died. I would've looked so insensitive."

It wouldn't have been good. "So, you kept quiet."

"Yeah, but I didn't realize how difficult it'd be. The way everyone doted on me and worried about why I hadn't cried. It was suffocating. I didn't want it, but I couldn't say anything. And before you think I have no heart, her death *did* affect me, just not as a partner. We lived together, she was someone I once loved, and while we didn't work out, I never wanted any harm to come to her."

"I understand."

"Do you?" Hannah looked at her with the same pleading eyes she'd had when she'd come to Late Bloomer.

Vanessa nodded, her initial anger subsiding. They weren't that different, the two of them. They both mourned Bren's exit from the world, just not as her lover. "In hindsight, I made a lot of assumptions." She could thank her past issues rearing their ugly heads for that.

"I could've been more forthright, but once I wedged myself into that situation, I couldn't see a way out." Hannah put a hand on the doorknob. "Anyway, September is a long way off. I hope you'll let me prove myself until then."

Vanessa didn't know exactly what that meant, but she appreciated that Hannah didn't pressure her. She nodded.

Hannah opened the door. "Thanks for responding to my text. I didn't want to leave things the way they were."

"I'm sorry I overreacted." Due to the weather or as an olive branch, she wasn't sure which, but Vanessa offered her an umbrella from the stand in the entry. "Here."

"It's not far."

Vanessa pushed it into her hands. "It's coming down hard."

Hannah took it, and Vanessa watched from the doorway as she got in her car. As Hannah's taillights receded into the darkness, Vanessa went inside.

Perhaps going to California and hearing what Georgina Kaplan had to say would allow Vanessa to work through some of her lingering issues regarding trust and forgiveness. And going with Hannah? Their common history, if she could call it that, gave them a bond. Hannah was kind, energetic, and intelligent with an infectious personality. Not the worst option for a traveling companion.

She climbed the stairs. Yes, she found Hannah attractive. Who wouldn't? Vanessa froze just inside her bedroom.

In light of the information she'd just learned, Hannah might not be so off limits after all.

The thought of being with someone made Vanessa's chest tighten, and she needed a minute before she could breathe easily again. It *would* be nice to get to know Hannah better, and not everything had to end in a relationship. People had sex all the time with no expectations. She smiled at the image that came to mind. But when it came to Hannah, and if the opportunity presented itself, would Vanessa be satisfied with only something physical?

Either way, she began to think of Hannah in an entirely different light.

Chapter Seven

Hannah entered Late Bloomer, the door held for her by a short man in a tweed blazer exiting with a vase of coral-colored roses. "Thank you." She gave him a smile. It made maneuvering her way into the shop with her hands full a little more graceful.

She'd waited before contacting Vanessa again after the nearly disastrous ending to their evening a week ago, but she'd woken this morning needing to see where things stood regarding the trip they'd discussed. If Vanessa no longer wanted to be involved, Hannah could go by herself at an earlier date, but hopefully, that wouldn't be the case.

Inside, the coolness was a relief from the unusually warm June day. She should unbutton her suit jacket to take better advantage of it. The heady, perfumed air surrounded her, and for a moment, as she waited to be noticed by a staff member, she longed to bottle it so she could take it with her. What a difference from the sterile environment of her office that smelled of industrial cleaner.

An older woman wearing the store's embroidered polo shirt offered the gentleman ahead of Hannah assistance, and the young man at the other end of the counter looked up and came closer. "Good morning. How can I help you?"

"Hello. Is Vanessa available to speak for a few minutes?"

"I believe so." His nametag read Cai. "One moment, ma'am." He disappeared into the back.

Seconds later, Vanessa followed him out and stopped short, the swinging door hitting her backside. "Hannah."

As Vanessa brushed off her apron in what looked like a habitual move, Hannah thought she caught her gaze flick from Hannah's skirt to her charcoal gray heels before raising again. Was she checking out her legs? No. Probably just the shiny newness of her shoes, or perhaps their height had drawn her attention.

"Hi." Hannah offered her a to-go cup from Seismic. "One latte, since you didn't get to enjoy your last one."

Vanessa stepped forward and took it. "Thanks, but I hope you didn't come here just to deliver this."

"That, and this." Hannah held out Vanessa's umbrella. "Thanks for letting me borrow it." It furthered her excuse to stop by today, although, since entering the store and being reminded of its amazing scents, she had a legitimate one.

"You're welcome." Vanessa took it and tucked it under the counter.

With a glance at the array of colorful flowers surrounding them, Hannah said, "And I'd also like a bouquet." Okay, so that hadn't been part of her plan, but was it wrong to want to take a little piece of the wonderful fragrances and colors with her?

If surprised, Vanessa hid it as she set the coffee down. "Any special occasion?"

"No." Hannah hesitated, then settled on the truth. "They're for me, for my office. I'd like something pretty to brighten the space, and I love how it smells in here."

"We have pre-made ones in the case behind you."

Hannah turned, fingering the hem of her jacket, suddenly unsure what to do with her hands. The vibrant arrangements were gorgeous, but her curiosity at Vanessa's talent won out. "Do you have time to make me one?"

"Of course." Vanessa gestured to the rows of buckets overflowing with bright blooms. "Do you have a color or flower preference?"

"No." She reconsidered. "Well, not too much pink."

"Coming right up."

As Vanessa walked around the store, Hannah followed. Watching her deftly pluck some blooms but not others had Hannah wondering, but that wasn't the purpose of her visit today.

"Also, I wanted to see if you're available for lunch on Saturday. I thought we could discuss the trip again. Do you work weekends?" She almost crossed her fingers, hoping Vanessa's answer would be no.

"Sometimes, but I run a volunteer program at a youth garden on Saturdays from ten to one. I'd ask Raymond to handle it—he teaches the gardening elective during the school year—but he'll be at his son's semi-final soccer match. I'll be turning kids away this week as it is."

"What do you mean?" Hannah hitched her purse higher and folded her arms.

Vanessa added some greenery to the assortment. "There's a maximum youth-to-adult ratio, so any child who arrives after that number is reached has to be sent home."

"These kids show up on a Saturday morning to volunteer during their summer, and they get turned away?" Hannah stifled her disbelief. What if the youth leadership program she'd attended each summer as a teen hadn't been there? Where would that have left her? Certainly, with less confidence. And likely wracked by boredom for three months while her parents focused on the company's needs. She credited it with where she was today almost as much as she did their influence.

Vanessa laid her selections on the counter. "Rules are rules." She snipped the ends with a pair of scissors and began to arrange the flowers in a simple glass vase.

"That's ridiculous." Hannah paced as Vanessa worked. "How old are they?"

"Middle school." Vanessa tied a violet ribbon around the neck and continued to move the stems around.

Hannah stopped. "What if I volunteered with you? Then we can have lunch afterward and talk."

"Why would you offer to do that?" Vanessa's forehead wrinkled.

"You wouldn't have to send any of them home." Obviously.

"It happens all the time. We both can't be there every weekend." Vanessa fitted the base into a cardboard box, likely to keep the arrangement upright during the ride to Hannah's work.

Should Hannah speak what crossed her mind? Would she be able to make time for it? She'd have to. It was important, so she'd figure out a way. Hannah moved closer. "What if you had three adults supervising every Saturday?"

Vanessa studied her. "Do you even like gardening?"

"I don't know." Hannah leafed through a notebook covered in daisies to hide her discomfort. "I've never done it." She returned it to its place.

"The district requires volunteers to be fingerprinted."

Hannah's body buzzed. Vanessa hadn't discounted her offer. "Fine." She faced Vanessa and couldn't believe how vibrant her order looked. "Tell me where." Hannah lowered her face into the petals and inhaled. "This is beautiful."

Vanessa's eyes narrowed. "You know I'd be willing to meet for lunch another day to talk about the trip, right?"

Hannah looked up, caught off guard by Vanessa's admission. She swallowed to make sure her voice didn't waver. "I didn't, but I'm happy to hear it."

"You know, you seem to have missed something important."

Hannah's thoughts raced. "I did?"

"Yes." Vanessa pushed her hands into the front pocket of her apron. "I might not have said yes the other night, but I didn't say no either."

"Oh." Hannah's head spun. She hadn't thought of it that way. A warm tingle deep inside made her smile. "I see." She wanted to look away from Vanessa's quiet study of her, but she didn't. "How much do I owe you?" She reached into her purse.

"Consider it a gift."

That hadn't been her plan when she'd asked, but one look at Vanessa told her she shouldn't argue. "That's sweet of you." She lifted the bouquet carefully. "Thank you." Hannah's phone buzzed, and she checked it. "Work. Gotta run. Sorry." She grinned and backed toward the door. "Don't let your coffee go cold."

Vanessa mock saluted with a short nod.

"Fingerprints. Text me." With a little wave, Hannah pushed out the door, making the bells jingle behind her. Would Vanessa remember? Hannah would have to rush things in order to be able to start this weekend.

As she walked to her car in the heat, she considered their conversation. She didn't want Vanessa to think her offer to help at the garden was an attempt to convince her to go to California. Hannah had volunteered in the community since she was a teen. It wasn't until her parents retired that she'd gotten so busy she'd had to quit temporarily, and now seemed like a good time to start up again. And while the hours she spent each week at her last position unboxing dry goods in the back of the food bank had been needed, she'd longed to work directly with people. Kids were a bonus. So, regardless of what was going on between Vanessa and her, this wasn't a quid pro quo situation.

Aside from that, what had held Hannah's attention so much the other night that she'd missed that Vanessa hadn't actually told her no?

❖

FLOWERS AND GEMSTONES

On Saturday, Hannah pulled her Lexus into the parking lot of Kikisoblu Middle School. If someone had told her a week ago she'd be gardening with a bunch of teens—or were they tweens?—she'd have requested her temperature be taken. But here she was, in jeans and a T-shirt, with a jacket thrown in the back in case the sky opened up. Would they do this if it rained? She hoped not as she envisioned caked mud on her car's floor mats.

Hannah got out. Vanessa had told her to go around back. Asking what she should bring hadn't occurred to her. Next time, she'd be better prepared. This week's priority had been rushing to get fingerprinted. Late yesterday afternoon, Vanessa let her know she'd been cleared. So, here she was, out of her element, as Vanessa would discover before long. The closest Hannah could come to identifying any plants would be pointing out the grass on the football field and some sort of pine trees near the teachers' parking lot. Hopefully, her ability to work hard and learn quickly would earn her points.

As she entered the gate that had an open padlock hanging from it, she took in the six-foot-tall fence. Was it to protect the garden from deer or vandals? When she spotted a group of people in the far corner, Vanessa stood out, her blond ponytail blowing in the wind as she leaned on a shovel watching Hannah approach.

"Glad you could make it."

Something in her tone made Hannah think Vanessa had doubted she would.

"I hope your students are good teachers. I'm afraid I'm going to need a crash course in all this." Hannah waved her hand at the rows of beds.

"They'll show you what you need to know." Vanessa handed the shovel to the girl next to her and came closer. "I will, too." She eyed Hannah. "Right now, this group is doing some weeding, and those over there are going to plant seedlings. You can choose where to start."

An Asian girl with green-streaked hair ran up to Vanessa. "You said I could turn the compost bin this week. You didn't spin it, did you?" She bounced on the balls of her feet. "I've been taking progress shots every week for my video. Do you think it'll go viral? I mean, it might if there's lots of worms when I turn it. Right?"

Vanessa laughed. "No one's touched it. I saved it for you." As the girl raced off, Vanessa turned to Hannah. "That's Vesper. Most of the other kids' excitement will be at a much lower level."

Hannah nodded. "Okay, good." She was already a little overwhelmed participating in something so foreign to her, and four shots of espresso didn't contain that much energy.

"C'mon. I'll introduce you to the others."

By the time they'd made it around the garden, Hannah had almost memorized all the names. But could she match Zaiden, Ger, Haylee, Samantha, Hector, Noor, Isla, Jawan, and two Ellies with the correct child?

"So, planting or weeding?" Vanessa asked.

Her eyes weren't visible behind her sunglasses, but Hannah could feel them on her. She'd already decided. "I'll pull weeds. I don't want to kill any seedlings on my first day."

Vanessa smiled. "Okay, join that group over there then. Do you want me to come with you?"

"No, I'll be fine." Hannah headed toward the kids bent over the raised beds.

When she approached, they quieted, but her rueful request for help to identify what was a weed and what wasn't seemed to earn her pity points. After forty-five minutes, she had a bucket nearly full of the bad guys, a shirt damp with sweat, and joints that screamed they hadn't seen much more than desk work in way too long.

"Oh, God." Vanessa stood above her. "Come with me."

Hannah rose and moaned as her knees cracked. She cringed with mortification. A worse thought struck her. Had Vanessa seen the bucket? What if Hannah screwed up and pulled all the wrong green things? She hadn't questioned the kids when they'd told her what were weeds. She sighed. Had she been initiated by a practical joke that would end up with Vanessa mad at her? It'd actually been fun so far, and she hated to think this might be the first and last time she'd be welcomed here.

Vanessa led her to a shed in the farthest corner. Its doors hung open, and a utility sink with a hose hooked up to it stood beside it. "Over here." She turned on the water and clutched Hannah's hands. "These are a mess. Why didn't you grab a pair of gloves? There should've been a pair in the wagon."

Hannah looked down at her hands. They were streaked in green, and dirt caked her nails. She'd destroyed her manicure, and an angry red line ran the length of her index finger. All of that aside, they were cradled in Vanessa's warm clean grasp. At the restaurant, she'd noticed the tiny scratches and cuts that blemished Vanessa's skin from her fingertips almost to her elbows.

"What's wrong with yours?"

Vanessa raised her eyebrows. "Mine?"

"All the marks." Hannah motioned with her chin.

"Oh." Vanessa said, as though she'd forgotten they were there. "Roses, mostly. We have to strip the thorns every day. Gloves help, but they still poke through. Then there are knives and clippers. All hazards of the job." She pulled Hannah closer to the sink. "Let's get you cleaned up."

Instead of letting her do it herself, Vanessa stepped in front of her and drew one of Hannah's arms around her. She gently began washing away the dirt and stains, the water from the hose tepid from soaking up the heat of the sun.

Hannah smiled to herself. Was this some maternal instinct, maybe a result of working with and being responsible for kids? But when she realized how close her breasts were to Vanessa's back, all thoughts of maternal *anything* fled her mind.

At this proximity, Hannah could smell Vanessa's shampoo, something tropical that made her think of piña coladas on the beach. Warmth built in the small space between them, and Hannah carefully kept what little distance remained.

Vanessa washed her other hand while Hannah stood there not knowing what to do, a rare occurrence for her. She didn't want to embarrass Vanessa by drawing attention to their situation, especially since she seemed to be the only one aware of it. And while they were currently out of sight of the rest of the group on the side of the shed, what if one of the kids walked around the corner and saw them like this? Wouldn't that be worse?

To Hannah's relief, the water cooled, and Vanessa turned it off. "Hang on." She disappeared into the small building, then returned with a rag. "It's not pretty, but it's clean. Dry off and come inside."

Hannah used the makeshift towel as she followed.

"I should've given you a pair of gloves." Vanessa glanced over her shoulder.

"*I* should've thought to bring some." Discomfort oozed from Hannah's every pore.

Vanessa bent and unzipped a backpack. "You can use some of mine." She handed her a green pair, stained, but smelling of laundry detergent. "Did you remember sunscreen?"

"No." Hannah gripped the gloves. "It's not really sunny out."

"It doesn't matter." Vanessa retrieved a bottle and, before Hannah could react, began spreading lotion over her cheeks and chin. "Close your eyes."

Hannah started to pull away, then found herself relaxing into Vanessa's tender touch and the nearness of her. The scent of coconut—presumably, what she'd gotten a whiff of standing behind Vanessa outside—mingled with the earthy pungency of potting soil.

With the same soothing strokes, Vanessa applied it to her neck and the tops of her ears. "Arms."

Now clean, Hannah could do this herself. Was Vanessa using it as an opportunity to touch her? Was she enjoying it as much as Hannah?

"You can open your eyes. I'm done with your face," Vanessa said, a hint of laughter in her tone.

Okay, so she'd drifted a bit. Hannah cleared her throat. "Thanks."

"Nice bucket of weeds." Vanessa wiped the remainder of the sunscreen on herself. "I think I'll keep you." Her expression turned serious. "Are the kids behaving? If they get wild, just let me know."

"They've been great." So, they hadn't pranked her after all. "The one girl sitting to the side and watching has been a bit quiet though. Is that normal?"

Vanessa frowned. "Which one?"

"Short hair. Black and gray flannel."

"I know who you mean. Samantha." Vanessa grabbed her gloves. "I'll walk you over there."

By the time Hannah and Vanessa got back to the group, the kids had begun a new row. Hannah was way behind. They'd each doubled her output.

Vanessa walked around the four sections they'd already completed. "These look fantastic. Did you all notice how much taller the beans have gotten since last week?"

"I take a photo every week to document it. I think I'm going to make a time lapse." The compost girl stood.

Vespa? Versa? Hannah struggled to remember.

Vanessa moved toward her. "Let's see them, Vesper."

Vesper. It was going to take Hannah a few weeks to learn their names.

After complimenting her shots, Vanessa bent to pull a few missed weeds as she wandered toward where Samantha sat on the edge of the farthest bed.

From the wagon, Hannah grabbed a kneeling pad she now noticed everyone else using, then brought her bucket to the end of the row near the two of them and pulled on her gloves. She got the attention of the white boy across from her, not an easy task with his hair hanging into his eyes. "So, the weeds over here, do they look the same as the ones over there?"

"Yeah." He grinned. "These are the tomatillo seedlings. The beds are labeled at the ends if you ever wanna know what's up."

Hannah blinked a few times at all the green things growing before her. She cleared her throat, knowing she was about to show how ill-suited she was for this task. "They all look the same to me. How am I supposed to tell them apart?"

He reached over. "See how these leaves have little things poking out, kinda like a steak knife? Those are the tomatillos."

Good God. Was she going to have to get her reading glasses from the car? Hannah leaned closer. Whew. Serrated edges. She could do this. "I see. Tell me your name again?"

"Zaiden."

"Thanks, Zaiden."

On the periphery of the garden, Vanessa sat beside Samantha. "Are you not feeling well today? You can call your dad to get you if you need to go home."

"I'm fine."

"Then why aren't you helping? You're usually one of my best weeders." Vanessa's warm tone reminded Hannah of when she'd helped her with the box.

"Because of those. I'm not wearing them, and I can't find any others."

Hannah glanced over to see Samantha pointing at a pair of bubble gum colored gardening gloves on the ground a few feet away.

"Because they're pink?" Vanessa looped her arms around her knees.

"Yeah. There's no way in hell I'm wearing them."

Vanessa pulled off her own brown ones. "You look like you might wear the same size I do. Want to try mine?" She held them out.

Samantha hesitated, then took them and slipped them on.

Hannah wished she didn't have to pay such close attention to what she was doing and could watch the exchange more closely. Vanessa's compassionate way with the kids intrigued her.

"Yeah, these are good." Samantha flexed her fingers. "Thanks."

"Sure." Vanessa stood. "Next time, just tell me if something is wrong, Samantha, so you don't miss out participating. Okay?"

"You can just call me Sam when I'm here."

She'd said it quietly, but Hannah filed it away. Didn't like pink, didn't want to be called the feminine version of her name.

"Sam." Vanessa paused a moment, as though trying it out. She must have been putting things together in *her* mind, too. "I can do that. Anything else I should know, like regarding pronouns?"

Sam shook her head. "No, my dad wouldn't go for that. He doesn't even like me using a nickname."

"Maybe he just needs a bit of time to get used to the idea."

But Sam had already risen and picked up a bucket from the pile. "I'm going to do the tomatoes."

Hannah looked at Vanessa, and Vanessa shrugged.

As the two groups had made progress, they'd come together in the middle of the garden. Instead of going back to where she'd been working, Vanessa retrieved the piece of foam she'd been using to cushion her knees and dropped it beside Hannah. She peered in Hannah's bucket. "You look like you need help."

"Really? Zaiden, how full is yours?" Hannah craned her neck to see.

He tipped it toward her.

Twice as much. Damn.

"Maybe I do," she said to Vanessa as she threw a handful of weeds into hers. "But these are really hard to tell apart."

"Yeah, I might need to grab my readers for this bed." Vanessa rose and came back a minute later. She slid on a pair of black-framed glasses. "Much better." She quickly pulled three or four weeds in succession.

Hannah tried not to stare. If Vanessa had intended to take sexy up a notch, she'd succeeded. Hot librarians had nothing on her. A cool breeze would be nice right about now.

Hannah shook those thoughts away. "It's the worst when your vision starts to go."

"You too?" Vanessa glanced at her.

"I began to notice last year."

"We're probably close in age. How old are you?"

Hannah leaned back. "Forty-six. You?"

"Forty-eight."

"Wow, you're like nearly as old as my grandma." Zaiden's mouth hung open.

"Is that a problem?" Vanessa arched an eyebrow at him over the top of her glasses.

"No." He bent his head, the sweep of hair covering his face again.

In the final hour, Hannah filled three more buckets with Vanessa's help, but she'd definitely need some ibuprofen to get through the rest of the day. Even her aching knees and back couldn't dampen her anticipation of having lunch with Vanessa, though.

❖

After all the kids had left, Hannah waited for Vanessa to lock the shed and then the gate.

Instead of heading toward their cars, Vanessa motioned toward the bleachers. "Mind if we sit? Sometimes I just need a few minutes to decompress."

"I'll follow you."

Vanessa climbed midway up before choosing a seat. "What'd you think?"

Hannah laughed and sat beside her. "It may take me a month or two to get up to speed, but I liked it. The kids all seem nice, and being outside feels good. I'm cooped up in my office too much."

"Yeah, they're great." Vanessa stretched out one leg. "There's an elective class during the school year, but those here in summer do it because they want to. They don't get credit for it."

"Oh, wow."

Vanessa gazed at something in the distance with a faraway look in her eyes. "This was my junior high, back in the day."

Hannah turned to her. "Really?"

"Mm-hmm. Kissed my first girl under these very bleachers." Vanessa pointed to a nearby building. "Eighth grade English was in that corner room on the second floor. Ms. Brandt. Back then, the gardens were much smaller and part of an after-school program she supervised. I had a mad crush on her, so of course, I joined. She encouraged me, not only out here, but in school, too. I was fortunate she showed interest. I didn't have much of that at home." She grew quiet.

Hannah wanted to know more about what had made her suddenly so melancholic. "I'm sorry to hear that. Your parents didn't care about academics?"

"It's just my mom. My dad left when I was seven. We'd been a pretty normal family up until then, or at least so I thought." She held up her hands. "Apparently, he left us for a cocktail waitress who worked at the bar near his office."

"I'm so sorry you went through that." Hannah wished something she could say would let Vanessa know how much she cared and hated the thought of her hurting, even if it had been years ago.

Vanessa took down her ponytail and ran her hand through her hair, untangling the ends. "My mom had to take a job at a twenty-four-hour diner and worked the graveyard shift."

"Who'd you stay with?"

Vanessa just looked at her.

"Oh."

"She'd bring me orders the kitchen had messed up or left under the heat lamps too long, or she'd grab junk food from the convenience store as an afterthought. Usually, she'd be falling into bed or having a few drinks as I left for school."

Hannah took her hand. "That must have been difficult for you, especially being so young."

"I could've handled that. The worst was how she completely changed. When my dad was with us, she was caring, interested in me. She cooked and cleaned and made me after-school snacks. Normal mom stuff for the time. But that all stopped. It was like living with a different person. She became bitter and critical, when she even noticed me at all. I'm sure she was depressed, but she refused to get help."

"What'd you do?"

"What could I do? I was a kid." Vanessa stared at the school. "At first, I missed my dad. When I became a teenager, I realized how selfish he'd been, and missing him turned to hatred. He'd disappeared, not even helping us financially. I suppose I didn't hate *him* as much as what his actions had done to us, how they'd ruined our lives." Vanessa slipped her hand from Hannah's with a gentle squeeze. "What about you? Did you have the most annoyingly perfect parents?"

"Not perfect, no. How about I fill you in over lunch? I'm getting hungry."

Vanessa stood and brushed off her jeans. "Are we clean enough to be seen anywhere?"

"At the place I have in mind, yes. Wait here." Hannah felt Vanessa watching her as she hurried down the bleachers before Vanessa could say anything. At her car, she retrieved the picnic basket she'd packed from her trunk, then headed back.

When Hannah returned, Vanessa smiled at her from the bottom step. "You're sneaky."

Hannah grinned. "I had a feeling I might end up looking like this. How about under that tree over there?"

Once the food was unpacked and spread out, Hannah sipped her iced tea with her head tipped back to enjoy the sun that had presented itself to accompany their meal.

"So, tell me about your parents." Vanessa unwrapped a sandwich.

"Jumping right in, I guess." A passing cloud cast a shady spot on the grass as Hannah considered what to share. "Years ago, before I was born, my parents started the company. They specialized in wedding and engagement rings, but sold other items, too, as you know from your necklace purchase."

Vanessa nodded.

"I suppose I can't complain too much about my relationship with them. As far as I know, they love and are committed to one another, although they've always been more concerned with work than family life. They weren't the best role models for how to balance an intimate relationship with a career or how to be emotionally available to family, but they showed me how to focus on running a successful business at an early age."

"That's all they cared about?" Vanessa looked surprised.

"At least talked about. At home, at headquarters. You name it." She gave a little shrug.

"You went to the office with them?"

Hannah laughed. "I have pictures of me walking around the executive suite in diapers. I practically grew up within the company's walls. As I got older, I spent time working in every division to learn the ins and outs. It might not have been a normal childhood, but they included me in it at every step."

"And now you're the boss." Vanessa smiled.

Hannah thought about why that had come to be and hoped her voice didn't waver. "My mom had a stroke. It was enough to scare my dad. They took an early retirement and moved to Palm Springs."

"I'm so sorry. Did they come to the funeral?"

"No." Hannah paused to dip a pita chip into the hummus, then pop it into her mouth. "They were on a cruise in the Mediterranean at the time, and after how hard they worked all their lives, I refused to let them cut it short. They were obviously worried about me and still don't know the details that you discovered about the day Bren died. But they saw I was holding it together, and apparently, it was enough to assure them I was fine." She debated about sharing the next part, but Vanessa already knew one of the darker decisions she'd made in her life. "I delayed telling them about her death so they couldn't get back in time."

Vanessa gasped. "Hannah."

She'd underestimated Vanessa's shock, judging by her slack jaw.

"So, they think she died days after she did? What if they find out at some point, or look online to read her obituary? What are you going to tell them?" Vanessa's eyes had widened so much that white ringed her pupils.

"I was thinking of them."

Vanessa looked across the school grounds, and Hannah could feel the disappointment radiating off her. "You took away their right to make that choice for themselves. How would you like it if someone did that to you?"

Was Vanessa's reaction in part due to her experience with Bren? Vanessa and Bren hadn't mutually decided that marriage wasn't for them. Bren had simply abandoned her in front of her friends and family.

"I struggle with doing what I think is for the best versus letting others make decisions." Hannah took a bite of her sandwich.

"I can see that." Vanessa's tone had cooled.

The sudden vibration of Hannah's phone made her glance at it. Her head of IT. The text explained his second in command had just turned in his resignation. Who did that on the weekend? She sent a quick response and stowed her phone. She'd deal with it after lunch.

"Everything okay?" Vanessa watched her over the rim of her soda.

"Just work stuff."

"On the weekend?"

"Twenty-four seven, it seems." Hannah needed to change the subject, so it didn't return to the sticky issue surrounding her parents. "About the trip to San Francisco," she tried to sound casual, but after all, it was the reason for this lunch, "I think we should take my car. If we go, that is. It'll take us thirteen hours if we travel down I-5. The route along the coast is far more scenic, but it'd be closer to twenty hours, and even longer with stops. The driving tends to be more intense with all the curves, too. That seems a bit much."

"It does." Vanessa scooped up hummus with a carrot.

She didn't bring up not going, so Hannah relaxed a bit.

"Plus, I-5 takes us through Ashland," Vanessa said. "I could show you my farm, if you want."

"Since when do you have a farm?" Hannah wadded her wrapper around the crusts.

Vanessa raised her eyebrows. "Twenty years, give or take. Well, technically it's not mine. I co-own it with my best friend and her husband. Sonja and Jeffrey are my business partners. They manage the farm and greenhouse that supply many of the store's flowers."

"The same best friend you lost your—you know…"

A lovely flush reddened Vanessa's cheeks. "Yes, the one and the same. You'll meet her. I'm sure they'd let us stay with them if we'd like. They have the room."

Hannah picked up her phone. "Seattle to Ashland is about seven hours. That'd be the perfect place to stop for the night. You'll ask her if she minds?"

"I'll call her later." Vanessa bit into a chip.

This road trip was beginning to sound like a sure thing. After Vanessa's initial reaction to finding the note in Hannah's car, she wasn't certain Vanessa would agree to go, even though they'd appeared to talk through it.

"So, same time next week?" Hannah leaned back, enjoying the sunshine.

Vanessa blinked. "For what?"

Hannah ran her hand down her dirty shirt. "Gardening."

A slow smile spread across Vanessa's face. "Same time every week."

Hannah could hardly wait.

Chapter Eight

Vanessa stood beside her car in the cool shade of the ponderosa pines that lined the teachers' parking lot. Hannah had shown up this morning with the gloves Vanessa had given her last week, armed with sunscreen, a hat, and her glasses. And she'd done great remembering most of the kids' names, teased Zaiden, and weeded like a pro. Vanessa had even convinced her to plant a few seedlings after she assured Hannah she wouldn't kill them. The most difficult part of the day had been remembering to split her time among all the participants, even though she would've preferred to stay by Hannah's side.

"What sounds good for lunch today?" Vanessa ran a couple of restaurants through her mind but had no preference.

"Would my place be okay?" Hannah hesitated beside her Lexus. "I feel gross and want to change. I can loan you something, too. Then I can either make us lunch or we can go somewhere."

"That's fine." She gestured to Hannah's dirt-streaked jeans. "But only one of us is wearing half the garden home."

Hannah looked down, making a couple of futile swipes across her clothing. "I haven't discovered your secret yet." She shot her a smile. "Give me time. Want to ride with me? I'll bring you back later if you're comfortable leaving your car."

"Sure." Vanessa got in, dropping her backpack at her feet. She sank into the plush leather seats with a contented sigh. "Oh, your car is comfortable. I'm glad we'll be taking it on the trip."

Hannah glanced at her before she pulled from the lot. "Do you want to do some of the driving?"

"As long as you trust me with your car."

"I trust you."

The way she said it made Vanessa wonder if they were still talking about the trip. She must have pondered it longer than she thought because the next thing she knew, Hannah had turned into her own driveway and killed the engine.

"I can't park in the garage right now. I've started packing Bren's things, and it's cluttered with boxes. It's taking longer than I expected to finish."

Vanessa got out, slinging her backpack over her shoulder. "I don't have anything planned the rest of the day. Do you need help? Unless it's too personal."

Hannah stopped. "You'd do that?"

"Sure." Vanessa waited for her at the walkway. "I know it's not easy. I did it once before, granted, under different circumstances."

"Thanks." Hannah pulled her keys from her pocket. "I'd really appreciate that. Zara was going to come over sometime this weekend, but she's been trying to catch up on work."

Inside, the cool air smelled the way Vanessa remembered, as if the last scent had been Hannah emerging from the shower. It welcomed her in a pleasant way. She dropped her bag by the door and followed Hannah into the living room.

"I'm going to change. Feel free to pull anything out of the refrigerator that looks good. I just bought sandwich fixings. Give me two minutes, and I'll be right down."

"Take your time." Vanessa wandered into the kitchen. To her surprise, a Chinese evergreen plant sat on the windowsill above the sink. She was certain it hadn't been there the last time she was here. She gently stroked the pink and green leaves. It looked healthy, and a light press of her finger into the soil told her it hadn't been over-watered. Pride suffused her, and she smiled. This was the only plant she'd seen in Hannah's home. Did it have anything to do with volunteering at the garden? Vanessa's chest tightened. Or with her? She quickly washed her hands. Sandwiches needed to be made.

"Okay." Hannah entered just as Vanessa was choosing which sliced cheese to use.

When she turned, she stopped short. Hannah hadn't just changed, she'd put on a form-fitting pair of yoga pants and a racer-back tank that clung just as snugly. Vanessa swallowed and forced her attention to their lunch.

Hannah stepped beside her, their arms brushing. "I'll take over."

Vanessa nodded, glad for the excuse to put some distance between them. "I'll get plates. Where do you keep them?"

In no time, they relaxed on Hannah's deck, enjoying delectable ham sandwiches and grapefruit sparkling water. When they finished, Vanessa sat on the living room floor while Hannah brought her Bren's items. She folded clothes, taped and labeled boxes, and when ready, one of them took them to the garage.

Hannah deposited another armful of items onto the coffee table. "I hadn't even realized this stuff was in the back of the closet."

Vanessa's heart jumped at the sight of a long, slim box she hadn't seen in years. A light layer of dust covered it, only smudged where Hannah had touched it. Vanessa picked it up but couldn't bring herself to open it.

"It's a pen." Hannah flipped her hair over her shoulder with a toss of her head. "A nice one."

"A Montblanc." Vanessa lightly touched the top. "I gave it to her as an engagement present."

Hannah sank to the floor beside her. "I didn't know." She put her hand on the box. "What do you need? You can have it back if you want. Who knows how long this probate thing will take, but the court doesn't know what's here. Take it if you want it."

Vanessa handed it to her. "I don't." She didn't even want to see it. The night she'd given it to Bren came rushing in. She drew her knees up and wrapped her arms around them. "You know, I was the one that proposed."

"You did?" Hannah slid it out of sight behind her.

Bless her.

"She said she needed some time to think about it." Vanessa laughed, the sound more sardonic than she'd intended. "I should've known then, seen the red flags."

"No one could've predicted how things turned out."

"No, but I was so naive. I'd had prior relationships but none as long or as serious. The store and farm consume so much of my life. When she finally agreed to marry me, I was so thankful, I bought her the pen. How pathetic is that?" She scoffed. "Oh, to go back and do things differently."

"Everyone has instances in their lives they wish they could do over." Hannah grew quiet.

"Do you?" Vanessa shifted to face her.

Hannah laughed. "Only about five hundred." She leaned back and extended her legs. "For this conversation, everything about my relationship with Bren was a bit off from the start. She pursued me, and I've always been the one to make the first move with women. But she was attractive, and I found her interest in me intoxicating."

Vanessa remembered the heady feeling.

"As I got to know her, I discovered she was as hard-working as I was and understood the time demands of my company. That was a plus, since other women I dated didn't. I was a vice president back then." Hannah stood and extended a hand to her, sliding the box containing the pen underneath the couch with her bare foot. "Let's get some wine."

Vanessa allowed herself to be helped to her feet.

In the kitchen, Hannah poured two glasses of Sancerre and slid one toward her. "We'd dated about a year around the time my parents retired, and as CEO, my involvement in the company naturally increased. She began complaining about my long hours."

"Was some of it because you revamped everything?" Vanessa settled onto a stool, and Hannah sat beside her.

"No, not right away. I spent almost a year letting everyone acclimate to my new role. While I wanted to make the changes I'd been incubating for most of my adult life, I knew the importance of letting the staff get used to the idea of me being the boss. Many of them have been there since I wore braces."

"That was smart." Here Vanessa was, hanging out with her ex-girlfriend's girlfriend—ex-girlfriend? Whatever Hannah was, there had to be a bad lesbian joke in there somewhere.

"Necessary, in my opinion. My first major initiative was introducing a new Pride line of engagement and wedding rings for queer couples. I needed everyone to trust me and be on board for it to be successful."

Pride? Hannah impressed her on so many levels. "And was it?"

Hannah smiled. "We're still in the developmental stages. Even though my parents had me fast-tracked for leadership, I always enjoyed design. While I leave that to the professionals, I'll have input in how the line looks."

Vanessa rested her chin in her hand. "And what are you envisioning?"

"Well, we've always been happy assisting queer couples in finding the right rings for whatever occasion, but I noticed we kept getting requests for ones that featured a rainbow of gemstones." She traced a line across her finger where a wedding band would go. "The issue is sourcing the right gems. A wedding or engagement ring needs to be the highest quality and durable, since it's usually worn all the time. Finding gems that fit that description in each color takes time."

"So, these rings will have colored gemstones instead of a diamond?" Vanessa didn't know if she'd want a wedding ring like that, though she didn't see herself ever getting married. Not after what had happened.

Hannah shook her head. "Not necessarily. Most will have a diamond, and the other jewels will be accent stones."

Vanessa smiled. "I think it's great you're doing this."

"It's far from being done, but it's in the works." Hannah sighed. "But back to my original story. I hadn't implemented any of this, and Bren was already frustrated by my work hours. She found this house and suggested we both move in to maximize the time we had together, and I agreed to placate her, something I'd definitely do differently in hindsight. It was much sooner than I would've preferred. I'd never lived with a girlfriend before."

"Really?"

Hannah laughed. "I work a lot. Before Bren, I went on one date, maybe two, with a woman and was content with that. There was a sense of relief knowing they didn't want any more from me than what I gave them, because I didn't have much more to offer."

Vanessa tried to digest this latest information. They were so different in that way. She'd made a fool of herself in her desire to marry Bren.

"So, when Bren asked, I agreed even though I didn't want to." Hannah indicated their surroundings with a sweep of her arm. "She loved this house, and with my hours and her spending more and more time in San Francisco, it seemed the thing to do if we were going to try to make things work."

"Did it help?" Clearly not, but Vanessa wanted to give Hannah a safe place to share the difficulties of her relationship with Bren.

"For a while." Hannah sipped her wine, then stared into space for a few moments. "Then she became distant and more secretive, and I didn't know why. I thought it might just be the shine and newness wearing off, or that's what I told myself. Bren traveled to San Francisco more and more. I tried to broach the subject many times but only received irritated reassurances that everything was fine. It got worse, but by then, I was neck-deep as CEO. Even though I felt like I was already living alone, I didn't have the time and energy it'd take to break up with her, find a new place, and move out. It had to wait."

"You couldn't stay here and ask her to go?"

"This place isn't me. It's so dark and outdated." Hannah gave her a rueful smile. "I don't even want to be living here now." Then she brightened. "Enough about that. I talked to some friends in San Francisco. They have an Airbnb on Telegraph Hill I usually stay in when I'm in town. They said it's available the dates we'll be there if we want it."

"Oh." Vanessa started at the sudden change of subject. Or was it that she'd assumed they'd get hotel *rooms*—emphasis on the *s* at the end. Did she want to share a space alone with Hannah, even for a few days?

"It's a three-bedroom. Don't worry." Hannah laughed, lightly touching her leg. "I won't pull one of those only-one-bed scenarios on you."

"I wasn't worried." Her face and neck warmed with the fib.

Hannah grinned as she withdrew her hand. "It must be the wine making your cheeks turn that cute shade of pink."

It was too much. The closeness, the teasing, the confusion and tension she didn't know how to cope with when Hannah was near. Was Hannah interested in her, or did she flirt with everyone? *Was* she flirting?

Hannah was gorgeous and interesting and fun. She probably could have just about any woman in King County whenever she wanted. What would she see in Vanessa?

The afternoon had gone on too long. Vanessa needed some space. She would stay a few more minutes, then ask Hannah to drive her back to her car. The temperatures would drop soon, and she could go for a long run to clear her head and gain some perspective. The last thing she wanted to do was make another one of those decisions they'd been discussing that she wished she could do over.

❖

Vanessa jogged in place when the light at Mercer Street turned red. She wiped sweaty strands of hair from her cheeks, and a glance at her phone informed her she'd missed a call from her mother minutes before. Only a few blocks from home, she preferred to have the conversation there, away from the noise of traffic. Besides, if it were important, her mother would've tried again.

And again. And again.

She hadn't jogged two blocks before she felt her phone vibrate. There it was. She slowed to a walk. Cool-down time, apparently.

"Mom. What's going on?"

"I can't believe you didn't answer. It's an emergency," her mother said sharply, skipping any greeting. "You should've called me right back."

The volume of her voice made Vanessa hold the phone a few inches from her ear. She rubbed her forehead. "I'm on a run and didn't feel the first call. Are you hurt? What's the matter?"

"The house is flooding." Her mother's heavy breathing muffled the whoosh of the passing cars. "I'm going to slip and break my leg. Get your ass over here."

Vanessa's stomach tightened. She picked up her pace. "Where's the water coming from?"

"The kitchen. It's everywhere."

"Can you shut it off at the main valve?"

Her mother huffed. "Have you forgotten who you're talking to? I can't turn the handle with my arthritis."

Of course. Vanessa should've known better than to ask. Odd how that didn't hinder her mother from twisting off the caps of whiskey and vodka bottles. "Okay. I'll be there as soon as I can. Sit on the patio until I arrive." She sped up.

Her mother made a disgruntled noise. "For how long? This is my house."

Technically, Vanessa owned the condo, but bringing that up now wouldn't get them anywhere pleasant. "I don't want you to slip and fall. I'm almost home, and I'll come right over."

"Well, hurry up." The pitch of her mother's voice climbed to a shriek. "If I fall and die, it'll be on your conscience."

Vanessa stifled a sigh. How bad was it really? "Just sit out back. I'm on my way."

At the sudden silence in her ear, she looked at the screen, seeing the connection had been terminated. She called back but didn't get an answer. The second try yielded the same result. She broke into a run. Had her mother fallen? More likely, she was ignoring her, a passive-aggressive tactic she often employed.

At the end of her driveway, she glanced at her front door and considered a quick swipe of a towel and change of clothes, but thought better of it. If this was truly an emergency and her mother was hurt, the guilt would eat Vanessa alive. She jumped into her car and headed for Tacoma.

When Vanessa let herself in, heart racing, she stopped short. Her mother lounged in her favorite leather recliner, slippered feet crossed, a rocks glass with a small amount of amber liquid beside her. "What the hell, Mom? I sped over here thinking there's some emergency, and you're relaxing with a cocktail?"

"It's just Jameson."

The exuberant sounds of the game show on TV grated on Vanessa's nerves, but her mom didn't bother to lower the ridiculously high volume.

Her mother scoffed. "Besides, what was I supposed to do? You took your sweet-ass time getting here."

Vanessa motioned to her running shorts and tank top. "I didn't even stop to change. And I told you to wait outside."

"Go." Her mother flapped a hand toward the doorway across the room. "In there. Water everywhere."

Vanessa bit back a retort and entered the small but modern kitchen. It took her a couple of seconds to notice the puddle on the floor in front of the sink. It had seeped onto two of the square-foot tiles. Surely, no more than a quarter of a cup. She clenched her teeth, counting to ten. *Stay calm.*

She returned to the living room. "You manipulated me into rushing over here for a few drops?"

"What if I fell and broke my hip at my age? Do you know how dangerous that is? Or, you don't give a shit." Her mother spat out the last words, then threw back the rest of her drink.

Cirrhosis of the liver was dangerous, too, but Vanessa didn't have the energy to go there again.

With a sigh, she returned to the kitchen and tossed down a towel before kneeling and opening the cupboard. The recycling bin overflowed with empty alcohol bottles. She pulled it out, the glass clinking loudly, and squeezed her head and shoulders under the sink. A drop fell from the hose connected to the faucet's sprayer. She rose and turned it on, then examined it, finding the leak where the connection had loosened. After hand tightening it, she tested it again. Sealed. She let it retract.

With annoyance, she cleaned up, then put the towel on the washing machine. "It's fixed," she said, returning to the living room.

"About fucking time. I need a refill. I've been stranded out here an hour."

Based on the coarseness of her mother's language, this wasn't her first drink. Vanessa tried to blink away the beginning of a headache. "You know, next time it's something minor, you don't need to lie about it being an emergency. Just tell me what's going on, so I can deal with it appropriately. I would've liked to shower and change."

Her mother whipped her head around with surprising quickness. "I'm so sorry I interrupted your precious leisure time. I could've been dying. You didn't even answer."

Vanessa pointed to the small device on her mom's wrist. "That's why you have Life Alert. For emergencies. This wasn't one."

"How would you know? You have no idea how long I spent mopping up gallons of water before you got here. Me, at my age, on my hands and knees cleaning up the mess because my daughter is too preoccupied doing who knows what."

Her mother's tan slacks appeared bone dry, and Vanessa assumed the mop was no different. She'd seen zero evidence of wet towels in the laundry room aside from the one she'd deposited there. These were games her mother played, dares for Vanessa to call her on her lies, and if she did, the fallacies would only multiply to the absurd. With this many years of experience, Vanessa knew there was no way to win.

Her mom glared at her. "Were you with a woman? Is that why you ignored me?"

Vanessa bristled. "I was jogging." Again, she gestured toward her clothing. "Not that what I'm doing or whom I'm with is any of your business." Thoughts of Hannah rushed in, but she shelved them for later.

"Well, since you're never here when I need you, and I have no idea when you'll grace me with your presence again, sign me into Netflix." Her mother tossed the remote at her.

Vanessa caught it against her chest. "Where's your notebook? I've given you the password at least seventeen times." At her mother's shrug, Vanessa picked up the pad near the phone and wrote it down. "And I'm here every week weeding your flower beds. I bring you groceries and fix whatever needs fixing, just like today." All more than her mother had done for her when she was young.

"Francine's daughter got her a caregiver who comes every day. I'm too embarrassed to tell her my good-for-nothing daughter would never do something so thoughtful." She ignored the note and remote Vanessa set on the table beside her.

Vanessa wasn't going down that rabbit hole again. She heard some version of that story every other month. Surely, all these women living on fixed incomes didn't have home health assistants. Besides, her mother didn't need one. While she had ailments commensurate with her age, she wasn't *that* old. She still went out with her walking group four times a week and had plenty of energy to socialize, especially at events where drinks were being served. Personal hygiene and light housekeeping hadn't become issues yet. And she could cook for herself. Vanessa wasn't paying a nursing student to play Canasta all day. People her mother's age lived all around her if she wanted companionship.

But the truth of it stung. All her mother wanted *her* around for was to wait on her and take her abuse.

"I'm going home. I need a shower." Vanessa hesitated at the door. Her mom didn't look away from the TV, so she let herself out. She'd long ago learned not to expect any gratitude and tried not to let incidents like this get her down, but it never seemed to get easier. Knowing her mother didn't want to spend time with her as much as she desired more money or someone to handle repairs and run errands was difficult to accept.

Part Two

Chapter Nine

Vanessa marveled at how quickly three months had passed, being busy at the shop with all the special events, volunteering at the garden with the kids every Saturday, and lunch with Hannah afterward each week. They'd even managed a couple of dinners and an art show for which Hannah had a plus-one invitation. The only dark cloud had been her mother's bouts of bitterness and criticism, but there wasn't anything new about that, except when Vanessa informed her she'd be out of town. But now the time was here.

She hadn't been sure about this trip for most of the summer, but the closer it'd gotten, the more she found herself looking forward to it. Now with the height of the wedding season behind her, she could get away and actually enjoy it.

By the time she and Hannah reached Olympia, Vanessa had learned two things. Hannah drove fast, and she sang. If they weren't having a conversation, Hannah was belting out a song. She'd even convinced Vanessa to join in a time or two.

As they reached Capitol Lake, Vanessa melted into the comfortable seat, pushed her shades higher on her nose, and crossed her legs. The warm sun on her arms and the lavender-scented air freshener Hannah had clipped to the vent helped her relax.

They'd called Georgina a couple more times in the preceding days but hadn't had any better luck than on prior attempts. "Are you nervous?"

Hannah glanced at her. "A little." She paused a moment. "I mean, I got to thinking last night that all the time you and I have spent together has been with other people around or at our houses where there are close neighbors.

Vanessa tilted her head, a bit confused. What was she getting at?

"But now we're going to be alone. I realized you could be an axe murderer."

Vanessa snorted. "I find swinging an axe in a car to be difficult." She gently pinched Hannah's earlobe. She'd learned how ticklish Hannah could be, and purposely chose something she hoped wouldn't endanger them.

"Hey." Hannah twisted away. "Don't mess with the driver."

Vanessa chuckled. "I meant confronting Georgina."

Hannah laughed as she settled in behind the wheel again. "It's not news they were having an affair. I just have some questions and want to see who she is." She paused. "I have something I've been wanting to ask you, though."

Surprised, Vanessa studied her. Their conversations had grown so easy, and they'd shared so many things, but she still had secrets and supposed Hannah did, too. If Hannah was uncomfortable about asking, maybe Vanessa should be careful. "Why haven't you brought it up before now?"

"The timing's never seemed right."

"And it seems right now?"

Hannah didn't answer, her eyes fixed on the road.

Vanessa fidgeted. How bad could it be? Hannah didn't know anything about the two things Vanessa *really* didn't want to tell her about, how bad things were between her and her mother and her attraction to Hannah.

"I'm sorry. Never mind," Hannah said softly. "It's none of my business."

Vanessa wavered. She was curious now. "Go ahead."

Hannah gave her a quick look. "Are you sure?"

Vanessa nodded, still cautious but willing to give it a try.

Hannah inhaled and adjusted her hold on the steering wheel. "Will you tell me what happened the day you were supposed to get married?"

The question broadsided Vanessa, and she struggled to draw a breath. Why did Hannah need to know that now, after all this time? She straightened in her seat and swallowed hard. "It's exactly like it sounds, Hannah. I'm sure you've seen it in movies."

"Sorry. I just wondered." Hannah banged her palm on the steering wheel. "What the hell was she thinking?"

Vanessa startled at Hannah's angry reaction. *She*, meaning Bren? Vanessa decided to go with the first question, since it proved to be easier.

"My mom was there, and all my friends from over the years. I invited everyone from work and shut down the shop for the day. All our mutual friends came, too, along with most of Bren's softball team. We booked the University Unitarian Church. It's a gorgeous building if you've never seen it." She stared out the window at the businesses as they flew past them.

Hannah squeezed her knee. "You don't have to talk about this if you don't want to. I'm sorry I asked."

The touch soothed Vanessa. "It's okay." And it really was. As difficult as it was to discuss it, to relive it, Vanessa found she didn't mind Hannah knowing. She wanted Hannah to have an idea of the events that'd made her who she was today. And maybe it'd do her good. "We decided to do the thing where we didn't see each other that day until the wedding. I was getting ready in one room in the church, and she was supposed to be doing the same in another. When it came time for the ceremony, two of Bren's teammates answered our friend Clare's knock. They said all of Bren's things were gone, and so was her car."

"Did you call her?"

"Others did. She wouldn't answer her phone. Her stylist said Bren sent her away, saying she wasn't needed. The poor woman assumed Bren simply wanted to do her own hair and makeup. Apparently, no one knew how to tell me. They hoped they'd find her before I found out. At some point, they realized they couldn't stall me any longer. They elected Sonja as the one to break the news." Vanessa recalled the look on Sonja's face. She'd immediately known something was very wrong, yet she couldn't have imagined the gravity of how devastating the information would be.

Hannah took her hand. "What happened?"

"What do you mean? She was gone."

"Not with her. With you. How did you react?"

Vanessa dug up the long-buried memory. "I remember being numb, not understanding. Just sitting there, not caring that I was crushing my dress. Sonja convinced me not to give up hope, and they tried to find Bren for another hour, a few of them even driving around looking for her car. When they couldn't, I knew keeping all the guests waiting any longer wasn't right. The irony of me, not Bren, standing up in front of the church apologizing to them made me want to smash windows."

"Be glad I wasn't around then." The fierceness in Hannah's tone had Vanessa turning to look at her. A muscle twitched in Hannah's jaw.

Was she this protective of all her friends?

That day, and in the ones that followed, Vanessa received sympathetic looks and heartfelt condolences about how she didn't deserve this terrible thing that'd happened to her. Except from her mother. True to form, *she'd* blamed Vanessa, reacting with her usual vitriol. She could still hear her, this many years later.

What'd you do to make her dump you? How humiliating. Must be karma. You destroyed my marriage. Ran your father off and ruined my life. You don't deserve to be loved. I bet she's with someone else right now.

Prophetic? Had her mother been right? Had Bren ran into another woman's arms? Vanessa bit her tongue until the pain overpowered the sharpness of the memory. "I never saw her again," she managed.

"What?" Hannah shot her a sidelong look.

"Bren sent me a vague text apologizing but didn't respond to any of my return messages, and someone picked up her belongings but wouldn't tell me where she was."

"Jesus Christ," Hannah said through gritted teeth.

Vanessa turned her attention back to the scenery, notably the snow-covered peak ahead to their left. "I think I need to be done with this for now."

"I'm sorry I asked." Hannah's tone dropped in obvious remorse. "I shouldn't have."

"No, I'm glad you did and that you know now." Vanessa's emotions began to settle. "I just need to put it back into the past again."

"Okay, and thank you for telling me. So, change of subject. Let's take a selfie with that mountain behind us. I should probably know which one it is." Hannah's comically upbeat demeanor made Vanessa smile.

"It's Mount Hood. We're not far from Portland."

Hannah found a place to pull off and took a photo of them, each with an arm around the other's waist.

Vanessa had to admit they looked good, the sun on their faces and their different shades of blond hair blowing in the wind. "Will you text me that?" She received it before they got back to the car. While she would've liked to look at it a bit longer, the thought of doing so in front of Hannah made her stomach flip-flop. It'd have to wait.

"Would you like to drive?" Hannah hesitated in front of the Lexus. "It's fine if you don't. I just thought you might like to switch it up."

Vanessa changed direction, going to the driver's side. "We're stopping for snacks, if you allow eating in your car."

Hannah rolled her eyes. "I vacuum the floor mats every Sunday. A few crumbs mixed with the dirt aren't going to hurt." She got in the passenger's side. "I thought about getting things to munch on, but I didn't know what your favorite travel treats might be since we haven't done this before. At least I brought the water."

They fueled up in addition to buying far too much junk food for two people, and an hour later, with empty wrappers and half-full bags stuffing the available nooks and crannies, Hannah fell asleep. Vanessa realized it when the singing stopped.

She glanced over at her. Hannah's head was turned toward her, her lips slightly parted. Vanessa tried to angle the visor so it shaded her face, but the sun was in the wrong spot for it. Asleep, she looked so relaxed and peaceful. Tiny freckles that Vanessa hadn't noticed before dotted her cheeks. Her beauty was remarkable, asleep or awake.

After driving for a while, Vanessa gently shook her leg. "Hannah. Hannah, do you need a rest stop? There's one coming up in two miles."

Hannah stirred and pulled off her sunglasses. "Oh, hi." She smiled. "I think I dozed off."

Vanessa laughed. "You definitely did. Rest stop? If so, I need to change lanes."

"I'm good," Hannah curled up in the seat, her body turned toward her. "Do you need me to drive?"

"No." She gave Hannah's knee a squeeze. "I can get us all the way to Ashland, if you want. I've done it many times."

"Maybe I'll sleep a few more minutes," she murmured.

Vanessa was about to answer, but the ragged breath Hannah drew in told her she'd already drifted off. She lowered the volume of the music so it wouldn't disturb her.

Driving had always calmed Vanessa. She loved watching the scenery change, seeing the countryside at various times of year, all the farmland and ranches along this route. And after experiencing Hannah's car, she better understood Hannah's love of speed. The ride was so smooth, Vanessa hardly realized when she'd reached numbers that would surely earn her an expensive ticket. She backed off the gas. Once the traffic wasn't so heavy and there weren't so many trucks around, she'd figure out the cruise control.

A warmth beneath her palm drew her attention, and she glanced down. Her hand still rested on Hannah's knee. The gesture had been natural with Hannah awake, but now that she slept, it seemed wrong, so Vanessa shifted her grasp to the gear shift. Touching her had been nice though, comforting. Would she have kept it there if Hannah had stayed awake? Probably not. It would've become awkward at some point. But what would it be like to be able to touch Hannah whenever she wanted?

Her phone vibrated to save her from that spiral. Vanessa checked the screen. Her mother. She winced, having hoped to make it to Ashland before hearing from her, some place where she could move out of earshot of Hannah. She never talked on the phone while driving without being connected by Bluetooth, but with her mother's increasingly fragile health, she had to answer. After accepting the call, she held the device to her ear. "Mom. Is everything okay?"

"No, it's not, but you'd know that if you ever dragged your ass over here."

This was a standard line in every call, so Vanessa skipped over it. "What's wrong?"

"My daughter's an ungrateful little bitch. That's what's wrong. I could be dead on the floor, and you wouldn't give a shit."

Vanessa suppressed a sigh. "Has something happened, or are you just being dramatic? I told you I couldn't weed this weekend because I'd be gone."

"So, my home, the one thing in my life that brings me pride, has to look like garbage because you're off on a *trip*?"

The pride dig cut deep, but she wouldn't let it show. "It's not even a week. I'll be back soon and do it then. No one's going to notice a few stragglers among the peonies in that brief time."

"*I* notice. And after everything I did for you, how I broke my back keeping a roof over your head after your father ran off, this is how you repay me. You don't even know the things I had to do to make sure you ate."

Oh, she knew. She must've heard it a thousand times. How hard could it have been to grab a bag of chips when she stopped on her way home to buy booze? Vanessa had been grateful for times like those. At least those mornings her mother had remembered her. Most days there was no breakfast at all. She bit the inside of her lip to stave off further descent into the past. "Mother."

"Don't 'mother' me. I gave up my life for you, my dreams, and this is what I get in return? You selfish bitch. Always putting what *you* want first."

A firm grip on her arm startled her. She jerked her head to the side and found Hannah's face close to hers, pure rage in her eyes, her other hand on the steering wheel beside Vanessa's.

"Pull over. Now."

"I'm hanging up, Mother." Vanessa passed the phone to Hannah to end the call.

Hannah slid the hand on her arm across her shoulders. "Turn on your signal. Just slow down and ease off the road. You got this."

"There's no place to pull over." She glanced in her mirror at the semi-truck following them. That's when she realized how badly she shook.

"You're going to reduce your speed as much as you can. Don't worry about who's behind you. Then slowly ease onto the shoulder as far over as you can get. I'm going to take over from here."

Her soothing tone calmed Vanessa. "I'm sorry." Vanessa rapidly blinked as she decelerated, trying to keep her welling tears from obscuring her vision. "I'm so sorry."

"There's no need for you to be sorry." A hardness had returned to Hannah's voice. "Right up there, where the mud turns to gravel. Pull over there."

When Vanessa did and came to a stop, she almost missed the "Good girl" amidst the noise of passing cars. She couldn't ever recall someone saying that to her.

"Stay right there. Don't move." Hannah got out. She waited by the back bumper until a string of cars passed, then came up the side, opened Vanessa's door, and reached across Vanessa to unfasten her seat belt. "C'mon. Out you go." She led her around the car and into the passenger's seat. "Buckle up."

Vanessa still trembled but managed the task.

Behind the wheel, Hannah waited almost a solid minute until she was able to pull back onto the interstate.

Vanessa stared out the windshield. She'd regained her composure as much as she could, but the dread of talking to Hannah, of her knowing she'd put them in danger and broken the law in the process, was too much. So, she counted the mile markers instead, and when she arrived at five, she spoke. "I'm sorry, Hannah."

"Stop saying that."

"But I am. This is your car, and I should've been paying closer attention. It's just that my mom is getting up there in age, and I always answer in case something's hap—"

"You think that's why I'm mad? Because you weren't hands-free? God, Vanessa." Her loud sigh filled the car.

Vanessa's apprehension skyrocketed, and she had to swallow before speaking. "Did you, uh, overhear any of the conversation?"

"Probably most of it. Music doesn't bother me, but I'm a pretty light sleeper when it comes to other noise." Hannah shrugged. "I didn't know what to do. Eavesdropping wasn't my intention, but it's not like I could leave the room."

Her mother's words, her condemnations and accusations, the names she'd called her, replayed in Vanessa's mind. And Hannah had heard it all. Nausea began low in her abdomen, then grew stronger, her mouth filling with saliva. "Pull over. I'm going to be sick."

"Jesus." Hannah glanced at her, looking stricken. "Hang on. Can you make it to that exit?" She accelerated and gripped Vanessa's hand.

Vanessa could only nod and squeeze back hard. She concentrated with all her might on the brush of Hannah's thumb across her knuckles.

Hannah took the offramp and skidded to a stop on the side.

Vanessa was out of the car and retching near the rear bumper when she felt Hannah rubbing her back. When she straightened, Hannah handed her a tissue. As she wiped her mouth, she let her tears fall. Hopefully, Hannah would think they were from the exertion and embarrassment of emptying her stomach on the side of the road. And there was that. But she cried for so much more. For the mother she used to have and lost. For the child she'd once been, innocent and carefree. Those days were long gone. She hardly remembered them, and yet, it still hurt badly when she did.

"Put it in here." Hannah held out the to-go cup she'd gotten at the last stop, and Vanessa deposited her garbage. "Now drink some of this." She handed Vanessa a bottle of water. When she'd drunk as many sips as she could muster, Hannah capped it and put both items on top of the car. Then she turned to Vanessa and pulled her into a tight embrace and held her.

Vanessa merely closed her eyes and inhaled the intoxicating scent of Hannah's hair. For a long moment, here in Hannah's arms, she believed things might be okay.

"You don't deserve that, you know." Hannah's soft voice near her ear made her tear up again.

Vanessa pulled away. "It's complicated."

"It doesn't matter. No one deserves that." Gently, Hannah wiped under Vanessa's eye with her thumb. "Especially you."

With the way Hannah looked at her, the depth and affection in her unwavering gaze, Vanessa almost believed Hannah could see inside her, see the things Vanessa had fought so hard to hide, to forget, to unlearn. See the years of what she'd endured as both a child and an adult, when she'd had no one to turn to and so little self-worth she'd let it happen. What must Hannah think of her now?

"That's a beautiful dress. I don't think I told you that."

Hannah's soft smile made Vanessa's empty stomach do a little flip, and in an instant, the air between them changed, charged with something hotter than the sun on Vanessa's shoulders and more forceful than the winds whipped up by the trucks hurtling down I-5 not far away. Not quite understanding it frightened her. "We should get back on the road. Sonja's expecting us for dinner." Vanessa reached for the door handle.

Hannah didn't respond, only took the drink containers off the car and got inside. She maneuvered them back onto the interstate and sang an entirety of a lengthy song like nothing had happened. "So," she said finally, "you can explain to me what makes it complicated, or I'll be forced to sing to you the remainder of the trip."

"I like your singing." It was true. Hannah had a full, rich alto she found captivating.

"Oh, I don't mean my normal versions. I'll serenade you like the guy at karaoke who's had three too many lemon drops and thinks his rendition of 'Wonderwall' is going to get him laid when it's the cringiest thing on the planet."

Vanessa couldn't help but laugh imagining it. She had to admit Hannah had a talent for lightening the mood.

"It's settled then." Hannah raised a fist in the air. "Complicated. Go."

The jovial atmosphere dissipated as Vanessa debated where to start. A drink of water bought her a few seconds. "I told you my mom changed after my dad left."

"You did."

Vanessa leaned her elbow on the window. "She always had opinions, but it wasn't until my dad abandoned us that she became so overly critical."

"What I caught wasn't overly critical. It was cruel."

Vanessa didn't respond.

"And you were only seven." Hannah uttered the words like they tasted terrible.

"When I was around eleven or twelve, my mom came home after her shift one morning. She was drinking whiskey as I made myself breakfast. She started in on me, and in my nervousness, I spilled an entire box of cereal." Vanessa could still see the precious Rice Krispies, a rare treat, scattered over the stained linoleum. She hadn't eaten them since. "It set her off."

"How so?"

"The usual insults. How I was worthless and not good for anything, but this time, she went further. She admitted she blamed me for ruining her marriage and her life. Apparently, she'd wanted an abortion when she found out she was pregnant with me, but my father convinced her not to because he believed it was a sin. But then he escaped to greener pastures, leaving her to raise me. In her eyes, if she hadn't had me, she'd still have a marriage, a husband, friends she'd lost when she'd had to begin working, dreams she might have fulfilled, etcetera. You get the idea. I've never been able to do anything right in her eyes."

"It's like a game you're destined to lose from the start."

The tension in Vanessa's shoulders ebbed with her relief at Hannah's evident understanding. "It feels like it sometimes."

A call appeared on the screen above the console. "I'm sorry. I have to take this. It's my assistant." Hannah tapped the name before Vanessa could say anything.

Surprised by the abruptness of the end of their conversation, Vanessa tightened her arms around her torso. Hannah had wanted so much to hear about this part of Vanessa's life, and yet, here Vanessa was, alone in the emotional sediment it'd stirred up. On the other hand, she was used to dealing with the aftermath of interactions with her mother on her own. She could do it again. She just needed a few minutes to breathe and recover.

Chapter Ten

Hannah still reeled from being awakened by the venom in Vanessa's mother's words. Who talked to their child like that? Who talked to *anyone* like that? She couldn't imagine what Vanessa had gone through growing up.

Hannah had been blissfully dreaming of the moment her breath had caught that morning when she'd picked Vanessa up, and Vanessa emerged in a sleeveless floral dress. Its wide straps crisscrossed her chest, revealing a tantalizing glimpse of cleavage. She'd noticed Vanessa's assets before. How could she not? They were more generous than any Hannah had ever had the pleasure of holding, and whether Vanessa was wearing a simple T-shirt or a dressier blouse, Hannah was aware of how they moved beneath the fabric, how the material clung to their curves, and well, just about everything about them. Her breasts were worthy of starring in a Clare Ashton novel.

But the pleasure of the dream had shattered when Hannah had seen the pallor of Vanessa's face. Hannah's rage rose with each accusation and cutting remark, doused only when she'd noticed Vanessa shaking and the car drifting over the line.

Later, as she'd driven them southward, she'd gotten Vanessa to open up a little, but Hannah could tell the ordeal had sapped her strength. She let her rest and then doze, covering her with her jacket in case the air conditioning chilled her. It seemed such meager protection against the terrible things Hannah would like to shield her from.

They'd stopped in Eugene to eat sandwiches. But now, as they neared Ashland, the nourishment seemed too long ago. Hannah picked through the snacks they had left, but nothing appealed to her.

"Hungry?" Vanessa looked at her.

"A bit, but I can wait."

"It'll be worth it. I promise. They love to grill. Sonja already asked me if you eat meat." Vanessa tapped her phone's screen. "We're only forty-five minutes away. It's not exactly in Ashland, of course."

"So, you come here often?"

"No." Vanessa smoothed her dress over her thighs. "I aim for once a quarter to check up on everything, but they know what they're doing."

Hannah adjusted her visor against the sinking sun. It'd taken them longer to get here than she'd anticipated, but she didn't regret the couple of selfies they'd stopped to take or the time Vanessa had needed after talking with her mother. As long as they appeared before dinner, she wouldn't feel guilty for keeping Vanessa's friends waiting.

Even with Vanessa's phone call from hell and Hannah having to deal with a work issue, it hadn't been a bad day. She'd enjoyed traveling with Vanessa. As road trip companions went, she was amicable and pleasant to be around. It turned out, they liked similar music, and she'd even gotten Vanessa to loosen up and sing with her a few times. The memory made Hannah smile all these hours later.

"At the next exit, you're going to turn left at the stop sign." Vanessa pointed.

The green farmland gave rise to the bluish mountains in the distance, and only a few white clouds interrupted the picture-perfect sky. Hannah could see the allure of living in a place like this. Soon, Vanessa instructed her to turn under a wooden gate.

"Stop."

Hannah hit the brakes. "Did I run over something?"

"No, but the road to the house isn't paved. Your car will get filthy. I'll call and have Jeffrey pick us up." Vanessa moved wrappers, presumably looking for her phone.

Hannah put a hand out to stop her search and eased her foot onto the gas. "It's fine. A little dirt won't hurt." A few minutes later, when the washboard road rattled her teeth, she worried more about her shocks and suspension than dust on the paint job. The section was overdue to be graded.

"There's Sonja." Vanessa rolled down the window and waved as Hannah brought the car to a stop in front of a two-story green farmhouse.

A woman with dark hair and strong cheekbones wearing a Deschutes Brewery baseball cap pulled up beside them on a red four-wheeler as

Vanessa got out. She flew from the seat and had Vanessa in a hug before Hannah killed the engine.

Hannah waited off to the side, giving them time to enjoy their reunion.

Sonja cupped Vanessa's face. "You look good." She glanced down. "And look at this dress. It's fantastic, but I hope you brought something more suitable if you're going to walk through the fields."

"Of course. I wanted to be comfortable on the drive."

Hannah raised an inner eyebrow. Comfort wasn't what came to *her* mind when looking at Vanessa's outfit.

Vanessa let go of Sonja and turned to Hannah.

A bright glow highlighted Vanessa's delicate features. With her curls blowing in the gentle breeze, and the tease of cleavage the dress allowed, Hannah found her absolutely stunning. She looked away, her eyes burning as if she'd stared at the sun.

"Sonja, this is Hannah Baros. Hannah, Sonja Wong-Nyland."

"Ah, yes. The jeweler." Sonja stepped back and gave her the once-over. "Vanessa's told me about you."

The way Sonja said it left Hannah wondering exactly what Vanessa had relayed. "It's lovely to meet you." She tried not to think about the main thing that stood out from what Vanessa had told *her* about Sonja. Hannah gestured around her. "This place is gorgeous." All kinds of scents greeted her, earthy herbaceous smells, the light hint of wood smoke in the air, and the sweetly floral fragrances likely coming from the flowers that bloomed near the home's entrance.

"We love it." Sonja hooked her arm through Vanessa's. "Jeffrey's in the north field. He'll be a bit. I was about to start dinner. Hungry?"

"We're definitely ready for food."

Hannah wasn't sure if the smile Vanessa gave her was due to her search for a snack in the car or something else.

They got their suitcases, and once inside, Sonja pointed to the stairs beyond a rustic living room. "Show Hannah where she can put her things and freshen up if she'd like. I'm going to change and clean up, too. Join me in the kitchen in a few minutes."

Hannah followed Vanessa to the second floor.

She stopped outside a small bedroom decorated in white with pops of denim. "This is you. I'm just next door. The bath is there. It's just the two of us sharing it."

"Okay." Hannah parked her roller bag near her bed.

Still in the hall, Vanessa gathered her hair high on her head, then let it tumble over her bare shoulders, her breasts rising and falling with the motion. "I'm going to change. Do you want me to wait for you before I go down?"

"No need." Hannah silently mourned the impending loss of the fabulous dress. She covertly appreciated it one more time before it disappeared. "See you in a few."

Vanessa closed the door with a smile.

Hannah grinned. Was it just her? Or were things changing between them?

Chapter Eleven

When Vanessa entered the kitchen, Sonja looked up from where she arranged crackers and carrots around some sort of dip. Dinner ingredients covered one end of the island, including a raw marbled steak that looked large enough to feed a dozen farmhands.

"Here." She pushed the plate toward Vanessa. "Something to snack on while I get this going."

Vanessa took her favorite stool on the end and sighed. Not that her dress hadn't been comfortable, but it felt good to put on sweats, and she didn't have to worry about potentially showing too much.

Seconds later, Hannah appeared in the archway separating the kitchen from the living room still wearing jeans. The tendrils around her face were damp and clung to her skin. Even with no makeup, she looked so beautiful, it'd taken Vanessa a moment to recognize the difference.

"Sonja made us a snack." Vanessa rose and moved behind Sonja, who gave her room to pass. "Do you want something to drink?"

"Whatever you're having."

Hannah took the stool beside the one Vanessa had vacated, and a little thrill ran through Vanessa at the thought of having her near. It was natural. They'd become accustomed to being close in the car all day. Vanessa didn't usually feel the need for proximity with anyone.

Sonja glanced up from where she sliced green onions. "We haven't gotten that far. There's red wine, sparkling water, there might be some iced tea left, or—"

"Wine sounds good."

"I agree." Vanessa opened the cupboard where Sonja kept glasses. "What about you?" She leaned into Sonja's line of sight.

"My water's around here somewhere."

Vanessa spotted it beside the sink and put it on the island.

"Darn. I forgot to light the grill." Sonja turned to her. "Vanessa, could you get that for me?"

Sonja's look of innocence was so pure, Vanessa couldn't help but be suspicious. She gave her a warning glare, picturing little daggers shooting from her eyes as she switched tasks.

Sonja ignored her, instead scraping the skin from a large chunk of ginger with a spoon.

"I'd love to," Vanessa muttered.

"So, Hannah," Sonja said as Vanessa left.

Vanessa only closed the screen on the slider, but the grill was too far away on the deck for her to hear any of the conversation inside. With their decades of friendship, she should've known Sonja would try to corner Hannah. The fact that Vanessa had brought a woman with her proved too much of a temptation, even though Vanessa had clearly explained who Hannah was and the reason for the trip. When Vanessa returned to the kitchen, she found them laughing.

"Sonja thinks you and I should show up at Georgina's door in T-shirts that say Girlfriend One and Girlfriend Two."

"A little riff on Dr. Seuss," Sonja added.

Vanessa slid onto her stool. "What would that make her?"

"Girlfriend Three?" Sonja minced two cloves of garlic.

Its pungent scent made Vanessa's stomach growl. She pulled the appetizer plate between her and Hannah and snagged a cracker.

"Or patient zero," Hannah said dryly, before crunching into a carrot.

Her quip had them all laughing, but Hannah made a good point. As Vanessa watched Sonja measure soy sauce and a few other ingredients into a bowl, she pondered the truth of it. Who had Bren dated first? Her or Georgina? Her hunger gave way to queasiness, and she pushed the plate closer to Hannah.

"I'm going to let this marinate." Sonja set the beef on the back counter. "I should've done it earlier, but we were having a plumbing issue in the greenhouse, and I didn't get up here as early as I would've liked."

"Everything okay?" Vanessa didn't like to hear about problems that could potentially cost a lot to solve.

"My brilliant husband fixed it, but it put us behind today." She washed her hands. "Speaking of Jeff, I'd normally make steamed rice to go with this, but I promised him baked potatoes tonight. I can make rice, too, though, if you'd like."

"Don't do any more work on our account. Potatoes are great," Hannah said.

A door banged. "Where's my beautiful wife?"

"Kitchen, baby."

With his usual flair, Jeffrey stopped in the doorway, his cowboy hat clutched to his chest. "I must have done something good in another life to be greeted with a sight like this." He flashed his boyish smile that made his face beam.

"It's good to see you, Jeff. You're looking well." Vanessa had missed the two of them.

He moved around the island to kiss Sonja on the cheek.

"Oh, baby, you need a shower before you greet anyone else." Sonja eased away from him. "And we need to fix your line-up soon, too." She ran her thumb along where his hair met his forehead. "It grows so fast."

"Vanessa, good to see you," he said. "And you must be Hannah. Apologies, but my wife just told me I stink, so I'm going to clean up before I give her a hand."

"Grill's heating and the steak's marinating," Sonja called after him as he left the room.

"I'll make the salad," he said, his voice fading.

In less time than it'd ever taken Vanessa to shower, he was back, and after a quick hug for her and a handshake for Hannah, he pulled cucumbers and red onions from the refrigerator. Beside him, Sonja wrapped clean potatoes in foil.

"Gotta take out the seeds," he said, scraping out the middle of the cucumber with a spoon. "Can't have you ladies burping all night."

Under the counter, Hannah gave Vanessa's leg a little pinch.

Vanessa looked at her in a silent question, but Hannah just smiled. When Hannah moved her hand again, Vanessa caught it, holding it against her thigh. There'd be no more of that. She glanced at Sonja, who was busy with dinner, and when she turned back to Hannah, that playful grin had disappeared, replaced by something very different. Desire? Arousal?

Vanessa looked away. Ridiculous. They'd been hanging out together occasionally all summer. She would've noticed a change like that.

"Baby, do we have any sesame oil?" Jeffrey rummaged in the pantry.

"It's already out."

He turned, a bottle of rice wine vinegar in his hand. "Oh, there it is." Once he'd added the sliced onions, he shook a little of both over the mixture, then added a handful of sesame seeds. He fitted a tight lid on the bowl and shook it in all directions, doing a little circular dance, then poured it onto a plate. After taking a few quick slices of the scallions Sonja hadn't used, he sprinkled them on top. "There. We're fancy like that."

Vanessa laughed. She'd been so entertained watching him, she only realized she was still holding Hannah's hand when Jeffrey came around the island to put the salad on the table.

She released it.

"Whatever you put on the steak smells delicious." Hannah slid her touch from Vanessa's thigh.

Her skin tingled where Hannah had been touching her.

Sonja dried a cutting board. "I wish I could tell you it's a recipe, but I just sort of throw things together based on what I have on hand."

"Oh, no worries. It was simply a compliment. I don't really cook."

A sly smile crept across Sonja's face. "She does." Sonja motioned in Vanessa's direction. "You should ask her to cook for you sometime. She's fantastic in the kitchen."

Daggers. All the little daggers.

Hannah smiled at Vanessa. "I've seen some evidence of this."

"Well, good for you. She tends to reserve her skills for special occasions."

Based on Sonja's gleeful expression, Vanessa was in trouble. Hannah had unknowingly provided ammunition Sonja could use to tease and torment later. And Vanessa had no doubt both would be coming her way.

Strangely, dinner passed without a single jibe, only excellent food and the camaraderie of old and new friends, if she and Hannah could be considered such. She wasn't sure what they were to each other.

"You'll have to check out the ground we've cleared for the new greenhouses," Jeff said, relaxing back after pushing his plate away. "The site work's almost finished. They'll pour the foundations in the next week or so."

"I'm sorry dinner took so long." Sonja leaned back against Jeff's arm that he'd rested across the top of her chair. "Your tour will have to wait until morning."

Outside, twilight had descended, casting the trees and bushes in the backyard as dark, indiscernible shapes.

"That's fine." Vanessa rose and began clearing the dishes. "I'm excited to see the progress and show Hannah the fields and the hothouse."

Hannah stood to help her. "We don't need to be any place at a certain time tomorrow. We'll drop by Georgina's whenever we get there."

"With or without matching T-shirts?" Sonja finished her water with a smirk.

Jeffrey pushed back his chair. "I'm going to leave you three to your private jokes and go feed my dogs." He kissed Sonja and stepped outside. A sharp whistle brought their beloved golden retriever Duckie and border collie terrier Patches scrambling around his legs.

Sonja took her glass to the sink where Vanessa began loading the dishwasher. "There's ice cream in the freezer if you two want dessert. I doubt either of us will be up much longer." She turned to take the leftover steak and potatoes from Hannah. "Farmers' hours, you know. Is there anything I can get you before I turn in?"

"Go to bed." Vanessa waved her off. "I know where everything is. We'll clean up."

Sonja slid the plate onto the counter. "I appreciate it. Breakfast is at sunrise if you're interested."

Hannah laughed. "Does that have a corresponding time on a clock?"

Vanessa made eye contact with her, and they shared a smile. "Don't worry. You'll smell it, and if you don't, I'll wake you." She caught Sonja's raised eyebrows before she turned back to the sink.

When they'd finished in the kitchen, they quietly retreated upstairs. It was earlier than Vanessa usually went to bed, and probably the same for Hannah, but driving made her tired. Combine that with the emotional toll of the call with her mother and Hannah overhearing it, getting a few extra hours of sleep suddenly didn't sound so bad.

She hesitated before her door. Hannah had taken her hair down again, and the glossy waves curled around the tops of her shoulders. Vanessa wondered what they'd feel like between her fingers. "It's been a long day."

"It has." Hannah leaned against the wall. "We don't have to drive as far tomorrow."

"You don't have to take a tour of the farm if you don't want to. I like to check everything out when I'm here, but if you want to sleep—"

"I'll go with you." Hannah's lips pulled into a lazy smile. "I better get some rest if I have to witness a sunrise."

Vanessa had been considering asking her if she wanted to go back downstairs for another drink, but she'd taken too long. "Okay." She waited for Hannah to make a move toward her room, but she didn't.

"Yeah." Hannah's gaze flitted around her face before dropping to her lips. "Okay." Finally, she pushed off the wall, but she still didn't leave. The tip of her tongue darted between her lips.

It happened quickly, but it brought Vanessa's attention to her mouth—her lovely mouth—and her perfect lower lip, now glistening under the hall light.

God, this was Hannah, the woman who'd lost her partner just a few months ago, even if she said she'd mourned Bren long before that. Vanessa took a step back. "Well, good night then."

Hannah blinked slowly, then nodded. "Good night."

❖

Vanessa only had time to unzip her suitcase before a soft knock startled her. Sonja was probably fussing, reminding her to jiggle the guest toilet's handle if it didn't stop running or offering ice cream one more time. But it wasn't Sonja.

It was Hannah.

"Hi." Vanessa held the door in one hand.

Hannah slowly pushed it open until she stood in the doorway. Her eyes were dark, searching. She stepped closer, slipping an arm around Vanessa's waist.

Vanessa couldn't breathe. Hannah's touch seemed to have short-circuited whatever part of her brain was responsible for such mundane things.

Hannah gently stroked her cheek, then slid her fingers behind Vanessa's neck, holding her in place. She leaned in, and Vanessa closed her eyes when Hannah's soft lips brushed hers. It felt so right. Hannah moved against her, and Vanessa leaned into it, pressing back. A flick of Hannah's tongue had Vanessa opening to her, letting her in.

Vanessa forgot the past and blanked on the future. Only the goddamned perfect present of this exquisite kiss existed. They might have kissed for seconds or minutes, but they kissed long and slow, and she didn't ever want it to end. She was semi-aware of Hannah's soft hair between her fingers and her body pressed against hers, but Hannah had inundated her senses too much for anything more to register.

Hannah broke the kiss far too soon for Vanessa's liking. She pressed their foreheads together, and their breaths came hard and fast as they shared the air between them.

"That's better." Hannah's voice had dropped, more raspy than Vanessa had ever heard it. With her face flushed and eyelids heavy, Hannah took a step backward and smiled. "Good night, Vanessa."

Vanessa stood unable to move until the click of Hannah's closing door broke her trance. She waited until she heard Hannah use the bathroom and presumably go to bed, then did the same. But when she crawled under the covers, sleep eluded her. After that kiss, knowing Hannah was on the other side of the wall made her wish they weren't sleeping in separate rooms in someone else's home.

Chapter Twelve

The morning sun warmed Hannah's bare arms. Before her, rows of green appeared to stretch as far as the tree-covered mountains in the distance.

Beside her, Vanessa plucked a weed. "The pumpkins will support the local stands as Halloween gets closer. Jeff and Sonja sell some of them where the driveway meets the main road. An honor pay system. It doesn't bring in enough to merit someone working it." She seemed so at home here, in the middle of a field with the sunshine making her hair glow and talking about flowers and plants.

"What about gourds?"

"Yes, they sell a few, and dried corn stalks and hay bales, too. Sonja dreams of having an actual establishment, a produce stand of sorts one day. Perhaps not year-round but open as much as possible. She's plotted a spot for it down where I suggested you pull your car over. Local artisans could sell jams and jellies, cheeses, honey, even beeswax candles, but the main draw would be our organic fruits, vegetables, and flowers." Vanessa walked down a row.

Hannah followed. "Why haven't you done it yet?"

"Money." Vanessa stopped to pick a small purple flower. She threaded it into Hannah's hair, then smiled. "C'mon. This way." She took Hannah's hand, her skin warm and soft, and led her toward the largest building on the property.

Hannah wasn't sure what to make of the handholding. Neither of them had brought up her ill-conceived kiss the night before. She didn't know what'd come over her. Maybe it was the closeness they'd experienced during the drive or perhaps simply having to exist in the same vicinity of Vanessa in that dress for so long, but Hannah had gone to her room needing more. She'd awakened this morning with the realization of what a bad idea it'd been.

While she was familiar with short-term physical intimacy, she got the feeling Vanessa wasn't. So, that wasn't happening. Of all the people Hannah had met in her life, Vanessa appeared to have more goodness and purity than most. Hannah wasn't about to ruin that by using her to satisfy a need, and anything beyond that was impossible. Hannah had made a mess of the one serious relationship she'd been in, and she wouldn't do that to Vanessa. No, it was time to return to what made her most comfortable. Before Bren, she'd been content to share a night or two with a beautiful woman and leave it at that. She could do it again. It's not like she had time for dating, anyway. She slipped her fingers from Vanessa's.

Vanessa opened the door to the greenhouse, and they stepped inside.

A wall of fragrance hit Hannah. Loamy, floral, fruity. The warmer temperature and the high humidity made it difficult to breathe. It was like stepping into another world.

"This is incredible."

"Isn't it?" Vanessa wandered along, touching leaves and petals or occasionally pressing her finger into the soil. "That's why we're building more. This is the most important piece of the puzzle." She stopped to pull a curled hose from above and misted some plants Hannah didn't recognize. "Without this," Vanessa waved her hand, indicating the metal and glass above, "our growing season would be much shorter. Some flowers we wouldn't be able to grow in this climate at all. Crops would be subject to late or early frosts or hailstorms that could wipe them out completely." She retracted the hose.

"What percentage of your flowers do you grow?" They'd been walking for a while, but Hannah still couldn't spot the far end.

"About sixty percent. Without this, I'd be purchasing wholesale."

As they approached a man wearing a Crocodile Dundee type hat, he broke into a huge grin. "I hoped to say hello to you on your visit."

"Jorge, so good to see you." She hugged him. "Is Marina walking yet?"

"She's everywhere. Her mama gets nada done. Did you know they're having another?"

Vanessa turned to Hannah with a chuckle. "Jorge is a proud granddaddy."

Hannah smiled. "That's wonderful." As Jorge and Vanessa reconnected, Hannah touched the flower Vanessa had put in her hair, wondering what it was.

"Ready?" Vanessa touched the small of Hannah's back, reclaiming her attention. "Jorge was one of our first hires here," she said as they moved away.

"Are most of your workers Hispanic?" Hannah had only noticed two white people so far. The rest had all been brown-skinned.

"Latino? Yes. I don't know how we'd manage without them. I honestly don't know who we'd hire."

"How do you know if they're," Hannah lowered her voice, "citizens?"

Vanessa stopped and stared at her a moment. "How do you know if *your* employees are? We ask for paperwork and documentation, same as you. Many of them are migrant workers, but that doesn't mean they're illegal." She turned and started walking again.

Hannah had to pick up the pace to keep up. "What's the difference?"

"Migrant workers move from farm to farm, usually when crops need to be harvested. There's a hierarchy. The oldest and most respectable farms get them first. If the owners don't treat them fairly or nicely, they're going to be moved down the schedule."

"So, they'll all leave soon?"

Vanessa shook her head. "Not all. Some are full time, like Jorge and his family. It just depends."

Finally, Hannah could see the large doors at the end of the greenhouse.

"Let's finish up here, and I'll show you the You-Pick berry patches." Vanessa touched her arm. "Then we should probably get on the road."

❖

As they neared the Bay Bridge, Hannah braked for the traffic that crept through the East Bay. "There she is." She pointed across the water to where most of the Golden Gate Bridge was visible beneath the marine layer that hid the tops of the two great towers.

"Beautiful." Vanessa gazed out the window. "And look at all the sailboats."

Kite boarders and windsurfers also dappled the water between the shoreline and Treasure Island.

"It is, no matter the weather." Hannah changed lanes. "How long has it been since you've been here?"

"Hmm." Vanessa tapped her chin with her fingertip. "Probably at least seven years."

It'd likely been with Bren. The thought made Hannah want to help her create new memories, better ones, to take back with her.

Once they'd successfully maneuvered past the toll booths, the speed of traffic increased. Hannah shook her head as they passed the skyscraping Salesforce Tower she still hadn't grown accustomed to seeing as part of the skyline, and on her left, the Giants baseball stadium made her recall how Bren had always said she'd take her to a game there but never had.

"There." Vanessa pointed, looking between the screen on the dash and the signs above the roadway. "That lane will take us to Daly City."

Hannah changed freeways. It wasn't even four o'clock yet, but experience reminded her that rush hour started much earlier in San Francisco, and she was happy to be leaving the downtown financial district.

When they reached the suburb and she turned onto Louvaine Drive, Hannah immediately looked for a parking space. Even during the day, cars lined the curbs. Residents must take public transportation to work.

"There." Vanessa motioned to the opposite side of the street.

Hannah made a U-turn at the next intersection and pulled into the spot. She kept the engine running. "Are you sure you want to do this? I can go alone if you're having second thoughts."

Surprise flashed across Vanessa's face. "I came all this way. There's no way I'm not seeing this woman now." She opened her door.

Hannah hadn't been sure. Vanessa had been quieter than usual once they'd left Ashland, and Hannah kept kicking herself for complicating things by kissing her, as nice as it'd been. *Nicer* than nice. Divine. It'd occupied the majority of her thoughts on the drive. Hell, maybe *she'd* been the quiet one. Way to make things even more awkward.

Hannah winced and got out. The homes in the neighborhood were older and on the smaller side but well-maintained. Utility lines crisscrossed the street. Hannah locked the car, and they walked the half block to the Kaplans' home. The clouds and fog now obscured the sky from view, and a slight chill hung in the air. "Shall I do the talking, at least at first?"

"Yes." Vanessa grasped her wrist as if in solidarity, then let go.

They stood on the small porch of the whitewashed single-story home, and Hannah rang the bell.

A boy answered, his eyes deep set and inquisitive. He had beautiful dark skin and looked to be twelve or thirteen, close in age to the kids she'd gotten to know at the garden.

"Hi, is Georgina home?"

He turned and yelled. "Mom. Someone's here for you."

A woman appeared behind him, Latina and curvy, her orange shirt making her skin seem to glow. Blond highlights streaked her chestnut brown hair, and she wore a fashionable pair of tortoiseshell glasses. She barely spared them a glance.

"Noah, go spray the stain and put this in the washer if you want it for tomorrow." She tossed him a royal blue shirt with yellow trim.

He caught it and disappeared through a doorway but not before giving Hannah and Vanessa a once-over.

"Hi," Hannah said, "I'm—"

Georgina held up her hand, effectively silencing her. She stepped outside, forcing them down the steps, and closed the door behind her. "I wondered if you'd come here," she said, her voice nearly a whisper. "My son is home. You can't just show up whenever you want. If I wanted to talk to you, I would've taken your calls." She set her jaw.

"I'm sorry," Hannah said, "but we'd really like to speak with you. It's important. This is Vanessa Holland—"

"I know who you both are." Georgina glanced between them, then behind her, as if considering her options. Her shoulders drooped. "Fine. Come by tomorrow at ten. Noah will be at practice. I'll give you an hour."

Hannah took a step back. "Thank you."

They turned and walked to her car. When Hannah glanced back, Georgina still stood on the doorstep.

"That could've gone better," Vanessa said.

Hannah started the car. "She didn't say no or yell at us. Let's consider it a win." She pulled into the street.

"She's gorgeous." Vanessa crossed her arms over her chest.

Hannah laughed. "I knew she would be."

Vanessa turned. "Why do you say that?"

"Look at you." Hannah gestured toward her.

"I could say the same," Vanessa said quietly.

Again, tension filled the air, as if both were thinking about the kiss. Unfortunately, Hannah's thoughts were likely different from Vanessa's. She had to break the heavy silence. "How about some food and taking in a sight or two?"

"Do we need to check into the Airbnb?"

"It has a keypad. We can arrive whenever." Hannah turned westward, knowing the route would take them past the zoo and north along the coast. "Let's find a place where we don't need reservations."

By the time they'd finished eating at the chalet-style restaurant overlooking Ocean Beach, the fog had burned off and the sun setting over the Pacific dusted the wisps of clouds near the horizon with shades of rose and gold. Hannah pulled into the parking lot above the Sutro Baths.

"I've never been here." Vanessa leaned forward, peering over the dash to the shoreline below.

"Oh, perfect." Hannah got out and pulled their jackets from the back seat. "We'll need these." She held Vanessa's open for her.

"What is this place?" Vanessa looked around as they made their way down the steps that descended to the beach.

Hannah breathed in the salt air. "It's the ruins of a giant indoor pool complex." She led Vanessa toward the rectangular rock foundation now filled with seawater. Graffiti covered almost every inch of the crumbling stone. Above, the famous Cliff House lorded over the park. Beyond, barricades kept people from venturing where the waves crashed against the rocks. But in between, greenery abounded, and ice plant and small ferns fought for space. Bright yellow flowers dotted the vegetation.

"Dune tansies," Vanessa said, leaning down to examine them.

Of course, Vanessa would notice. It was beyond endearing. When she straightened, tossing her hair from her face, Hannah reached for her hand and drew her closer.

Vanessa, with vibrant questioning eyes, no longer studied the foliage but her.

The shattering of each wave crashing on the rock and shore should've been jarring, but it wasn't. It provided an oddly comforting soundtrack to whatever was happening between them. Hannah inched closer. Neither looked away. But with no warning, the ocean pulled back its power and coughed up an enormous wave with a great roar.

Vanessa yelped and buried her face in Hannah's neck, embracing her tightly.

Hannah blinked to clear the cold spray from her eyes, but she didn't need to see to bask in the pleasure of Vanessa in her arms.

"That was unexpected," Vanessa said, lifting her head and wiping the mist from her cheek. "Sorry," she mumbled, looking at her.

Against Hannah, Vanessa's warmth contrasted with the cool ocean air. This close, Vanessa's sweet scent drifted over her, and their chests rose and fell with the same quick, shallow breaths.

Vanessa had threaded her arms beneath Hannah's jacket and now clutched her shirt. "Hannah," she whispered.

Hannah barely heard it, maybe because of the thundering waves, or perhaps because all she could think about was kissing her. It hadn't been a smart idea last night, and it certainly wasn't now, but Hannah's willpower was slipping with Vanessa so close.

"The tunnel's down here," a boy shouted, running past. Two more followed him.

Hannah stepped in front of Vanessa, shielding her from the intruders she hadn't noticed descending the hill, but with their fishing rods in hand and youthful exuberance, they hardly seemed a threat. She put some distance between her and Vanessa.

The last boy, who looked older than the other two, kept his focus on the sand as he passed them. "Sorry," he said.

Hannah wasn't. The interruption had saved her from making another mistake. She turned to Vanessa and motioned to the path. "Shall we?"

Vanessa's quiet and curt, "Sure," cut sharply through the evening breeze. Was she upset?

As Hannah climbed the stairs, she pulled her coat tighter against the biting wind, shoving her fists beneath her arms to keep her from doing something ridiculous like holding Vanessa's hand again. "Now that we've met Georgina, are you nervous about tomorrow?" she asked, desperate for a topic that would lead them away from their almost kiss.

"Not really. Just don't know what to expect."

Hannah didn't either. "She clearly didn't want to talk to us while her son was around. Do you think she'll be more willing when he's gone?" They reached the parking lot.

Vanessa stepped around to the passenger's side. "I have no idea. Guess we'll find out."

Silence filled the car on the drive to Leslie's place on Telegraph Hill, and Hannah did her best not to squirm. By the time they arrived, the sky had grown dark. Thankfully, the condo had space to park one car, or finding a spot on the tiny winding streets would've been a nightmare.

Inside, Leslie had left a living room lamp on, and the space welcomed them with warmth and vanilla-scented air. Like most vacation rentals, the décor was regional, the walls plastered with prints of the Golden Gate

Bridge, Fisherman's Wharf, and Coit Tower. Red crab knick-knacks lay strewn throughout. At least it wasn't the lighthouse and seashell kitsch that covered most coastal Airbnbs.

Once they'd stowed their bags in their respective rooms, Hannah searched the refrigerator. "There's wine and beer. Or water, if you'd prefer." She'd have to thank Leslie for stocking drinks and snacks.

"What're you having?" Vanessa turned from the window.

"Cabernet."

"I will, too, then." She returned to the view. "If that's Alcatraz, what's over there?"

"Angel Island." Hannah brought their glasses to the chairs in front of the large window. "The Ellis Island of the west."

They nursed their drinks while admiring the stunning vista, but what lay between them weighed on Hannah. They were here for a purpose, and she needed to remember that. The goal remained. Talk to Georgina, get some answers, and go home. Once there, everything would return to normal.

Vanessa shook her head. "Can you imagine looking at this every day?"

"I'd get zero work done." Hannah reached for her phone. "Speaking of which, I need to coordinate picking up the diamonds tomorrow. I'll probably shower and head to bed after that." She stood. "The remote for the TV is on the end table, and if you get hungry, Leslie put snacks in the cupboard beside the refrigerator."

"Thanks." Vanessa's cool delivery didn't include eye contact or a good night wish.

Hannah couldn't help but feel she'd done something wrong, and she had. What had she been thinking kissing Vanessa last night? She retreated to her room.

It didn't take long to schedule the diamond pickup. It was simply a matter of completing the wire transfer and determining a time to swing by the dealer's offices. Then she got ready for bed.

When she returned from taking her glass to the kitchen, the sound of a shower brought her to a halt as she imagined warm water sluicing over Vanessa's body. She tried to shake the vision and pulled the towel from her own wet hair. After hanging it on the back of the door, she sank onto the foot of the bed to check her phone.

Usually, she'd still be answering emails at this hour, and she considered booting up her laptop to do just that, but a quick glance at her inbox told her they could wait. If her assistant were more competent, Hannah could assign some of them to her. She had no idea why her parents had hired Annika. Hannah's mother had done almost everything herself, which is probably why Hannah inherited that practice, and the most her father had asked of Annika was bringing him coffee and making copies. Hannah either needed Annika to start pulling her weight, or she needed a new assistant. She'd been so hesitant to rock the boat her first year at the helm, but that was over. It was time to start making changes.

"I expected you to kiss me tonight."

Hannah jumped at the sound of Vanessa's voice. Vanessa leaned against the doorway in a satiny robe that clearly told Hannah what was—or rather wasn't—underneath.

"What?"

"Tonight. I thought you'd kiss me." Vanessa gave a little shrug and straightened. "You did last night. Before we were interrupted, I thought you might on the beach." Vanessa's half smile looked stiff. "But you didn't." Her face fell.

"Vanessa." Hannah clutched the bedding.

"It's understandable if you're still mourning." Vanessa came closer. "If that's the case, I'll return to my room."

She looked so damned beautiful, her hair slightly damp and a sparkle in her eyes.

"It's not. Like I said before, I'd grieved Bren's loss long before she died. You're…" Hannah faltered. How could she explain?

Vanessa stopped in front of her, holding Hannah's gaze. She slipped a bare foot between Hannah's, her skin warm to the touch. "I'm what?"

Hannah took a deep breath. Best to get it out there. "You're too good," she said with emphasis. "Too sweet, too pure. I sleep with women and never see them again. We already know each other and work together in the garden. I'm not going to have a one-night stand with you. You deserve better than someone messed up like me." She fiddled with the end of her belt. "And I can't offer you anything more. You saw the mess I made with Bren. I don't know how to be in a relationship."

Vanessa brushed her knuckles down Hannah's cheek. "Many single people could say the same."

"It's different with you," Hannah whispered.

"It doesn't have to be. We're here. I liked kissing you, and I think you liked it, too." Vanessa nudged Hannah's legs apart until she stood between them. She cupped Hannah's face. "I haven't wanted to do this with a woman in a long time. I tried but couldn't. Can we just let it be what it is and enjoy one another tonight?"

Vanessa was talking about so much more than a kiss. Thoughts sped like racing cars down the freeway of Hannah's mind. She wanted to. Oh, God, how she wanted to. If the kiss had been a mistake though, what was she about to do here? Five years, since Bren? Christ. They still had thirteen hours of driving together. What if it was awkward with a capital A?

All logic and reason evaporated when Vanessa leaned down and kissed her.

As Hannah relaxed into it, she slipped her fingers around the backs of Vanessa's knees, caressing the soft skin there.

With the sureness and tenderness that accompanied most things Vanessa did, she threaded her hands into Hannah's hair, tipping her face up, like she couldn't get enough of her.

Hannah had been reliving their kiss from the night before all day, but the magnificence of the reality of right here and now came crashing in on her. She didn't want to stop, ever, and still she broke away just enough to draw a breath. "Are you sure?"

Vanessa straightened and pulled the tie around her waist until the knot fell loose. "Never more certain." She inched open her robe.

Hannah trailed her gaze down the strip of bare skin Vanessa exposed, from the soft inner curves of her breasts, over her gently sloping stomach, to the fine hairs at the junction of her thighs. With one finger, Hannah drew the panel of silky material until Vanessa's nipple came into view. Her breath caught. The sight entranced her, a beauty so divine sculptors expertly captured similar spectacles in marble. But when Hannah cupped the supple warmth of Vanessa's breast, any thoughts of cold, hard stone fled. When she looked up, Vanessa's eyes were dark with evident desire.

"You're so beautiful," Hannah whispered, caressing Vanessa's hardened nipple.

Vanessa sucked in a breath and closed her eyes but grasped Hannah's hand. "Before we go further…well, I should warn you." She sat beside Hannah. "Sometimes I have trouble reaching orgasm. I don't want you to be disappointed or think it has anything to do with you."

Hannah entwined their fingers. "I'm not sure that merits a warning." She tried for a reassuring tone. "I simply want you to enjoy the experience."

"I do." Vanessa smiled. "I just can't always get to the finish line."

"Is it the same when you're by yourself?"

Vanessa blushed, then let out a short laugh. "It's different when it's just me."

"That's good." Hannah raised their joined hands and pressed her lips to the back of Vanessa's. "That tells me the engine is in working condition, if you'll excuse the terrible metaphor. So, we'll just take our time, and see how things go. As long as you're enjoying what we're doing."

With a quiet sigh, Vanessa looked up. "Thank you. And I already am."

Hannah leaned in and kissed her, curling an arm around Vanessa and drawing her closer. As she moved her mouth against Vanessa's and was invited in through her parted lips, she rested her fingertips on Vanessa's collarbone. Her skin was so soft and delicate, and Hannah ached to strip off Vanessa's robe and explore her everywhere at once. But there was something deliciously erotic about discovering Vanessa's secrets inch by inch.

When Hannah moved her mouth to the sweet spot below Vanessa's ear, Vanessa moaned and tilted her head back, allowing Hannah easier access.

Hannah groaned as she left a trail of little nips down Vanessa's neck. But it was more than arousal. Vanessa hadn't given herself to anyone in years, and yet, here was Hannah, alone with her, exploring her intimately, the recipient of such a treasured gift. How had she gotten so lucky? Whether good fortune or something else, she was grateful, and even more so when she opened the robe fully to reveal Vanessa's other breast.

She gazed in awe, unable to speak or even breathe.

Then she couldn't wait a second longer. Hannah jumped up, tugged Vanessa to her feet, and yanked down the covers. When she turned around, Vanessa's piercing green eyes were hooded, and a blush bloomed on her chest. Hannah stepped close, thrilling at the heat radiating between them, then smoothed her palms down the sides of Vanessa's neck, and pushed the robe from her shoulders.

Vanessa caught it in the crook of her arms, then let it drop to the floor. She stood before Hannah more confidently than anyone Hannah had ever been with. And rightly so. She was gorgeous, a vision Hannah could gaze upon for hours, but this wasn't a museum, and Vanessa wasn't a piece of art. She was a living, sensuous woman with needs.

And by the way Vanessa was devouring her with her eyes, Hannah was clearly what she needed.

With a sly upturn of her lips, Vanessa pulled the belt at Hannah's waist until her robe fell open. But she didn't take it any further.

Was she toying with Hannah, waiting for a precise moment when she'd flip the table and own her? Hannah didn't care. Vanessa could take whatever she wanted. For now, she was allowing Hannah to take the lead.

Slowly, with the reverence Vanessa deserved, Hannah slid her hands beneath Vanessa's hair and pushed it off her shoulders, then lay a tender kiss atop each one. She dipped her head to Vanessa's sternum and did the same.

Vanessa inhaled, her breasts lifting as though begging for attention, but she let Hannah continue.

When Hannah kneeled and left an open-mouthed kiss on Vanessa's stomach, she was rewarded with a sharp intake of breath and the thrill of Vanessa's hand in her hair. She moved lower still and sucked gently at the soft skin of Vanessa's leg, then trailed her lips across to the other side, her own need surging when Vanessa jolted as Hannah brushed across her center. Hannah couldn't get enough. She caressed the backs of Vanessa's legs with her palms and slowly licked a path along the silky skin of Vanessa's inner thigh. When she could take no more of her own burning desire raging through her body, she pressed her forehead against the slight bump of Vanessa's belly, her breathing ragged and fast.

Vanessa pulled her in more tightly, both her hands in Hannah's hair, stroking, clenching and releasing, and running her fingernails along her scalp. "Please?" The word came out in a hoarse whisper.

Hannah rose. "Lie down."

Vanessa moved to the center of the bed and positioned a pillow beneath her head. She met Hannah's gaze as she drew up her knees, then let one drop to the mattress, opening herself to Hannah.

Yep. Hannah was about to be owned. With a flick of her shoulders, she left her robe on the floor and climbed atop her. The sensation of the length of their bodies pressed against one another with nothing in between stole her breath. The way their breasts fit perfectly together and Vanessa's leg slotted between hers almost overwhelmed Hannah. Emotion flooded her. Had she ever felt anything so deeply?

Vanessa pulled her down, and their mouths met again.

Hannah needed more. She abandoned the sensually exploratory nature of the previous kiss. This one was fast and frantic, almost rough at times, and Vanessa responded in kind, but when their teeth clashed, Hannah reined herself in. Hadn't she just said they could take it slowly?

Vanessa was clearly as aroused as Hannah, but there was no reason to rush toward an orgasm. Vanessa had been honest about sometimes having trouble in that department, so Hannah wanted to do everything she could, not only to give her the best chance of reaching that goal, but to have a mind-melting climax at that.

Hannah softened the kiss, then eased away. She stared into Vanessa's eyes as she sat back and removed her rings before setting them on the bedside table.

Vanessa followed her every move intently, then pulled Hannah to her again. She palmed Hannah's breasts as Hannah settled a leg between hers.

Hannah moaned at Vanessa's wet heat against her thigh.

Vanessa kissed her again, this time gentler yet insistent, as she thumbed her nipples into hardened points.

The pleasure heightened Hannah's need. When Vanessa lifted her head and took one between her lips, then into the warmth of her mouth, Hannah clenched her eyes shut and reveled in the sensation.

She let Vanessa worship her other breast, and when Vanessa finally slowed, Hannah realized she'd been grinding herself against her with each suck and nip. She was too close to coming. Hannah stilled herself and grasped Vanessa's wrist, then touched her lips to the inside. She captured the other before interlacing their fingers, then pressed their hands into the mattress near Vanessa's shoulders.

Vanessa's eyes widened when she moved between Vanessa's thighs.

"My turn," Hannah whispered.

Without a word, Vanessa wrapped her legs around Hannah's waist and pressed against her.

Hannah arched with a rush of desire. *Slowly. Take it slowly.* With restraint, she rocked her hips into Vanessa as she sucked along the tender column of her neck to the hollow of her throat and grazed her teeth over the gentle rise of her collarbone. She released Vanessa's hands to follow the curve of her breast with a single finger before tenderly massaging it.

God, her imaginings of a moment like this, as good as they'd been, had fallen so short. She kissed around Vanessa's nipple, then flicked it with her tongue.

Vanessa tightened her hold on the back of Hannah's neck. "Oh, yes."

Hannah closed her eyes, relishing the moment.

When she drew Vanessa's nipple into her mouth, Vanessa gave a sharp cry and held her close.

"More."

Happy to comply, Hannah sucked harder, then gave it a little nip.

Vanessa planted her feet on the mattress and pushed against Hannah in time with the rapid gasps of her breathing.

Hannah lifted her head, pressed her hips into her, and admired the rosy point that seemed to be begging for more. She kissed her other breast, then worked her way over her ribs, then her gently sloping stomach. After licking a line up the curve where her thigh met her body, Hannah traced the glistening flesh between Vanessa's legs, parting her with the tip of her finger. *So beautiful.*

Hannah lingered at her opening, marveling at Vanessa's wetness and enjoying her grip in her hair. Hannah wanted to taste her, wanted it so badly her vision swam, but she had to wait just a little longer. She moved up beside Vanessa and pulled their bodies flush.

But Vanessa was clearly done waiting. She claimed Hannah's mouth and kissed her hungrily.

Who was Hannah to argue? She ground hard against Vanessa's thigh. "Touch me," she whispered, her jaw clenched.

Vanessa cupped her face, studying her, then rolled her onto her back. She raked her gaze over Hannah's naked body. "Where?"

Her voice was husky, lust darkening her eyes. Hannah groaned. "Anywhere. Everywhere. I want *you*. Your hands. Your mouth. Your fingers inside me. I want all of it."

With a single nod, Vanessa tapped Hannah's hip. "Turn over."

Hannah blinked. She hadn't been expecting *that* but obeyed.

She waited. What was Vanessa doing? Was she taking her in, learning her body? Did she like what she saw? She couldn't see much. Hannah's breasts were pressed into the mattress, her legs closed.

Finally, Vanessa's first touch.

A light brush of Hannah's hair from her nape made her jump. Then Vanessa's warm breath and press of her soft lips.

"So nice," Vanessa murmured, leaving kisses along her shoulders and back.

Hannah's mind emptied, her focus consumed by the physical. Not knowing Vanessa's intentions heightened her senses. Every new touch a surprise, every little kiss or lick that surely would've been pleasurable had she been able to see, intensified to heated arousal. Featherlight brushes of fingertips along Hannah's sides made her ache for them on her breasts, her nipples. She tried to rise, to turn over, but a firm hand between her shoulders pressed her down. A light tap to her inner knee made her part her legs.

The bed shifted, and Vanessa moved between Hannah's thighs. "Open more for me, beautiful."

Hannah did. She forced herself to relax her grip on the pillow. Her breathing came hard. She'd never been this turned on.

The soft tickle of Vanessa's hair swept down from Hannah's shoulders. Tender kisses along her spine followed. She tried to squeeze her legs together to relieve some of the pressure, but Vanessa kneeled between them.

Vanessa squeezed Hannah's ass and moaned with obvious appreciation, then stretched out on top of her. "You feel so good."

Again, Hannah tried again to close her legs, desperate for some way to ease the ache, but Vanessa kept a knee in place. With a groan of frustration, Hannah attempted to wriggle against it.

Vanessa laughed softly.

"I'll give you what you want. Just ask." She kissed Hannah's jaw and snaked a hand beneath her to pinch her nipple.

Hannah cried out and thrust her hips into the bed, then arched for purchase against Vanessa's leg again. Only moments ago, she'd been in control. Hadn't she? Now, she was a heaving, hot mess. "Please make me come."

Vanessa kissed her neck, sucking and licking her way to the curve of Hannah's shoulder.

The wet heat of her mouth made Hannah crave it one place above all others.

Vanessa sat up, straddling one of Hannah's thighs, then glided her hand over Hannah's spine, past the dip of her lower back, and between her legs.

Hannah tried to rise again, but Vanessa held her in place. She moved her fingers through Hannah's wetness, barely grazing the underside of her clit, then flirted with her opening.

Hannah stilled and held her breath, hoping Vanessa would understand. She did. Vanessa entered her, slowly, sweetly.

"Oh, my God." Hannah shuddered and clenched around Vanessa's fingers. She lifted her hips to take more of her, press into her harder.

Vanessa waited, leaning forward to kiss the area between Hannah's shoulder blades and rake her teeth over the tender skin where it covered bone.

When Vanessa sat back and thrust into her again, a guttural cry of pleasure tore from Hannah's throat. She ground her hips into the bed until Vanessa gave her more. What had been desperate arousal was now *need*, raw and primal. Her orgasm loomed, but she couldn't get to it. Vanessa held all the power, and Hannah loved it.

Vanessa rotated the fingers inside her, making Hannah tighten around them and lift her hips.

"Again," Hannah pleaded, but she got only a quiet, low laugh in response. But the new position offered much more.

Vanessa rubbed Hannah's clit with a thumb while she gently slid deeper into her, then out, then deeper still.

Hannah nearly wept in relief.

For hours—likely only minutes—Vanessa pleasured her, taking her to the edge, pulling her back, making her beg, all the while soothing and reassuring her. The feeling teetered between being excruciating and euphoric. Hannah had never felt so cared for and safe.

"Turn over," Vanessa finally whispered. She was on Hannah instantly, reclaiming her, licking and sucking her breasts, filling her once more, then withdrawing and adding another finger.

Hannah lay back, giving herself over completely. When Vanessa's warm breath touched her swollen flesh, Hannah gasped. She was so close.

Vanessa licked a wide path upward from the base of her fingers with a satisfied moan.

Hannah wanted to remember the image of Vanessa's face buried between her legs, the way her blond corkscrews fell over her forehead, and how she wrapped her arm around Hannah's thigh as though she'd settled in for the night. Hannah fought to keep her eyes open to sear every instance into her memory, but the pressure built at the base of her spine, swelling with every flick of Vanessa's tongue and pump of her fingers. When it became too much, she grabbed Vanessa's hand and surrendered to a shattering orgasm.

Vanessa stayed with her as Hannah returned to Earth. She left sweet kisses all along her inner thighs, over her belly, everywhere except where Hannah was too sensitive.

When Hannah's ability to speak resurfaced, she tugged Vanessa's arms. "Come here."

Vanessa crawled up her body, sitting up and straddling her waist. She gathered her curls atop her head, then let them fall. Her voluptuous breasts swayed with the motion.

Hannah watched, riveted. "I love when you do that."

"Do you?" Vanessa smiled. "And do you love *this*?" She leaned forward, planting her hands beside Hannah's head, and began to rock against her.

Hannah did indeed. She let Vanessa's nipples brush her palms with each pass, and they hardened from the friction. The slickness of Vanessa's arousal on Hannah's stomach told her she was loving it too. Hannah gripped Vanessa's hips and urged her back a bit so she had something firmer to grind against. "Now do that."

Vanessa began to move again, her eyes widening. "Oh. That's good." She gyrated her hips and let her head fall forward. Soon, her skin glowed with a sheen of perspiration. She thrust harder.

Hannah wanted Vanessa to come, and she wanted to see her come like this, so stunning and uninhibited. So different from what most people saw, from even what Hannah had seen before tonight. And *tonight* might be her only chance. Hannah grasped Vanessa's hips and lifted up into her. "Is this enough? Do you need more?"

Vanessa sagged, her first sign of frustration, but didn't stop. "I don't know." She shook her head. "Maybe."

"Raise up," Hannah said, sliding her upturned hand between them.

When Vanessa settled on it, she seemed unsure, but then her eyes lit up. "Oh." She thrust against Hannah's fingers.

At this angle, Hannah couldn't reach far, but when Vanessa moved, Hannah curled and slid them just inside her.

Vanessa's hair fell onto Hannah's face and chest, her breath warm on Hannah's cheek.

They worked it like that for a while, Vanessa sometimes sliding onto Hannah's palm, and when she did, Hannah entered her to a wondrous little gasp.

Then, without warning, Vanessa lifted her hips with a jerk. "Harder," she panted.

Hannah took it up a notch, able to thrust faster and deeper with more room to maneuver. Vanessa shifted her weight onto one arm and reached between her legs, but Hannah beat her there. "I've got it." And within a few seconds, she had the sheer exhilaration of watching Vanessa unravel above her.

Vanessa collapsed on top of her, her face buried in Hannah's neck.

Hannah ran her hands up and down Vanessa's sides and back and over her ass, giving it a two-handed squeeze. Along Vanessa's hairline, she pressed tender kisses. With all the patience she could muster, Hannah gave Vanessa a full two minutes to recover, then flipped them. She went right to the source, spreading Vanessa's legs and tasting her for the first time.

With a soft, "Oh," then, "Oh, yes," she tangled her fingers in Hannah's hair.

Hannah moaned. She couldn't get enough, but she'd agreed to Vanessa's invitation of one night of pleasure. Would it extend the length of their stay, and if it didn't, how would she bear it?

Chapter Thirteen

Seated on the sofa beside Hannah in Georgina's living room, Vanessa truly appreciated the awkwardness of the situation. She'd been apprehensive heading into this, but she'd had no idea.

"We need to wrap this up before eleven." Georgina crossed her legs where she sat across from them in a worn but inviting blue armchair.

Vanessa suspected they owned a cat based on loose threads on one side.

"Noah's practice gets over then." Georgina jiggled her foot.

She hadn't offered them coffee or water, and Vanessa didn't expect she would.

"We don't want to keep you any longer than necessary." Hannah opened her bag and retrieved the birthday card Georgina had sent Bren. "We found this, so obviously, we have questions." She leaned forward and handed it to her.

Georgina took it but immediately dropped it onto the coffee table between them. "I didn't do that often, send things like that." She flicked a lime green fingernail at it. "Bren always assured me she destroyed them." She glanced between them. "I expected you to show up." She pointed at Hannah, then turned to Vanessa. "But you're a surprise. How do you even know each other?"

Shocked yesterday that Georgina knew who she was at all, Vanessa realized it didn't bode well for Bren not cheating on her, too. She swallowed her rising nausea.

"We met at the funeral," Hannah said.

Georgina recrossed her legs. "That must've been an interesting conversation."

"How'd you find out she passed away?" Hannah folded her hands and rested them on her knee.

"She didn't return my texts or calls that night. The last I'd heard from her was that her plane landed safely." Georgina shrugged as if trying for nonchalance, but the sheen of moisture that misted her eyes betrayed her. "I called her at work the next day. She didn't answer there either, so I called her office pretending to be a client. They told me what happened."

"I'm sorry for your loss."

At Hannah's soft words, Vanessa turned to her, intrigued. Hannah had been dating Bren when she died, yet here she was, extending condolences to this stranger with whom Bren had been cheating. Vanessa doubted *she'd* do the same in Hannah's position.

"Maybe you could start at the beginning, if you don't mind," Hannah said gently. "How did you meet?"

Georgina shifted her gaze out the window. "We grew up together in Stockton. In high school, I'd admired her for over a year. Then she asked me out, and we fell in love." She paused.

Maybe Hannah had patience for the story to unfold, but Vanessa didn't. She wanted to learn everything, but quickly, so they could get the hell out of there. Being in Georgina's home made her skin crawl. "So, what happened?"

"My mom died when I was young, and my dad became extremely religious." The life left Georgina's pretty face. She stared at the floor, clearly lost in memories. "He was a terrible father to begin with, but when he found out about us, he let his objections be known with his fists and boots."

Vanessa drew in a breath.

Hannah said nothing.

"I knew if I didn't get out of that house, I'd end up dead." Georgina hesitated. "Or pregnant," she whispered.

Hannah stiffened. "I'm so sorry. No one should have to go through that."

Georgina composed herself. "I had few options, but I had to do something. Jamal, my husband, is a year older and grew up in the same apartment complex. I knew he was in love with me, but I was in love with Bren, so we remained just friends." She touched her chin. "After my dad broke my jaw, Jamal, who knew everything, even about Bren, insisted we do something. He'd been working and saving since he'd graduated and planned to move to San Jose for college. He proposed, and I accepted.

Even though I was a junior, I was almost eighteen. We got married on my birthday, and I went with him."

"And Bren?" Now enthralled, Vanessa couldn't imagine how devastated she must've been.

"We were in the same grade, so she was still in high school and had no more options than I did at the time. Jamal could keep me safe in a way she couldn't, and she loved me enough to understand."

Vanessa tried to recall the decisions she'd made at that age. They didn't compare to what Georgina had been forced to do.

Georgina's features relaxed, and she smiled. "Jamal was just what I needed. He's intelligent, devoted, kind, and genuinely loves me. We both worked multiple jobs and lived in a cramped studio apartment, and once I finished high school, I attended college right beside him." She looked to the window again. "I grew to love him, too, though not in the same way I loved Bren." With a sigh, she faced them. "They're different people, and I love—loved—them differently."

"When did you start seeing Bren again?" Hannah shifted a bit closer to Vanessa, and their arms touched.

Georgina tilted her head. "I never stopped."

Stunned, Vanessa couldn't move, couldn't speak. Her stomach churned at the confirmation that Bren *had* been seeing Georgina when she was with Vanessa, too. *And* when she'd left her. Vanessa had known it was a possibility, but she hadn't expected her heart to pound so hard it threatened to burst from her chest.

"Did Jamal know?" Hannah's quiet voice helped anchor Vanessa.

"I had his blessing." Georgina leaned forward and massaged her temples. "Look, I didn't set out to be poly. Hell, I didn't even know it had a name back then. I just knew I loved two people, and they loved me back enough to realize I needed both of them. Each offered me something the other couldn't, and they wanted to see me happy." She wiped the corner of her eye. "I was very lucky."

"So, Bren and Jamal never…uh…" Hannah faltered. "You know."

Georgina frowned at her. "No. But he genuinely liked Bren."

"And you have a son?"

Obviously. Vanessa glanced at the front door where they'd met him. She fidgeted. She wanted out of there more than ever.

Georgina nodded. "When I was twenty-three, I had Noah. Suddenly, I had this wonderful little family and a full life. Jamal was my primary relationship, and we had a child. I knew I'd never leave them. By the time Noah was a toddler, Bren was working in Seattle, and we only saw each other when she had business in San Francisco. I loved her, but I knew she couldn't have been happy with the few days a month I was giving her. Bren assured me she understood and was fine with our relationship being secondary. She insisted what we had was enough. But we began to argue more. She became increasingly lonely and frustrated, and I knew she wasn't telling me the truth. God, I felt so guilty. While I still loved her, I wanted her to have what I had, so I encouraged her to date."

Vanessa did the math. "So, she began seeing me."

"And I think the two of you were happy, at least for a while." Georgina raised her eyebrow.

Vanessa gave a reluctant nod. "Enough for me to propose."

Hannah squeezed Vanessa's thigh.

Georgina glanced between the two of them again. "When you did," she paused, closing her mouth, then opening it, "it scared her. That's why she didn't accept right away. In her mind, saying yes to you meant losing me." She rubbed her forehead. "Look, I know what you both must think of me, and hopefully my explanations make everything a little easier to stomach. I'm sorry my relationship with Bren had to play a part in yours. As hard as we tried to extinguish our feelings for one another, we couldn't."

"Did you tell her not to marry me?" Vanessa couldn't look at Georgina. She focused on Hannah's hand on her leg.

"On the contrary. I encouraged her, hoping commitment would allow her to invest more deeply and give her some stability. Jamal was great, always taking Noah to Santa Cruz or the Sierras when Bren visited so we could have the weekend, but I knew I could only give her a fraction of what she wanted. She could have it all with you." Georgina picked at a chip in her polish. "In the end, it backfired, and she got spooked. I know she hurt you, and I told her you deserved honesty, but she was too embarrassed to face you again."

The warmth of Hannah's palm still resting on Vanessa's thigh soothed her, but tears stung her eyes.

"She sent someone to pick up her belongings."

"Mandy," Georgina said quietly, "from her softball team."

Vanessa snapped. She leaped to her feet and grabbed her purse from the sofa. "It must be nice, all these years, knowing everything about us when we knew nothing about you or even the woman sharing our lives and beds." Her voice cracked, echoing off the burnt orange walls as she hurried past Georgina and her shocked expression.

"Vanessa, wait," Hannah called.

Vanessa rushed outside, but Hannah didn't follow. She slowed. It'd warmed since they'd arrived. She pulled her sunglasses from her bag and walked toward the car.

Halfway there, Hannah called her name as she caught up. "Look at me." She tugged her elbow until she stopped. "Are you all right?"

Vanessa's knees wobbled, and she was thankful for Hannah's grip. "I...I don't know."

"Come on, let's get you to the car." Hannah looped her arm through hers.

"She knows we're leaving?"

Hannah laughed. "That was fairly clear. She apologized for not attending the funeral."

Vanessa couldn't imagine the circus that would've been.

As they neared Hannah's Lexus, a lanky boy rose from the curb. When he turned, Vanessa recognized Noah from their brief encounter yesterday. He wore the Warriors jersey Georgina had tossed him and held a basketball under his arm.

"You're from Washington." He pointed to Hannah's WATAGEM license plate with its Mount Rainier background. "Are you friends of Bren's?"

Present tense?

Georgina's son didn't know? Vanessa couldn't face this, not after what she'd just been through.

"We knew her, yes." Hannah unlocked the car and left Vanessa standing by the open door. She stepped back onto the sidewalk toward Noah.

"I was just wondering," he dribbled once, then again between his legs, "you know, if she's really gone." He hadn't looked up the entire time.

Oh, Jesus.

Bounce, bounce, bounce.

"'Cause I went to my cousin's funeral when he drowned. He looked so creepy, I knew he was dead. But Mom wouldn't let me go to Bren's to see her." When he shrugged, his bony shoulders looked like they'd break through his skin. "So, I thought maybe..." He trailed off, probably knowing the minuscule likelihood of his childlike wish being granted.

Hannah touched his arm. "I'm afraid it's true. She passed away. But no one got to see her, sweetie. Her casket was closed."

Oh, for fuck's sake. Why had Hannah brought *that* up?

"Yeah." Bounce. "Okay." He swiped at his eyes.

Vanessa breathed easier when he didn't ask why the casket hadn't—*couldn't have*—been open. But her heart broke for him. And for Bren, for all the complications she'd faced in her search for love. She'd been like a pinball, causing pain and damage wherever she ricocheted, even in death. Had she ever truly been happy?

"You know what though?" Hannah's tone brightened. "I know this." She leaned down until she could make eye contact with Noah. "I know she really, really liked coming to visit you."

He smiled despite his red eyes and teary cheeks. "She did?"

"Yeah." Hannah gave his elbow a squeeze.

In the sunlight, Vanessa made out the lightest peach fuzz on his upper lip. She supposed Hannah's statement wasn't *technically* untrue. The receipts proved it. Bren had obviously meant something to this boy, and it was only fair to assume he'd meant as much to her.

Noah sniffed and pulled his phone from his pocket. He tapped the screen with his thumb. "I can't be late." And just like that, as though their weighty conversation hadn't occurred, he turned and walked toward his house, head down, bouncing the ball with each step.

Hannah went around to the driver's side.

Vanessa studied his loping gait with her hand on the car door. How surreal. She'd met the woman who'd been the love of Bren's life. The woman she'd been with the entirety of their relationship. Vanessa had no idea how to sort the myriad feelings the last hour had whipped up.

She blinked back tears of her own and got in.

Chapter Fourteen

In the car, Hannah leaned her forehead against the steering wheel. "Christ." Had that really just happened? She sat back and started the engine. "Let's get out of here before Georgina chases us down for talking to him."

Vanessa didn't respond.

"Are you okay?"

Vanessa shrugged and stared out the windshield.

Hannah had asked after Vanessa bolted from Georgina's house but hadn't gotten much of an answer then either. "Here." She uncapped the water bottle in the cup holder and cringed at how warm it was. "Maybe drink something."

"I'm not thirsty."

Hannah let it go. If Vanessa needed a minute or two, she didn't blame her. It was a lot to digest. It wasn't even lunchtime, and Hannah was emotionally exhausted. Physically, too, but the overnight exertions had been well worth it. However, Vanessa's current mood made those memories seem fuzzy and distant.

When she neared downtown, Hannah tried again. "Hungry? There are lots of places to eat in SOMA. Chinatown's not far from where we're staying either."

"I don't have an appetite." Vanessa's bleakness concerned Hannah.

"Okay. I'm going to take us back to the rental. If you want, you can take a nap, and we can order in later. I know it was a lot, but if you want to talk about it, we can." Hannah inwardly cursed the heavy traffic, both vehicle and pedestrian. It didn't allow her to look at Vanessa.

Vanessa didn't respond.

Her demeanor perturbed Hannah, especially after what they'd shared last night. She disliked being beside someone, yet feeling a million miles apart. The stale rush of too many years of that with Bren washed over her.

When they reached Telegraph Hill, Vanessa shifted in her seat. "I think it's best if I go home. If you want to stay longer, I'll rent a car."

A chill coursed through Hannah. "I'm not leaving you. I dragged you into this, so if you choose to head home, we'll go today."

"What about the diamonds?"

"I already flew someone down to grade them. My job is to wire the funds and transport them. We can pick them up as we leave the city. I'll let my dealer know I'll be there soon."

Asking Vanessa to accompany her on the trip had seemed like a good idea at the time. If Hannah had known how meeting Georgina would affect her, she never would've suggested it.

Hannah hadn't wanted to bombard Georgina with questions from both of them right away and spook her before getting any information, but Vanessa had been so quiet at the house almost the entire time. At least until the end. Clearly, the news of the cheating hit her hard, though Hannah had suspected as much from Bren. How you do one thing is how you do everything, and all that. Still, Hannah had been so hurt when she'd first suspected Bren's infidelity and then when she'd gotten confirmation of it upon reading the card. Nothing had ever made her feel quite so inadequate as Bren's unfaithfulness. She wanted to absorb some of Vanessa's pain, help carry the burden, but she didn't know how.

They packed quickly and arrived at Union Square around one thirty. On the way, Hannah had eaten a granola bar Leslie had left for them. Vanessa ate nothing.

"That might be a spot." Hannah pointed ahead. "Never mind. Tow-away zone. Do you mind circling while I run in?" She'd asked Vanessa to drive for this very reason.

"No."

One-word answers seemed to be the most Hannah could hope for.

Less than ten minutes later, she waited outside the building with several velvet bags of diamonds in her coat pockets. She gripped them tightly, leery of pickpockets in this tourist-heavy area. Vanessa turned the corner, and Hannah darted out between two parked cars to meet her.

Hannah opened Vanessa's door. "Quick, switch me."

Vanessa scrambled out and into the opposite side as the driver behind them honked.

"Hold on." Hannah hit the gas. A constant beeping had her checking the dash. It grew louder. "Seat belt." She tapped Vanessa on the thigh.

As if dazed, Vanessa looked at her, then seemed to realize what was happening. She clicked it into place. "Sorry."

It wasn't until Hannah had driven through multiple counties and rice fields lined both sides of the interstate that Vanessa got out her phone. She spent close to ten minutes texting with someone.

Finally, she put it away. "Sonja said we can stay the night again."

"You sure?" Hannah glanced at her. "I'll drive you home, if you want."

"I'm sure, but is it okay if we don't talk for a bit?"

The comment speared Hannah like she'd impaled herself on rebar. She'd barely said two sentences to Vanessa since they'd left the city.

"Fine." It stung, and so did the goddamned tears that momentarily blurred her vision. Thus far, the ride back was the opposite of the trip down. Not wanting to bother Vanessa by asking if she minded music, they traveled in insufferable silence.

What would it be like once they reached Ashland?

❖

Vanessa feigned sleep in the passenger's seat. She'd finally reclined the back and curled away from Hannah when the tension between them had become unbearable. She couldn't help it, though. After Georgina's bombshell, she wasn't able to pull herself together. How quickly a beautiful day could be shattered without warning.

Vanessa had woken earlier that morning the same way she'd drifted to sleep, inhaling the sweet scent of Hannah's hair and skin. Snippets from their hours of passionate lovemaking had quickened her heartbeat. She hadn't initially realized what Hannah had done. Their long, languid foreplay, then Hannah's surrender of the lead to Vanessa had primed her for a luscious orgasm. Hannah's understanding and patience had been such a relief, Vanessa had been able to get out of her head and let go. Her subsequent climaxes had come quickly and easily, making Hannah light up like the Christmas tree on Pier 39 at the holidays. Finally, Vanessa had laughingly begged for mercy around the time the birds outside began to chirp.

But that seemed long ago.

Vanessa was being a bitch, but she didn't have it in her to care. Her swirling thoughts demanded her attention. Maybe Hannah would understand *this*, too.

All these years, Vanessa had wondered what it was about her that made Bren leave. Then, in answer to Hannah asking when she'd started seeing Bren again, as casually as a rose releases its petals, Georgina dropped those words. *I never stopped.* Hannah said she'd suspected Bren's unfaithfulness, but Vanessa had been clueless, just like her mother called her. On cue, there she was.

What'd you expect? You could never be enough for her. You weren't even worthy of her in the beginning.

Vanessa hugged herself until her mother's voice subsided.

But it all came rushing back. The humiliation that day, the way none of the guests would look her in the eye, and the smug look of satisfaction her mother didn't even try to hide. Even months later, the whispers and pitying glances from people whenever Vanessa ran into them forced her to change neighborhoods from Green Lake to Queen Anne.

She'd spent her life focused on being understanding and kind, accepting life's difficulties with grace, volunteering and helping others, and developing any decent quality her mother lacked, but apparently, they weren't so different. Bren cast her aside without a backward glance, just like her father had done to her mom forty years prior. And now, after seeing Georgina, with her voluptuous curves and perfect skin, it was no wonder Bren had chosen her over Vanessa.

And what about Hannah? Her mother probably had a point. If Vanessa hadn't been worthy of Bren, she certainly wasn't worthy of Hannah, no matter how much she liked her. Sleeping with her had been everything she'd hoped and more, and she'd finally snapped that chain of celibacy that'd weighed her down for so long. But was that all it was, or did she have burgeoning feelings for her? And had it been just sex for Hannah or something more? Vanessa wasn't up for a repeat performance of being left by a lover. Bren's betrayal had nearly destroyed her. Vanessa refused to go through that again.

The past five years hadn't been easy, but with the therapy she'd been in since early adulthood that had helped her discover how to be an uplifting voice, an ally for children who might be dealing with some of same issues she had, she'd persevered. Vanessa had brought back the youth garden in one of the most impoverished neighborhoods in Seattle. While initially an escape, something to focus on when her mother's voice got too loud, she found it fulfilling. And while counseling and gardening helped her manage the last half decade, she hadn't been able to be intimate with anyone. How could she? When she'd thought she'd had a breakthrough, taken a chance, and opened her heart to someone, Bren dumped her. And now she'd learned it wasn't enough Bren didn't want to marry her, but that she'd been in love with another woman all along.

Her wedding day rushed back vividly. Vanessa could almost smell the gardenia bridal bouquet she never got to carry, hear the steady murmur of voices asking what was the polite amount of time to stay, and see the minister sheepishly remove her stole in an alcove.

Until Georgina shattered Vanessa's carefully conceived world, Vanessa had thought she had a handle on things. Late Bloomer continued to grow, and so did the farm. And whether she needed to or not, she met with her therapist once a month. As it turned out, she wasn't doing fine at all. She'd merely buried her pain, leaving herself vulnerable to the utterance of those three little words.

Vanessa was spiraling, and after so much work to get where she was. She'd only known Hannah a couple of months. Maybe her attraction to her would fade with some distance. Surely, Hannah wouldn't want to keep coming to the garden if they weren't on good terms. Then Vanessa could get back to her store, her volunteer work, and the comfortable life she knew.

She'd move her next therapy appointment up two weeks, and knowing she'd be seeing Sonja today calmed her. Unfortunately, she wasn't strong enough to share these issues with Hannah, but Sonja would give her advice.

Chapter Fifteen

Hannah quietly opened Sonja's guest room door and padded to the bathroom. The scent of fajitas still hung in the air from the dinner that'd been awaiting them. This time, no one tossed around jokes about matching T-shirts or patient zero. The exchanges had been serious, almost somber at times, and Hannah had been grateful the dogs were allowed inside. Their playfulness and occasional begging drew attention from the elephant in the room. Hannah had hoped Vanessa would warm up once they arrived, but she'd remained reticent. Jeffrey, Sonja, and Hannah had carried the conversation.

Hannah had spent most of the drive and a good portion of the night wondering what went wrong. She'd satisfied her curiosity about Georgina, but had it been worth it? She certainly didn't regret the time spent with Vanessa, but she wasn't sure Vanessa would agree. Hannah hadn't expected to meet Vanessa when she did, nor did she expect to be attracted to her, but she shouldn't have slept with her. Even if talking to Georgina was what made Vanessa withdraw, having sex had irrevocably complicated things. Vanessa's demeanor on the road was that of someone seriously battling demons, but Hannah wasn't sure which kind.

When she finished in the bathroom, she waited until the temperamental toilet quit running, then stepped into the hallway and stopped short. The door to Vanessa's room stood open, the light off. Hannah had gone to bed around ten, mostly to accommodate Sonja and Jeff's schedule, but also to avoid the awkwardness. It had to be after midnight now. Despite her attempt at ending her evening early, sleep had evaded her. She tiptoed to the top of the stairs.

Muted voices from below filtered up, low and feminine.

Disappointment spread through her chest, then settled in her stomach.

She retreated to her room. Even if she'd been able to make out their conversation, she wouldn't have eavesdropped. Vanessa obviously needed someone to confide in, and it wasn't Hannah. To be fair, they hadn't known each other that long, and Sonja had been her friend for decades. Still, it hurt that the woman who'd woken up in her arms less than twenty-four hours ago didn't feel comfortable talking to her.

Earlier, Hannah had dismissed the prospect of her and Vanessa sharing a bed. She could read a room. Vanessa's one-eighty after meeting Georgina told her what the answer would've been without asking.

The only time Vanessa had spoken directly to her since they'd arrived was when she'd caught her wrist before Hannah retired for the night. "I'm going for a run. I'll explain more tomorrow," she'd said.

Hannah fluffed her pillow and flopped into bed. They never should've gone to San Francisco.

❖

Vanessa curled her legs under her on the couch she shared with Sonja. She hadn't showered from her run yet, but she needed Sonja's perspective on everything that'd happened, and she didn't want to keep her up any later than necessary. They'd had to wait until Hannah went to bed though. Duckie put his head on Vanessa's lap, and she scratched his ears.

"You got along so well the other night." Confusion strained Sonja's features.

Vanessa sighed. "I know. I've connected more with Hannah than anyone in a long time. That's the problem."

Sonja narrowed her eyes. "Explain that to me."

"I can't go down that road again."

"And by that, you mean dating?" Sonja's brow furrowed.

Vanessa nodded, happy to have Duckie to keep her hands busy.

"But using that logic, you're presuming said relationship will sour, or she'll leave you out of the blue, like Bren did."

"It's the chance of that happening that I can't handle."

"Okay." Sonja leaned her head back on the cushion. "What if I'd decided after you broke my heart all those years ago that I was never going to date again? I wouldn't be with Jeff."

Vanessa scoffed. "We had some very enjoyable sex, but you weren't heartbroken." At Sonja's silence, she did a double take. "You were?"

"If you recall, I wanted more, but you weren't ready for that. Knowing your mother now like I do, I understand, but it crushed me back then."

"You've never said anything." Vanessa stared at her.

Sonja shrugged and shot her a grin. "I got over it, eventually. Don't worry, I'm not lusting after you anymore."

Vanessa smiled. "I'm glad."

Sonja raised an eyebrow. "Though I'm not sure everyone in this house can say the same. I see how she looks at you."

Vanessa played with Duckie's fur. "We took care of that last night."

Sonja poked Vanessa's leg with her stockinged foot. "Good for you."

Her five-year dry spell was no secret, and Sonja had repeatedly encouraged her to keep trying.

"It was a mistake," Vanessa whispered, unable to make eye contact. "I shouldn't have done it, not with her. Now everything is messed up. And I won't be able to get myself in a better place with her around."

"It's only what you make it." Sonja leaned closer and gave Vanessa's hand a squeeze. "But tonight's dinner was more uncomfortable than when Jeffrey's parents are here. Surely, this is more than just regret."

"Georgina's news shook me. It brought up all the painful memories. If I hadn't had sex with Hannah, things would be much simpler right now."

"Well, the other night, you were happier being around her than any woman I've seen you with in years. Keep that in mind." Sonja patted the space between them, and Duckie jumped up. "Knowing you, you're going to make yourself miserable for a while, but consider Hannah's feelings in all of this, too. Don't kick her to the curb just yet."

"I can't be around her right now." Vanessa twisted the hem of her T-shirt, knowing what she had to do, even if a little piece of her would be ripped away when she did it.

When she retired to her room, she spent the night tossing and turning, dreading the next day. She'd promised Hannah an explanation but had no expectation Hannah was going to like it, and Vanessa wasn't up for a fight.

The following morning, everyone endured an early but awkward breakfast. And after saying good-bye to Sonja and Jeff, she and Hannah were on the road alone.

An hour into the trip, Vanessa still hadn't said much. She'd offered to drive, but Hannah had declined. Not surprising, considering the state Vanessa was in. The agitated bounce of her knee probably didn't help.

Hannah was likely wondering if she'd hold true to her word and talk about what was happening, so Vanessa turned in her seat. It had to be done. "I was horrible yesterday."

Hannah didn't argue.

"I'm sorry." Vanessa fiddled with her bracelet.

"I wasn't expecting your reaction. I mean, I kind of thought the visit might go something like that." Hannah gave an abstract wave. "You know, Georgina telling us things we hoped weren't the case. But I was prepared. I thought you were, too."

So fucking stupid. You couldn't put two and two together with a calculator.

Vanessa pressed her fingers to her forehead and counted to ten. When her mind quieted again, she glanced at Hannah.

Concern shaped her lovely features. "Are you okay?"

Well, that was the crux of it, wasn't it? "No, but I'm hoping to be at some point in the future." It took everything in her just to admit it. "I have a psychotherapist, and yesterday I requested moving up my appointment." She admired the sunlight glinting off the tops of the round bales of hay in the field beside the road as she figured out what to say next. "The visit yesterday? It sort of broke me."

Hannah lay her hand on Vanessa's thigh.

"What you know of my mother, what you heard, that's just a small sample. Her voice is in my head every day, and some of it's about Bren. How I was never good enough for her." Vanessa drew in a steadying breath. "I can't go into details, but that's only a fraction of what I've fought so hard to quiet. I've been managing, thanks to therapy, and running and volunteering at the garden helps, too, but finding out Bren had been with Georgina the entire time we were together broke the dam. Everything poured through again, all the things my mother says and my own doubts and fears as well." She sniffed and searched her purse for a tissue.

Hannah retrieved a packet from the center console and handed it to her. "I'm going to take the next exit. There's a rest stop. I want to look at you and give you my full attention while you're talking."

If only Hannah knew how much harder that would make this, but Vanessa couldn't tell her. She was barely hanging on.

Once she'd parked, Hannah turned to face her. "Okay. Go ahead."

Vanessa inhaled, collecting her thoughts. "I know Bren and I have been over for years, but finding that out yesterday made the betrayal fresh again. All the terrible memories I have of my wedding day keep rearing up." She wiped her nose. "The way I didn't want to believe people's speculation, and how I actually worried something bad had happened to her."

Stupid girl. I knew this wedding would never happen. What could she possibly see in you? I don't know why I even bothered coming.

Vanessa squeezed her eyes shut, then opened them. "And along with those images, I hear my mother's voice telling me how I'm not good enough. She's at full volume in my head right now."

Hannah squeezed her arm. "I'm sure you've discussed it with your therapist, but you know those things your mother says are horrible, right? It's emotional abuse. No one should be spoken to like that."

Vanessa nodded but looked away. "Yes, but I've heard them for over forty years. I worry they're ingrained in me."

"Why do you keep her in your life?"

Vanessa drew back. "She's my mother."

Hannah looked like she wanted to say more, but she didn't.

Vanessa twisted the tissue in her hands, delaying the inevitable for a few more seconds. "So, when we get back to Seattle, I need space."

"That's understandable." Hannah faced forward. "I'll leave you be this week and see how you're doing on Saturday. Maybe we could have lunch. When's your therapy appointment?"

"That's not what I mean," Vanessa said, ignoring the question. "These issues, they linger. Just because you or I would like them to be resolved in a week's time doesn't mean I can make that happen. Hell, I've been trying for five years, and here they are again. I need some time and space to figure things out, get myself in a healthy place again." She paused before delivering the line she'd been dreading. "I can't do that when I'm around you."

Hannah gripped the steering wheel, her knuckles whitening. "Oh."

Vanessa bowed her head and massaged her temple. "You make it so I can't think."

Hannah started the engine and shifted into reverse. "I see." She drove to the end of the lot and accelerated up the ramp.

In the silence, Vanessa could almost hear the machinations of Hannah's mind. The argument was coming. Based on what she knew of Hannah, it had to be.

"I like you. We seem to click. I think you're being a bit hasty in shutting me out. If you want to take a few weeks, that's great. Let's see where things stand then."

A few weeks? Vanessa would be lucky if she slept through a full night in the next month. She'd been here before. "I can't."

"Why? Can't you at least give us a chance?" Hannah glanced at her.

"Because I'm not like you. It takes me time to get over substantial things like the end of a relationship." The words flew out before she could stop them. And there it was, the final blow, the knockout punch to end the round.

And based on Hannah's silence, it'd done its job.

Chapter Sixteen

Vanessa took a moment to retreat to her office while Cai supervised the front counter. Fridays tended to be busy at the store, and today was no exception. She'd run seven miles, showered, and still been the first to arrive this morning, but her stomach rumbled as she sat. Her desk drawer held miscellaneous office supplies, two packets of soy sauce, berry lip balm, and an expired coupon for a car wash she threw in the trash, but not the granola bar she'd been hoping for.

She brought her laptop to life and glanced at her online calendar. The pottery class she'd registered for last week started at eight. It wasn't much of a Friday night, but it was something. It allowed her to get her mind off things she'd rather not think about. So did jogging, which she'd begun to do every day. But if she didn't find time for a decent meal before her lesson, she'd be on fumes by the time she eventually got home.

Dorothy popped her head in the door. "Cai wants you. And I moved all the new orchids up front."

"Thanks." Vanessa had been gone mere minutes, and Cai was one of her best customer service people. What could he need already?

When Vanessa pushed through the swinging door, it became apparent he didn't. Hannah stood with her back to them, looking over the orchids Dorothy had just received. Just seeing her gave Vanessa a little rush, along with a thread of annoyance.

"This really isn't a good time." Vanessa folded her arms over her chest.

Hannah turned. She looked smart in a classy black business suit and heels, and she'd had her hair trimmed. It no longer touched her shoulders.

"It won't take long." Hannah eyed her. "I texted you, but you didn't respond. I needed to make sure you're all right."

Vanessa had ignored the contact. She'd worried if she opened the door a crack, she might not be able to close it again. "I've been busy."

Hannah searched her face, then slightly shook her head. "I brought you a flat white and some almond biscotti." She handed Vanessa the offerings. "The guy at the coffee shop said they're some of your favorites, and you hadn't been in today."

Chloe burst through the swinging door. "Vanessa—" She halted. "Sorry, I didn't realize you were with someone."

"Chloe, this is Hannah Baros. Hannah, Chloe Tran. She manages the store for me." After they'd extended polite words, Vanessa addressed Chloe. "What's going on?"

"Since opening, we've had thirty-eight online orders for this weekend. Between those, the two weddings, and the three funerals, we're understaffed."

Vanessa considered what to do since she'd be at the garden for part of the day tomorrow and unable to help. "Ask Mi-young and Mi-sook if they want extra hours."

Chloe nodded a few times. "Yeah. Okay." She went to the back.

Vanessa set the cup and bag from Seismic on the counter where it wouldn't be in Cai's way as he helped a customer. She faced Hannah. "Maybe I'm wrong, but in your eyes, the trip helped you gain closure. For me, it opened old wounds. I told you I need some time to get things right up here." She tapped her temple. "While that's happening, I need to run the gardening program and ensure my business continues to be successful."

Chloe appeared beside them. "The Kim sisters said they'll do it."

"Tell them thanks." Vanessa took Hannah's elbow and led her into the greeting card alcove so they'd have some privacy.

"I feel for you." It was Hannah's turn to cross her arms. "I really do. I guess I don't understand why you wouldn't want to have someone around to lean on. Two is greater than one, you know."

"You don't seem to get it. I need space." Vanessa tried to keep her voice low. "I hear my mother's voice constantly. I don't expect you to know what that's like. How could you? Your mother sounds more normal than most."

Hannah appeared to recoil. "You're assuming a lot, since you know very little about her."

"Fine. I don't understand you, and you don't understand me." Vanessa had some awareness of wildly gesturing as she spoke, but her heart pounded and the blood whooshed in her ears. "I've told you I need time, and I'll take however long I need to work through this. No one is asking you to stick around for it." Vanessa knew she should stop there, but she couldn't seem to rein in her emotions. "Your problem is, you don't know how to listen."

Hannah opened her mouth to speak, but Vanessa beat her to it.

"You certainly didn't hear Bren when she complained about your job having priority. Instead, you moved in with her and kept your same MO when it came to your career. No wonder the two of you fizzled out. You're such a workaholic that you don't even realize that's what's in the way of you having a successful relationship." Vanessa hushed her voice. "I'm not the only one that needs to come to terms with my issues. If you're so bored waiting around for me, why don't you go tell your family and friends you were planning to break up with Bren the day of her death instead of lying about it?"

Hannah reddened, and her chest rose and fell with each audible breath.

Vanessa thought fire might come from her nostrils.

"Fine." Hannah smoothed her jacket. "You want me to leave you alone? Here I go." She brushed past Vanessa and pushed the front door open so hard the bells hit the glass, making Cai and the customer with him look up.

"Everything's fine," Vanessa said. What a lie. Why couldn't things just be how they were before?

Chapter Seventeen

Vanessa pulled into the teachers' parking lot on Saturday morning and braked, slamming herself against the shoulder belt. She had to be imagining the sight before her.

Hannah. On her phone. Pacing around her Lexus.

After what had been said yesterday? After Hannah had left in a huff? Alongside her confusion at being secretly pleased to see Hannah, her annoyance and desire to run away were equally strong. She parked a few spots away, not beside Hannah's car like she normally did. After gathering her bag and the tray of broccoli and kale seedlings, she decided to come back for the ten-pound bag of potatoes.

"May I carry that for you?"

Vanessa hadn't noticed Hannah end her call. The things she'd said to Hannah rang in her ears. It wasn't like her to lash out at someone like that. The road trip had taken an emotional toll on her, but that was no excuse for losing control of her tongue. Was she becoming her mother? No, Vanessa needed to do better and would. "I can come back for it."

Hannah picked it up. "I got it."

"Why are you here?"

Hannah shut the trunk. "Why wouldn't I be?" She appeared truly mystified.

Vanessa began walking toward the garden, and Hannah fell into step beside her, gently swinging the bag of potatoes. "For starters, I asked you to give me some space." Vanessa glanced at her. "But I apologize for yesterday. I was rude."

"I've thought a lot about what you said, and I'm sorry I reacted how I did. You made some valid points. Harsh, but valid." Hannah took the seedlings from her so she could unlock the gate. "For a brief time, I considered not coming, but I said I would, and I'm not going to abandon these kids. I made a commitment to them to be here each week. Whatever is going on between you and me is separate from this. If you truly never want to see me again, that's going to be difficult."

Vanessa hadn't anticipated Hannah's passion for the project. "I didn't say I never wanted to see you again."

All she got was a raised eyebrow in response.

When it came down to it, Vanessa couldn't act irrationally, even if Hannah being there confused things for her. The program was her priority. With the problems they'd had in the past finding adults to help, she'd be a fool to send a hard-to-get, dedicated volunteer away.

She unlocked the shed and motioned for Hannah to set the items on the sawhorse table she'd made from a repurposed door. "Actually, it's good you came. I won't have to turn anyone away. Raymond will be out for a while. He broke his leg yesterday on Mount Rainier after falling down a ravine."

Hannah leaned against the door frame. "Yeah. Ray called me last night."

Ray? Vanessa had never heard anyone call him that. But then again, she didn't even know they communicated outside of the garden. "He did?"

"Did you hear his son hiked out and led rescuers back to him?"

"I hadn't. I guess that's a testament to spending time outdoors. Branson basically grew up on that mountain."

"Hannah's here!" came a shout from the entryway to the garden. Ellie and SuAnn stopped to check something out in the first raised bed. Behind them, Ger adjusted his flat-brimmed hat, and Hector got out of his mom's car in the parking lot.

"They're always so excited when you come." Vanessa pulled on her gloves. "And you're a successful, positive female role model, just what some of them need." What kind of person would she be if she severed their connection with Hannah?

"Is that how you see me?" Hannah looked skyward, then held out her hand.

The ping of raindrops reverberated off the shed's tin roof. "You know I do." She busied herself digging trowels out of a plastic bin.

"I wasn't sure after yesterday. Or after the ride home, actually." Hannah stepped inside the shed.

In the confines of the small building, the walls seemed to close in on Vanessa. She couldn't breathe. Not with Hannah so close. She moved around her toward the door, but she caught Hannah's scent, so unmistakable, so unique. Vanessa would know it anywhere. She'd buried her face in it, felt the rapid pulse in Hannah's neck, her silky hair against Vanessa's cheek. It'd been one of the most comforting moments of her life. Now the memory brought a bittersweet pang.

Vanessa turned back. "People might have things they need to work on, but that doesn't mean they can't possess attractive qualities at the same time." She looked at the sky. "I don't know how long the rain will last."

Hannah studied her as she pulled on her gloves. "It doesn't matter. I'm here to stay."

"I'm seeing my therapist every week now instead of once a month." Vanessa didn't know why she'd felt the need to blurt that information or where it'd come from. A part of her wanted Hannah to understand what she was going through, even though she'd demanded space. Drops pelted her head and shoulders.

Hannah simply nodded and gave Vanessa a soft smile as she stepped outside. "Shall we greet the kids?"

The rain created difficulties, as it sometimes did. The kids were jubilant at first, but by the time mud covered their gloves, tools, and clothing, they'd lost some of their spark. Hannah allowed Ellie Number Two and Isla, who hadn't brought jackets, to do jobs inside the shed, like cutting the potatoes into pieces so each contained an eye, or little stem bud, they could plant.

Vanessa poked her head in. "You two doing okay?"

Isla looked up. "Yeah, we just fed the worms scraps. Ellie's going to clean the tray beneath the bin, and I'm wiping down tools."

"Nice job, you two. Remember to bring jackets next time, or text me if you need one, okay?"

Mumbles about forgetting and something about one being left at a friend's house followed Vanessa outside. She'd pulled her hair back earlier and was glad she did. Rain had soaked it down to her scalp, and it'd be stuck to her neck and face if she hadn't. Above, a spot of blue appeared, growing larger by the second as winds pushed the clouds east. Too bad the rain ended just as they were finishing up.

As she looked over at the kids cleaning up outside, dread materialized in her stomach. It was the last day for her existing students who were entering high school. She'd miss them, but she was proud of their growth and knowledge they'd gained during their time with her.

A few beds away, Hannah stood with Vesper. They'd been planting a new crop of carrots and radishes. Vesper rubbed her phone's screen on her jeans before holding it out. Hannah's eyebrows raised.

"Everything okay?"

"Look at this." Hannah turned the phone toward Vanessa.

It showed a delicate pair of earrings, ones that dangled a bit too much for Vanessa's taste, but otherwise pretty. "Very nice."

"She designed and made these." Hannah pointed at them. "Why didn't you tell me she was into jewelry? She has an Etsy shop."

"I honestly didn't know." Vanessa thought she was great at connecting with the kids and Raymond, but Hannah, with her copious charm and good-natured personality, managed to reach another level with them. Earlier, Hannah had mentioned offhand how "Ray" had been teaching her to count to ten in Salish. Perhaps they related to people in different ways, one not necessarily better than the other. Vanessa never would've known this side of Vesper without Hannah's involvement.

"How old are you?" Hannah handed Vesper the phone. "I mean, what grade?"

"Ninth." Vesper took a photo of the bed they were planting. "Well, in a few days."

"Any idea if your school supports internships?" Hannah moved beside Vanessa, so they both faced her.

Vesper's forehead wrinkled. "There's like a career program where you can work at companies. My cousin did it two years ago. She was at Amazon."

Hannah withdrew her wallet from the pocket of her jacket. "Well, if you're interested, I'd be happy to give you an internship at my jewelry company. You probably wouldn't be designing anything, but it'd be a wonderful experience for you if that's where your interest lies. Here's my card. Be sure and contact me beforehand so I can do everything I need on my end with the school to get approved."

Vanessa thought Vesper was going to cry, but she pulled it together. Even so, she stared in wonderment at the business card like it was the Hope Diamond.

"I heard a rumor it was your family's. I've seen the commercials before." Vesper looked at Hannah. "But I didn't know you were the CEO." Her amazement seemed to grow. "Does that mean you're the boss?"

Hannah laughed. "It does."

"Not your parents?" Vesper flicked her hair from her eyes.

"Not anymore."

"I saw one of your stores in the Glendale Galleria when I visited my grandparents. I wouldn't have to leave here to do the internship, would I?" A bit of fear seemed to creep across her features.

"Of course not, hon. Our headquarters are located downtown. It's easy to get to, even by bus."

Hannah's low, soothing voice managed to comfort Vanessa, and she wasn't even the one who needed it. It was one of Hannah's unique abilities.

"I'm like, high-key stoked about this." Vesper's grin grew wider. "My parents are gonna freak." She looked up. "Do you think I could do something involving social media? I have almost eight-and-a-half-thousand followers."

Hannah, clearly trying not to grin, glanced at Vanessa. "Let's discuss that once we get everything set up. A position in our marketing department is certainly possible."

Vesper turned to Vanessa. "Can I text my mom and tell her even though we're not supposed to be on our phones? It's almost time to go."

"Go ahead."

They watched her bounce away.

"I guess I'm finishing the radishes on my own." Hannah looked at the nearly completed bed.

"Sorry." Vanessa picked up Vesper's knee pad. "I'll help you."

The culmination of the storm and the sweet fragrance the showers had left behind allowed Vanessa to breathe easier. This was her happy place, the one area in her life that brought far more satisfaction than anything else. Being here while being forced to be around Hannah made the stress of the situation fade.

Together, they finished quickly. Hannah had come a long way since she'd begun volunteering. She needed little direction these days, and if she did, she must be asking the kids because Vanessa hadn't had to instruct her in some time.

"Soup," Hannah said.

Vanessa looked up. "What?"

"It's the perfect day for a hot bowl of soup, isn't it? Maybe a grilled cheese or some warm bread with it."

"You should have some, then." She gathered the tools and stood.

"You should come with me." Hannah crumpled the empty seed packet and stuffed it in her pocket. "I hate eating alone in restaurants."

Vanessa eyed her. "I'm sure even you could manage making that at home."

Hannah pressed her hand to her stomach. "I'm too hungry for that." She motioned at the neat-looking bed. "I worked hard today."

"You did." Vanessa's heart rate increased just having this conversation. Distance, she'd asked for distance. "Get takeout then."

"It's never hot by the time I get it home, or the sandwich is soggy." Hannah sighed. "It's just lunch, Vanessa. Eat with me. Don't read anything more into it. I'm starving."

Had Vanessa eaten that cardboard fiber biscuit on her way here, or had she forgotten? She couldn't recall. Her mouth salivated at the thought of biting into a crispy golden exterior with cheese oozing out, and creamy, slightly sweet tomato soup to dunk it in. She never ate one without the other. "I suppose I should eat." What was she doing?

"Good. That's settled." Hannah gave her a wry smile. "I don't want to say good-bye to our high schoolers. I'm going to miss them."

Vanessa's chest squeezed a little at the reminder. "Me, too. But many of them will come by and say hello next summer." She smiled, remembering. "They'll look different. New hairstyles, taller, less awkward, more filled out. The boys' voices get deeper. It's fun seeing them grow."

Hannah nudged her arm as they carried the tools to the shed. "You're incredibly good at this. I can tell your entire heart is in it."

"You've made a difference, too. Plus, the internship thing. That could be life-changing. You didn't have to do that, but you did." Vanessa laid her tools on the bench in the shed. Ellie and Isla had joined the others when the rain stopped. When she turned around, Hannah was right there. Vanessa took in Hannah's makeup-free face, her jacket covered in droplets, and the shaking of her hands. "You're soaked." She removed a lock of hair stuck to Hannah's cheek and tucked it behind her ear. She took Hannah's ice-cold hands in hers and rubbed them. "Let's finish up and get you warm."

"I meant what I said." Hannah managed to grasp her hands. "I want to be respectful of your needs. It's just lunch. Just don't…" She glanced away, out the open door, then back again. "Just don't completely shut me out, please."

Vanessa looked down. Neither had let go. "I have to look out for myself right now. I can't be anything to you." But even as she said it, fond memories of their time on the road and their night in San Francisco played in her mind like one of those first motion pictures where the timing was just a fraction of a second off. Even so, happiness washed over her. How long had it been since she'd known that feeling before she met Hannah? Or had she simply been content and existing? Vanessa wasn't sure. She also didn't know what Hannah wanted from her. It might be sex, or it might be something more. Unfortunately, Vanessa didn't have it within her to give either in the near future.

As if reading her mind, Hannah shook her head. "I'm not asking you for anything right now other than a meal together. This," she eased her hands from Vanessa's and motioned between them, "is enough. Just being in your presence."

Just being in her presence? Vanessa's insides reacted like a champagne bottle that had just been uncorked. But how could that be enough for anyone? Her thoughts drifted to how Hannah showing up this morning had made Vanessa's day so much better. Maybe it was that simple. But it wasn't fair to string someone along if Vanessa had no intention of making good on anything in the future. "I don't know…" It was presumptuous to talk about this, to assume this was something Hannah desired from her. "I'm not sure I can be in a relationship, certainly not now, and who knows what lies before us. I've seen what happened when my dad abandoned my mom and when Bren left me. I simply can't go through that again."

Hannah touched her cheek so lightly Vanessa wasn't altogether sure she'd made contact. "It's just soup." She smiled tenderly at her but it faded quickly. "Just don't push me away," she whispered.

"I'll still need space." Vanessa's eyes watered, and she blinked to avoid spilling a tear.

"I understand. I'll do my best to give it to you."

Vanessa smiled and lowered her gaze. "Thanks for the coffee and biscotti. You have no idea how much I needed them yesterday." When she looked up, Hannah beamed.

"I'm glad." She motioned to the door. "Shall we hug some high schoolers?"

Vanessa nodded and followed her outside. She really didn't know what she'd agreed to or what parameters had been put in place. Apparently, they'd figure it out as they went. The idea didn't bring the anxiety she thought it would.

Chapter Eighteen

Hannah sat on her living room floor and reinforced the bottom of another box with tape. Dozens surrounded her like a cardboard fortress. She could no longer see Zara across the room. "It's like déjà vu after doing this with Bren's stuff."

"Where'd you put all her crap?" Zara's head appeared over the wall of Hannah's bunker.

She pulled the empty roll of tape from the gun. "A small storage unit. I paid a company to do it."

Zara cleared some space to see her. "And then what? You just bleed money for it to stay there for how long?"

"Until the whole probate thing is done. I don't want any of it, even the furniture, but I can't get rid of it either." Hannah leaned back on her arms. "It's not that expensive."

"I could've helped." Zara's face crumpled a tiny bit.

Hannah twirled her finger around. "I was saving you for this. Overworking my unpaid labor is frowned upon."

"By whom?" Zara's eyebrows raised.

"By the unpaid labor." She ripped off another length of tape, securing another box's bottom, then added two more strips, just in case.

Zara came around Hannah's stronghold, cleared a spot on the floor, and sat. "You've been different since you got back. More agitated at work. Zoned out today. You know I worry about how many hours you spend there, but this appears to be about something else." She gently took the tape gun from Hannah. "That box has half a roll on it, and it has nothing in it."

While Vanessa assumed the road trip had brought closure for Hannah, it hadn't. Hannah had been out of sorts since returning home.

"I haven't had much rest." Hannah sighed. "I find myself lying in bed dwelling on things."

"Like what?"

"Oh, I don't know. Like realizing I was lied to during my entire relationship with Bren." With her suspicions, Hannah hadn't expected the confirmation of the ongoing affair to affect her, but it had. There'd been nothing truthful about their relationship from the start. Just thinking about it made her blood simmer. Frustration was a normal part of her job, but it didn't usually extend to her life outside of work. Occasionally, her irritation morphed into anger, like when she'd fled Late Bloomer. This wasn't like her.

"Learning the person you were in love with was unfaithful is a lot to absorb. Give yourself some time to work through it." Zara squeezed her shin.

Except that Hannah hadn't been in love.

She took a deep breath, hoping it would calm her racing heart. "If I tell you something, will you promise not to storm out before I can explain?"

Zara gestured at the cardboard surrounding them. "I don't think people usually storm *out* of a castle, do they?" Her face grew serious. "I promise. Out with it. You're scaring me."

Hannah folded her legs beneath her despite the protesting ligaments in her knees. "I haven't been fully honest with you." She capped and uncapped a Sharpie until Zara took it from her.

"Just say it. We'll work through it."

"Bren might have had a plethora of faults, but I'm no angel either." Hannah picked at a snag on the rug.

"Okay."

"I wasn't honest with her." She looked up. "I had a feeling something was off, but I didn't insist on discussing the changes I'd noticed in her because work was—"

"It's always about the job with you. All you've talked about the last week when you weren't complaining about your assistant is the new Pride line. Even during drinks. Continue." Zara made a hurry up motion.

"When she asked me to move in together, I didn't want to, but I did it anyway."

"Oh." Zara scowled and slowly shook her head. "Why? You hated this house."

"I know." Hannah shrugged. "It seemed easier to just go along with it. Now I wonder if we would've ended up in the same place if I'd spoken up. My inaction might've put her on a certain path. Maybe if I'd said no, she'd still be alive."

The doorbell rang.

Zara rose before Hannah could. "Hon, you did what you thought you needed to do at the time. You had no idea how things would turn out. But you could've told me." She paused a beat. "So, um…you might hate me for a few minutes, but remember you love me deep down, and that I ate that atrocious dish alongside you the night Bren passed away."

A second ring chimed.

What the…? Hannah hadn't even gotten to the part about her planned breakup.

When she heard a voice she recognized, she scrambled to her feet just in time to see Vanessa follow Zara into the living room.

Vanessa carried a pizza box, the aroma immediately filling the small space, and Zara held two six-packs of beer.

"Nice fort." A smile played around the corners of Vanessa's mouth.

"What are you doing here?"

Vanessa cocked her head toward Zara. "Your friend called in reinforcements. I brought my able body and sustenance." She set the box on the coffee table.

Hannah glanced at the floor where she'd been sitting. Her phone was missing.

Zara returned her glare with a wicked grin.

"You didn't say anything at the garden about moving." The downward tilt of Vanessa's eyebrows made her appear wounded.

Hannah shrugged. "It's not a big deal. I grew tired of living in this cave, and I have to be out before October first."

"I thought you owned it."

Zara watched them, her eyes darting side to side as she followed their conversation.

Thankfully, Hannah suggested renting somewhere after Bren admitted she had little in savings to put toward a down payment on a house. For half a second, Hannah had considered using her money to put a home in both their names, and Bren could help with the payments, but a niggling feeling had made her change her mind. If she hadn't, she'd have one more enormous knot to untangle right now.

"No, and I'm renting again, but a condo this time. It's in Belltown and has a beautiful view."

Zara set the beer on the kitchen table. "And it doesn't have to be forever if you decide you don't like it."

Hannah wasn't the type to think in terms of forever. She never had. Living in the moment was more her style. "Pizza first, then packing?" She lifted the lid on the box and smiled. Her favorite, sausage and pepperoncini. She elbowed Zara. "You're forgiven." She wasn't sure what'd inspired Zara to sneak into Hannah's contacts and text someone. Had it been whatever Zara had been sensing was off with her? "Where's my phone?"

Zara slid it from on top of the coffee maker and passed it to her.

Hannah scrolled through her messages. No texts had been sent to Vanessa today, so Zara had simply wanted her number. What had Zara told her to convince her to help Hannah move? It was ballsy, considering they hadn't officially met, only glimpsed one another at the funeral.

Vanessa handed her a paper plate, and they cleared off the table enough to eat.

"Do you usually have events on the weekends? Weddings and stuff?" Zara opted to use a knife and fork.

"Mmm." Vanessa dabbed at her mouth with her napkin before answering. "We have orders every day of the week, three hundred and sixty-five days a year. For events, it's simply a matter of delivering the flowers or whatever the order entails, and my drivers do that." She picked at the corner of her beer label. "Sometimes I'll fill in if the staff is shorthanded or if we have an abundance of orders. That happens mostly during the summer months." She leaned back in her chair and crossed her legs. "What do you do at Baros?"

"Reception," Zara said, not missing a beat.

Hannah almost spit out the drink she'd been swallowing.

"I make coffee, answer the phone, and order things like staples and pens. Some days I put cookies in the conference room if there's a meeting."

"You're friendly and have a great personality. I'm sure your visitors—"

Hannah couldn't take it any longer. She touched Vanessa's sleeve. "She's pulling your leg." Hannah poked Zara with her toe.

"Ow." Zara grinned and took another slice.

"She's the vice president of Marketing. She wouldn't know how to order office supplies if she had five hundred dollars riding on it."

Zara scowled, but her smile was right behind it. "True."

"What you described, though, that could be my assistant." Hannah covered her eyes. "She's absolutely terrible."

"Why don't you fire her?"

"Yes, Hannah, why don't you?" Zara returned her earlier poke in the leg before turning to Vanessa. "I keep telling her to, but the woman worked for her parents, and Hannah is a softie at heart, if you didn't already know."

"It's not that." Hannah picked off a burned pepper. "She's only doing what she's used to. My parents didn't ask much of her because my mom supported my dad. I've tried increasing her workload, and she gets confused and makes mistakes, or I walk by her desk and she's crying. Technology isn't one of her strong skills—"

"What is?" Zara muttered.

"So, I've been doing most of it myself."

"Which is a problem." Zara pointed her fork at Hannah. "You don't have the time to be managing your own calendar or answering every email. Annika should be administratively supporting you and doing a better job at gatekeeping. Anyone on staff—even outsiders—can walk into your office whenever they want."

Hannah tossed her crumpled napkin at her. "Including you."

Zara dodged it. "I bring you lunch. If I didn't, you'd go without most days."

Vanessa appeared amused by their back and forth. "It sounds like you need an experienced executive assistant." Her eyes sparkled. "You squabble like sisters." Her forehead creased. "I don't actually know if you have any siblings."

"A younger brother. He's a kindergarten teacher in Redmond," Hannah said, thinking she needed to text him. It'd been a while. He'd be thrilled she was working with kids.

Vanessa tilted her head. "He managed to escape the family business?"

"Never had any interest in it." Hannah shrugged. "My parents knew I did, so I think it took the expectation off him."

"What about you? Any siblings?" Zara twisted to drop her plate into the garbage.

"No, it's just me and my mom."

Hannah bit her lip to keep from saying anything about Vanessa's mother and tried to school her expression. Just thinking about that woman made her blood boil.

"Well, speaking of assistants, have I mentioned how fabulous mine is?" Zara wiggled her eyebrows.

"Every day since you hired her."

Zara made a face at her, then turned to Vanessa. "She's amazing. Before I ask her to do a task, she's already done it. She's proactive and anticipates my every move. Jen knows all these little tricks when it comes to my calendar, never overschedules me, gives me plenty of travel time to and from meetings, and everyone loves her." Her eyes glazed over, and she smiled. "Her hair is red, which usually doesn't do it for me, and she wears the prettiest midi dresses every day."

"Hey." Hannah held up her hand like a stop sign. "I don't need Helga leaving her HR dungeon in the basement to inform me of any potential sexual harassment issues in your department."

Zara waved her away. "I'm only looking and using my peripheral vision at that. You know I'd never do anything that would put me, or you, in that position. Or, God forbid, bring Helga to my doorstep." She grimaced, glancing between them. "Besides, Jen has a teenager. That's usually a no-go for me."

"You don't like kids?" Vanessa laughed when Zara scrunched up her face. "I can't believe how good Hannah is with them. They adore her."

Zara slowly turned to Hannah. "And whose kids would these be?"

Vanessa's eyes widened as she must have deduced Hannah hadn't shared anything about volunteering.

"Vanessa runs a garden program at a middle school. I've been helping out."

"You?" Zara gave a small laugh. "Gardening?" Her features fell. "Is this why you're never available for brunch on Saturdays?" She narrowed her eyes, as though the pieces had clicked into place for her, then stood and put her empty bottle under the sink.

Vanessa mouthed "I'm sorry" and looked horrified.

Hannah rose and met Zara as she closed the refrigerator. "Hey, I should've said something. Maybe I was worried you'd make fun of me. You know as well as anyone that I've never had a green thumb. Forgive me?"

"I should go."

Vanessa made to stand, but Hannah extended her hand as though it might hold Vanessa in place. "No, please stay." When Vanessa rose, Hannah desperately tried to think of some way to keep her from leaving.

"I'm going to check out your backyard and give you two a moment." She took her beer and slid open the back door.

Hannah turned back to Zara. "I'm sorry."

"How long has this been happening?" Zara crossed her arms.

Hannah looked up and mentally counted. "Uh, five months." When Zara's mouth fell open, she quickly amended, "Four months and a week."

"I'm your friend. If I decided to take dance lessons, would you make fun of me because you know I'm uncoordinated and clumsy?"

"No." Hannah grasped the back of a chair for support.

"You really like her, don't you?"

Hannah froze. How was she supposed to answer when Zara still thought she'd been in love with Bren in May? "I find her interesting."

"Yeah." Zara studied her. "I thought your weirdness might have something to do with her. That's why I asked her to come help. Now seeing you together, I get it." She pushed away from the counter where she'd been leaning. "I wanted to see how you'd answer my question. She's 'interesting,' huh? There's enough heat between the two of you to melt the cheese on the pizza that's gone cold."

Hannah swallowed. Her throat had gone dry. "Do you think badly of me, you know, for developing a crush so soon?" In reality, it wasn't soon at all, nor likely a crush. But Hannah was fighting against perceptions for which she had only herself to blame.

"Only you know when you're ready to move on." Zara's eyes held compassion now instead of the irritation they'd had a moment ago. "That's not for me to judge." She pointed her finger at Hannah's face before dropping it. "But I will pass judgment when you keep things from me."

The hair on Hannah's arms stood on end. "I'm sorry." Zara's reaction to the garden made her question how wise it was to divulge the bigger secret she harbored.

Zara squeezed her shoulder, then shooed her toward the open door. "Go tell her it's safe to come inside. I'm not packing all these boxes myself while you build a citadel."

❖

Hannah walked to the corner of the backyard where Vanessa was rubbing a leaf between her thumb and finger. "Hi."

Vanessa turned. "Hi."

Hannah motioned to the bush before them. "Is something wrong with my plant?"

"No." Vanessa turned. "I was just admiring your helenium."

Hannah hadn't known its name. "Do you have a favorite flower?" She admired Vanessa's tails-out button-up shirt over jeans look. "Or is that a strange question to ask a florist?"

A small dimple appeared on Vanessa's right cheek she'd never noticed before.

"Yes."

"To which question?" Hannah bit her lip.

Vanessa laughed, and the wondrous sound woke something that'd been dormant in Hannah for months. Years?

"Yes, I have a favorite." Vanessa stepped to the next bush and seemed to inspect it, too.

"Are you going to share?"

Vanessa plucked a weed that had managed to poke through the mulch. She tossed it behind a bush. "Orchids."

"Why them?" Hannah was grateful it was one she recognized. "Not that they're not pretty."

"I like what they symbolize."

Hannah followed as she moved along the line of foliage. "Which is what?"

"Many things. Beauty, grace, refinement, love." She looked at Hannah over her shoulder. "And thoughtfulness, among others. What about you?"

Hannah looked around her yard filled with gorgeous greenery and blooms she'd taken for granted. She should slow down and appreciate life once in a while. "I've never thought about it, but you did an excellent job selling me on orchids." She tucked her hair behind her ear.

A line formed on Vanessa's forehead. "Did I?"

"Yeah, they remind me of someone I know," Hannah said softly. She didn't miss the split second of surprise cross Vanessa's features. "If you had to pick a flower to represent me, what would it be?" Hannah asked, moving closer.

"You?" Vanessa's gaze seemed to wander from Hannah's hair to her shoes. She took her time before looking up. "Zinnias. They're gorgeous with bright, bold blooms."

It sounded like a compliment, probably was, and Hannah appreciated the sentiment, but it wasn't what she'd been asking. "Do they symbolize anything?"

Vanessa glanced back from where she'd wandered ahead, then took a drink and came to stand before her. "Absent friends, endurance, goodness, and lasting affection." Her steady eye contact almost seemed to dare Hannah to question it.

While Hannah wasn't thrilled to hear the word friend included, if that's all Vanessa could give her at the moment, she'd take it. Lasting affection, on the other hand, held possibility. Hannah realized she hadn't responded. She ran her fingers through her hair, trying to tame it in the breeze. "I didn't mean for it to get awkward in there."

"I'm sorry I said anything. I didn't realize she didn't know." Vanessa tipped the last of the beer into her mouth. The act highlighted her neck and the thin silver necklace that peeked from the V of her shirt. She'd left a couple of buttons undone, and the shirt gaped between the third and fourth where it was stretched tight across her chest. But Hannah picked that up out of the corner of her eye and kept her gaze above Vanessa's shoulders.

She'd missed that neck, though, the taut muscles she'd traced with her fingers, the blood pulsing through Vanessa's veins beneath her tongue, the subtle scent of perfume that lingered on her skin, and the way Vanessa made happy little sounds when she kissed the area just below her jaw. Hannah wanted to kiss her now. Standing in the sunlight, with her curls dancing in the breeze, Vanessa made it difficult to breathe.

"Are you okay?" Vanessa's eyebrows pulled together.

Hannah shook herself from her daydream. "I'm fine. You had no way of knowing." She didn't actually have a real reason for keeping the garden project a secret. Maybe she just wanted Vanessa to herself for a while. Without a third set of eyes, there was no scrutiny. Although, with Vanessa distancing herself to work through things, there wasn't anything to investigate. And yet, here Vanessa was, standing before Hannah, looking concerned.

Hannah leaned on the end of the wood and wrought-iron bench that had come with the place. "What did she bribe you with to get you to show up today? You brought the pizza and beer, so it wasn't that."

Vanessa swung the brown bottle between her index finger and thumb. "No bribe." She smiled.

Hannah couldn't let it go. "What'd she say?"

"Does what we talked about worry you?" Vanessa whispered as she passed, her breath warming Hannah's ear.

Excitement, and something more, jolted through Hannah. She swiveled so she could face Vanessa where she'd sat on the wooden slats. "Should it?"

A sly smile spread across Vanessa's face. "She didn't tell me anything I didn't already know."

"That's not fair."

Vanessa shrugged and finished peeling the beer label free.

"Whatever it was, thank you for coming. I know this goes against your needing-space edict."

"Edict?" Vanessa's face fell. "That makes me sound like such a bitch." She folded the label in half, running her thumbnail down the crease.

"No, it makes you sound like a woman sure of what she needs and confident enough to ask for it." Hannah gave her a sheepish smile. "Even if some people try to sneak through the cracks."

"You're rather difficult to push away." Vanessa fiddled with the piece of paper.

Hannah studied her shoes. "I feel guilty for bringing you into all of this. Since I'm the cause, the least I can do is stand by you while you work through the ramifications of the encounter. Again, two is greater than one."

Vanessa shook her head vehemently. "You are not at fault in any of this. We both know who is."

"Still, if I hadn't contacted you—"

"I'm glad you did." She handed Hannah the folded label, picked up her empty bottle, and walked toward the house.

She was? Hannah watched her until she'd gone inside. Vanessa had said some hurtful, if albeit true, things to her at the flower shop, but Hannah had quickly seen them for what they were. It strengthened her determination not to let Vanessa push her further away. The reflection Hannah did during the time they'd spent apart since the ill-conceived trip convinced her they might be really good together. Someone had to fight for them. Time and patience. That's what it was going to take. Time and patience. Vanessa wasn't ready for anything beyond being in the same vicinity right now, but perhaps one day she'd welcome the idea of something more. Hannah wouldn't pressure her, but she also wasn't about to walk away. Not from the most interesting and beautiful woman she'd ever encountered. She already knew Vanessa was worth the effort.

Hannah looked at the piece of paper she still held in her palm.

Vanessa had folded it into a tiny flower.

Chapter Nineteen

Hannah leaned against the side of the shed as the kids filed out of the garden's gate carrying heavy canvas bags. Vanessa had timed much of the harvest so they could take the cornucopia home for Thanksgiving for those who celebrated, and as a surprise for the families for those who didn't. She'd even printed simple recipes they could make with the different kinds of produce. To Hannah's surprise, every child had wanted a share of the bounty and the instructions to make the dishes Vanessa had created.

Vanessa came to stand beside her.

"Where'd you get the bags?" Hannah asked, not taking her eyes off the students.

"I asked a business to donate them."

Together they watched the last of the kids put the evidence of their hard work into the backs of their parents' cars, or stand in the school bus line with their totes laden with winter vegetables like beets, Brussels sprouts, radishes, carrots, butternut squash, zucchini, potatoes, parsnips, and cauliflower. She couldn't get over the proud looks on their faces. Hannah had declined her percentage, telling Vanessa to split it among the youth.

Vanessa swung her tote, filled with a smaller amount than she'd given the children, onto her shoulder. "Shall we?"

Hannah padlocked the shed and waited while Vanessa secured the gate. They continued toward their cars.

"This is far too much food for one person. Why don't you come over tonight? I'll make dinner. You should taste the delicious products of your hard work."

Hannah almost stumbled on the completely flat sidewalk. "Me?" Dinner kind of sounded like a date, or was she reading too much into it?

With a cute grin, Vanessa playfully turned in a circle as though looking for someone else. "You're the only person around, so I guess you'll have to do."

"Sure." Hannah had planned to work this evening, but she also had to eat. "Can I bring wine or dessert?"

Vanessa's eyes sparkled. "I'll never turn down a bottle of vino." She unlocked her car. "I have to run to the grocery store, or I'd invite you over now to hang out."

Hannah's phone rang, and she quickly pulled it from her pocket. It was her facilities manager, never a good sign. "Work. I need to take this, anyway."

Vanessa nodded. "Seven? Or six if you want to keep me company while I cook."

"Six sounds good." Hannah took the call. "Sharon, what's going on?"

It turned out, a lot. Hannah watched Vanessa turn a corner and disappear from sight as Sharon filled her in on the details of the malfunctioning HVAC system. While Sharon and her team fixed many problems that occurred in the buildings, this one appeared too great and probably would cost as much to repair as it would to replace. Ditching the twenty-three-year-old unit and purchasing a new one was the smart option, but installation likely wouldn't happen for days. That did nothing for the poor staff who were now at work in the building and would be around the clock until things were fixed.

Hannah took care of it as much as she could, but it was six thirty when she arrived at Vanessa's.

Vanessa opened the door wearing an apron. "Hi." She stepped back to allow her to enter. "I thought you might've abandoned me."

"Sorry I'm late. There was an issue at work." Hannah dropped her bag under Vanessa's coat rack.

"And it kept you after five?"

Hannah gave her a wry smile. "Problems don't care what time it is. And this is nothing. I'm often there until ten or eleven." She followed Vanessa into the kitchen where wonderful aromas greeted her. The small room exuded warmth.

"That's terrible you have to work so late. Did you solve the issue?" Vanessa pushed a plate holding slices of raw carrots and radishes and some kind of pesto dip toward her.

"As much as I could. We fabricated a temporary fix." Hannah took a bite. The crunchy bite of the radish with the herbed dip was like an electrical jolt to her taste buds. "That's fantastic," she said, pointing at the green sauce.

Vanessa eyed her. "Have you been home since I last saw you? You haven't changed."

Hannah shook her head. "No. We lost an HVAC system in the building that houses the support center. It's staffed twenty-four hours a day, seven days a week. While we don't need heating or cooling often in this climate, they do require ventilation, so we had to find a solution until we can get it replaced."

"What'd you do?" Vanessa slid what looked like a loaf of bread wrapped in foil beside a casserole dish already in the oven.

"We set up industrial fans and flexible ductwork to circulate fresh air." She sighed. "At least it wasn't a building that needs high security like the one that contains the precious metals and gemstones. Open doors and windows wouldn't be possible there. As it was, I called in extra personnel for the entrances to make the staff feel safe." She dropped her head into her hands. "I forgot to bring wine."

Vanessa didn't appear fazed. "There's some in the refrigerator. It'll go nicely."

Hannah rose and got it out. She screwed off the top. "Glasses?"

Vanessa pointed, and Hannah poured them each one.

"Do you want some clean clothes?"

Hannah assessed her condition. Covered in dirt from the garden and then cobwebs and grime from when she'd retrieved the units from storage, she had no right to be sitting at Vanessa's counter looking like she did. "I probably should."

"Would it be rude if I sent you to find something while I finished dinner?" Vanessa stirred a mixture she poured over spinach leaves.

"Just tell me where."

Vanessa pointed. "First door, top of the stairs. There's a laundry basket of folded clothes at the foot of my bed I haven't put away yet. You'll find options in there."

Hannah left her shoes by the front door and found Vanessa's bedroom. She flicked on the light. The walls were either off-white or a pale shade of lavender. Unlike the kitchen and living room she'd glimpsed on her way in, this room didn't have plants on every surface. It had a clean but lived-in look, with a sweater thrown over the back of a chair near the window and books on the bedside table. Antique botanical prints decorated the walls. Vanessa's scent lingered in the air, and Hannah closed her eyes and inhaled.

Not wanting to dally, she found a pair of sweats and a threadbare Supersonics sweatshirt that might be softer than anything she owned. She looked around for a place to change. Closing the bedroom door felt too personal, and she didn't want to invade Vanessa's private bathroom without asking. Instead, she took the items downstairs.

Vanessa must've heard her approach, for she called out before Hannah reached the bottom step. "Find something?"

"I did." Hannah lifted the pile to show her. "I'll just be a minute." She stepped into the half bath she'd glimpsed off the hall.

After leaving her dirty clothing folded beside her bag, she returned to the kitchen. She'd taken a few minutes to wash her hands and face, too, and had a little pep in her step that'd been missing ten minutes ago.

Vanessa looked up. "Better?"

"Much." She smiled and snagged a carrot.

"You could've changed in my bedroom," Vanessa said, the twitch of a smile showing her amusement.

Hannah leaned her arms on the counter. "I wasn't sure." She glanced around. "You really have an eye for color and design. You did a lot of the renovations yourself, right?" She hadn't seen much with the closed floor plan Victorian homes were known for, but what she'd viewed had been impressive, from the hardwood beneath her feet to the crown molding.

Vanessa stilled from where she'd been tossing vegetables in a bowl. "You have a good memory. Thank you."

Hannah nodded and took a sip of wine. "I should've told you this right away, but it smells divine in here. It made me realize how hungry I am."

A glow seemed to emanate from Vanessa along with her shy smile and flushed cheeks. "Thank you." Vanessa pulled the large dish and the foil packet from the oven. "Can you put this in the center of the table, please?" She pushed a trivet toward her. "Actually, if I could just hand you things..." And she did, passing them over the counter for Hannah to arrange on the table.

While Vanessa put the warm bread into a basket, Hannah placed the steaming entrée on the hot pad.

"Are you going to describe all these wonderful things?" Hannah gazed in awe at the meal before her.

Vanessa joined her, bringing their glasses with her. "Sit there." She took the seat opposite her. "This is a spinach, beet, and goat cheese salad. I roasted Brussels sprouts, potatoes, butternut squash, and parsnips and tossed them all together. The main dish is a zucchini and cauliflower gratin." She glanced up. "I thought meat might be overkill."

"Completely." Hannah stared at it all, especially the bubbly dish in the middle. "I'm warning you now. I might eat half of that."

Vanessa's sweet laugh bounced off the walls, multiplying the joyous sound. "Be my guest."

With an incredible amount of patience, Hannah finished her salad, tried the roasted veggies, and saved tasting the gratin for last. "Oh, my God." She shielded her mouth with her hand as she sucked in air. It was still fiercely hot. When she swallowed, she spoke. "We did well. I mean growing this stuff. And you did an amazing job cooking it. This is particularly fantastic."

"I'll send some home with you." Vanessa turned her attention to her food but looked pleased, the compliment adding to her glow.

"Better not, or just a little." Hannah hated to decline the deliciousness. "I'm traveling for work. I'll be in Vegas, LA, and San Diego, then joining my parents in Vail for Thanksgiving."

"When are you leaving?" Vanessa hadn't looked up.

"Saturday." The temperature in the room seemed to drop.

Vanessa raised her gaze, her gorgeous eyes holding something Hannah couldn't read. "When will you be back?"

Something had changed between them, and Hannah wasn't sure what. "The Sunday after Thanksgiving. Late."

After dropping her napkin beside her plate, Vanessa rose and filled a glass with water from the fridge. "It's just…you didn't mention it." She hadn't turned around to speak.

Hannah considered how she could phrase it without receiving any more of this—whatever—from Vanessa. "Neither trip impacted volunteering because of the holiday, but I planned to ask about your Thanksgiving plans tonight and tell you about mine."

Vanessa spun around. "And if I hadn't asked you to dinner?"

Well, she had her there.

Hannah stood and approached her. "Hey, what is this about?"

With a flick of her hand and a shake of her head, Vanessa said, "Nothing."

"It's obviously something." Hannah wanted to touch her, to take her hand, but she wasn't sure it would be welcome. "I wouldn't have left to see my parents without telling you I'd be gone."

Vanessa stared at her. "Really?"

"Really."

"What about the work trip?" Vanessa couldn't have appeared to wait for an answer more if she'd put her hands on her hips and tapped her foot.

Hannah walked a tightrope, trying to keep her balance with each tiny step forward. "I didn't know you'd want to know."

Vanessa motioned her back to the table. When they were seated again, Hannah waited for her to speak before resuming eating.

"What if something happened to you?" Vanessa picked a crispy sprout leaf from the mixed vegetables and chewed it, so Hannah stabbed a chunk of butternut squash.

Telling Vanessa her parents would be notified if she were to die probably wasn't the right answer. "Like what?"

Vanessa gestured into the air. "Delays, mechanical difficulties, a car accident, a tornado, a mugging, losing your purse. Anything could happen."

She'd apparently put a lot of thought into it. What *would* Hannah do? Taking care of everything herself, dealing with issues as they arose had been her life for as long as she could remember. She hadn't even told her parents about Bren when she should've, not that she was mentioning that now. "I don't know."

"Well, someone should know your whereabouts and make sure you safely get from place to place." Vanessa raised her hand when Hannah started to speak. "And don't say your assistant, because you've already established she's terrible."

"You also have a good memory." Hannah smiled.

Vanessa didn't return it. Her hand holding her fork shook. "I guess my point is, you can text me while you're traveling, you know, to check in, if there's no one else." Her plate suddenly had her entire attention, so much so, that Hannah was left with a view of the top of Vanessa's head, the careful part just to the left, her curls falling to each side.

Hannah took a moment to let the understanding sink in, and when it had, the undeniable inclination to ease Vanessa's concerns was all that mattered. She extended her hand across the table, palm up.

After staring at it a moment, Vanessa slipped hers into it and looked at her.

Hannah held her gaze. "There's no one else, Vanessa."

Vanessa nodded and seemed to steel herself. She squeezed Hannah's hand twice before letting go. "Finish your dinner before it gets cold."

Chapter Twenty

With the increased frequency of her therapy visits following the trip to San Francisco, Vanessa had been able to address some of her issues and, in general, her head felt clearer. If only it wasn't so expensive. And now she questioned how much she benefitted from the additional hours. She'd tired of the routine of being asked questions and dealing with the resulting emotions when she hadn't fully processed the session from the week before. But Dr. Martinez had helped her immensely over the years, and Vanessa had developed a respect and comfort with her so she had no intention of trying to find another psychologist.

"Vanessa, are you listening?"

She blinked, Dr. Martinez coming into focus. "I'm sorry. I was lost in thought for a moment."

"As I was saying, you discovered over the last couple of months that compartmentalizing your emotions versus analyzing and addressing them are vastly different things. In the first instance, you're simply shoving them in a figurative box and slapping on a lid. They still exist inside, fully formed and quietly alive, like a bear in hibernation. That's fine until something rips off the lid and the bear awakens. However, when you face headfirst the things that make you feel poorly, address why it is they have that effect on you, and find healthy ways to work through them, you're taking them apart piece by piece, breaking them into smaller bits, and they no longer have the power they once held." Dr. Martinez tried to tuck her chin-length brown hair behind her ear, but it fell forward again, perhaps due to the glasses she always wore during their sessions. "Does that make sense?"

Vanessa nodded. It did, but knowing and doing were light years apart, and while she owned the tools to do the challenging work, she needed to remember to use them.

"You seem distracted today." Dr. Martinez pushed her glasses higher as she studied her.

"I was thinking about someone." Her thoughts had drifted again.

"Can you be more specific?"

Vanessa picked at a hangnail. "Hannah."

"What made you think about her?" Dr. Martinez jotted something on her legal pad.

Vanessa took a moment to formulate her answer. "Remember how I told her I needed space?"

"She's not honoring that?" Another scribble.

"Actually, she has been." While Hannah had eschewed her initial attempt to push her away, she'd respected Vanessa's boundaries for the most part, and Vanessa gave her credit for that. Of course, she still volunteered, and Vanessa respected Hannah's dedication to the middle schoolers. How could she not? And like Hannah had said, she seemed content simply to be in her presence once a week, something Vanessa couldn't say about a single other person on the planet. "In fact, *I* suggested we spend additional time together. I invited her to dinner."

"How did that make you feel?" Dr. Martinez tilted her head.

"Asking her, or while she was there?"

"Let's start with how you felt when you asked her."

Vanessa closed her eyes, remembering the moment. "Nervous, a bit guilty." She opened them.

"How so?" The raising of Dr. Martinez's brow seemed to convey her surprise at Vanessa's answer.

"I used the excuse of wanting her to taste the vegetables we'd grown, when the truth was, I just wanted to spend a bit more time with her that day." Vanessa shifted in the leather armchair.

"And you don't feel that was fair to her?"

Vanessa scoffed. "It wasn't, not after I told her I needed time to process everything. I'm sending her mixed signals, but I can't seem to help myself."

"Was asking for space the only reason you tried to distance yourself?" Whatever Dr. Martinez wrote down took a moment, allowing Vanessa time to formulate an answer.

When she looked up, Vanessa spoke. "I'm obviously attracted to her. You know we slept together in San Francisco."

"And you enjoyed it." It wasn't a question.

Oh, God, did she. Enjoyed was somewhere around number two on a scale of one to ten. What she'd experienced had been a twelve. "Yes."

"And you're afraid this sexual attraction won't allow you to deal with the issues surrounding Bren and your mother."

Was it time to leave yet? Vanessa glanced at the clock. Eleven minutes remaining. Shit. No getting out of this one. "What frightens me," she clasped her hands in her lap to stop them from trembling, "is that the attraction isn't only sexual." There. She'd said it. The sound of Dr. Martinez's pen furiously scratching against the paper told her all she needed to know.

"Are you worried the feelings you have for Hannah will preclude you from finding the healing you know you have to do?" Dr. Martinez still hadn't raised her head, her pen moving line to line.

Was that the case? Vanessa turned to look out the window, at the trees now devoid of leaves swaying in the autumn breeze. "I don't…" She pressed her eyes closed. Teasing out the nuance of emotions in a situation like this left her exhausted, and she was sure to be of little help to her staff the rest of the day. "That's part of it. I've seen what a loved one leaving can do to the person left behind."

Dr. Martinez looked over the top of her glasses. "We established long ago that your mother could've grieved and chosen a different path for herself. She likely has untreated depression and, from things you've told me, alcoholism. While something terrible happened to her, yes, how she responded to it is on her. At any point, she could've asked for help, especially considering she had a young daughter to care for. Instead, she chose to live her life as a bitter, angry woman."

Vanessa nodded. She'd heard this before. "The voices aren't quite as bad anymore."

Dr. Martinez made a note. "We've talked about this, Vanessa. They're not voices you're hearing with your ears that no one else is hearing. They're intrusive thoughts. How often?"

Vanessa shrugged. "Less than once a day."

After flipping back a few pages, Dr. Martinez nodded. "That's an improvement. So, back to Hannah."

For the last minute or so, Vanessa had been hoping Dr. Martinez had forgotten about her.

"It seems that you're afraid that if you begin a relationship with Hannah...what?"

Vanessa possessed numerous fears. Where to start? "I guess, mostly I'm scared that if we begin dating, I'll grow too attached, and when she leaves me, it'll break me."

"I noticed you said when and not if. You believe she will?" Dr. Martinez glanced at her watch.

"That seems to be what happens more often than not." Vanessa wouldn't survive going through that again. Surely, Dr. Martinez should realize that.

"You could look at it that way." Dr. Martinez laid her notepad and pen on the table beside her. "Divorce rates are over fifty percent. People fall in and out of love. No one is perfect. But if you go in expecting the worst, are you even giving the relationship a chance?"

Vanessa stayed silent, not finding a suitable answer.

"How did it feel being around her when you invited her over?"

"Good. Great, actually." Except when Hannah sprung the news she'd be traveling and gone for a while. Vanessa touched the center of her chest where it ached.

"Instead, you could approach the situation by thinking about Hannah and asking yourself, 'Is she worth it? Do I care about her enough to consider that not being with her would be an even worse outcome?' If you genuinely love her, your love for her will be so great that you'll be willing to take that small risk, that one day she might leave you, but not being with her now simply isn't an option."

Love? Where did Dr. Martinez come up with that? Yes, she cared about Hannah, but she never said she loved her.

"Our time is up. Think about that between now and our next session. How do you feel about going back to once a month? I'm pleased your intrusive thoughts have decreased. You're making substantial progress." She stood and escorted Vanessa to the door. "You look well and seem to be in good spirits."

"I think that'd be good." Vanessa breathed easier. She hadn't had to suggest the change, nor address the love issue, at least today.

"I'm glad to hear it. Tell Ronald to schedule you in four weeks. Have a happy Thanksgiving." Dr. Martinez closed her door.

It took Vanessa a few minutes with Dr. Martinez's assistant, then a ten-minute drive to work before she'd left the heaviness of the session behind her. *Love.* She scoffed.

Once in her office, she took out her phone to catch up on anything she'd missed while she'd been gone. No texts from Hannah. She sighed, then chastised herself. What did she expect? Unable to stop herself, she scrolled to the photo of the view from the mountaintop in Vail Hannah had sent her yesterday. How many times had she stared at it, wishing she were standing beside her?

A call appeared on her screen.

"Raymond, how are you?"

"I've been better. I'm afraid I've got unfortunate news."

Vanessa immediately worried what other injury he might've incurred. Surely, he wasn't hiking on his leg already. "What is it?"

"The custodian just called. Apparently, the garden was vandalized overnight. Locks cut on both the gate and shed. They smashed windows, tore up plants, overturned some planters, and tagged a bunch of stuff."

"Oh, no." Her stomach knotted as she envisioned the damage.

"Yeah, probably high schoolers with nothing better to do. The police have been called. I'm heading over soon to see if anything was stolen."

Vanessa had pulled up the orders still outstanding for tomorrow as he'd been talking. "Damn. I can't leave right now. I had an appointment this morning, and I need to help my staff get caught up, or people won't be receiving flowers tomorrow. I can come by later."

"Don't worry if you can't make it. I'll stay while they make the report, and we can deal with the rest when we have time."

She didn't like that solution, but had little choice. Her garden, her poor little garden. The kids were going to be devastated. "Okay."

After hanging up, Vanessa stared at her phone. She wanted to call Hannah and tell her what happened, not to commiserate because she could do that with Raymond, but because talking to Hannah brightened her spirits, and she could use that right now. Plus, Vanessa had missed her while she'd been traveling, even if Hannah dutifully sent her departure and landing texts, and a few bonus ones in between. It felt like she'd been gone a month. But it wasn't fair to bring Hannah down during her time away with her parents.

Vanessa hoped Hannah was skiing in three feet of fresh powder and loving every minute of the whoosh of freezing air against her face as she raced down the slopes. Hannah deserved a vacation with how dedicated she was to her job. She was always working, day and night. And Vanessa bet Hannah being in Vail was no different. It was difficult to imagine her setting aside time for herself. Her company seemed to take priority over everything. As much as Vanessa liked and admired her, she wasn't too keen on that aspect of Hannah's personality. In the end, it didn't matter.

They weren't dating.

❖

It was four long, excruciating hours before Vanessa could leave work, and she tried not to speed on her way to the school. Raymond had left her a message saying it didn't appear anything was stolen. The vandals had been more concerned with destruction and leaving their mark. The police had photographed the tags but said it was unlikely anything would come of it.

Vanessa loosened her white-knuckled grip on the steering wheel. A garden. At a school. Who did something like that? Yet, she knew Raymond was probably right. She'd done stupid things as a teenager out of boredom, to impress others, or just for fun. But she'd never broken the law.

Once again, she braked hard after turning into the teachers' parking lot. There, in its usual spot, was Hannah's Lexus. And beside it, a white van that read Armand & Daughter.

Vanessa couldn't get out of her car fast enough. She jogged past the busted lock, spilled soil, and battered plants. An older man and younger woman were measuring the shed's windows. Broken glass littered the ground at their feet, and graffiti covered the walls. She skidded to a stop.

The woman turned. "Hi. Are you Vanessa?"

Vanessa nodded, surprised to find herself out of breath. "Is Hannah here?"

"I am."

Vanessa spun around, elation soaring through her upon hearing Hannah's voice. She wore rubber gloves and held a scrub brush and a can of something chemical. It was the only thing that stopped Vanessa from throwing her arms around her. "You're here."

Hannah smiled and held out her arms. "In the flesh."

"You're not skiing." In her peripheral vision, Vanessa noticed the young woman return to her task.

"My dad hurt his knee, not on the slopes, but getting off the chairlift. It was painful enough he wanted to have his doctor image it. My mom invited me to Palm Springs, but I saw the relief on her face when I declined." Hannah looked to the shed. "I wanted to come home and surprise you."

She'd succeeded. "Yeah, I wasn't expecting to find you here." She glanced at the two people working on the shed. "Or them."

"When I landed and turned on my phone, I saw Ray had left me a message. I came straight to the school knowing that if you weren't here yet, you soon would be." Hannah glanced at the destruction. "My heart dove into my shoes when I heard the news. The poor kids."

"Who are they?" Vanessa motioned with a raise of her chin.

"Jean-Paul used to work for me in facilities. When Natacha became old enough, they went into business as father and daughter." She set the brush and can on a crate and pulled off her gloves. "I'll introduce you."

Once Hannah had, Natacha addressed Vanessa. "We don't have windows this size, so we'll put in smaller ones with temporary frames around them until we can make some. As soon as we get both of these in, we'll help you remove spray paint."

"I want to fix the two beds whose sides were kicked off before we go, too," Jean-Paul said.

"Okay, you do that, and we'll deal with the graffiti." Natacha picked up a drill.

Someone's phone rang. Hannah pulled hers from her pocket. "Sorry, work. I have to take this." She walked toward the gate.

Within an hour, the makeshift windows were in place. Hannah and Vanessa scrubbed one side of the building and the front while Natacha took care of the other. Thankfully, the vandals hadn't tagged the back because it abutted the fence.

"You're quiet. Just upset?" Hannah sprayed more WD-40 on a streak of yellow paint.

Vanessa sighed. "I know I shouldn't be, but it feels personal. It better not have been any kids who've come through my program."

"I'm sure it wasn't." Hannah was quiet for a moment. "It means too much to them. I can see it in every participant I've worked with. It's understandable you're angry though."

"Not angry." Vanessa rubbed a particularly stubborn line of red. "Mostly sad. Disappointed." She blinked back tears that'd come out of nowhere.

Hannah stripped off her gloves again. She gently laid her fingers on Vanessa's arm. "Me, too. Come here."

"I'm covered in—"

"I don't care." Hannah pulled her into a tender embrace, and Vanessa found herself sinking into it.

Behind Hannah's back, she removed the rubber gloves and dropped them to the ground, not wanting to transfer any chemical onto her. With her hands bare, she could feel Hannah's warmth through her shirt. Other senses came alive, too. She caught the fragrance of fabric softener and some kind of hair product, and when she turned her face into Hannah's neck, she detected the sweet scent of Hannah herself. Vanessa tightened her hold on her, and their bodies met in that familiar way she'd almost forgotten. She closed her eyes, feeling how when she breathed out, Hannah breathed in, their bellies in sync.

Hannah sifted her fingers through Vanessa's hair, much like she'd done when they'd been in bed.

"You okay?"

Vanessa took a step back at the quiet question, but Hannah continued to rest her hands on Vanessa's shoulders. "I will be. Thank you for coordinating this, but there's not money in the..." The rest of her statement died at the fiery look in Hannah's eyes.

"I didn't do it with the expectation of being reimbursed."

Vanessa nodded. "Of course." She hooked her hands over Hannah's forearms.

"We're about done here," Jean-Paul said, coming around the corner.

They stepped away from one another.

"Thank you for everything," Hannah said. "It already looks so much better."

He looked around. "Yeah, most of the stuff just needs a bit of cleanup. I've seen worse."

He and Natacha loaded up their tools and left by the time they finished the shed. It wasn't perfect, and depending on how it looked in the full light of day, it might need a coat of paint. But it was fine for now.

"I guess you decided not to join Sonja and Jeffrey for Thanksgiving." Hannah glanced at her phone as Vanessa unwrapped the new locks she'd brought from work and forgot in her car when she'd arrived.

"I couldn't get away. It was too busy since I'd given some of my employees the time off they requested."

"So, no Thanksgiving plans?" Hannah looked around.

Vanessa followed her gaze, unsure what she was doing. "No."

"Since my holiday was cut short, and there seems to be enough vegetables still here, what would you think of re-creating that meal from a week or so ago? I've had dreams about it."

Vanessa froze, a lock in each hand.

"I mean, I'll help you cook, or at least chop things. I'm not asking you to do all the work," Hannah quickly added.

"That's actually a good idea." Vanessa dropped the padlocks and got a bag from the shed. "Help me pick what we need?"

In no time at all, they'd filled a tote with vegetables.

"I didn't buy a turkey this year." Vanessa waited for Hannah's disappointment, but it never came.

Instead, Hannah smiled. "I've never been a fan."

They secured the shed and gate, and walked toward their cars. All the talk of food made Vanessa's stomach express its audible disapproval. "It's a soup kind of night," she said, watching Hannah for her reaction.

Hannah grinned. "Oh, is it?"

"Unless you have plans." Vanessa gave a shrug she hoped appeared nonchalant.

Hannah stopped and pushed her hands into her back pockets. "Zero."

"Then, I should buy you a meal as thanks for today." Vanessa wasn't sure the invitation was a wise idea, but she'd spoken before thinking it through.

"As long as it's just dinner." Hannah's eyes twinkled as they stopped between their cars.

"It's just soup." Two could play this game. She'd missed their banter.

"Thank you, but I'll have to decline." Hannah held out her hands, palms up. "Unless you're willing to throw in a sandwich, too."

Vanessa grinned. "Get in. I'll drive."

As they left the school, Hannah received a call from work she had to take, but even that couldn't keep Vanessa from smiling. Hannah's early return had been a very nice surprise.

Chapter Twenty-one

When Hannah woke two weeks before Christmas with a sore throat, she couldn't believe her luck. With so much to do, it didn't stop her from going to work, but by lunchtime, her blouse stuck to her skin, and the floor tilted whenever she stood.

The last time she'd gotten sick had been on her thirty-seventh birthday. Whatever stomach bug she'd likely picked up on her way to New Orleans had stopped the party before it'd begun. Her friends had moped about the hotel suite with long faces until she'd insisted they take to Bourbon Street in her honor. When she returned home and stepped off the plane, she wondered how many tourists could say they went to the Big Easy and didn't have a single drop of alcohol.

When Zara entered her office, she caught Hannah with her hand down her shirt blotting perspiration from her chest.

"Okay. Wasn't expecting that." Zara dropped a folder on Hannah's desk. Her red-and-white-striped glasses resembled candy canes. "Here's the revised marketing strategy."

Hannah tossed the damp tissues and pulled another from the box. "Sorry." She wiped at her brow. "I think I'm coming down with something."

Zara took a step backward. "Don't you dare give it to me. I have a date with Derrick tonight and go home on Friday. If I show up to my mother's sick, she'll make me get back in my car. You know she's a total germophobe."

"Derrick?" Hannah sniffed and wiped her nose. "I thought you weren't interested in him anymore."

"I wasn't." Zara leaned against the wall. "He's all about finding serenity eighty percent of the time. It got boring after a few months."

Hannah would've lost interest long before that.

"Remember when I went on that retreat?"

"Yeah." It was when Hannah had asked Vanessa to be with her when she opened the box containing Bren's belongings. How had six months already passed?

Zara sighed. "I basically threw myself at him the entire time. All he wanted to do was meditate." She spotted the candy dish on Hannah's bookshelf and took a Hershey's Kiss. "But he contacted me a few weeks ago, saying he'd missed me in the weekly sessions and asked me to dinner. I thought I'd give him one more chance." She popped the chocolate into her mouth.

Hannah couldn't determine if Zara was swaying or if the problem was with her. God, her head ached.

"Hannah." Zara planted her hands on her hips. "Go home. You look like hell. Instacart some Pedialyte and NyQuil, and crawl in bed."

"I have work to do." She sneezed.

"It can wait." Zara flicked a finger at the folder on the desk. "Or, since you asked for that to be printed like you've turned into your dad, take it with you."

Hannah tried to pick up the folder. It took three tries.

Zara lifted Hannah's coat from the back of her door. "Get your bag. I'm having Annika drive you home."

Hannah glared at her. "Are you trying to kill me?" she whispered.

"Then go, but you're not staying here." Zara tossed her jacket at her. "Think of how much productivity you'll lose if you get half the company sick."

Okay, so Zara knew the one argument that would seal the deal. "Fine." Hannah stood on wobbly legs and held onto her desk until the room stopped spinning.

"Jesus." Zara pressed two fingers to her chin. "You can't drive, and I have a department meeting in thirty minutes. Who can I ask to take you home?"

Hannah collapsed into her chair. "No one. That's so wrong."

"I'm sure there are many people who wouldn't mind. Give them a bonus for their time."

Hannah shook her head. "It's not about that. The optics are bad. It looks like they have to say yes if they want to keep their job or stay in my good graces. That's not fair to them."

"I don't want to put you in a ride-share in this state. You look like you're about to pass out, and I'd worry about your safety." Zara pressed her lips together. "What about Vanessa?"

"God, no. I don't want her seeing me like this." Hannah blew her nose and rested her forehead on her desk. "I think I'm dying."

"I'm texting her."

Hannah raised her head so fast the room spun. Zara had her phone out. "No!"

Zara hesitated. "Tell me a better option."

With a huff, Hannah laid her head on her arms. "I don't have one. I can't think."

"Hang on. She's typing."

Hannah groaned. "I thought you deleted her number. I'm all sweaty. What's she going to think?"

"That you're sick?" Zara tapped at her screen. "She'll be here in fifteen minutes. Let's get you downstairs."

"She's leaving work in the middle of the day? Did you even ask her if she could?" Hannah examined a wet spot on her sleeve. Was it sweat, drool, or snot?

Zara scoffed. "Of course. I'm a professional. Now sit up, so I can help you."

"Find a paper bag and cut some eye holes in it for me. I'll wear it over my head until I get home."

That earned her a laugh.

"It'll be fine. She sees you covered in dirt and mud every week."

At least the kids were already out of school, so Hannah didn't have to worry about missing garden time. "That's different." She let out a little sob. "This time the gross stuff is coming out of *me*."

"She's simply driving you home. You'll survive. I promise." Zara held open her jacket.

"Too hot." Hannah waved it off and managed to stand.

Zara carried it along with Hannah's bag and held her elbow all the way to the lobby.

"Would you like to sit?"

"Yes, please." Why did she sound like such a baby? She really needed to pull herself together, but her muscles ached and her head was in the process of exploding. Sweat coated her upper lip.

Zara guided her to a sofa, then proceeded to pace between her and the main entrance.

"Go." Hannah waved her away. "I know you have your meeting."

"I'll tell Jen to cover for a few minutes if necessary." Zara typed, then pocketed her phone. "Have I mentioned how amazing she is?"

From where she'd rested her head on the back of the couch, Hannah asked, "Who? Vanessa?"

"No, silly, although she's a champ for coming to get you. I meant Jen." Zara let out a slow breath and whispered, "You should see the dress she's wearing today. It's not even tight, but the way it shows off her legs and—"

"Do not finish that sentence." Hannah raised her head. "Do you hear yourself?" She studied Zara, who'd stopped in front of her. "I can't have this. I'm serious."

Zara glanced around. "I was quiet."

Charles, the only other person within earshot, spoke on the phone and paid them no attention.

"I'm sharing this with you as your friend and not your employee. She gets my engine revving, that's all," Zara said.

Hannah let her head fall back. "Zara." It came out sounding like a moan. "You've got to stop."

"Fine. I won't talk about her anymore."

Eyes closed, Hannah tried to point at her, but she didn't know where Zara was with her constant pacing. "And no objectifying either."

"You know," Zara had taken the seat beside her based on the proximity of her voice, "you're no fun when you're in boss mode."

Good. That wasn't Hannah's aim. Running the company was serious business, and she placed importance on operating at the highest levels ethically and morally. It's why she'd convinced her parents to transition to lab-grown diamonds years ago. Zara might be a vice president, but as close as they were, she didn't realize everything Hannah dealt with or the pressure that came along with the job. Hannah could be fun on her off time.

At the sound of screeching tires, Hannah opened her eyes.

Vanessa flew inside and looked around. When she spotted them, she hurried over and sat beside Hannah. "You poor thing. You must be miserable." She held the back of her hand to Hannah's forehead, and Hannah closed her eyes at the cool touch.

"She wouldn't give me a bag." Hannah motioned toward Zara.

"Are you going to vomit?" Concern filled Vanessa's voice.

Hannah shook her head and winced as her brain ricocheted in her skull. Poor decision. "No."

Vanessa must have looked to Zara for help.

"She's worried you'll be repulsed by her, so she wanted to wear a paper bag over her head."

"I'm disgusting." Hannah covered her eyes with her arm.

Vanessa laughed, and the lovely sound made Hannah feel a tiny bit better.

"You just caught a bug. Let's get you home." She managed to get an arm behind her, and it took their combined efforts to get her to her feet. "I'm illegally parked out front, but don't worry, I know the CEO," she said into Hannah's ear.

"I've got your things." Zara followed them.

Hannah wobbled, but Vanessa's steady arm around her waist kept her upright.

"Almost there. You're doing great."

Zara held the door for them. "Are you going to be able to get her inside by yourself? She's not in the best shape."

"Don't worry. I've got it under control."

Vanessa's quiet assurance let Hannah's worries float away. Pain pounded inside her head, and even the light from the overcast sky hurt her eyes. Vanessa would get her home safely, and then Hannah could crash. Until then, maybe she could close her eyes for a few seconds.

The sudden forward motion of the car startled her. "I need to tell Zara good-bye."

"You already did." Vanessa rubbed her leg. "We're almost there. Just sleep."

Hannah cracked open her eyes. Huh? They weren't at headquarters anymore. Pain and brightness forced them closed again. Vanessa would wake her when they arrived at her condo.

"I need you to go up a few steps for me. One foot at a time, okay? I've got you."

Her building had an elevator. "Where are we?" She forced herself to look around. Her hand rested on a finial, and above, she recognized a bracket. A Victorian. "This isn't my place."

"That's correct. Now lift your foot and lean on me."

Even in her downgraded state, Hannah recognized how good Vanessa's body felt against hers. "Why did you bring me here?" She made it to the porch despite being in heels and the ground undulating.

Vanessa leaned her against a wall to unlock the door. "You're sick, and I'm going to take care of you. Everything I need is here." She pulled Hannah upright. "C'mon. Let's get you inside."

They made it as far as Vanessa's living room, where Hannah fell into a chair.

"Originally, I planned to put you in my bed, but I don't think you can manage an entire flight of stairs." She handed Hannah a couple of pills and a glass of water. "Take these. They'll help with your fever."

Vanessa covered the couch in a sheet and retrieved pillows and blankets. She faced Hannah, hands on her hips. "What do you want to do about your suit? It can't be comfortable."

Hannah slumped further into the chair and massaged her aching temples. "If I can borrow something, I'll change."

Vanessa arched an eyebrow. "Can you manage that alone?"

It didn't matter if she died trying, Hannah wasn't about to let Vanessa see her in her sweaty, naked state. "We'll see."

"I can help you." The corner of Vanessa's mouth pulled into a half smile. "It's nothing I haven't seen before."

Hannah rested her head against the cushion. "I'll be fine. May I have a bag for my clothing?"

"Do you want me to hang it up?"

Vanessa would have to wring it out first. "No, thanks. I'll have it dry-cleaned."

"Here are the sweats you wore last time. I chose a T-shirt for you though, so you don't get overheated." Vanessa laid them in her lap.

How had she moved so fast? Had Hannah lost track of time again? She grasped the clothes. If she rested a minute or two, she'd find enough energy to change.

Her first heel coming off startled her. Had she fallen asleep?

Vanessa removed the second one. "Let's get you out of that jacket. You'll feel so much cooler."

Hannah twisted away. "I'll do it. I'm gross." Her throat felt raw.

"You can barely move, darling. Let me help you."

Her arm slid from one sleeve. "Please." She couldn't recall ever being so mortified.

Vanessa hesitated. "If you really don't want me to touch you, I won't. But I'd like to get your fever down, and this isn't helping. I think you're hallucinating. You're pretty out of it."

Hannah reconsidered. Heat poured off her. "I'm really sweaty. I'm sorry."

"Hmm." Vanessa pulled the jacket off her other arm. "I didn't seem allergic to it in San Francisco, did I?" Her low chuckle seemed to be right by Hannah's ear.

Oh. It took Hannah a moment to realize what she meant. They'd never discussed that night. Neither had brought it up before today.

Vanessa worked quickly, pulling the shirt over her head as soon as she removed her blouse. She unhooked Hannah's bra through the material and slid it out one sleeve. Hannah's skirt followed, and Vanessa helped her stand to finish pulling up the pants. She deposited her on the couch with pillows propping her up.

Before Hannah closed her eyes, she noted the box of tissues and water beside her. Moments later, or perhaps longer, something cool touched her face. When she reached up, she discovered the soft dampness of a washcloth and Vanessa's hand.

"Let me. Relax." Vanessa lowered Hannah's arm to her side, where she gently held her wrist. The slow press of the blissfully soothing cloth resumed along Hannah's cheeks, chin, neck, and brow.

Had anything ever felt so amazing?

Vanessa left it lying across her forehead. "Sleep. I'm going to make you something to eat."

The tenderness in her words would've made anyone drift off with the marvelous sense of being cared for. But what had been the light touch to the top of Hannah's head? A kiss?

The next thing she knew, Vanessa was pulling her upright.

"Lean forward." She took Hannah's weight and wedged another pillow behind her.

The darkness outside hadn't been there the last Hannah remembered. "What time is it?"

"Close to nine. Your fever came down a degree or two. Can you manage to eat if I help you?" Vanessa sat beside her, their hips touching. She picked up a bowl from the coffee table.

Despite her stuffy nose, the tantalizing aroma and sight of the chicken noodle soup made Hannah's mouth water.

At her attempt to take the bowl, Vanessa hesitated. "Are you sure you can hold it?"

Hannah nodded. "I think so. The sleep helped. Or maybe it was the medicine."

After she handed her the soup, Hannah expected Vanessa to leave her to eat, but she remained where she was, watching her. Hannah ate a spoonful and moaned. "How is this so good?"

Vanessa smiled. "Stock made with vegetables from our garden."

Our? "You made this?" Of course, she did. What couldn't Vanessa do? Hannah took another bite, this one bigger.

"Mm-hmm. While you were sleeping."

"Where's yours?"

Vanessa blinked a few times. "I suppose I could eat with you." She rose and returned with a matching bowl and some crackers.

"I'm sorry you had to leave work." Hannah wanted to crawl under the area rug remembering how Zara had called Vanessa to take her home.

"I wondered how long it would take before you felt the need to apologize. When it comes to setting work aside for things that are important, I have flexibility." She ate a spoonful of noodles but continued to study her.

Hannah couldn't help but wonder if that was a dig, but she didn't want to read too much into it. Halfway through her bowl, she reached her max. "Sorry, I managed as much as I could. It was delicious."

"I'm glad you liked it. I was worried you wouldn't want anything." Vanessa took their dishes to the kitchen.

The room twisted. She really did have a fever. Hannah slid down until her head rested on the pillow. The pounding inside it had stopped, but it took so much energy to do the smallest thing. Even her eyelids felt heavy.

The next thing she knew, the room was dark. Light came from the kitchen, and the sound of running water. Voices, too. Vanessa's. Hannah would know her silky-smooth timbre anywhere. And the other, more difficult to make out but brittle and biting, Hannah had heard before. Vanessa's mother.

"So, I'm supposed to drive a car that's unsafe because you're too cheap to help me?"

"Mom, it's a headlight. I already sent your stipend for this month. How did you go through that much money already?"

A wave of heat rushed over Hannah, but this time it wasn't due to her illness. Vanessa must be talking to her while cleaning up, her phone on speaker. Hannah didn't want to eavesdrop, but where was she to go? She honestly didn't know if she could crawl to the bathroom by herself.

The water stopped, making the conversation clearer.

"You have no idea of my expenses. The bills, the doctors' visits. It all adds up. Which you'd know if you were ever around and not spreading your legs for any woman who shows you attention."

Hannah winced. Did Vanessa's mother actually believe the horrible things she said?

"Why'd you need to see the doctor?"

It sounded like the life had been sapped from Vanessa. Hannah would feel the same if she were in her position. Hell, she felt that way now, simply overhearing the vile woman.

Silence.

"Mom?"

"I haven't lately. Just in general, not that it's any of your business."

A pan clanked in the sink. "Last I checked, I pay all your bills except your cable, so it *is* my business."

"I have debts you don't even know about. You think you're so smart and know everything."

Hannah wanted to scream. Vanessa was one of the least arrogant people she'd met. Her mother was horrid. She hated that Vanessa let her talk to her like that.

"So, are you giving me the five hundred or not?"

For a headlight? Hannah would've leaped from the couch and through the phone line if she'd been able.

"Is that the only reason you called?"

A beat of silence. "You get your greediness from your deadbeat father, keeping everything for yourself while I live in poverty. After all I did for you."

Greedy? Vanessa's Accord had to be at least ten years old. Hannah scoffed and tried to take a sip of water to relieve her scratchy throat, but in her weakened state, the condensation on the glass made it slip through her fingers. It hit the wooden floor, splashing everywhere.

"I'm ending the call now, Mother."

When Vanessa entered the room, Hannah was hanging over the edge of the couch trying to dab at the spill with a handful of tissues.

"I was thirsty." Hannah attempted to sit up, but Vanessa had to help her. "I hope I haven't ruined your floor."

"Let me grab a towel. It'll be fine if I get it right away." She went to the kitchen. When she returned, she quickly wiped it up. "How long have you been awake?" The unnatural pitch of her voice told Hannah she knew she'd been overheard.

"Long enough." Hannah threw her arm over her face.

"I thought you were out." Vanessa sat on the edge of the sofa again. "She called while I was doing the dishes, so I put it on speaker. I'm sorry it woke you."

Hannah shook her head and let her arm fall. "I don't think that's what did." In the dark, she couldn't see Vanessa's face well enough to get a read on her. Sweat drenched Hannah's back again. Her vision swam, so she closed her eyes.

"It's almost time for more pills."

Something cool filled Hannah's palm. Long fingers, tiny scratches. Vanessa's hand. Had she taken it, or had Vanessa put it there? Even if she had, Hannah could claim she didn't know what she was doing in her sickened state, and it was true. The comfort of it almost made her forget everything that ached. "She's wrong, you know."

"Who?" Vanessa's hand tensed under her caress.

Who else? Hannah opened her eyes. "Your mom."

"About what?" Gently, Vanessa assessed Hannah's fever with the back of her hand again, then trailed her fingers along her temple, tenderly brushing stray hairs from her face.

"Everything." Hannah tumbled into darkness before hearing if Vanessa responded.

Chapter Twenty-two

With the meeting of her department heads looming in less than fifteen minutes, Hannah took the opportunity to remove her shoes beneath her desk and wiggle her toes. She should've chosen a more comfortable pair, but these matched her cherry red suit, and with Christmas only a week away, being festive never hurt anyone. Although, if she had to listen to Annika play that infernal Wham! song at her desk one more time, she might need to shove a few holly berries in her bleeding ears.

She checked her texts. Nothing from Vanessa. Hannah hadn't expected one but couldn't resist looking. They hadn't seen one another since Vanessa had driven Hannah to work to pick up her car last week, though they'd texted a few times. Vanessa had checked to see how she was feeling morning, noon, and night the first couple of days.

Regardless, Hannah needed to focus less on Vanessa and more on her upcoming presentation. Initially, when the garden project changed from Saturdays to Thursdays with the start of school, this meeting had conflicted with volunteering. However, moving her execs to a different day had been fortuitous. Her team seemed more energetic and responsive earlier in the week since they'd made the transition. Hannah needed to remember to shake things up once in a while to find better ways of working.

After retrieving her compact from her purse, she checked her makeup, ensuring her Dynamic Ruby lipstick hadn't exceeded its boundaries with a swipe of her thumb.

The holidays had crept up on her so fast. She supposed that's what happened when someone was as busy as she'd been. The tree lot she'd passed this morning made her think of Vanessa's farm and what it might be producing. The negative associations she'd formed after the trip had been slowly fading as each month passed. She'd been left with a majority of positive memories, when she stopped to think about it. Ones that held her attention hostage at inopportune times. In fact, it was this same gathering last week in which she'd caught herself remembering the way Vanessa had stood in the doorway in San Francisco, exuding sensuality through her posture, the sweep of her long legs beneath the short robe, her tantalizing display of cleavage, and the way the satin clung to her every glorious curve.

Zara appeared in the doorway, holding her laptop. "Almost ready?"

Hannah blinked, returning to the present. "I am." She felt around for her shoes.

"I just wandered right in. Not a soul in sight out there." Zara pointed toward where Annika's desk apparently sat empty.

"There's not?" Hannah had been tortured by that song for no reason.

Zara cocked an eyebrow. "No. You don't know where she is?"

"No. She takes her lunch from twelve to one."

"I wish you could hang out in my office for two hours. You'd leave with your jaw dragging on the floor."

"I just need to get through this Pride ring launch before I can focus on that, so let's go meet with everyone." Hannah had finished her presentation late last night, or more accurately, early this morning. Granted, it would've gone a lot faster if she had an assistant who could create an attractive slide deck.

Zara fell into step beside her, and their heels clicked against the tile as they headed toward the conference room.

"Since I had to drag you out of here when I left at six forty-five last night, I'm making you leave at five today and have a drink with me at that new rooftop bar that opened a few blocks from here."

Hannah let out an irritated sound. "Six."

Zara grabbed her elbow before she could enter through the heavy wooden door. "Five thirty. I'm not kidding."

It was easier to acquiesce than draw attention. "Fine. First round's on you." She walked inside.

While it went smoothly for the most part, questions about the new line made the meeting run late. Helga and Jing, the head of Diversity and Inclusion, contributed to the discussion around expectations for employees and the new commercials featuring real queer couples.

When Hannah got back to her office, it was almost four, and Annika was at her desk. She didn't have time for a conversation about where Annika had been earlier. With only ninety minutes before Zara dragged her away, she had a lot to accomplish. She closed her door.

❖

When the bartender set their drinks in front of them, they looked more like Hannah's high school chemistry experiments than cocktails women in their mid-to-late forties would order.

"The bourbon's in here," he said, pointing to a pipette. "You can control how much you squeeze in."

Why wouldn't she use all of it? Surely, they were designed so the amount mixed a revolver in the correct proportions. Hannah smiled sweetly at him. Last she checked, she was paying him to make her drink, not being forced to do it herself.

"Isn't this fun?" Zara kneed her.

A gimmicky short-lived craze, overpriced, and probably far more popular with tourists and guests at the hotel beneath them were more apt descriptors, but she hummed an agreeable sound that probably got lost in the thumping music.

At least the view was spectacular. The rotating lights of the Great Wheel, the islands in the distance, ferries crossing the sound, and the sky slinking into shades of gold and fuchsia made it worthwhile.

"I've been thinking about Jen."

"What about her?" Hannah approached the conversation with caution. The line between CEO and best friend was often blurred. They'd known each other for decades, and she wanted to support Zara, but she had a company to look out for, too.

"You know I like her, right?" Zara stared at the ice cubes she'd sent swirling in her glass.

Hannah needed to feel this out. "I've picked up on that. Or at least I knew you found her attractive."

"More than just that." Zara turned to her. "That's why she needs to be your assistant."

The determined look in her eyes told Hannah the importance of this conversation. "But I already have one."

"Yes, and she certainly doesn't deserve the salary she probably gets for the work she doesn't do. But I can't have Jen working for me, so I'm willing to make a trade."

A glance at Zara's glass told Hannah she hadn't consumed any alcohol despite her odd behavior. "You know how terrible she is. How's that going to solve anything?"

"I have hiring and firing privileges within my department. I'll bring her over, train her, inform her of the expectations for the job, and if she doesn't meet those, I'll put her on a performance plan. It's more than she deserves in an at-will employment state. Don't worry. I'll run it by Helga first. If Annika can't meet the minimum standards, I'll let her go." Zara lifted her glass. "Do you see how serious I am? I'm willing to venture into the HR dungeon." She took a sip. "Mmm. Not bad."

"You want to date Jen?"

Zara held up a finger. "I want the *option* of dating her. Hell, I just want the opportunity to be able to flirt with her a little, see if the attraction might be more than one-sided. I was at Pacific Place last weekend and saw three or four things I thought she'd love, but I can't give them to her because they'd look too personal coming from a boss to a subordinate."

Usually, Hannah was scrambling to find gifts before Christmas. December kept her busier than other months, and shopping always slipped her mind. Not this year. She'd bought Vanessa's gift over a month ago and nearly vibrated when she imagined the look on Vanessa's face when she gave it to her. Thought had gone into it. Again, something she wasn't used to. Her parents often received whatever attractive boxed set of cologne or perfume the department stores featured, or something of that nature. Zara was a little easier to buy for, her love of chocolate and anything bright and quirky making for easy options.

"So?" Zara studied her.

Hannah returned to the conversation at hand. The switch would allow her to get rid of Annika, and she could really use Jen's skills, if they were as good as Zara claimed them to be, especially with the upcoming launch. And if Annika didn't work out, it wouldn't be Hannah having to fire her parents' former assistant. "Let's do it. First of the year."

"Really?" Zara's squeal turned heads, and the look on her face informed Hannah she hadn't expected her to agree.

"I could use the help, and who am I to get in the way of love?"

"Hey, no one said anything about love. I'd just like the possibility of seeing what's underneath her sexy dresses, at least for now."

Hannah scowled. "What happened to meditation man?"

"Exactly. That's all he cares about." Zara's finger hovered an inch away from Hannah's nose. "After our date, he suggested stopping at a park so we could have a mini session."

"Are you sure that's what he meant? Maybe it was a double entendre." Hannah tried not to cringe.

"Oh, no. It wasn't." Zara threw back a mouthful of her cocktail. "We meditated, though I insisted on only ten minutes."

Hannah grimaced. "Yikes. Okay, then. Monday morning, we'll inform Jen and Annika of the switch."

"What should we tell them is the reason?"

"We'll tell them I need an experienced EA, which Jen is. Annika might have been assistant to my father while he was CEO, but she's never worked for any other C-level execs. She performs receptionist duties at best." She turned to Zara. "That's another option. Charles notified me he plans to go back to school next fall. If Annika can't manage in her capacity as your EA, we could consider her for the front desk."

Zara scoffed. "You'd have to glue her down."

"I'd need to set firm expectations. I did a poor job of that when I took over, reluctant to rock the boat until everyone adjusted to me being CEO. Looking back, it was the wrong move. I allowed her to take advantage of me."

"Jen will take a lot of tasks off your plate. I think you'll find you have much more time for the important things." Zara motioned for the bartender.

"Everything's important. The success of the company rests on the decisions I make."

"Sure." Zara rolled her eyes. "But you have dozens of highly intelligent professionals supporting you whom you should be letting have more control. Let the experts in their individual fields make ninety percent of the decisions. Make the crucial remaining ones." When Hannah didn't answer, she continued. "Think of it this way. The president of the United States isn't deciding if whole wheat or sourdough rolls are served at the White House Correspondents' Dinner."

She had a point.

"Two more, ladies?" The bartender bussed their empty glasses.

"For me, yes." Zara turned to her expectantly.

Hannah nodded. "Same, but I don't need the…" She pinched her forefinger and thumb together.

"No pipette. Got it." He moved down the bar.

Zara threw an arm around Hannah's shoulders. "Things are going to improve for you and me next year. I just know it." She kissed her on the cheek. "I'm going to pee." Zara slid off her stool, took her purse, and wandered away.

She hadn't been gone twenty seconds before a brunette took her spot. Her hair fell to the middle of her back, and the dip of her dress went almost as low in the front.

"I noticed your girlfriend left. Mind if I join you?"

At earlier points in her life, Hannah would've been ecstatic to have this opportunity, but the woman's appearance didn't generate the same response tonight. "My friend, and she's in the restroom."

"Ah." The brunette didn't relinquish the seat. "I'm glad to hear you're not together, although if I'm honest, I was hoping she'd gone."

"Your drinks." The bartender set them on the bar, not seeming to notice Hannah's company had changed.

"Could I borrow your pen?" The woman took it from him and flipped over a coaster. She slid it toward Hannah. "My number. I'm staying at the hotel tonight and tomorrow night. I hope to hear from you." She disappeared just as Zara returned.

"Um, who was that?" Zara hung her purse under the bar.

Hannah glanced down. "Melanie, apparently." She folded the thick cardstock in half and pushed it away.

"I see." Zara scanned the busy room. "There used to be a time when you were excited to get a woman's number."

"And where she's staying." This time, the proposal had stirred nothing in Hannah. Had she been working too much? Perhaps being sick had thrown her off her game. Thoughts of Vanessa's hand on her forehead, the way she brushed stray hairs away from her face, and generally took care of her for two days came rushing in.

Zara touched her elbow. "She likes you, too."

"You barely saw her." And Zara had caught none of their short conversation.

"I wasn't talking about the brunette." She sampled Hannah's drink.

If Zara hadn't been talking about Melanie, was she referring to Vanessa?

"Did you see how worried she was when she came flying into the lobby?" Zara raised her eyebrows. "Or how quickly she managed to get beer and pizza and show up on moving day?"

Hannah glanced over. "How fast?"

"She made it there in thirty-five minutes."

Damn.

"You were basically strangers and asked her on a road trip, and she went." Zara sipped her own drink this time. "I know you like her, too, beyond sleeping with her because she's hot, because she most definitely is." She let out a long whistle.

Hannah watched the bartender make a margarita and plunge a test tube of tequila in it before she answered. "Yes, I like her."

"Then do something about it."

"I can't." Hannah rubbed her forehead.

"Why not?"

She looked at Zara. "I promised her I wouldn't. What she learned on the trip was traumatizing, and she asked me to give her space."

Zara looked at her through narrowed eyes. "So, you show up every week to garden with her?"

"I made a commitment to those kids. It's simply a bonus that she's also there."

"And she doesn't seem to mind?" Zara frown made her appear she didn't believe it.

"I don't think so, but even if she did, she's not going to turn me away because she knows me being there each week is good for the program. She told me as much." Her body warmed thinking back to when Vanessa had shared her opinion of her as a positive role model.

Zara seemed to contemplate it a moment. "Did she say for how long?"

"No. She's working through some stuff." Hannah shrugged. "It doesn't matter. She can take as long as she needs."

"You really mean that, don't you?"

"I do." Why would she want Vanessa to take a step she wasn't ready for, when she wasn't in the right headspace, or not at a point where a relationship might be a positive thing in her life?

"And you're not impatient? Don't tell me you've gone without sex since San Francisco." Zara's eyes grew huge.

"If I wanted it, I could have it." Hannah flicked the bent coaster. "I want more."

Zara nodded, and a faraway look came over her. Finally, she laughed. "Yeah, I get that. Thanks again for switching assistants with me." She lifted her cocktail.

Hannah clinked glasses with her. "Here's to exciting changes for both of us."

Chapter Twenty-three

Vanessa assessed the two crimson poinsettias she'd placed on either side of her fireplace. In the background, Bing Crosby softly crooned, putting her in the holiday spirit. She moved the flowers to the mantel, then down again after deciding they competed with the green garland she'd strung just below it. Usually, she didn't do much decorating for Christmas. It was just her, after all, but fussing was better than picking up her phone for the sixteenth time when her desire to call Hannah became too strong.

The small tree she'd placed on a table in the corner glowed with strings of white lights. Ornaments or simplicity? Tradition won out, and she pulled the small box from the plastic storage container. Inside, the mostly homemade creations appeared innocent, but the reminders they evoked were not. She carefully lifted one out and discarded the protective tissue. The center featured a smiling, gap-toothed photo of her in an ugly striped shirt surrounded by green and red elbow macaroni. Second grade, she knew, without turning it over. The genuine smile had been for Miss Ammen, with her long dark hair and love of headbands. Vanessa's crush had been massive.

The warmth of the memory faded as she unwrapped each one and hung them on the branches. These were things a mother should own, should want to keep, but hers had thrust them at her one Christmas when Vanessa dropped off her gift, saying, "I'm decluttering. Getting rid of old junk." Initially, Vanessa had wanted to throw the box in a dumpster between Tacoma and home, but a severe rainstorm negated the impulse. She was glad it had. Like with Miss Ammen, they held positive remembrances she cherished, even if her mother didn't.

With the living room decorated and the packaging put away, she longed for something to keep her mind busy. A quick search of the TV showed a few holiday movies playing, but she'd missed the start of them, and none streaming were ones she hadn't already seen. She turned it off.

Her phone on the coffee table called to her. She wondered what Hannah was doing.

Hannah's parents were in the Bahamas, but Zara had invited Hannah to *her* family's Christmas Eve celebration in Everett, though Hannah had insinuated she didn't want to go. Apparently, Zara's father's political beliefs and his penchant for discussing them made it stressful. Had she gotten out of it?

Sonja and Jeff had invited Vanessa to the farm. Spending the holidays there in the past had been fun, with giant bonfires and too much spiked eggnog and hot buttered rum. She'd thanked them but declined. This year, Sonja's parents were visiting from Hong Kong, and while Vanessa knew they'd never make her feel like an outsider, the couple deserved to have some time alone with them since they saw each other so little.

Just thinking of Jeff's tasty drinks made her stomach rumble, so she went to the kitchen. The refrigerator held little. With the Christmas season so busy, she had no time to shop, and now stores wouldn't be open. Poor planning on her part, but the hollow ache in her belly didn't care. The pantry offered little more.

Her phone beckoned again. Was her need to talk to Hannah so strong because of the holiday, and most people had loved ones around? Vanessa was no stranger to being alone, so it didn't seem like loneliness was the cause of her yearning to make contact.

She called Hannah. The phone rang twice.

"Hi, you."

Hannah's ebullience lifted Vanessa's spirits. "Hi. What're you doing?"

A pause. "I'm actually at work finishing up a project."

"On Christmas Eve?"

Hannah laughed. "Yeah, it's a ghost town around here. I think I'm the only one in the building."

"I guess this means you decided against Everett."

"Work needed to be done, and I couldn't deal with the pontificating." Hannah cleared her throat. "Are you in Ashland or Seattle?"

"I'm at home." Vanessa made a split decision. "And I'm starving and didn't have time to go to the store. If I ordered a pizza, would you be interested in eating half?"

"Do you think any places will be open?"

She hadn't considered that. "I thought you could order one every day of the year, but I'll check it out. Does that mean you're in?"

"Definitely. I was about to leave here, anyway. Could you get some of the cinnamon dessert things if they have them?" Hannah's voice dropped a level below raspy.

Vanessa's skin tingled. "Mm-hmm." Opening her mouth to speak might've resulted in her voice cracking.

"Nice. I'll head out soon. Shall I try to pick up some drinks if I can find someplace open?"

"No, I'm stocked in that department. Just bring you." And what a gift it would be. Already, Vanessa's evening had improved simply by hearing her voice.

"Hey, I have a small Christmas present for you. Is it okay if I give it to you tonight? I planned to run it over tomorrow if you were in town."

Vanessa wondered what it was. She hadn't been expecting anything even though she had something for Hannah. "Of course, I can give you yours, too."

"Does half an hour work?"

"Whenever you'd like. I'll be right here." Thirty minutes seemed too long to wait, but Vanessa wasn't about to tell her to hurry. "What toppings do you want?"

After discussing the order, they hung up. Vanessa googled her favorite place and thanked Santa they were open. The estimate for the delivery time almost coincided with Hannah's arrival.

Hannah pulled up twenty-three minutes after they'd hung up, not that Vanessa had been counting. She wore a dark green, double-breasted suit and heels.

Vanessa hadn't been expecting that. "Look at you." She made a point of closing her mouth.

With a smile, Hannah held out her arms and made a production of doing just that. "What?"

"You look really nice. I thought you'd be in jeans if no one was at headquarters today."

Hannah stepped inside and deposited a tall bag on the floor. She slipped off her heels and put them beside it. "No one in my building, at least this late. People are always working, even on holidays, I'm afraid. There's no getting around that when offering customer service. They get extra pay though, if that helps wipe the sad look from your face." Hannah took her chin and playfully gave it a little shake before moving past her. "It's so pretty and festive in here."

"Thanks." Vanessa's thoughts lingered on Hannah's touch. "The food will be here soon. Do you want something comfortable to change into?"

Hannah sank into the sofa. "Aren't you tired of me borrowing your clothing?"

"I don't think my bras will fit you, so at least they're safe." Vanessa winked. "Follow me." In the laundry room, she opened the dryer and pulled out lounge and sleepwear options, the non-sexy kind, though Hannah in any of her clothes tended to make her feel things. "Take your pick. You can change in here or the bathroom."

The doorbell rang.

"Hurry. I'm starving."

"You better not start without me," Hannah said.

Vanessa threw a look over her shoulder, catching Hannah averting her gaze from her ass. She shivered.

They ate on the couch. The TV softly played, but they never settled on any particular show, spending the time talking instead. When Vanessa returned from storing the leftovers, Hannah flipped through Christmas movies.

"Do you want to watch *Love Actually*? I adore it."

So did Vanessa. "Emma Thompson."

"When she finds the necklace..." Hannah's eyes widened.

"And then he doesn't give it to her?" Vanessa clasped a hand to her chest. "I should get the tissues now."

She opened the ottoman and retrieved an afghan. When she settled beside Hannah, she spread it over their legs.

"I don't have any crocheted blankets." Hannah ran it between her fingers. "I forget how comforting they are."

Vanessa studied it. "I think it's knitted."

"Did someone make it for you?"

She shook her head. "I bought it, but isn't this what knitting looks like?"

"I don't think so. Doesn't crochet use two..." She batted her forefingers together.

"Lightsabers?" Vanessa asked, biting back a laugh.

Hannah narrowed her eyes. "Smartass. No, those needle things."

"I honestly don't know, but I think this is knitted."

"Crocheted." Hannah's lips curved into a mischievous smile.

Vanessa couldn't stifle her own. "I guess we have to agree to disagree if we're ever going to watch the movie."

Hannah lightly rocked into her before hitting play.

Vanessa settled in, warmed by their banter. Or, if she were honest, heated by their closeness. Either was fine with her.

❖

The next thing she knew, pins and needles shot through her arm beneath her. She tried to move but couldn't. The gentle rise and fall of her head and the cushion of a body against her front soothed her, but where was she? Gradually, the haze of sleep melted away. Sandwiched between Hannah and the back of the sofa, she lay half on top of her with the afghan covering them. She rose slightly. The TV was off, the only light in the room the soft glow from her little Christmas tree.

"Go back to sleep, sweetheart." Hannah's garbled words hit Vanessa smack in the chest.

Was Hannah fully awake? Vanessa fought to steady her breathing at the unexpected endearment.

Hannah began to rub her back as Vanessa freed her pinned arm and returned her head to Hannah's chest. At some point, she'd thrown her leg over Hannah's hip and her good arm around her waist. Hannah's breast nestled below her chin, and this close, her scent, warmth, and softness overwhelmed Vanessa's senses.

"You missed the end of the movie." Hannah continued the slow caress of Vanessa's spine, her voice clearer now.

Her touch made Vanessa's eyelids heavy, but she managed a small laugh. "I've probably seen it twenty times."

"That explains why you were out so fast."

Oh, no. How quickly had she fallen asleep? And had she draped herself over Hannah in the process? Embarrassment burned in her cheeks. "Are you uncomfortable?"

Hannah's touch faltered. "I'm perfect."

Relief flooded Vanessa, and she relaxed into Hannah's embrace. This was nice, something they'd shared briefly in San Francisco, but truth be told, they hadn't done much sleeping or cuddling. So, she let herself enjoy the moment. If only her eyes and brain weren't so tired. She fought against it for a few minutes, but when Hannah's hand stilled and her breathing evened, Vanessa followed suit.

❖

Vanessa took the leftover pizza from the fridge and put a slice on a plate. "Do you want your breakfast warmed?" she called when she heard Hannah's footsteps on the stairs.

Hannah came into the kitchen, her hair wet, face scrubbed clean, and wearing more of Vanessa's clothing. "Just the cinnamon twists. I like cold pizza." She moved around Vanessa to the cupboard beside the sink. "Want coffee?"

"Sure." Vanessa had taken the time after her shower to dress, comb her hair, and put on a little makeup, so she hadn't had a chance to fix herself a cup.

Hannah pulled out two mugs and filled them. She added creamer and handed one to Vanessa. "Merry Christmas."

"Merry Christmas." Vanessa tapped their mugs together before blowing on hers and taking a sip. The microwave dinged, and she handed Hannah her plate. "The pizza's on the table. I'll be right there."

She heated hers and joined her. "I'm sorry it's not pancakes or something better."

"It's one of my favorite foods, and I enjoy it this way. " Hannah looked at her. "Am I keeping you from something today?"

"No. You?"

"No. I'd probably just be working." Hannah tossed a piece of pepperoni into her mouth.

Vanessa assessed her. "You spend too much time there. On your phone or laptop, too. Don't you worry about burning out?"

Hannah leaned back in her chair. "You sound like Zara. Are you two texting again?"

"Not since you were sick. I just worry about you." Vanessa tried to hide her vulnerability by lifting her coffee to her lips.

"Do you normally see your mom today?"

So much for any discussion of Hannah's work/life balance. "I'll drop off her gift either tonight or tomorrow. She usually spends the day with a few of the women who live in her complex."

Hannah's brow wrinkled. "Does that upset you?"

"You've heard her. What do you think?" There *had* been a time when Vanessa would've loved to spend Christmas with just the two of them, but that dream had died decades ago. "Don't worry, she feels the same."

Hannah gave a quick nod. "Fair enough."

There wasn't anything fair about her relationship with her mother, but Vanessa didn't point that out.

"Would you like your gift?"

Vanessa grinned. "I thought you'd never ask."

Hannah skipped into the living room to retrieve it from under the little tree.

"Would you please grab both of them? Be careful with it."

Hannah returned, then set Vanessa's present to her on the table. She handed Vanessa the gift bag. "You go first. I've been dying to give it to you."

Vanessa carefully opened the sealed top and gasped. "A purple phalaenopsis." She lifted the plant out against the sting of tears. "Orchids are the diamonds of the flower world, and these are some of the most highly adored."

Hannah beamed.

Vanessa set it on the table, then stood and kissed her on the cheek. "I love it. Thank you." She returned to her chair. "Now you."

Hannah took her seat and pulled the box Vanessa had carefully wrapped closer. "It's heavy." She tore off the paper and peeled back the tape on the lid. As she removed the gift and the surrounding tissue, her eyes grew bigger. "It's beautiful." She held up the speckled green pot.

"I thought you could put the Chinese evergreen in your kitchen in it if you don't have something for it yet. I made it in my pottery class." She'd wondered if a handmade gift was lame, but Hannah seemed to like it.

"It's still in its sad plastic container." Hannah turned it over and traced the VH inscribed into the bottom with her fingertip. "I can't believe I own an original Vanessa Holland."

"They're rare. I only made two before I stopped going." Vanessa turned her orchid to face her. "This will look nice in the first pot I made, even though the piece didn't come out perfectly round." At first, she'd thought she'd enjoyed the class, but as the weeks passed, she admitted she simply appreciated that it distracted her from thoughts of Hannah, and as time went on, she hadn't needed that anymore. How long ago that seemed. Now they were spending Christmas day together.

The morning meandered into afternoon, and with gifts exchanged, they settled in the living room under the twinkling lights of the tree and watched the football game. When Vanessa found a lasagna in the freezer, she decided delivering her mother's gift could wait until tomorrow. She stepped outside to call her, wish her Merry Christmas, and let her know. She didn't want Hannah overhearing another of her mom's rants. Thankfully, she got her voicemail.

After dinner, they started another movie. The day had been so relaxing, it wasn't long before Vanessa let her eyes close. When she opened them, Hannah was gone. She rose, angry at herself for falling asleep—again—and for caring that Hannah hadn't woken her to say good-bye. She stuffed the blanket into the ottoman. It had been such a lovely day until now, too.

The sound of the front door opening made her jump. She rushed to the entryway.

"You're awa—" Hannah stopped, her eyes going wide. "What's wrong?" She closed the door and ran her hands over Vanessa's shoulders.

Vanessa only shook her head and tried to step away.

"Oh." Hannah eased back. "You thought I left. I just went outside to make a work call."

As Hannah said it, Vanessa noticed Hannah's heels still under the coat rack. Her relief that knowing she hadn't gone was replaced by a slight irritation that she was working on Christmas. "It's fine."

Hannah caressed her cheek. "I understand how something like that might affect you. I wouldn't have left without waking you."

"Really?" Vanessa looked into her eyes, reveled in her tender touch, craved the feel of her body against hers. Other than accidentally falling asleep on the couch together, they'd rarely been this close since San Francisco.

Hannah brushed her knuckles along Vanessa's jaw. "Really."

She shouldn't, but Vanessa wanted more. She fisted her hands into the bulky sweatshirt material at Hannah's waist and pulled her closer.

Hannah's pupils grew large with arousal. "Space. You wanted space," she murmured, blinking slowly. "Tell me to go, and I will."

Only a few inches, if that, separated them, and it was too much.

Hannah flicked her tongue over her lips, leaving them glistening.

Vanessa's ragged breathing seemed to echo in the small alcove as she tried to make sense of it all. Of Hannah, standing before her smelling of Vanessa's conditioner, looking so inviting in Vanessa's clothes, her hand warm and gentle on Vanessa's face. And yet, looking so unsure.

Then Vanessa knew. It had to be her. She'd been the one to make the pronouncement, to put the brakes on. And while Hannah might not have disappeared into her own life, she certainly hadn't pressured Vanessa into anything more than she wanted to give. If this moved forward, it had to be Vanessa's call.

"Tell me to go." Hannah's words contradicted the desire in her eyes. Their noses brushed. Vanessa couldn't find her voice.

"Ask me to stay," Hannah whispered.

Vanessa kissed her hard.

Unleashed, Hannah responded, nearly bending her backward as she returned it.

They devoured one another, their mouths hot and greedy, their hands roaming, like they'd been restraining themselves from this very moment ever since they'd returned from San Francisco. Hadn't they?

Vanessa slapped the air until she found the light switch that plunged the foyer into darkness, then yanked Hannah's shirt over her head. She admired her breasts, then pressed her against the wall. She cupped her face and met her eyes. "This can't mean anything. Do you understand?"

Hannah blinked, then again, looking dazed. She nodded.

"Tell me you understand." She wanted Hannah, but offering her more now wasn't fair. *This* was all she had to give.

Hannah turned her head and kissed Vanessa's palm. "I do."

Vanessa brought their lips together again. She'd missed this, the headiness of Hannah moving against her, the heat of her skin under Vanessa's fingertips. She moved her mouth down Hannah's chest and sucked her nipple as she slid her hand beneath the waistband of Hannah's sweatpants. Her fingers found their destination, and they both moaned.

Hannah widened her stance and pushed into Vanessa's touch.

Vanessa entered her at the same time she switched her attention to Hannah's other breast, drawing a strangled cry from her. She could have spent all night right there in her entryway, unraveling Hannah, but when Hannah dug her fingers into Vanessa's back with a guttural, "Please," she relented. Together they extricated Hannah from her sweats and Vanessa added another finger.

"Touch yourself," Vanessa whispered.

Hannah did. Her eyes fell closed.

"Open your eyes, darling." This, just this—Hannah, so beautiful, so tight around her fingers, breathing like she'd run a six-minute mile—electrified Vanessa.

"I...I'm not sure I can stand." Hannah grasped Vanessa's shoulders.

Vanessa kissed the soft swell of her breast. "I've got you. All you have to do is come for me."

"Kiss me again."

She did, slow and long and deep, and Hannah came. After a moment, Vanessa helped slide her sagging body down the wall, then sat on the second stair beside her and ran her fingers through Hannah's hair.

Finally, Hannah opened her eyes and stretched. With a sultry look, she moved between Vanessa's knees, "Take off your shirt."

Vanessa pulled it over her head.

"Your bra, too." Hannah waited, her hands on Vanessa's thighs, watching every move. "Very nice," she murmured at the sight of Vanessa's bare breasts.

The huskiness of her voice made Vanessa even wetter.

Hannah leaned forward, holding Vanessa at the waist. She licked a line up Vanessa's stomach and over her chest until Vanessa drew her into another kiss.

Vanessa wove her fingers into Hannah's hair, wanting to prolong the sublime while needing to end the torture. When Hannah gently pushed her back and pulled off her yoga pants, Vanessa rested her elbows on a higher step and watched as Hannah descended between her legs. At the first touch of Hannah's tongue to her center, she moaned and let her head drop back.

Hannah licked and sucked in no apparent hurry, occasionally flicking her tongue inside her. When she filled Vanessa, the delicious stretch combined with her gifted mouth was too much. Vanessa's foot flailed, kicking over the brass umbrella stand with a clang.

"Fuck me, please." Vanessa gripped a baluster, the fingers of her other hand in Hannah's hair.

Hannah's eyes were closed, her face serene, and she was so goddamned beautiful.

What were they doing? Was this a mistake?

Vanessa shut her mind to the questions and allowed herself to be led into pleasure. But it never progressed beyond that.

Then it hit her. No matter how good this felt or how skilled Hannah was, *it* wasn't going to happen. She wanted to sob in frustration.

"Hey," she said, gently pushing Hannah away.

"Did I do something wrong?" Hannah sat back on her heels, but she didn't remove her fingers.

Vanessa closed her eyes. "Not at all. I just don't think I can get there." She offered Hannah a sad smile. "Quickies and I have never been a good mix."

Hannah looked thoughtful. "But you can give yourself orgasms. Right?" She took Vanessa's hand and pressed it to her center. "I'll help, or I can just watch. It's up to you."

Vanessa had already begun to move her fingers in small circles. "You sure?"

Hannah laughed as she lowered her gaze from Vanessa's face to the apex of her legs. "Of course. I want you to feel good. Whatever you need, just tell me."

"Move like you were before."

Hannah began to thrust in time with Vanessa's movements.

Kisses along her thighs, her knees, and close to where she frantically rubbed helped bring her along. The orgasm she thought impossible moments before was building. Vanessa wanted to sing with joy.

Hannah cupped her breast, squeezed, then played with her nipple. She pinched and tugged, and when Vanessa's yesses piled atop one another, Hannah curled her fingers into that perfect spot.

Vanessa tensed and shattered.

Hannah continued gentle thrusts as Vanessa finished with a few final strokes, eking out every last sensation. At length, she removed her fingers and cradled Vanessa on her lap. She left tiny kisses along her forehead as Vanessa's breathing slowed.

Eventually, they parted and started pulling on their clothing.

Once dressed, Hannah gathered Vanessa into a loose embrace and kissed her slowly.

"Thank you for the orchid," Vanessa said after breaking it off. "No one's ever given me flowers before."

Hannah held her at arm's length. "You're kidding."

"Bren was never the type." She gave a short laugh. "But you already knew that. And with others, maybe they thought since I'm around them all the time, I wouldn't want any." She tightened her hold on Hannah. "But I absolutely adore it."

Hannah simply kissed her again. When she pulled away, she smiled. "I love my one-of-a-kind pot you made me."

Vanessa didn't want her to go, but they separated, and Hannah began to gather her belongings. When she had, Vanessa walked her through the house.

Hannah winced, her hand on the doorknob. "My knees are letting me know I'm too old for sex on wooden floors." She grinned. "No matter how good it is."

"I'm so sorry. I should've told you to pull the rug over or gotten you a pillow." Vanessa's face burned.

Hannah ran her thumb over Vanessa's cheekbone. "That would've taken the spontaneity from the moment. I'll be fine." She opened the door.

"What if there's permanent damage?"

Hannah smiled, pausing on the porch. "You'll have to take care of me." She descended the steps.

Vanessa let out a long-suffering sigh. "I'll have to drive you everywhere. Work, your doctors' appointments, the store. But then I'll feel guilty about all those vehicle emissions, so you'll probably need to move in with me if it's a chronic condition."

Hannah's eyes widened. "What will your neighbors say about the two white-haired old ladies living together?"

"They'll probably say, 'Look how cute those lesbians are. The younger one wears whatever the older one knits for her.'"

Hannah laughed. "Crochets."

They smiled at one another as Hannah slowly walked backward to her car. "Merry Christmas, Vanessa."

Vanessa's body still hummed. Merry Christmas, indeed.

Chapter Twenty-four

The bounce in Hannah's gait as she climbed Vanessa's stairs mirrored her spirits. When a longtime supplier called at the last minute offering her tickets he couldn't use to the New Year's Eve party at Chihuly Garden and Glass, she accepted but anticipated having to go alone or possibly drag Zara along. Hannah had tempered her hope Vanessa would accept her invitation, but to her surprise, she had, even after Hannah informed her it required formal attire.

Hannah hadn't seen her since Christmas, and the unexpected happenings in Vanessa's foyer had filled her dreams—and waking hours—for days.

Moments after Hannah knocked, Vanessa opened the door wearing a midnight blue, off-the-shoulder gown.

Hannah grasped the door frame for support. "Wow, you look fantastic." She appraised Vanessa, letting her gaze sweep from her perfectly styled up-do to her matching heels. "How'd you manage this in such little time?"

Vanessa laughed, the lightness in her voice making Hannah's breath catch in her throat. "Probably the same way you did. You look beautiful." She reached out to feel the fabric of Hannah's black dress. "Gorgeous."

"Thank you." She followed Vanessa inside, trying not to look too closely at the bottom of the stairs, recalling what'd occurred there the last time she'd been here. "I'm told we'll be able to see the Space Needle fireworks through the glass ceiling, or we can find a place in Seattle Center to view them."

"It depends on if we want champagne at midnight. I doubt they'll allow us to take it outside."

Hannah had been hoping for more than bubbly when the clock struck twelve. "Or, I could show you my new place. I have a bottle chilling in my refrigerator. Belltown is only a few minutes by car."

"I'd like that." Vanessa smiled. "It'd give me an opportunity to see how your plant looks in the pot."

"Oh, he loves it. I think he's grown two inches."

"He?" Vanessa bit her lip, hiding her smile.

Hannah nodded. "Ralph. He's thriving." Would a glass of champagne turn into something more? She hoped so, but she knew Vanessa would need to make the first move. Even though Hannah had agreed to the "this can't mean anything" statement on Christmas, it'd been harder than she'd anticipated to stay true to her answer.

"You're too cute." Vanessa squeezed her arm. "Let me grab my clutch, and I'll be ready to go."

"Take your time." She already missed Vanessa's fleeting touch.

Vanessa's phone rang before she'd taken two steps. She retrieved it from the table. "Hospital?" She frowned at the screen before accepting the call. "Hello?" The frown turned into a scowl. "Where is she now? For how long?" She paced in front of the window. "I see. Yes, I know where it is." Vanessa pulled the clip holding her hair in place, and it tumbled to her shoulders.

Hannah's morale fell with it.

"I'm on my way." Vanessa hung up.

"Is everything all right?"

"My mother slipped and broke her hip. She had to undergo emergency surgery. They said she'll be admitted for a few days, but when she's stable, they won't release her unless a family member is able to care for her around the clock. If not, they'll send her to a rehabilitation facility."

"You've got to be kidding." Bitterness filled Hannah's mouth.

Vanessa turned. "No." She kicked off her shoes and undid her bracelet, dropping it on the table.

"You're actually going to do it?" Hannah wished her incredulity hadn't leeched into her tone quite so much, but it was only a fraction of what boiled inside. "Send her to the rehab place. She won't be able to get up your stairs, anyway."

"I'll put a hospital bed in my living room so she can convalesce. She's alone and the only family I have." She faced Hannah. "When my father left, she could've abandoned me, too, but she didn't. I'm taking her in. She's my mother."

"She certainly hasn't acted like one." Hannah put her hands on her hips. "You might've been better off without her."

Vanessa turned away. "This isn't your concern."

"It involves you, and I care about you." Reasoning with Vanessa wasn't working. It was time to be brutally honest. "People don't talk to someone they love like that."

Vanessa froze. "I don't need your input in this. I can handle it myself."

Hannah came around so she could look her in the eye. "And by that, do you mean let her emotionally and verbally abuse you?"

"I'm helping her out." Vanessa threw things in her bag.

"For weeks? Months? I can't believe you're considering this. How can you put yourself in that situation after everything your mother has said and done to you? Look how hard you've worked in therapy to get past this."

"Why are you doing this?" Vanessa's expression held both anger and disappointment.

"I've heard her. She's horrible. You're not that little girl seeking her mother's approval anymore. You don't have to do this." Hannah tried to touch her arm, but Vanessa pulled away.

"You don't know everything about my childhood. You weren't there. Besides, who are you to tell me what to do?"

Hannah didn't know *what* they were to one another. They weren't dating. Friends didn't fit. Two people who'd had sex seemed the closest match, but they felt like so much more than that. She glanced at the time. "I have to call my sapphire dealer soon, but we can discuss this more when I'm done."

"Tonight? Typical." Vanessa scoffed. "Putting work first, like having a conversation with me isn't as important." She shook her head. "You know what, I can't deal with," she drew a circle in the air in Hannah's direction, "any of this right now, anyway. I have enough on my plate, and you clearly don't understand. Why don't you just go."

Hannah held up her hands, palms out. "I can reschedule the call. Let's talk."

"Just go, Hannah." Vanessa didn't so much as glance at her.

"When will you be back?"

"I don't know." Vanessa looked up. "Don't concern yourself with it."

The remark hit like an arrow to Hannah's chest. Whatever they had was slipping away, and she was unable to stop it.

"I'll see you out." Vanessa moved past her and held open the front door.

"Vanessa," Hannah gave it one last attempt, "won't you reconsider?"

Vanessa stared at the floor. "I'm going to be busy. I'll reach out at some point when I have time. Until then…" She didn't finish.

Hannah knew no call or text would be forthcoming. "Please don't do this." She no longer meant Vanessa taking in her mother. Her lungs couldn't expand, her chest was so tight. She stepped onto the porch.

"I need to leave soon." Vanessa closed the door.

Hannah dragged herself down the same short sidewalk she'd nearly skipped up mere minutes ago. She got in her car and, once she'd left Vanessa's street, parked so she could call Zara. Hannah planned to play the pitiful best friend card, hoping Zara would ditch her plans and get drunk with her. Before hitting send, she reconsidered. Just because *her* night, and near future, were ruined, it wasn't fair to wreck Zara's, too.

Hannah drove away, the sinking feeling in her stomach compounded by the knowledge that as Seattle ushered the new year in, instead of kissing Vanessa, she'd be watching the Space Needle fireworks from her bed with a bottle of Veuve Clicquot.

Chapter Twenty-five

As she neared hospital room 645, raised voices told Vanessa exactly which open door it would be. Her mother sounded much like she did when she'd had two or three drinks too many. Vanessa paused just outside, steadying herself for the onslaught of emotions sure to overwhelm her.

"Get your filthy hands off me."

So much for her mom coming out of surgery drowsy and mellow.

"Mrs. Holland, you can't pull out your IV. If you continue to do so, we'll have to restrain you."

Her mother's acidic laugh bounced off the hard surfaces. "I'd like to see you try." A slap cracked in the disinfectant-scented air.

"Mother." Vanessa stepped into the room. "That's unacceptable."

"Look who's finally graced us with her presence. Took you long enough. You never could get anywhere on time."

Vanessa ignored her mother's blatant lie; she hadn't been late for anything in years. Not since a flat tire caused her to arrive at Dr. Martinez's office five minutes past her appointment time, and she'd called ahead to let them know. She turned her attention to the nurse, on whose cheek, crimson imprints of her mother's fingers had bloomed. "Are you all right? I'm so sorry."

A male nurse stood near the wall, almost cowering, his eyes huge.

The woman, whose badge read Nadine, touched her face. "I'd like to tell you it's the first time it's happened." Her gray-streaked red hair was in disarray, as if she'd been in a struggle.

"She hit you twice?" Shock must have been written all over Vanessa's face. She glared at her mother, who looked even older in her hospital gown, her white hair flattened to her scalp. What wasn't different was the disdain in her eyes. "I'm her daughter. Please accept my apologies."

"It's—"

"Never wanted kids," her mother said to no one in particular, talking over Nadine, who'd started to respond to Vanessa. "Didn't have much of a choice." She appeared fascinated by the ceiling.

Nadine stepped closer to Vanessa. "Only once. Unfortunately, it's a hazard of the job, even when we're trying to help them. She's been quite a handful since coming out of surgery. They just transferred her from recovery. Sometimes the medication chills them out, sometimes it amps them up. But I have to report it."

Vanessa knew from experience it was just a normal day for her mom, not due to anesthesia or painkillers. "Again, I'm so sorry." She turned. "Mother, let her help you. I'm sure being restrained or sedated would be more unpleasant." Vanessa dropped her bag on a chair. She wasn't even sure if something like Valium was an option for a post-surgical patient, but she felt the need to help the staff in whatever ways she could.

"Mrs. Holland, I'm going to stop the bleeding and reinsert your IV."

"Touch me and I'll sue you." Her mother tried to spit on her, but luckily for Nadine, she missed.

"Mother!"

Nadine spun and walked out of the room.

The young man edged closer to the door.

Vanessa knew the only way her mother would be filing any lawsuits was if Vanessa paid for the attorney, which wasn't happening. She moved around the bed and ripped open a packet labeled gauze. "Hold still." She pressed it against the trickle of blood where the IV had been inserted.

"I don't need your help." Her mother struggled.

Vanessa maintained the pressure. She'd remind her mother of this the next time she wanted more money, funds she rarely approved over the monthly stipend since her mom spent it on alcohol. There never seemed to be a lack of it in her home, the bottles lined up on top of the refrigerator. Like with the burned-out headlight bulb that cost fifteen dollars, twenty with labor, Vanessa paid the mechanic or business directly whenever she could. "How long have you been a nurse?" she asked the young man.

He cleared his throat. "I'm in school doing my clinical rotation. I'll graduate this spring."

"A fucking baby." Her mother's words sliced through the small room. "They can't even give me a real one."

A flush appeared on his light skin.

"Sorry," Vanessa said. "You're not the only person she talks to this way." Usually, she received the brunt of it.

"Why are you even here?" Her mother tried to pull her arm free. "Go home. I don't need you." She turned to the man. "She likes to pretend she's a good daughter."

Before Vanessa could respond, Nadine entered, followed by a white man in matching black scrubs who managed to dwarf her even while wheeling a cart.

"Okay, Mrs. Holland," he said. "I hear you're being stubborn." He parked the cart near the head of the bed. "My name's Brian. I'm going to put your IV back in, and if you give me any problems, you're going to end up wearing a pair of my fancy bracelets." He pointed to the restraints. "Please step aside, miss."

Vanessa moved away as her mother eyed the lined cuffs. The sight of them or Brian's size must have been enough to convince her to cooperate. He had her hooked up in no time.

Nadine administered something in a port below the bag of saline. "They're bringing you food soon. If you're feeling nauseated, let me know, and I can give you something."

Vanessa had to admire the woman for returning after being slapped and spit at and still doing her job with dignity and grace.

Nadine moved closer to Vanessa and spoke softly. "Usually, just the sight of the restraints inspires cooperation." She raised her voice. "There's a cafeteria downstairs that's open until eleven if you want anything. After that, it's vending machines and coffee." Nadine cleaned up the supplies.

It was after ten thirty. Vanessa should run down to see what food they had to offer, but knowing she should be eating passed hors d'oeuvres and drinking champagne with Hannah, her appetite faded.

"Go." Her mother waved her away. "Get out of my sight."

"I'm not hungry." Vanessa almost said she was fine, but that was eons from the truth. Thinking about Hannah and the way they'd parted left her numb.

"Well, I don't want you sitting here. I wasn't good enough for you to spend time with when you were in high school and running around with those sluts. All you cared about was hanging out at that boy's house. I used to tell my boss it was a miracle you never got pregnant. Thank goodness I warned you to keep your legs together. You must've listened for once."

Vanessa closed her eyes. When she first had sex was none of her mother's business. "You shouldn't call people that. We liked being at Alexi's house because he had a pool. And as you well know, I'm a lesbian."

No answer came from her mother, who'd fallen asleep with her mouth open. Vanessa didn't know if it was sheer luck or Nadine's doing, but she breathed easier.

On the way, she'd been hoping that whatever drugs her mother had received would soften her. Clearly, that hadn't been the case. She cringed at how Nadine blamed the meds for her mother's inexcusable behavior. Vanessa's face heated knowing the staff would quickly find out her mom was always like this. She took a book from her bag and tried to read.

A short time later, a middle-aged man brought in a tray containing broth and Jell-O. Vanessa motioned for him to leave it. Her mother would wake if hungry. She wasn't about to disturb the temporary peace.

Vanessa glanced at her phone. Twenty minutes until midnight. She was supposed to be with Hannah, looking at art and the way Hannah's dress exposed one leg to mid-thigh. Instead she was here, miserable. Had Hannah gone without her? If she had, did she take someone else? Or if she went alone, would she meet someone? And what would she do when they rang in the new year? Would she kiss another woman even though it should've been Vanessa in her arms?

Her chest ached.

When it came down to it, she didn't have the right to know and barely a right to wonder. She'd pushed Hannah away, likely for good this time. However, Hannah had refused to understand the situation. Vanessa had little choice. Dealing with her mother was going to take everything she had, and instead of supporting her, Hannah had tried to talk her out of it.

"You saw them bring this crap and didn't do anything about it? Worthless..." Her mother pushed the tray of food onto the floor.

Vanessa's reprieve was over.

❖

Vanessa rose from the uncomfortable chair in the corner of her mother's hospital room and answered Sonja's call.

"Hi. How are you holding up?" Sonja's cheery voice soothed her.

"As good as can be." Vanessa ignored her mother's scornful gaze and left to talk elsewhere. The second day had seen much the same as the first, and her mom had only been awake an hour. Wait until she found out the physical therapist was on the way.

"Is she treating you decently? Is she right there?" The weight of the apprehension in Sonja's voice could topple the Space Needle.

"Not anymore. I'm walking to the cafeteria. I was going to grab some breakfast soon, anyway." Her concern warmed Vanessa. Sonja's interest in her mother's welfare had waned decades ago, and Sonja wasn't the type of woman to pretend otherwise. It was one of the things Vanessa liked about her. There was no pretense. "I'd like to say she's in rare form, but it's only her usual acerbic nature, though the staff doesn't know that yet. I'm sure if she's here much longer, they'll be consulting psychiatry."

"That may not be a terrible thing. I've been saying for years she needs to be on antidepressants."

"At the very least." Vanessa hated to think of the poor person who would receive her mother's wrath when she figured out what was happening. "I can't imagine she'll take anything." She swerved to avoid a doctor when she turned a corner.

"If they can convince her, perhaps she'll change her mind after experiencing what meds can do for her." Sonja's hope and positivity were other aspects of her personality that had always drawn Vanessa to her.

"Perhaps." But even if medication improved her mother's dark moods and outlook, would that make up for everything Vanessa had endured for over forty years? She might be flesh and blood, but Vanessa wasn't sure their relationship was salvageable. Time had etched her razor-edged remarks and biting insults into Vanessa's memory, and no amount of wishing they'd never been uttered could make her forget. In the end, pharmaceuticals would simply mask what her mother thought about her. Vanessa had no doubt her mother believed whatever flew from her mouth. "How do the greenhouses look?" She needed to focus on something lighter.

A happy sound squeaked from Sonja. "So good. Jorge should have all the cameras operational by this weekend, so you can see for yourself whenever your dear heart desires."

"You'll tell me what app I need?"

"Of course. The glazing we installed on the house for the orchids and other indirect-light lovers looks great. They seem to be thriving."

"I can't wait to see them." Vanessa found herself smiling as she poured herself a coffee.

"How's the orchid Hannah gave you doing?"

Vanessa froze. Answering carefully was necessary, or she'd be having a conversation she'd rather not have right now. "It's loving its new spot."

"That was a very thoughtful gift. And Hannah? How's she?"

Shit. "Fine. I think." Vanessa balanced a doughnut on her cup so she could hand the cashier her credit card.

"What's that mean?" Sonja's tone changed.

"It means I assume she's fine."

Sonja sighed. "Are you two not talking or something?"

Vanessa chose a private table in the corner. The metal chair made a scraping sound as she pulled it out. "Or something."

"Out with it, Holland. I don't have all day. There's a farm to run, in case you've forgotten."

"Hannah was there when I got the call about Mom. She freaked out that I planned to take her in. I was trying to juggle everything and didn't need her making things more difficult, so I asked her to leave." Vanessa intentionally didn't mention telling Hannah not to call, even if she hadn't used those exact words.

"Oh, Vanessa, tell me you didn't." The exasperation and disappointment in Sonja's voice came as a surprise.

Vanessa didn't answer. She broke off a piece of doughnut but left it on the napkin. "I had to. It's not easy dealing with this. You know I keep my distance from Mom as much as I can, so even the thought of her living under my roof is stressful."

"Yes, but," another sigh, "you two were practically dating."

"What?" People turned to look at her. "No, we weren't," she said, quieter this time.

"Think about it. You're more intimate with her than anyone in your life."

Intimate?

"She's the only person you've had sex with in the last year, and you spend time together every week," Sonja said, her voice rising at the end.

"The garden doesn't count. That's to help the kids."

"Is it? What about the sleepover, the lunches, the impromptu dinners? You spent Thanksgiving and Christmas with her, for goodness' sake."

"We were supposed to go out last night." Vanessa didn't know why she shared the information. It was only ammunition to fuel Sonja's argument.

"Where?" Sonja's voice dripped with suggestion.

"Chihuly Gardens. Some special event. Food, drinks, fireworks." Her skin chilled. She should've been downtown with Hannah on New Year's Eve, dancing and having fun, then moving things to Hannah's condo where they might've enjoyed more than champagne.

"What did you plan to wear?"

"I wore my dark blue dress." At Sonja's lack of response, Vanessa racked her brain. "The one from Dorothy's wedding. I sent you a photo."

"Ooh, the sexy one. What do you mean you wore it? I thought you didn't go."

"I had it on when she arrived to pick me up. That's when I got the call." The one that had ruined everything. Or was it *her* who had turned things upside down between them? It hardly mattered now. What was done was done.

"You let her see you in that slinky thing and then told her to leave? That poor woman." Sonja tsked in her ear. "Don't you think that was harsh? Couldn't you have said you'd talk later or something?"

"I tried to explain, but she refused to understand." Just reliving the exchange made her heart rate increase.

"I'm not sure *I* understand."

Vanessa set her coffee down. "What's that supposed to mean?"

Silence greeted her.

"Sonja?"

"It's just that…well, I'm not sure how to say it."

"Just spit it out." Vanessa rested her forehead in her hand, already knowing she wasn't going to like what was forthcoming.

"Ask yourself if your mom would do the same for you."

Vanessa raised her head, and the room blurred into colors and shapes. She rubbed her face. "Touché."

"I didn't mean to hurt your feelings."

"You didn't." Vanessa composed herself. "You're right. She wouldn't."

"She doesn't treat you well."

"I know. Trust me, Hannah has pointed that out many times." Vanessa worried her napkin.

"Good. She's worth keeping around. You should listen to her."

"It's not like that between us."

"Isn't it? Tell me, when you get good or bad news, who do you think to call first, her or me?"

Vanessa wasn't going to hurt Sonja's feelings by answering.

"And that Christmas gift? She obviously went to some trouble to find you something meaningful."

"It's just a flower." A gorgeous one, and Hannah had known orchids were her favorite.

"Is it? Do you know what I got my coffee klatch? Bath bombs." Sonja's little laugh made her smile, and Vanessa joined in.

"Who doesn't enjoy one of those now and then?"

"That's not the point." Sonja must have covered the microphone, but Vanessa still heard her yelling at Duckie not to drink out of the toilet. "Anyway. Think about why you keep your mother in your life when she treats you terribly, yet you keep pushing Hannah away when she seems to care a great deal about you."

When Sonja put it like that, it sounded horrible. "Okay, I will."

"That was easier than expected."

"I agreed to think about it. Everything is up in the air right now, and I have things to do before I can make any gigantic life decisions. I need to rent a hospital bed and have it delivered, go to my mom's place and get some of her things, and on top of it all, I'm missing work. When life has slowed a bit, I'll deal with Hannah."

A lengthy pause followed, and Vanessa glanced at her screen to see if their call had disconnected. It hadn't.

"Keep in mind, by the time you get around to it, it might be too late." Sonja's dejected tone caught Vanessa off guard.

"You're acting like we've split up. You know we weren't together, right?"

"So you say." Sonja was quiet for few seconds. "Jeffrey just texted. I need to help him with the watering. I'll check in on you tonight. Love you."

"Love you, too. Give him a hug for me." Vanessa ended the call and sipped her coffee. It was decent for a hospital cafeteria and the singular bright spot in her morning.

Chapter Twenty-six

"Close the door, please," Hannah said to Zara, not wanting Jen overhearing anything from her desk. The first few days of the Great Assistant Switch had seen some difficulties, most of it on Zara's end, especially when Annika had transferred almost all of Zara's calls to Hannah on Monday. Since then, things had gradually smoothed out, and strangely enough, no one seemed happier than Zara.

She dropped into one of Hannah's guest chairs. "You beckoned, m'lady?"

"You're in a good mood."

"I am." Zara wore a tennis-ball-yellow pantsuit. She stretched out her legs and folded her hands behind her head.

Hannah pulled her purse into her lap. "Where'd I put my sunglasses?"

Zara fake laughed. "Hilarious."

Hannah returned her bag to her drawer. "How are things in your office?"

"We're working out some wrinkles. I expected a learning curve."

"Are you having regrets?"

"Not at all." Zara grinned and motioned with her thumb over her shoulder. "Jen smiled at me and said she's missed my face. You might have to summon me more often."

"She was a little thrown off when I initially mentioned the switch. Apparently, she liked working for you quite a bit." Hannah gave her eyebrows a little wiggle.

Zara's expression brightened. "Really? That's good to know."

"I thought there might be tears. In fact, she was so upset about leaving you, I had to give her overnight to consider it. While I desperately need her skills, I didn't want a disgruntled employee."

"Something must've made her come around." Zara got a far-off look in her eyes.

Hannah smiled. "I mentioned she'd still see you around, being in the same building, and since you two were friendly, you could even meet for lunch whenever you wanted."

"And she knows I never eat with my direct reports." A slow smile formed on Zara's face.

"Exactly."

Zara grinned. "Well played." She rose and took a chocolate from Hannah's dish. "When does your garden project resume?"

"School resumes next week." Hannah wasn't looking forward to it.

"Do you plan to go?"

Hannah took a moment to answer. "I think so."

Zara tossed the wrapper into the trash. "Does Vanessa know you'll be there?"

"No." Hannah wiped imaginary dust from her desk. "I considered not going or sending someone in my place, but I should stay true to my word."

"I'm not sure she's going to see it that way."

No, she and Vanessa didn't agree on much these days. That would involve talking. "It doesn't matter."

"Are you hoping to make her angry?" Zara sat again.

"Me?" Hannah's irritation flared, which didn't take much. It had been lurking just beneath the surface since New Year's Eve. "I had nothing but good intentions. Her mother is downright cruel. She pushed *me* away."

"So, that's it for you two stubborn women?"

"Vanessa's dealing with some difficult issues and will continue to unless she makes changes." Hannah spun the two gold bracelets she wore. "Besides, she said some hurtful things, and I'm not at a place of forgiveness yet. I have feelings, too."

Zara studied her. "How's her mom doing?"

"No idea. We haven't spoken, and she's made it clear she doesn't want me reaching out."

A knock sounded, and Jen poked her head in. "Excuse me."

"Come in."

She glanced between them. "I'm sorry for interrupting, but your three o'clock is here."

"Thanks. Will you please offer her something to drink?"

"Of course," Jen said with a smile. She'd likely already done it. Whenever Hannah retrieved someone waiting for her, Jen had already taken care of them. Zara hadn't been exaggerating when she said how good Jen was at her job.

Zara watched her until the door closed.

"You're so bad."

Zara smiled and stood. "Time for me to go. I emailed you the shot list for the Pride line shoot. Take a look at it, and let me know if you have any changes before end of day. Don't forget, or it could delay the June launch."

"You know what?" Hannah stopped her with a raised hand. "Since the blowup with Vanessa and with Jen now assisting me, I've had a bit of time to reflect." Too much time. "I have things I need to work on, too."

"Like?"

"The hours I spend at this job created friction with Bren, and Vanessa mentioned it, too. So, I've decided to find a work/life balance." She needed to take a look at her own self-worth, both in relation to Vanessa and her career. "I'm always tired and worry about burning out." Hannah rose. "I don't need to make every decision, especially when you're more than capable. I'm sure what you've created is fantastic. Send it off if you're confident with it."

"Really?" Zara pretended to take her temperature, but Hannah ducked away.

She laughed. "Get out of my office. I have an appointment."

"Drinks tonight?" Zara opened the door.

It wouldn't hurt to leave at a decent time. "Five thirty? Somewhere I can order a cocktail without smoke bubbles or pipettes, please."

"You got it, boss."

As Zara left, Hannah patted herself on the back on her first few tentative steps in a new direction.

· 238 ·

Chapter Twenty-seven

When Vanessa exited the elevator, her mother's screech filled the corridor. Vanessa broke into a jog.

Upon entering the room, she found the physical therapist and a nurse at her mother's bedside. A wheelchair stood nearby.

"I'm not going anywhere. My hip is broken, you fools. Broken! I don't know who you idiots are, thinking I should be using it." Her hair stood on end, and her gown twisted to one side, likely from her struggling.

"Mrs. Holland, I told you, it's important to begin rehabilitation as soon as possible to maintain the strength you had prior to surgery."

Her mother turned to Vanessa. "Do you believe these fucking imbeciles? I've just gone under the knife, at my age, and they want me to walk the halls."

The physical therapist faced Vanessa with an exasperated expression. "I'm sure you realize this is necessary," he said. "We're only taking her downstairs to take a few steps between the bars."

"Let them help you, Mom. They're right." Vanessa dropped her bag on the chair where she'd spent too many hours.

"Of course, you side with *them*. You wouldn't recognize loyalty if you tripped over it." Her mother folded her arms.

"Let's try this again. Don't you want to get out of this room for a bit? Surely, you'd enjoy a change of scenery." The nurse pulled back the sheet, but her mother grabbed for it.

"Get the fuck away from me." She turned to Vanessa. "You're worthless, standing there while they tear my clothes and hurt me. I don't know why I had you." She flailed a hand at her. "If I'd had the abortion I wanted, I'd still have my husband, and you wouldn't have ruined my life."

A banging started behind Vanessa's brow, and she hoped the hospital employees were too busy to notice what was likely a blush heating her cheeks. "Mom, really. Just cooperate."

The physical therapist ignored her mother's diatribe and hooked his hand beneath her arm. "Let's get you up, Mrs. Holland."

She shoved him in the chest.

"You two should go, for your safety." Vanessa faced the nurse. "Could you please let Dr. Kapoor know I'd like to speak with her when she has a moment?"

"She's in surgery and won't round until later." The nurse straightened her scrub top.

"That's fine."

They took the wheelchair and left the room.

"If you keep assaulting the staff here, you'll be slapped with charges." Vanessa was done with this, the daily struggle, the verbal insults. It was demeaning enough when it was the two of them, but others overhearing it made her wish she could magically whisk herself away. It wasn't quite as bad as the couple of times Hannah had overheard her mother, but close. It'd been part of the reason Vanessa had been so harsh with her. She knew she couldn't take her mom in and risk Hannah witnessing anything like this.

"If they keep putting their filthy hands on me, they can expect more of the same." Her mother refused to look at her.

"Everyone is trying to help you, me included." Vanessa moved her bag to the floor and sat.

Her mother scoffed. "Don't pretend you understand what I'm going through. I didn't ask for any of this."

"You never do." Vanessa glanced at the television where it played a rerun of *Judge Judy*.

"What's that supposed to mean?" The lines around her mother's lips deepened, making her look even harsher.

Vanessa straightened. "Everything happens to you. Don't think I don't know why you fell off the step stool. I know what you keep on top of the refrigerator."

"You don't know shit."

"You're eternally the victim. You've never taken responsibility for your lot in life." Vanessa shifted uncomfortably, not from the chair but the direction of the conversation.

"How could I? I was stuck with a baby I didn't want. My husband ran off with a whore, and I had to work my fingers to the bone so you'd have a roof over your head."

That didn't take long. "And that's what it was." Vanessa didn't look away. "A roof. Not a loving home, not a place where I was safe or cared for. No nurturing, no physical affection. Half the time, there wasn't even food."

Her mother hurled her cup at her. "You ungrateful little bitch."

Vanessa ducked, then stared at the water dripping down the beige paint. Her mom missed her target, but her lack of physical control seemed to be mirroring her decades-long verbal degradation.

"I'm not doing this." Vanessa stood, her legs shaking. "I've put up with this far too long. I'm not doing it anymore." The room started to spin. "I was going to let you recover in my home, but not if this is how you act."

"You're so dramatic. No wonder you're single."

Vanessa bent and retrieved her bag. "I'm stopping at the nurse's station and telling them to release you to the rehabilitation facility when it's time. They'll be better able to care for you." She hoped they had a psychologist on staff.

"Don't threaten me. You may be in your forties, but I'm still your mother. Sit your ass down."

Vanessa turned to look at her. "I'll pay whatever insurance doesn't cover like I normally do. Please don't contact me."

A string of expletives and slurs followed Vanessa out of the room. As she neared the group of nurses huddled around a counter watching her approach, silence fell.

Then her mother screamed, "You better send that fucking money every month," showing her true colors right until the end.

Relief washed through Vanessa. The money had always been the easy part.

Chapter Twenty-eight

When Vanessa approached the school garden on Thursday, she was neither surprised to see her order of gravel piled outside the gate, nor that Hannah had shown up early. Class didn't start for ten minutes.

Even though Vanessa worried she'd crossed the line and blown it for good, Hannah had already demonstrated her dedication to the kids, so Vanessa had no doubt she'd be here today. She wasn't sure it pleased her. It was sure to be uncomfortable, and it's not like they could talk with the youth around.

Vanessa entered the open gate. Hannah had loaded a wheelbarrow and taken it inside. She'd begun to spread some of the load over the weed barrier they'd cut into strips to fit between the beds. Her plaid cotton shirt hung on a nearby fence post, and she wore a tight navy tank top. She hadn't noticed Vanessa yet, so Vanessa took a moment to watch her throw shovelfuls of gravel. In the rare January sunlight, sweat glistened on Hannah's arms and the pink tops of her shoulders. That's when Vanessa noticed she'd already completed the path one bed over. How long had she been here?

Vanessa walked around the plot of potatoes so she could enter her vision without frightening her. "Morning."

Hannah wiped her brow with the back of her glove. "Hi."

"It looks good." Vanessa dared to come closer. "You're starting to burn." She tapped her own shoulder, then pulled her sunscreen from her bag. "Come here."

"I'm fine." Hannah pulled her baseball cap lower.

"You're already pink." She squirted some into her palm and rubbed her hands together. "Okay?"

Hannah gave a little nod.

Vanessa smoothed the lotion over Hannah's shoulders. She admired—despite Hannah's lithe body—her deceptive strength, something Vanessa easily felt as she worked the cream into Hannah's upper arms.

Hannah wouldn't look at her. "I already did my forearms."

"Okay." Vanessa rubbed the excess on her own.

"Thanks." Hannah scooped more gravel and hurled it toward the cabbage patch.

Vanessa pulled out her gloves. "Thanks for coming today."

"You knew I would." Hannah continued to toss the small rocks down the path.

"I did." Vanessa walked to the shed and returned with a rake. She began evening out what Hannah had distributed.

"You don't have to help. I can do it." Hannah dropped the shovel and began pushing the empty wheelbarrow toward the gate.

"I have other things for the kids to do today. This is what I planned to work on."

Hannah turned. "You obviously want to keep me at arm's length. I got the message loud and clear. I'm not here to spend time with you." She resumed walking.

Vanessa's belly flopped, and she pressed her hand to her stomach. The kids would be here soon, limiting their ability to talk, but did it matter? She had no idea what to say to Hannah. The things she'd said the last time likely cost Vanessa the chance of having anything more than this.

After leaning the rake against the fence, Vanessa retreated to the shed and sat on an upturned bucket. She rested her elbows on her knees and covered her face. She couldn't tell Hannah that she'd been right. That her mom was just as horrible as Hannah thought. That Vanessa's offer to take her in had failed in spectacular fashion before it'd come to fruition. Her ears burned.

"What are you doing?"

Vanessa rose so fast, the bucket toppled over. "Nothing."

Hannah moved to where her backpack sat on the makeshift table. "I just need my water." She pulled it from the sleeve and downed half of it.

They watched one another warily.

"Laying the gravel *would* go faster if we both worked on it," Hannah finally said.

Vanessa searched her face in the dim light but couldn't get a read on her. "It would."

Hannah righted the bucket. "Ray and the students are on their way."

"Right." Vanessa grabbed her gloves and headed outside.

Raymond approached. "How was your Christmas?"

"Very nice." It was New Year's Eve that had blown up like a firework finale. "Yours?"

"Good, good. Branson got spoiled again by his grandparents. Hey, I was hoping both you and Hannah would be here today. Would you mind if I took this time to start grading their papers on global warming they just turned in? I gave them extra time to finish over break."

"No problem." Other than now she had one less buffer between her and Hannah. Vanessa glanced down. "How's your leg?"

"Good as new," he said, grinning. "I'll pop down just before the end of class. I really appreciate this." He headed for the gate.

Ellie with the dark hair bounded up to her. "Mr. Sandcrane-Ochoa said we're going to plant flowers at the end of the rows this spring to attract pollinators. Can I help pick which ones?"

"Within reason, yes," Vanessa said. "We'll have to look at which varieties can withstand full sun, are affordable, and butterflies and bees like best."

"I really like those drippy heart-looking ones. My nonna has them in her garden," Ellie said.

Hannah skirted around Vanessa with a hand to her lower back.

Vanessa nearly closed her eyes at the sensation. Brief touches might be all she'd have left after what she'd done. "Bleeding hearts," she murmured. "I'm familiar with them."

Chapter Twenty-nine

With her to-go mug in one hand and her purse on the opposite arm, Hannah pushed through the front doors of Baros's headquarters. Charles waved from where he spoke on the phone. She smiled and strode past his desk.

"Hannah."

Upon recognition of the voice, she halted, one of her pointed Manolos wobbling beneath her.

Vanessa.

Hannah turned to find her rising from one of the chairs in the reception area. "Wh...what're you doing here?" This was her turf, and the unexpectedness of Vanessa greeting her on a Monday morning left her ill-prepared.

"I brought you coffee, the one you like from Seismic." Vanessa held out a cup. "And a blueberry muffin. I know you sometimes forget to eat." Instead of her usual work polo, she wore a flattering cream blouse and navy pants. Had she dressed up to come here?

Hannah lifted her mug. "I already have one. Thanks anyway."

Vanessa's expression fell. "Just the muffin then?"

"Vanessa!" Zara rushed toward them and enveloped Vanessa in a hug.

Emotions battled within Hannah. Anger at Vanessa for showing up when she'd told Hannah to stay away, delight at seeing her again, a twinge of excitement at the amazing way she looked, and jealousy that Vanessa was currently in Zara's embrace, not hers. Could their hug last any longer? Just when she was about to head upstairs, Zara pulled back.

"What a surprise to see you."

"I stopped by to bring Hannah coffee and a pastry, but it seems I'm too late." Vanessa held them out. "How about you?"

Zara's eyes gleamed. "Sugar and caffeine? Yes, please." She grabbed them.

Technically, Hannah had only declined the drink, and the fact that it mattered to her irritated her more.

"How've you been?" Zara glanced at Hannah, then back to Vanessa, clearly picking up on the awkwardness.

"Fine. The store was a bit slow the first half of January, but it always is. Everyone spends too much at the holidays and tightens their belts in the new year. But it's picking up again. How are you?"

Hannah flinched at the reference to the new year but noticed Vanessa provided no information of a personal nature.

"I'm great. Hannah and I switched assistants. We're adjusting, but I think we're both getting what we want from the exchange."

"That's good." Vanessa looked at Hannah. "You needed support. From the sound of it, you were doing everything yourself."

Hannah couldn't answer. Even if it were a veiled condemnation of her work hours, being this close to Vanessa, catching the scent of her perfume she only wore occasionally, wanting to touch her so bad she ached, Hannah couldn't formulate a response.

Vanessa's chest rose on a large inhalation. "I need to get back. Good seeing you both. Enjoy the coffee." She crossed the lobby.

"That was…weird." Zara took a sip. "Oh, hell. That's good." She looked at the logo. "Why have I never had this before?"

"It's a mom-and-pop place around the corner from her store." Hannah headed for the elevators, and Zara followed.

Once inside, Zara leaned against the wall as it ascended. "I don't get it. Why aren't you two talking?"

"Because she kicked me out and ended it with, 'I'll call you. Don't call me.'" Vanessa hadn't phrased it exactly like that, but her meaning had been clear.

The doors opened, and they walked slowly down the hall. "Despite that, you went to the garden. How'd that go?"

"We didn't really talk." Hannah almost mentioned the sunscreen, but didn't know if it meant anything and didn't need Zara's speculation. She stopped outside her office suite, where inside, Jen already typed away.

"At least it's equivalent." Zara continued down the corridor.

"What do you mean?"

"You both look miserable," she said over her shoulder.

As Zara turned the corner, Hannah glanced down, expecting to see the gaping hole in her chest. She was…mostly fine. Just empty.

"Hannah?"

She spun to find Jen studying her.

"The first interview for the VP of Operations position is in a few minutes. The candidate is in the conference room."

"Right. Thanks." Hannah needed to pull herself together. Seeing Vanessa couldn't affect her like this. She had things to do. "Could you please do me a favor? Vanessa Holland. You'll find her address in my contacts. Send her a short, polite email letting her know she can schedule time to see me through you."

"Of course."

Hannah needed some warning should this ever happen again.

Vanessa had looked stunning in her attractive outfit, her hair curlier like it was in the mornings. But she could've been wearing anything. It wasn't Vanessa's looks that had affected her.

Hannah's chest ached with how much she missed her.

❖

On Wednesday morning, a yellow, orange, and purple bouquet on Hannah's desk greeted her. It was there before she arrived, "delivered by a blonde just before eight o'clock," Charles said when Hannah called to ask. She recognized crepe-like carnations and delicate lilies, but didn't know the names of the other blooms. Their sweet fragrance permeated her entire office. Instead of the small note usually accompanying floral deliveries, a greeting card sat propped against the glass vase, her name on the outside.

She recognized the handwriting.

Her meeting with the head of her design team to discuss how the Pride line was progressing started in fifteen minutes. Should she wait to read the note? If whatever was written inside upset her, Hannah wasn't sure there would be enough time to recover. In the end, it didn't matter. She'd reschedule if necessary. There was no way she could sit through this meeting not knowing what it said.

Hannah sat on the corner of her desk and slit it open. A watercolor rendition of the Space Needle adorned the front. Vanessa's flowing script filled the inside. Hannah briefly wondered how many other recipients of floral deliveries in the Seattle area had been lucky enough to read Vanessa's beautiful cursive over the years.

My dear Hannah,

I chose this card because it made me think of you, even if the memory is bittersweet. When I close my eyes, I can still see you in that gorgeous dress you wore on New Year's Eve. I was a fool not to hang up the phone and spend the evening with you. I see that now.

I've made many mistakes in my lifetime and will surely make more. Perhaps the greatest has been staying in the same cycle of emotional abuse I've been dealing with for over forty years. I'm working on that now, and I'll continue to put effort toward finding a healthier way of living. As I'm sure you know, it's not going to be a quick fix.

I owe you an apology for the things I said, and certainly the manner in which I said them. If you're amenable to the idea, someday I'd like to express my regret and ask for your forgiveness in person, hopefully not in a schoolyard or your lobby. This isn't something I would normally hope to accomplish in writing.

I'd also like to express how sorry I am for showing up to your work without notice. It's a lousy excuse, but I wanted to see you, and I understand that coordinating with your assistant to find a suitable time is a better option.

You seem to be working on changes yourself. I noticed you didn't stop once while volunteering Thursday to take work calls. And I'm happy to hear you have a qualified assistant to rely on now. You deserve that. You deserve many things.

I'd like to make it clear that despite what I said in my emotional state, I don't want you out of my life. Please call or text me whenever you like. The last three weeks have brought much introspection, a lot of self-chastisement, and the realization that you and I might be really good together—if I haven't ruined things beyond repair.

Running twenty miles this week hasn't gotten you out of my mind, so instead, I'm sending you this.

Apologetically yours,
Vanessa

Hannah pushed the intercom button. "Jen, can you please reschedule this meeting to this afternoon?"

With that dealt with, she sank into her chair and read the card again. It contained enough information that she'd probably be mulling it over the rest of the week. *Good together.* Those two words alone would consume much of her day.

While she appreciated the card and the sentiments contained therein, one simple note wasn't going to fix the issues between them. Besides, how hard could Vanessa be working on things when her mother was still living with her? Or had her mom recovered and returned home?

Still, Vanessa's words held possibility, and Hannah would cling to that, even if neither of them was ready for more. Her breathing became shallow. Vanessa cared about her. Hannah had assumed it for some time, but seeing it in writing made it real.

Hannah tucked the note into her purse, retrieved her phone, and sent Vanessa a text.

Thank you.

She had so much more to say, but she didn't need to be rushing into anything in such a fragile emotional state. That would have to do, for now.

CHAPTER THIRTY

Vanessa finally took a proverbial breath after working two straight sixteen-hour days. Valentine's passed without any fanfare, at least in her personal life. However, the holiday was easily her highest profit day of the year, with Mother's Day second and Christmas close behind that. Neither she nor Hannah mentioned it the prior Thursday in the garden, and Vanessa couldn't help but wonder if perhaps Hannah was seeing someone. After all, the short acknowledgment Hannah had sent her after she'd delivered the bouquet and card had been generic. She tried not to let it bother her and left two more bouquets with Hannah's receptionist in the following weeks, with both generating similar responses. They never talked about them, nor the card, while volunteering.

Last week, she purposefully didn't send flowers, pride getting the better of her. The other arrangements could be written off as gifts to brighten Hannah's office. If Hannah was no longer single, sending her a bouquet right before the holiday symbolizing love made Vanessa appear too pathetic.

Finally standing up to her mother had brought her a sense of relief, a weightlessness she'd never known. It'd been difficult at first, with guilt and thoughts of betrayal eating at her. But something changed, and what she'd originally seen as disloyalty transformed into something resembling self-preservation. Along with it came a lightness that carried over into other aspects of her life. Despite wondering if Hannah had moved on, Vanessa had never felt better.

In the first few days, her mother had called multiple times. She'd left voicemails, and fifteen seconds into listening to the first one, Vanessa deleted all of them. She consoled herself with the knowledge that she wasn't completely turning her back on her only relative. Any outstanding balances from her mother's hospitalization and rehabilitation came to her, which she paid. And the stipend she'd been sending for close to twenty years continued to come out of her bank account on the first of each month. Other than that, she had no interest in seeing or talking to her mother again. Certainly not after witnessing the positive effect on her mental health.

Dr. Martinez noticed, too. And while she'd been leery of Vanessa's impromptu decision without any prior consultation, she also acknowledged the improvement in Vanessa's overall demeanor and attitude.

So, to celebrate getting through the busy holiday, Vanessa planned to spend her off days in Ashland. She hadn't visited Sonja and Jeffrey since she'd been there with Hannah. The installation of the cameras in the new greenhouses allowed her to travel less, but she still liked to oversee what was happening in the fields, especially with spring just around the corner.

After adding her toothbrush to her overnight bag, she sent a quick text to Hannah.

Going to be in Ashland for two days. Want anything?

Vanessa tossed her phone on the bed. This early in the morning, Hannah was probably already at work and in meetings. It pinged as Vanessa packed her charging cable.

Only a favor

Vanessa sent a question mark.

Let me know when you land? If there's no one else...

Vanessa smiled as she replayed their prior conversation in her head.

And tell S & J hi

Vanessa typed a response.

Will do. I'll text you.

She stared at it, not wanting to lose the connection so soon.

Safe travels. See you Thursday.

Vanessa sat on the end of her bed, and only then did the gradual ache in her cheeks make her aware she still smiled. Then a thought sobered her. Just because *she* wasn't romantically involved with someone, it didn't mean Hannah wasn't. Although, if Hannah were, would she have asked Vanessa to text her?

Vanessa didn't have time to dwell on it. If she wasn't out the door in the next ten minutes, she risked missing her flight. The TSA lines could be so unpredictable.

However, it didn't take her long, and the flight to Medford was smooth, despite the small plane. As they taxied to the terminal, she texted Hannah.

Landed safely

Hannah's response of *Makes my day* gave her goose bumps. By the time Vanessa deplaned, she'd put Hannah's text behind her. With only her carry-on, she didn't need to claim any luggage, and Sonja's white Ford F250 was easy to find among the few cars waiting curbside. She climbed in and tossed her bag on the seat behind her.

"Hi." She kissed Sonja on the cheek. "Thanks for picking me up."

"Any time. No Hannah?" Sonja waited for a van to pass, then pulled into the lane.

"What?" Vanessa hadn't mentioned her.

"I thought you might've brought her along." Sonja glanced at her as she navigated toward the on ramp.

"Why would you think that?"

Sonja patted her leg. "Wishful thinking."

They got on I-5, and dust billowed behind a tractor plowing a field on Vanessa's side of the freeway. "If I'd known you wanted to see her, I could've asked her."

"The wishing wasn't for me." With a loud slurp, Sonja finished what looked to have been an iced coffee. "I was hoping you'd brought her for *you*."

Vanessa pressed her palms to her thighs. "What's that mean?"

"You two have chemistry. Jeff and I both saw it."

Fence posts whizzed by Vanessa's window. "Yes, but I wrecked everything because I didn't do what I should've done years ago."

"But now you have." Sonja squeezed her hand. "So, what's your plan?"

"Don't laugh."

Sonja did. "You can't start with that. How can I not?" At Vanessa's silence, she eased away. "Sorry, it's out of my system. Go ahead."

"I'm taking a page from her playbook." It sounded so stupid when said aloud.

"You'll have to explain. Is that a sports thing?"

Vanessa took a deep breath. "When I pushed Hannah away, she did small things that showed me she cared. One day, she brought me coffee. When the garden was vandalized, she came straight there. Even showing up for the kids each week means something to me, and she knows that, which isn't to say she's not primarily there for the youth. She quietly stayed in my life, unobtrusively, never pressuring me. So, I'm attempting to do the same."

"How?" Sonja's eyebrows drew together.

"I brought her coffee and a muffin, though that didn't go well. I didn't have a plan, just showed up at her work. She didn't seem to appreciate it."

"No offense, darling, but what is the fine line between doing nice things and, well, stalking?"

"God, Sonja." Vanessa pushed her hair from her face. "You make me sound like a criminal."

"I'm serious."

The answer was easy. "If she asks me to stop, I'll stop. No reason needed." Vanessa dug in her bag for her sunglasses as the cloud cover burned off. "I left flowers for her at the front desk and a card once. And if I want to see her, I'll contact her assistant, like she asked."

"Whoa." Sonja made beeping sounds. "Back it up. Flowers? A card?"

"Bouquets, about once a week. One with a note—well, letter—apologizing for my behavior. I didn't want to wait too long without doing so, and I thought she'd be more receptive to something in writing, although I said I'd like to say I'm sorry in person one day."

"You see each other every Thursday. Why not then?"

Vanessa leaned against the window. "Because it's not a conversation to have around the kids. It needs to be the two of us."

Sonja signaled and took the exit. "Do you think that'll happen?"

"I don't know," Vanessa whispered, fear overwhelming her. She composed herself. "She's angry and has every right to be. It'll take time to mend what I've done."

"What'd she say when you told her you cut contact with your mom?"

Vanessa shifted in her seat. "I haven't said anything. We're not yet at the point of talking much. I sent her a letter, we've had a few innocent texts, and we only discuss the kids and plants while at the school." As she recalled their last communications, she reconsidered. Innocent might be the wrong word.

"How's any of this going to help the situation?" Sonja turned into the farm. "You two need to talk."

"Part of me thinks she'd be better off if I walked away."

They came around the bend, and in the distance, the four greenhouses made for a magnificent view. Vanessa's spirits lifted.

Sonja brought the truck to a halt halfway up the long drive. With it in park, she turned in her seat. "You seem made for one another. If my darling husband can see it when he can't find the milk in the fridge, there's something special between you and Hannah. Don't give up so soon."

Vanessa leaned against the head rest. "It's not easy. I've already been burned once."

"What then? Live the life of a spinster? Fill your home with flowers and cats?"

"There's nothing wrong with either of those." Vanessa shot her a glare.

"I didn't say there was." Sonja cupped Vanessa's cheek. "You might be afraid to love again, but think about how indulging your insecurities will affect her. If you two really have something, you'll be crushing the chance for *her* to have the possible love of a lifetime." She put the truck into drive. "Not to mention yourself."

It was a lot to consider. "I probably ruined things. She was furious, though she's calmed. It's going to take time."

Sonja pulled up to the house. "No one said it would be simple."

No, but when had Vanessa's life ever been? She needed to fix the situation, even if it took her out of her comfort zone. If anyone was suited for the task, it was her. It was Hannah who usually moved them forward. Now it was her turn. Because while she'd found a new sense of self-confidence and clarity of mind with her mother out of the picture, Vanessa couldn't honestly say she was happy. Not how she was around Hannah. Even spreading gravel beside her brought a simple joy to Vanessa's life that'd been lacking. Vanessa couldn't go back to the same dull, meager existence when Hannah brought so much light into her life. She wanted to be with Hannah, if there was still a chance of that happening. "Are you familiar with phototropism?"

"I was wondering when you were going to return from your," Sonja wiggled her fingers in front of Vanessa's face, "million-miles-away trip." She lightly tapped Vanessa's leg. "I might be a business major, but I live on a farm, if you haven't noticed."

Vanessa smiled. "Just like plants bend toward the light, I'm like that with her. I can't help it. Something about her draws me to her, and it has nothing to do with her attractiveness."

"She's quite beautiful though. Very sensual. It's something about the way she moves."

"Hey." Vanessa pointed toward the fields. "You have a husband out there."

Sonja grinned. "I can still admire." She opened her door and put one foot on the running board. "Are you ready to see your new greenhouses?"

Vanessa grinned and hopped down from the truck. She'd dreamed about this day for years, and the four beautiful concrete, steel, and glass structures held so much potential. It was hard to imagine the heights her business might reach five years from now. "Absolutely."

Chapter Thirty-one

Hannah listened to Jen give her the day's agenda. "Your calendar is up to date. You have the finance meeting at nine. The printouts are in the orange folder. You have Alison Booker at ten, Vanessa Holland at ten forty-five, and Zara at elev—"

"Vanessa?" Hannah shivered despite the room being warm.

Jen referred to her screen. "A fifteen-minute meeting. Said she didn't need much time." She looked up. "Is something wrong?"

"No." Hannah's heart rocketed through her chest. "Just caught me by surprise." Forcing Vanessa to make an appointment now seemed silly. If the intention had been to give herself forewarning, it did little good. She was just as thrown by hearing Vanessa's name as she would've been by Vanessa walking in the door.

"After lunch..." Jen continued her overview like she did every morning, but Hannah stopped listening.

Vanessa would arrive in a few hours, and Hannah couldn't imagine why. The bouquet Vanessa had delivered to the front desk on Monday still looked fresh, and its subtle fragrance perfumed her office. She'd grown fond of the arrangements, and in the times between one needing to be discarded and a new one arriving, the barren feeling of her space distracted her. Should she buy a plant for work? Ralph was thriving at home. With all the knowledge she'd gained in her months of volunteering and being around Vanessa, she could totally rock being a two-plant mom.

"Hannah?"

"Yes?" Hannah spun away from the window.

Jen smiled. "Need anything else from me right now?"

Hannah pulled her laptop closer to demonstrate her intent on working. "No, thank you."

"Okay, I'll be confirming your appointments for tomorrow." She pulled Hannah's door shut behind her.

As soon as she left, Hannah opened her desk drawer and flipped through it. There it was. She slid the magazine out and tucked it under the folder Jen had left for her. With that taken care of, she turned her attention to work. Or as much work as she was going to get done with thoughts of seeing Vanessa on her mind.

Somehow, in those few hours, Hannah managed to respond to all her emails and successfully get through her meetings. Behind her closed office door, she combed her hair, retouched her makeup, and ran a lint roller over her black pants and mint green shirt. She added water to the vase and was tidying her desk when a knock sounded.

Jen stepped inside. "Vanessa Holland is here."

"Please show her in." Hannah struggled to keep her voice steady.

Jen stepped aside, and Vanessa appeared in the doorway with a paper bag.

"Come in." Hannah rose, then realized she had no idea how to greet her. After an awkward second or two, Hannah quickly embraced her.

Vanessa blushed. "Hi." The simple blue midi dress she wore was the perfect cut for her physique. Its color brought out the intensity of her eyes and made her hair appear even more platinum.

Hannah directed Vanessa to one of the chairs and turned its mate toward her before she sat. "I was surprised to see your name on today's schedule."

"Yes, I suppose you were." Vanessa softly smiled. "I was missing you yesterday, and Thursday seemed a long way away. But I won't take up much of your time."

Hannah had been expecting flowers or a coffee, not that. "That's nice of you to say."

"I'm not just saying it. And it's about time I apologized to you in person." Vanessa played with the bag still in her hands. "I shouldn't have treated you that way, especially since you were only looking out for me. It's not an excuse, but I was overwhelmed and lashed out at you."

"I got your card." She touched Vanessa's hand. "This isn't necessary."

"It is. I treated you terribly, and I'm so sorry. I shouldn't have told you to leave, and I definitely shouldn't have asked you not to contact me." Her eyes shone, but she didn't allow her tears to fall. "I honestly don't know what I was thinking."

Likely, Vanessa had been thinking about her daughterly duty and the torrent of verbal abuse that would follow if she didn't take in her mother. She certainly hadn't wanted to hear what Hannah had to say, hence the reason for their stalemate. "What's in the bag?"

Vanessa still clutched it in her hands. "I brought you a sandwich. Since I failed at bringing you coffee, I thought you might like something for lunch. Lou's started making caprese paninis. You ordered the salad once, so these made me think of you. If you already brought somethi—"

"I didn't." Hannah took the bag from her grasp before she mangled the contents. "Thank you." She set it on her desk. "I have something for you I keep meaning to bring to the school, but since you're here..." She eased the *Horticulture* magazine out and handed it to Vanessa. "I earmarked an article about companion planting. Apparently, if you grow certain plants near one another, you get a better yield. It can help control pests, too. I thought we could try it this spring." Hannah looked up to see Vanessa smiling sweetly at her. "You already knew this, didn't you?" Her excitement at sharing the information with Vanessa plummeted.

Vanessa squeezed her arm. "Yes, but you're adorable." She ran her finger over the address label on the front. "You have a subscription?" Fine lines creased the corners of her eyes.

Heat rushed to Hannah's face. "I've learned a lot." She should've pulled the sticker off.

"The November issue." A smile played around Vanessa's lips. "I guess you have."

Hannah had no defense when Vanessa was like this. Playful, teasing, a bit flirtatious. She never had.

Jen poked her head in. "Hannah, your eleven o'clock is here. She's a few minutes early."

Hannah stood, and so did Vanessa.

"I should go." Vanessa gazed at her, something unreadable in her expression. "Thanks for the magazine."

"You don't have to take it." Hannah reached for it.

Vanessa turned her body to block the attempt and tucked it under her arm. "I plan to read it front to back. We have planting to do. March is almost here." She smiled. "Enjoy your lunch."

Hannah followed her. "Thanks for the sandwich." It was all she could do not to hug her again.

"You're welcome." Vanessa stepped into the outer office. "Hey."

Zara embraced Vanessa. "How are you? I didn't expect to see you here." She glanced at Hannah.

"Good. I was just dropping something off." She touched Zara's arm. "I won't keep you from your meeting." With a little wave, she headed for the elevators.

Zara followed Hannah into her office. "Did you know she was coming?"

"Yes." Hannah dropped into her chair, the conversation with Vanessa having taken everything out of her. "She had an appointment."

Zara raised her eyebrows. "Does she often do that?"

"No, this is the first time." Hannah pushed her pens into a neat row. "Since I asked her to."

A low chuckle rumbled from Zara. "Oh, Hannah. What am I to do with the two of you?"

Hannah ignored the question. "So. Photography?"

"Yes. Work. Of course." Zara opened her laptop. "Did you look at the proof sheet from the first session?"

"I did. Looks great. Like I told you, you don't need to run things like that by me. I trust you."

Zara narrowed her eyes. "You say that, but I'm having a hard time believing it."

Hannah laughed. "I've left here every night this week by five thirty. Believe it. I don't know how I existed with no work/life balance before now." She leaned forward. "Hiring Estella as the VP of Operations was eye-opening. I never realized how many calls I received about problems after hours."

"Glad it's working out." Zara glanced toward the bouquet in front of the window. "More flowers this week, I see. Many of the women and some of the men in this building are jealous, me included." She glanced at the door. "I wouldn't mind getting a bouquet, let alone dozens of them."

"There haven't been *that* many." Hannah jutted her chin in the direction of the door. "Plus, I thought you would've made a move sooner."

Zara studied her keyboard. "It's a bit complicated. Now isn't ideal."

"Would you like to talk about it?" It wasn't like staying on the topic of work had been successful.

"No. Another time." Zara gestured at the bag. "What's in there?"

"Vanessa brought me a sandwich." The scent of warm bread and basil greeted Hannah when she opened it. "Share it with me?"

"Absolutely." Zara pulled her chair closer. "It smells amazing."

Hannah unwrapped the monstrosity. "It's still warm." She offered Zara some napkins. "And we're going to work when we're finished. Agreed?"

"Sure." Zara picked up one end, and mozzarella strung between the two halves. "If I can still move."

They ate for a few minutes without talking, and Hannah hoped Jen couldn't hear the sounds they made. She probably wondered what they were doing behind the closed door.

Finally, Zara pushed away the remnants and sat back. "I'm out. That was better than sex."

"It was good, but not *that* good." Again, images of Vanessa invaded her thoughts.

"Ew. I can almost read your mind." Zara wiped her mouth. "You know, speaking of which, it might be time to cut Vanessa some slack."

"I don't believe we were talking about her at all."

Zara motioned around the room. "Hand-delivered flowers, coffee, sandwiches. She's obviously trying to tell you something."

Hannah looked at the arrangement. "I don't think she personally delivers them."

"She absolutely does. I run into her occasionally." Zara rubbed her forehead. "I don't know a better way to describe it, but sometimes she looks so forlorn. I never know what to say to her."

Hearing that made Hannah's heart do a little twist. "I don't think either of us is ready to move forward yet." She looked away. "I'm not sure I'll ever be."

Zara took the remnants of both their lunches, bagged them, and set it all aside. "Look at me. I'm calling time out on employer/employee right now. This is your best friend talking to you." She leaned her arms on the desk. "I'm going to be honest with you, and you need to listen."

A chill made the fine hairs on Hannah's arms stand up.

"I think you've developed real feelings for Vanessa." When Hannah started to speak, Zara held up her hand. "Let me finish. Yes, you've had past relationships," she used air quotes, "but you never had anything truly serious until Bren. You hadn't even lived with a girlfriend. And Bren had to convince you to move in together when you clearly weren't ready."

Hannah stared out the window. No, she'd never lived with a lover, never wanted to. Never felt the need to wake up next to someone. Until—

"This is a big step for you. Your relationship with Vanessa is different from any you've been in before. But you two can't keep dancing around one another. One or—better yet—both of you, are going to have to open up and be honest about what you want. You weren't truthful with Bren, and it affected things between you."

Images of eating lasagna in Vanessa's cozy kitchen, sipping wine in her backyard, and falling asleep tangled together on her couch scrolled through Hannah's mind. She looked down so Zara wouldn't see the emotion in her eyes.

"What you're feeling is new and scary, but that's okay. That's how you know it's real. But it's time to be honest with her."

Honesty. The word reminded her of other instances in which she hadn't been truthful with those important to her. She looked up. "You forget Vanessa continues to let her mother treat her the way she does. I don't know if I can be with a woman who doesn't value herself."

"Have you talked to her about it?" Zara looked at her intently.

Hannah stood and dropped the bag into the trash. "Yes, and she basically told me to go to hell."

"I'm not talking about then." Zara sagged into the chair. "Christ, hon."

"I'll think about it." Hannah sat again, this time in the chair beside Zara. "As hard as it is to admit, as much as I like Vanessa, she might not be right for me." Fuck her lip for quivering as she said it.

Zara recrossed her legs and tapped Hannah's knee with the side of her shoe. "That's all you'll hear from me on the matter. You know her better than I do, and you certainly know your own needs."

Hannah wasn't sure she did, on either front. Vanessa was an enigma in some ways, with her steely reserve and quiet manner. Every time she'd opened up, Hannah had felt like she'd been bestowed a rare gift. And Hannah didn't understand her own needs. She'd once thought it necessary to live with Bren, even when something inside had screamed to be steadfast and say no.

Bren's name reminded Hannah what she'd needed to do for months. "Speaking of honesty, I have something I need to tell you."

"Oh?" Zara's brow furrowed.

"God, I don't even know how to begin." Hannah pressed two fingers into her temple and squeezed her eyes shut.

"Please just say whatever it is. You're scaring me. Are you sick?"

"No, nothing like that." Hannah wrung her hands. "I haven't been forthcoming with you."

Zara's eyebrows shot up. "About?"

Hannah shook her head like it might tumble her thoughts into place. "When Bren died that day, I had plans. I was in my car, on my way home."

"Okay, slow down. What?" Zara touched her leg.

"I was on my way to break up with her." Hannah wiped at an unexpected tear. Where had that come from?

"Break up with…" Zara's jaw went slack. "That same day?"

Hannah nodded. "I had notes I'd rehearsed and everything."

"That means…you…weren't in love with her?" Zara stared at the framed Leighton Vaughn painting behind her desk, though she seemed to be looking through it.

"No. I hadn't been in some time."

"But you pretended you were." Zara turned, hurt and anger flashing across her features.

"No. Yes. I don't know. I was about to end the relationship, but all of a sudden, troopers were on my lawn. I didn't know what to do. What would everyone have thought if she'd just died, and I said, 'Aw, well. I was going to break up with her, anyway'?"

Zara didn't speak for almost half a minute. "You didn't cry at the funeral. Or at all, at least in front of me. I was worried sick about you. Now I know why." She laughed, but tears filled her eyes. "I'm supposed to be your best friend."

Hannah took her hand. "I wanted to tell you, but I was terrified of what you'd think of me."

"So, why now?" Zara eased away from Hannah's grasp.

"I came to realize that not being truthful, even by omission, hurts those around me. My relationship with Bren had enormous problems, but my dishonesty also caused issues between us." Hannah sniffed. "I've hurt you by keeping this from you, as I have my parents and others. You haven't gotten the true version of me. I'm tired of living with the guilt, knowing that this thing exists between us that shouldn't be there. You mean the world to me and deserve to know what really happened that day."

"Yeah." Zara nodded. "Okay." She stood and pulled a tissue from a box on the credenza behind Hannah's desk and carefully wiped at her eyes.

"I'm so sorry." Hannah wanted to touch her, hug her, but the aura radiating from Zara didn't make her seem receptive.

"I often wondered how you lasted as long as you did with her. She never seemed right for you." Zara didn't face her. "I blamed it on the way you met, the way she chased after you. Once that excitement dissipated, there wasn't anything left, no foundation upon which to build."

Hannah considered it. "You may be right." What a mess she and Bren had been. Hannah's heart went out to her, despite the harm Bren had caused. She'd tried repeatedly to find a substitute for the woman she couldn't fully have and had never succeeded.

"In a way, I understand why you did what you did, not telling anyone. But me? This is going to take some time to absorb. It's a lot." Zara quietly blew her nose. "I'm your best friend. I expected to be inside the circle of confidence." She stepped around Hannah's desk. "I'm going back to my office. Let's talk later."

"Zara." Hannah stood. "I'm so sorry."

"I know. I just need to think. Don't worry. You know I love you and can't stay mad at you for long." In the outer office, Jen cheerfully bade good-bye to her, but Zara's tone didn't reach the same level of enthusiasm.

When Jen entered, Hannah hadn't moved.

"Everything okay?"

Hannah forced a smile. "It's fine."

"Can I bring you anything?" Jen waited expectantly.

"No, thank you." It was times like this when Hannah wanted to talk to Vanessa, to lean on her for emotional support.

It took every drop of her willpower not to reach out.

Chapter Thirty-two

When Vanessa pulled out of her spot behind Late Bloomer, Sonja's name popped up on her console screen. "Hi."

"Hey, you. I had a few minutes and thought I'd try to catch you on your way to the school." Sonja's chipper voice cut through the gray day like a sunbeam.

"You succeeded. I just left work."

"Oh, good." In the background, a dog barked. "Just checking in. I haven't heard from you since you left over a week ago."

That long? "It's been unusually busy at work. Apparently, February weddings are in vogue again."

"How's Hannah?"

Vanessa had been waiting for the question. "She's fine. Volunteers every Thursday without fail."

"And?" The expectancy in Sonja's voice held a stop-messing-around quality. "How's your plan going?"

"I took her a sandwich yesterday, but I'm not making much headway." Vanessa was glad Sonja couldn't see the dejection probably written on her face.

"Why do you say that?"

"There's been some improvement but not as much as I hoped. She's put up her walls, and I don't know how to knock them down."

Sonja laughed. "A sandwich? My dear, you're going to need to do better than these token treats and bouquets, no matter how gorgeous you make them."

"I apologized in person for my behavior. That counts for something."

"Finally." Sonja made some sort of noise. "What'd she say?"

Vanessa recalled the awkward conversation. "Not much. She said it was unnecessary because I'd given her the card."

"Maybe that's true for her."

"Perhaps." It hadn't felt like it though. Hannah had been holding back. Vanessa had seen her do it before. "Regardless, it needed to be done."

"I agree."

"When it comes down to it, though, I've hurt her one too many times." Vanessa swallowed the sick feeling creeping up her throat. "I may have no recourse."

A pause ensued, and Vanessa could almost hear Sonja thinking.

"I'm not convinced of that. You're going to have to up the ante. If she's worth it to you, you need a plan beyond flowers and coffee."

Vanessa debated whether to say anything, but her curiosity to know Sonja's opinion won. "I'm going to ask her to have dinner with me on my birthday." Would it allow them to reconnect and find that spark again?

"Does she know it's tomorrow?"

"No." Vanessa hadn't mentioned it. Neither of them had. She wondered when Hannah's was.

"Just prepare yourself. She may have plans."

The unsaid lingered in the air. *With another woman.*

"Well, good luck, and tell me how it goes. In the meantime, I'm going to brainstorm some ideas for you."

Vanessa laughed. "Oh, no. I can't wait to hear what you devise. Hey, I'm nearing the school and need to find parking. Can we chat later?"

"Sure. Love you."

"Love you, too." Vanessa hung up and found a space a block over. As she cut across the teachers' parking lot, she tried to ignore the pang in her chest. Hannah wasn't there. Granted, it wasn't time for class yet, but Vanessa was running unusually late. Chloe had caught her with an important question right as she tried to leave. She and Hannah usually arrived fifteen minutes early to open the garden and set up.

Her phone vibrated.

Vanessa stopped and looked at it. A text from Hannah.

Sorry, can't make it. Burglarized last night. Gems taken.

The weight on Vanessa's chest wouldn't allow her to breathe. She looked up when she heard her name. Raymond trekked from the building to the still-gated garden, his dark ponytail bouncing behind him. The students followed. Vanessa broke into a jog and met him at the entrance.

"Hi." He grinned at her. "We don't usually beat you here." His smile faded. "You all right?"

"I need to go." She waved her phone. "There's an emergency. Can you handle things today?"

"Sure." He pointed. "I have a college student observing this week. He's fingerprinted and everything. We're good. Do what you need to do."

"Thank you." She hugged him and took off running.

❖

When Vanessa arrived at Baros's headquarters, she parked in front of the No Stopping sign and bollards protecting the front and jogged into the lobby.

Charles looked up with a smile. "Hey, Vanessa."

"Please don't let them tow my car. I'll bring more flowers for your girlfriend next time."

"You got it."

She bolted to the elevators and smashed the button until the doors opened.

When she arrived on Hannah's floor, she raced down the hallway and only slowed when she careened into Jen's office. Before Vanessa could reach Hannah's open door, Jen blocked her path, springing from her chair with surprising agility.

"You can't go in there."

Vanessa tried to duck around her. "I just need to see her." She gasped for breath even though the hallway couldn't have been more than sixty feet long.

"You don't have an appointment."

Vanessa tried to see around the door frame, but Jen held up a hand.

"I can't let you in. You can take a seat ov—"

"What's going on?" Hannah appeared behind Jen, the lines on her forehead marking her confusion. "Vanessa. Why aren't you at the school?"

This time, she darted past Jen and cupped Hannah's face. "Are you all right? What happened?" She skimmed Hannah's arms and searched her top to bottom looking for…what? Blood? Cuts? Holes? "Were you hurt?" Vanessa touched her face again, willing her to say something.

Hannah glanced at Jen. "Reschedule my next meeting and hold my calls, please." She led Vanessa into her office and closed the door.

"Are you okay?" Vanessa needed Hannah to say something.

Hannah took her by the shoulders. "I'm fine. Look at me. I'm fine. Okay?" She wrapped Vanessa in an embrace.

Shaking replaced her gasping. "Your text. I drove here as fast as I could. I was so worried something bad had happened to you." She'd missed the comfort of being held by Hannah.

Hannah pulled back. "Darling, it was a burglary not a robbery." She rubbed Vanessa's arms.

"No one held you at gunpoint?" Vanessa only became aware of her tears when Hannah wiped them away. "Or knifepoint?"

"No." Hannah tenderly appraised her.

"I figured you'd left late last night and someone surprised you in the dark."

Hannah smiled. "I don't make it a habit of carrying jewels around. And would you believe I leave every day by five thirty? I've made some changes. I have a new VP of Operations, so I'm not the one dragging fans out of storage after hours. I redid our company hierarchy, and I delegate more." She pointed toward the door. "Jen, my new assistant since I switched with Zara, will have my job if I'm not careful. She's incredible."

"Not bad to look at either, I imagine." Vanessa focused on the tan carpet.

Hannah tipped her face up with a single finger to her chin. "I wouldn't know. And if I *were* caught looking, Zara would probably put my head on a stake."

"Oh." Things clicked into place. "Is that why you swapped?"

"One of the reasons, yes, though nothing has happened between them, to my knowledge, so please don't say anything."

"Of course not." Vanessa took a breath to calm her still-racing heart, but it came out shaky.

"You were worried." Hannah tucked a couple of curls behind Vanessa's ear.

"Yes. What happened?" Vanessa gently rested her hands on Hannah's waist, and Hannah didn't move away.

"We discovered ten precious gems missing. It's looking like it's probably an inside job. The police just left. They're working with my security team to check camera footage and badge entries to try to determine who did it." Hannah led them to the chairs in front of her desk. "Here, sit. Would you like some water?"

Vanessa welcomed the seat, even if it meant letting go of Hannah. The wobbliness in her legs hadn't stopped. "No, thanks. I'll be fine. I'm sorry for my overblown reaction."

Hannah sat. "It's nice to know you care."

A heavy ball formed in Vanessa's belly. "You didn't know?" Was she that opaque?

"I had an inkling." Hannah's lips curved into a small smile.

Now that she was calmer, Vanessa was able to take her in. Hannah was always attractive, but here, her air of professionalism and designer clothing only heightened her appeal. Today's gray houndstooth suit was no exception.

"Look at you," she said, "making all kinds of changes."

Hannah looked pleased, though her confidence faltered. "Not just at work. Yesterday I told Zara and my parents the truth about the day Bren died."

Vanessa's pride in Hannah warmed her, and the weight in her stomach eased. "How'd they take it?" It couldn't have been easy.

Hannah tipped her head to one side. "So, so. Zara's hurt, and she has a right to be. We talked a little this morning, and I'm working on mending things with her. My parents scolded me like I was eight years old. They'll probably discuss me all day, and whatever comes of that, I'll hear about it tonight."

Vanessa squeezed her hand. "You did the right thing."

"Yes, though it should've been sooner." Hannah's eyes glazed over, and she seemed to become lost in thought. "Who's at the school with Ray and the kids?"

"He has a student teacher or something with him."

"Damn." Hannah rubbed her face. "I'm going to miss two weeks in a row."

A jolt of something unpleasant cut through Vanessa. "Why?"

"I'm traveling for work next week. I won't be here on Thursday. It's not something I can rearrange, or I would."

"It's all right." Vanessa hoped the universe would forgive her harmless lie. The thought of Hannah being away stirred the nest of hornets in her chest. "If there's no one else, perhaps you could text me when you land…and stuff."

Hannah closed her eyes, and when she opened them, she softly said, "Vanessa, there hasn't been anyone since I met you."

The hornets transformed into brilliant fragile-winged butterflies alighting on Vanessa's insides.

"I turn forty-nine tomorrow," she said quickly.

Hannah sat taller in her chair. "Oh. What're you doing for your birthday?"

Vanessa had only one thing in mind. "I'd like to spend time with you. Perhaps dinner?"

If her request surprised Hannah, she didn't show it. "Why don't I take the afternoon off?"

"What about work?" It seemed too good to be true.

Hannah eyed her. "I told you. I've made changes. Some things are more important."

Like *her*? Is that what Hannah was trying to say? "I'd really like that."

Hannah rose. "I'll find something for us to do, unless you have suggestions." She offered Vanessa her hand.

"No preferences. Time with you is my only request." Vanessa stood, and they faced one another.

"Two Pisces. That explains a lot." Hannah gave her one of those genuine smiles that made the delicate lines around her mouth and eyes crinkle.

"Really? When were you born?"

Hannah walked her to the door. "March fourteenth." She ushered her into the outer office. "I'll text you later about tomorrow."

"Okay."

Jen glanced at their clasped hands, and Hannah slid hers free.

Vanessa hesitated, still heavy with emotion and hating to lose sight of Hannah so soon after reassuring herself she was safe. But Hannah had a burglary to solve, and Vanessa could still make the last half of class if she hurried. "I'm glad you're all right."

"Thanks for checking on me." Hannah shoved her hands into the too-small pockets of her pants.

Vanessa smiled as she took a few steps backward. "Two is better than one, and all that."

A little ripple of amusement traveled across Hannah's features. She pointed down the corridor. "Skipping is fine, but no more running in my halls," she said with a grin.

Part Three

Chapter Thirty-Three

Vanessa waited for Hannah in one of the patio chairs on her front porch. Hannah insisted on driving since it was Vanessa's special day, and she'd offered to pick her up at the store at noon, but Vanessa informed her no one worked on their birthday at Late Bloomer. So, Vanessa flipped through the issue of *Horticulture* Hannah had given her and tried not to scan the street for her Lexus every thirty seconds.

When Hannah pulled into her driveway a few minutes before noon, Vanessa couldn't help but be surprised Hannah had been able to leave work on time. After grabbing her jacket, Vanessa slid into the passenger's seat. "Hi."

Hannah smiled. "Happy birthday. Ready to have some fun?"

"Thanks, and yes. Am I dressed appropriately for whatever we're doing?" Goose bumps broke out as Hannah's gaze swept over her.

"Perfect." Hannah threw the car into reverse. "You look very nice."

"Thank you." Vanessa hadn't been sure what to wear, so she'd chosen a powder blue linen shirt and her nicest pair of jeans.

"Do you want to know the plan, or would you like to be surprised?" Hannah headed south.

"Surprise me." She usually liked to know what to expect, but she trusted Hannah.

"Then sit back and relax. We'll be there soon."

When Hannah turned into a parking garage downtown, Vanessa sat forward in her seat. "Are we really going there?"

Hannah smiled as she took a ticket from the automated machine. "Where do you think we're headed?"

"The Convention Center." It was within walking distance, and Vanessa vibrated with anticipation.

"Oh? What's there?" Based on Hannah's grin, she knew exactly what was taking place.

Vanessa unbuckled, unable to get out of the car fast enough. A dinging sounded. "Are we going to the Flower and Garden Festival?" The annual Northwest event was the second largest show in the nation.

"We might be." Hannah pulled into a space vacated by a minivan.

"I haven't been able to go in years." Vanessa wondered how long Hannah would tolerate her visiting the different booths, on-site gardens, and maybe even a seminar or two.

As if reading her mind, Hannah said, "This is your day. I didn't plan lunch because the website said they have food booths, so we can nibble on things there. And we can stay until closing if that's what makes you happy."

Vanessa remembered. "Amazing food. Chocolate, pickles, coffee, alcohol. All kinds of goodies. But if you want a real meal, we should eat beforehand."

"Do you?"

Vanessa curled her hand around Hannah's elbow as they walked toward the stairs. "No, I'm happy with this." And grateful they'd seemed to find a comfortable space in which to exist together, if only for today. It brought back pleasant memories of when they'd been in San Francisco, though she couldn't stop the foreboding thought that her happiness would transform like Cinderella's coach into a pumpkin come midnight.

"Perfect." Hannah briefly touched her hand.

And it was.

Hours later, they retrieved the two flats of plants that Vanessa had purchased from different vendors and Hannah's small floral arrangement from the package check station and loaded them into the trunk. Vanessa's cheeks hurt from smiling. It had been one of the best times in recent memory, probably since the day they'd spent in San Francisco.

As Hannah navigated to the parking garage exit, she asked, "What was your favorite part?"

Vanessa let out a whoosh of air. "Oh, how am I supposed to choose? I always love the artistic display gardens. How are they able to create those in just a few days? They're incredible. The Survivors and Thrivers seminar on hearty garden plants was informative, too. So was the one on the Human Impulse to Garden." She turned at Hannah's low laugh. "What?"

"I wish I weren't driving so I could see your face. You're so excited."

"You saw me all day."

Hannah paid and exited the garage. "Yes, and I was entertained by your enthusiasm the entire time."

"How about you? Did you enjoy anything, or did I drag you along for," Vanessa checked the time, "six hours? Wow. No wonder I'm starving."

"Me, too. We're going to get food next. To answer your question though, I had fun. I liked the talk on the secrets of growing flowering houseplants. But my favorite was the seminar on how to make flirty floral arrangements."

"Because it was Bubbles & Blooms, and they served champagne?" Vanessa teased her, but she'd witnessed Hannah's investment in making her own charming piece.

"No. You know those things, but it's new to me. I wasn't aware so much went into it." She glanced at Vanessa. "Thanks for allowing me to do that. You were probably bored."

She hadn't been. In fact, she'd been so enthralled by Hannah's interest in her profession that she'd enjoyed observing her. "I loved it. Watching you create such a beautiful arrangement in such little time was impressive. You have natural talent."

"Thanks. That means a lot coming from you."

They'd probably driven less than a dozen blocks, right into the heart of downtown.

"Are we going to the waterfront?"

Hannah laughed. "For someone who didn't want to know about today's agenda, you sure have a lot of questions."

"I'm just excited."

"Is it too touristy?" Hannah turned on her signal, and Vanessa spotted another garage.

"No. I'm ecstatic, actually."

"Good." Hannah made the turn.

"I grew up here, but as a kid, I never did many of the things most Seattleites eschew. We didn't have money, and my mom being who she is, I didn't have many friends because I wasn't comfortable bringing anyone home. I led a sheltered life."

Hannah took her hand. "I never would've guessed. You seem well-rounded and worldly."

"I've traveled as an adult and tried to become cultured." Vanessa recalled her childhood. "But I'd never left the state until I went to college. I'm not sure my mother ever has. For all I know, she's never been out of King County."

Hannah parked. "Then, tonight, we're going to play tourists."

She'd avoided responding to Vanessa's mention of her mother.

Once out of the garage, Hannah offered her hand. "Hang on to me. It'll be easier getting through this Friday night crowd."

Vanessa wondered if that was the only reason. It was busy, but it wasn't comparable to Times Square at any time of day or night. Still, the waterfront was a popular place, and people flocked to it.

"It's probably too late to see them throw fish at Pike's Place," Hannah said.

"That's okay. I've been there because of the farmers' market." She laughed. "Mostly because I wanted to check out what flowers the competition sold."

"Of course, you did." Hannah squeezed her hand. "C'mon, let's find food. Your choice. I'm buying."

They walked along Alaskan Way hand in hand, and for as hungry as they claimed to be, didn't hurry.

Vanessa slowed. "I wouldn't mind seafood." All the bustle and noise coming from the restaurants on the piers drew her in. "I haven't had oysters in a long time."

"This way then." Hannah tugged her toward the crowd, and the aroma of fresh sourdough bread filled the air. "How about here?"

They scored a small table with a view of the water and ordered a dozen oysters, half Kumamotos and half Olympias. Since the place was crowded, their starter took a while, but the steaming clam chowder bread bowls arrived right behind them.

Vanessa blew on the soup and closed her eyes at the first spoonful. "Mmm, so creamy." When she opened them, Hannah waved her hand in front of her mouth. "Did you burn your tongue?"

"Mm-hmm," Hannah said, taking a drink of beer. "It looked and smelled so good, I couldn't wait."

The food wasn't the only thing that looked good. The black leather jacket Hannah wore over her tan blouse was a surprising and welcome addition. Her honeyed hair brushed her shoulders, and the perfection of the image before her had Vanessa concentrating extra hard on her meal.

With the open-air design of the restaurant and the breeze blowing through it, Vanessa was thankful she'd brought her jacket. The sun had set before they'd finished at the Flower and Garden Festival, and by now, true darkness heightened the bright glow of island lights and the ferries as they shuttled cars and passengers across Elliot Bay and the Sound. Not far away, the Great Wheel slowly rotated in a kaleidoscope of colored lights as it loaded and unloaded passengers.

"You're shivering. Come over here." Hannah scooted closer to the window, making room for Vanessa on the interior. As Vanessa moved her chair to the other side of the table, Hannah pulled her bowl across. Before Vanessa could sit, Hannah eliminated the three to four inches of space Vanessa had left between their seats so when Vanessa sat, their legs touched. "That's warmer, right?"

"Yes." She picked up her spoon. In so many ways. Holding hands had been one thing, especially under the pretense of getting through the crowd, but they'd rarely had this much contact since she threw herself at Hannah after the burglary, and before that, the escapade in her foyer that felt like a decade ago.

"I thought going on the Great Wheel after this would be fun." Hannah glanced outside. "There aren't as many people out now, and it's February, so I wouldn't think it'd be too busy." She turned to Vanessa. "Have you ridden it?"

"No. I've never been on a Ferris wheel."

Hannah looked like she could be knocked over with a sourdough baguette. "Then we must."

"Have you been on it?"

The sheepish look on Hannah's face foretold her answer. "I've always been too busy. I heard the views are great, though we won't be able to see the mountains in the darkness. We'll have to come back in the daylight."

Vanessa didn't want to put too much weight into the thought of them spending more time together. Other than working with the kids, they'd interacted little the last few months. Hannah had dutifully texted her while traveling, before she took off, when she landed, and—what Vanessa considered bonuses—when Hannah arrived at the hotel or returned after a late dinner meeting. However, Vanessa wasn't twenty-two anymore, and she'd had enough life experience to know these things meant little. She'd have to work for anything meaningful and lasting between them, and her time and energy didn't guarantee results.

Still, she could enjoy tonight.

And she did, for the most part. Her first experience with a Ferris wheel went much like she'd expected. The vibrant views of lit downtown buildings and the lights across the water had been pretty. While standing on the pier waiting to board, she'd found the LED light show on the wheel itself entertaining. However, after the attendant directed them into one of the cabins, he ushered in a father and his two teenage daughters behind them. A small child could've sat in the space Hannah left between her and Vanessa, and they said little more than short exclamations over the pleasing sights.

When they disembarked, they slowly walked back the way they'd come. Hannah didn't take her hand this time, and while it was less busy, Vanessa had a feeling that wasn't the reason. They passed the piers, gift stores, restaurants, and sweet shops until they reached the garage where they'd parked across from the cruise ship terminal and ferries.

"Feel free to say no, but I bought you a small cake if you'd like to see my place. If not, I can bring it to you tomorrow."

Hannah had moved months ago, but Vanessa still hadn't seen where she lived. They'd been planning on going there on New Year's Eve before Vanessa's mother broke her hip and everything had gone to hell.

Vanessa stopped. "What kind of cake?"

When Hannah turned, she sported that genuine smile that made her attractive age lines appear. "Chocolate, of course."

"I should probably check on Ralph, too. Is he still liking his new home?" They resumed walking.

A low chuckle preceded Hannah's response. "I'm surprised you remembered his name. You've only met once."

"He's very memorable." Vanessa took a chance and looped her arm through Hannah's. Hannah didn't pull away or acknowledge it, leaving Vanessa unsure of her opinion on the matter.

When they reached Hannah's building, Vanessa took in her surroundings. "We probably could've walked."

"True. Pier 70 is only a block away." Once inside the elevator, Hannah selected the top floor, which didn't surprise Vanessa.

Hannah's condo sported a modern look, with white walls, warm wooden floors, and black window casings. "This is definitely more you," Vanessa said, wandering through the open living area.

"Yes, I need the light."

Hannah read a few of the spines on the bookcase. Classics, thrillers, romances. Candles with blackened wicks dotted the coffee and end tables. "Do you miss Fremont?"

"You know, it's funny. Sometimes I used to be able to hear the elephants trumpeting at night in the zoo if I had a window open. I miss that. Oh, there's Ralph." From her spot in the kitchen, Hannah pointed to a table near a south-facing window.

Vanessa touched a leaf. "Look how big he's gotten. You're going to have to stop treating him so well, or I'll have to make you a new pot."

"Are you still taking classes?"

Vanessa looked up. "No, but I'd make one for you."

Hannah broke eye contact and rummaged through an open drawer. "That's nice of you."

Was that a blush on her cheeks? Vanessa walked closer but couldn't be sure. She turned her attention to the dessert. It wasn't a typical birthday cake, but a small work of art from a high-end bakery whose name she recognized on the box. Someone with immaculate handwriting had piped "Happy Birthday, Vanessa" on top. Perfect chocolate curls surrounded it.

Hannah pushed a single white candle into the ganache above the lettering. "To represent the last wonderful year of your forties."

"Thank you for not setting the place afire with forty-nine of them. Please, don't sing though."

"Was I that bad on the road trip?" Hannah frowned and flicked a lighter on and off.

Vanessa shook her head. "No, you have a beautiful voice. It just makes me uncomfortable having that much attention on me."

"It's no more of my attention than you usually have."

Vanessa could read volumes into that sentence if she desired.

Hannah lit the candle and pushed the cake toward her with a smile. "Happy birthday."

Vanessa blew it out.

Hannah cut them pieces, and they ate standing in the kitchen. When they finished, Hannah boxed up the rest. "For you to take home," she said as she retrieved Vanessa's jacket from a hook near the door.

As far as Vanessa knew, Hannah didn't work on Saturday, but for whatever reason, the evening seemed to be ending.

Traffic was light, and they arrived at Vanessa's in a little over ten minutes. Hannah pulled into the driveway.

"Was your porch light on when you left?" Concern filled Hannah's voice.

"No." Vanessa undid her seat belt while protecting her cake. "I forgot." She didn't want the night to be over. The entire day had been so lovely, so perfectly catered to her. And Hannah had been beside her throughout.

"I'm walking you to your door. I don't like that I can't see past those hedges."

Once on her porch, Vanessa set the box on the same chair on which she'd waited for Hannah all those hours earlier. She unlocked the door and turned. Hannah was right there, looking as fine as she had all night in her casually elegant way. "I had a wonderful day. I've never had a birthday like this. Thank you."

Hannah smiled. "I'm glad you enjoyed it. I couldn't believe my luck when I found out the Flower and Garden Festival was going on."

A fluttering inside Vanessa's chest made her leave the cake where it was. She closed the distance between them, resting her hands on Hannah's waist. "Would you like to come inside?" When Hannah didn't answer right away, Vanessa slid her arms into Hannah's jacket, and warmth poured from Hannah's body into hers.

"Vanessa." Hannah's voice sounded strained.

Vanessa looked at Hannah's lips, not for the first time tonight. She'd admired them while Hannah sipped her beer, smiled at her in her condo with a bit of chocolate on her lower one, and now, when they looked so soft and kissable in the glow from the streetlight. Her body took that moment to remember what Hannah's mouth could do, and a surge of arousal left her weak-kneed. It hadn't been in her plan, but now that they were standing here, she knew what she wanted. She lifted the hem of Hannah's shirt until her fingers met the heated skin of Hannah's back. Vanessa caressed the exquisite softness. "Stay the night."

Hannah pulled away, though she held one of Vanessa's hands between hers as she did. "We're not there yet."

Vanessa stepped closer and rested her palm on Hannah's cheek. "We've been there before."

"That, those times, were mostly about sex." Hannah looked down.

Mostly? But the sting of rejection hit, even if it brought new questions about what they were to one another.

"We both need to work on things, try to get ourselves to better places." Hannah met her gaze and traced her cheek from temple to jawline. "The next time we're together, if there's a next time, I'd like to make love to you."

It took a moment for Vanessa to comprehend, and when she did, the overwhelming sensation squeezed her lungs. She simply didn't have a response for that.

It turned out, she didn't need one.

Hannah embraced her tightly, and the press of lips against the side of her head were followed by a whispered, "Happy birthday, Vanessa." And then Hannah was gone in a series of nimble steps down Vanessa's front walk and into her car.

Numbly, Vanessa picked up the box and opened the door. It'd been a wonderful day, one of the best. Even being turned down couldn't detract from that. Too late, she realized her plants were in Hannah's trunk. She could've called, asked Hannah to come back, but Vanessa preferred to leave the night as it ended. Besides, it'd give her an excuse to see Hannah tomorrow.

Chapter Thirty-four

Hannah looked up from her attempt at building a bean trellis when someone squealed just inside the garden's gate. Vanessa had wrapped her arms around a woman. It wasn't until she let go that Hannah recognized Sonja, and relief filled her.

"I can't believe you're here." Vanessa squeezed her again. "Why didn't you tell me you're coming?"

Hannah rose and dusted herself off.

"I couldn't surprise you if you knew of my plans." Sonja turned to her. "Hannah, it's good to see you." She opened her arms.

Hannah held up her hands. "I'm filthy."

"No more than she is." Sonja embraced her.

Based on Sonja's size, Hannah had first assumed she'd be delicate, but she'd proven to be pure muscle stretched over a steel frame. She could probably snap Hannah in two. Maybe there was something to that farming thing. "It's nice to see you again."

"You, too." Sonja patted her arm. "Put me to work. What can I help with?"

Vanessa stood smiling, hands on her hips. "How'd you know which school?"

"My dear, you talk of *almost* nothing else." Sonja winked and walked past her to pull a pair of gloves from the supply wagon. "Need some help with that trellis?"

Hannah glanced at the mess of wire, zip ties, and twine. "It looked easier on the YouTube video."

"You've made a good start. Once we get it attached to the side of the bed, you'll see it take shape."

Vanessa returned to mixing worm castings into the soil, and past her, Raymond pulled the kids aside for an obvious teachable moment. Hannah caught snippets about pH and fertilizer.

"I heard you treated Vanessa to a very nice birthday."

Sonja's nonchalance seemed genuine, so Hannah shelved her initial wariness. Not every best friend was as meddlesome as Zara. "It was nothing. Luckily, she's easy to please."

"Only because it sounds like you put some thought into it. Jeffrey gives me expensive gifts each year, some of them probably made by your company, but I doubt he considers what would make me happy."

In that case, Hannah had knocked it out of the park. She'd put immeasurable thought into what Vanessa might enjoy, and the garden show occurring then had been fortuitous. She'd been less confident about the waterfront idea, but Vanessa had seemed quite excited by it. That Sonja had compared what Hannah had done for Vanessa to a husband's gift for his wife wasn't lost on her. "I got lucky. If the festival hadn't been happening, Vanessa might've ended up going roller skating." Hannah's heart skipped a beat when Vanessa looked at her and winked.

"Did you fly or drive?" Vanessa sat back on her heels as she addressed Sonja.

Sonja clipped the end of the wire. "Flew."

"You rented a car? I would've picked you up."

"Then I wouldn't have been able to see your shocked expression turn into happiness, would I?" Sonja looked at Hannah. "She doesn't get it."

Hannah smiled, remembering the times *she'd* been the one putting a joyous look on Vanessa's face.

By the end of class, Hannah and Sonja had constructed a fine-looking trellis. It ended up sturdier than if Hannah had built it herself.

As the kids filed out the gate, Sonja tossed her gloves at Vanessa who caught them and tucked them in the shed before Hannah locked it.

"Is that Italian restaurant I like still open?" Sonja wiped her brow. "Let me treat you both to dinner tonight."

"Oh, I couldn't," Hannah said. "You two go ahead. I'm in dire need of a shower." She looked up to meet Vanessa's intense stare. Had she done something wrong?

"Nonsense." Sonja put an arm around her as they walked toward the gate. "You're joining us. Don't worry. None of us are going looking like this. Let's go clean up, and we'll text you the reservation time. You can meet us there."

Pasta sounded terrific, and Hannah's hard work today justified the calories. "All right."

Sonja clapped. "It's settled then. Where are you two parked? I took my chances in the teachers' lot."

"I'm a street over." Hannah pointed.

"Me, too. I'll walk with you." Vanessa turned back to yell at Sonja who'd stopped by a white sedan. "Did you bring your house key?"

Sonja gave her a thumbs up.

Hannah and Vanessa headed toward their cars.

"Did you get everything from the garden show planted?" Hannah's palms sweated. Was it because the temporary buffer Sonja had provided was gone? Hannah and Vanessa had managed to volunteer last week with no problem. What was happening now?

"Most of them. I haven't decided where to put the last two."

Hannah stopped beside her Lexus.

"Thanks for agreeing to come. Sonja likes you." Vanessa smiled. "I'll text you in a bit." She trailed her hand along Hannah's lower back as she passed.

As she patted her pockets and felt around in her backpack for her keys, Hannah watched Vanessa walk down the sidewalk. She froze. Her cars had come with keyless entry for years. Strange how plans of an impromptu dinner had her so disoriented.

❖

Two hours later, clean and refreshed, Hannah closed her menu and set it aside. Their server, Lisa, as she'd introduced herself, offered the first taste of wine to Sonja, who'd chosen the bottle, then poured all three glasses. She efficiently took their orders and disappeared.

Like her, Vanessa and Sonja had showered and changed. Sonja wore a black tunic and matching pants for a clean and classy look. But it was Vanessa in her crimson silk shirt and dark pants that screamed stylishness and sophistication. It took concentration for Hannah not to stare at the onyx and gold necklace dipping low between the buttons Vanessa had left undone.

Sonja peeled back the white napkin in the basket in front of her. "I hear your business was burglarized."

The aroma of baked bread reached Hannah. She took a piece when Sonja offered. "Yes. They made an arrest this week."

Vanessa touched her arm. "Who did it?"

"One of our jewelers was caught on camera in Tacoma pawning a handful of gems that matched some of the ones taken. When they brought him in for questioning, he confessed. They found the rest in his apartment."

"Why'd he do it?" Vanessa's fingers remained on Hannah's sleeve.

"Sports betting. He only planned to borrow them to pay off his debt and buy them back when he made the money, or so he said. Fortunately for us, he'd been unaware of a random inventory check that discovered them missing."

Vanessa leaned against the banquette behind them. "I'm so glad it wasn't something more sinister." She appeared deep in thought.

An uncomfortable silence followed as they nibbled on items from the breadbasket.

"So, the greenhouses are doing well?" Hannah grasped for conversation topics.

Sonja lit up. "They're fabulous. Hasn't she shown you any of the feeds?"

"I haven't had the chance." Vanessa took a long swallow from her glass.

"Well, they're coming along nicely. This is going to be a stellar year for us. They'll allow us to do so many things we've only dreamed about." Sonja finished her explanation with such finality that another long pause ensued.

Hannah shifted in her seat. She licked her upper lip and tasted sweat. These lulls were intolerable. She turned to Vanessa. "How's your mom? Is she doing better?"

Vanessa's eyes widened, and the muscles in her neck went taut as she swallowed.

Sonja cleared her throat. "Pardon me. I need to use the ladies' room." She snagged her clutch and wandered toward the back.

Vanessa said nothing, just sat frozen with her lips slightly parted.

"Sorry. That's none of my business." Hannah turned her attention back to…well, she didn't know, so she made sure the ends of her knife and spoon aligned with the table edge.

"Actually, I want you to know." Vanessa twisted her napkin. "The answer to your question is, I'm not sure, because we're not speaking."

"That has to be awkward with her staying with you."

"She's not. She never has."

Vanessa's terse delivery set off alarms.

"What?" Hannah tried to reconcile this with what she'd thought the last few months.

Vanessa rapidly blinked. "I sent her to the rehab facility."

"Why didn't you tell me?" All this time, Hannah had been operating under the assumption that Vanessa was still allowing herself to be verbally and emotionally tortured.

"Many reasons. First, I didn't want you thinking I made the decision to win you back." Vanessa softly laughed. "Not that I had you in the first place, but hopefully you understand what I mean." She looked at Hannah. "I did it for me. Since then, I've worked hard in therapy, weekly until recently. I had a lot of issues that needed to be dealt with, like abandonment and guilt. Where in the past I'd compartmentalized and avoided them, this time I actually needed to address them. It's helped. I rarely hear her voice—I mean, have intrusive thoughts—anymore."

"I see."

"Do you?" Vanessa leveled her gaze on Hannah.

"No." Hannah's rapid breathing gave away her lack of composure. "Here, I'd been thinking that no matter how attracted to you I am, maybe you weren't the right woman for me because you'd never break that cycle of abuse. What if I'd moved on? Dated someone else?"

Vanessa looked away. "I thought about that. A lot actually. It was a risk I had to take. I had to believe what we have is stronger than that."

"You should've told me. I would've understood."

"You would've wanted to move forward, and you had work to do, too." Vanessa tapped her on the leg. "Look at all the positive changes you've made in your life since the beginning of the year. While you were wondering if I might be right for you, I'd been asking myself if I'd be content dating a workaholic, knowing I was always going to come second. I don't believe the answer would've been yes two months ago."

The extra time Hannah had been given might turn out to be worthwhile. "So, you cut your mother out of your life and never looked back?" How difficult that must've been.

"Not exactly. I sent her to rehab and asked her not to contact me." Vanessa sighed. "Of course, she didn't comply at first, but she's stopped calling. I'll admit, it's not a complete break. I still give her a stipend to live on each month and pay her bills."

"What's going to happen when you need those funds some day? Are you going to take care of someone who treated you terribly at your own detriment?"

"I don't need the money." Vanessa took a sip of wine and glanced toward the back of the restaurant. "There must be a long line."

How much time Sonja needed in the restroom didn't concern Hannah right now. "You might. What's going to happen when your Honda dies?"

Vanessa shrugged. "I'll buy something."

"How?"

Vanessa narrowed her eyes. "I get the feeling you think I'm hard up for money."

How to respond without offending her? "It must be at least ten years old."

"Oh, Hannah." Vanessa laughed. "Bertha's been great to me, and I love her. She runs well and gets great gas mileage. Why do I need a brand new car?"

"But—"

"I own my home, Late Bloomer, and the entire block it's on, including the building Seismic is in. All those businesses behind me lease their spaces, and I have a commercial property management agent who takes care of that."

"Oh." Hannah wanted to crawl beneath the table.

Vanessa smiled. "I've been making six figures since I was in my twenties. So, you see, providing for my mother, especially if it means I don't have to have any contact with her, is well worth the expense to me." She looked around. "Where's Sonja?"

Lisa returned and deftly unfolded a stand, then slid a tray onto it. As she placed plates of pasta in front of them, she said, "Your friend said to tell you she's taken care of your bill. She's going to bed early." As if to prove her point, no third entrée appeared. "And you're supposed to order dessert." She leaned closer. "You know, I couldn't help but notice you seem to be having an involved discussion. I know when my wife and I need to talk like that, it doesn't help to know people nearby are listening. We're not seating any more parties on the patio, and the last party is leaving if you'd like to move to a more private table outside."

Hannah raised her eyebrows, and Vanessa nodded. "Thank you."

"You two gather your things. I'll bring your food and drinks out." She reloaded the tray.

Hannah retrieved their jackets they'd draped over the extra chair, and Vanessa followed her outside. When Hannah sat at the one table beneath a glowing red heater, to her surprise, Vanessa lifted the chair on the opposite side and plopped it down beside hers. Hannah moved over to make room.

"It wouldn't hurt us to talk." Vanessa scooted in.

"True." Hannah was still smarting from finding out Vanessa hadn't told her about her mother. Was this how Hannah's parents and Zara had felt when she'd concealed how she'd been about to break up with Bren?

"We have so much to discuss." Vanessa slipped her hand over Hannah's thigh. "I've been wanting to ask your opinion about the best way to sell my engagement ring."

Intrigued, Hannah tilted her head. "Let me see if I can find you a private buyer. But why now?"

"It's finally time to move on. Why would I keep something that only conjures up bad memories? Besides, the money is going to be put to good use. I ordered new gloves and enough tools for each of the kids. And I bought a compost bin that can hold four times as much."

"Okay, loves. Here's your food." Lisa unloaded everything. "I'll check on you in a bit. I'm supposed to bring you another bottle of wine, so bottoms up." She tucked the tray beneath her arm and picked up the stand.

"Thank you." Hannah admired the sight of the city lights glinting off the water, then glanced at her meal. The orecchiette had sounded so delicious earlier but now did nothing for her.

Vanessa's phone vibrated. "Sonja. She's at the house and says not to be mad. She has the best intentions." Vanessa sent a text and put it away. "I know you're upset with me, but try to eat something. The fresh pasta here is fantastic."

Hannah picked up her fork and moved a few pieces around.

"Maybe you'd like mine better. Want to try it?" Vanessa held a piece of rigatoni inches from Hannah's face.

Hannah parted her lips and took the morsel from Vanessa's fork. The rich meat sauce complemented the noodles perfectly. "That's amazing." When Hannah looked up, she caught Vanessa staring at her mouth.

Vanessa quickly looked away. "It's my favorite dish, but I like yours, too."

"Here." Hannah offered her a bite and did no better ignoring the way Vanessa's gorgeous lips closed around it.

When they'd eaten half of their meals, Vanessa folded her napkin. "You know, we're past due for a real conversation."

Hannah couldn't agree more. "It's not that I haven't wanted to. It didn't feel right leading you on—leading both of us on—if I thought we didn't have a future. At the same time, I couldn't completely stay away from you." She smiled. "Yes, I'm fond of the kids and dedicated to the program, but that's not entirely the reason I volunteer each week."

Vanessa toyed with the pendant she wore. "I'm glad to hear that. At times, I worried it might be."

They were careening toward something Hannah found both exhilarating and terrifying, but she wouldn't have gotten off the ride if her life depended on it. "I couldn't be too close to you though. When you invited me to stay the night of your birthday, I almost caved." She pushed her plate aside. "And maybe you're right. If I'd let you in more, I would've been so focused on you, I wouldn't have made the changes I did." She took Vanessa's hand. "Not that I wasn't thinking about you constantly."

Vanessa smiled and ran her thumb over Hannah's fingers. "All these years—"

The door leading to the restaurant opened, and Lisa beamed at them. "How're we doing, loves? Are you interested in dessert?"

Hannah shook her head.

"I think we're fine. Will we be keeping you if we sit for a while?" Vanessa asked.

Lisa poured the rest of the wine between their glasses. "Not at all. I'm closing. Are you ready for your second bottle?"

"This will be fine. Why don't you take it home? Do you need us to say something to the manager?"

"Love, if I bring a bottle of this fancy wine home, my wife will probably do a cartwheel after being in the kitchen all day. We own the place. Been running it for twenty-three years now."

"You two enjoy it then." Vanessa pulled her drink closer. "We're going to chat a bit."

"That's sweet of you. I'll check on you in twenty or so."

Vanessa turned to Hannah. "How are you?"

"I'm not sure. There are so many emotions whirling around inside me."

Vanessa tucked a lock of Hannah's hair behind her ear. "On New Year's Eve, after I asked you to leave, I went straight to the hospital, and I heard my mother berating the staff even before I found her room. It took me a few days, but I realized you'd been right about her, not that I hadn't known it for some time, but accepting it was another matter. She was never going to treat me any differently."

Hannah gently touched her cheek.

Vanessa captured her hand and kissed her palm. "All these years I'd been looking to her for approval. And even if I didn't want to admit it, I desperately wanted her to love me. Standing there in her room, I realized

I no longer craved those things, at least not from her. I'd already found all of them in you, plus so much more."

Had Hannah heard correctly?

Vanessa squeezed her hand. "You care about me, encourage me, and believe in me. For years, I didn't think I wanted or needed love in my life, but I was wrong. I was managing, but I wasn't content and definitely wasn't happy. Then you came along, chasing me through a cemetery."

Hannah laughed. Oh, God. This conversation was really happening.

"But I made a grave mistake, no pun intended, and I wasn't sure you'd ever forgive me for what I said and did on New Year's. So, when I didn't take my mother in, I couldn't tell you. Plus, you needed time to work through your hurt and anger. And in the process, you began making changes, and I was so damned proud of you." Tears welled in Vanessa's eyes as she caressed Hannah's face. "And even when I pushed you away, we seemed to grow closer, if by smaller degrees. You got into my corners, threw back the blinds, and let in the light. I realized I was intimate with you in so many ways, more than I was with anyone else, and withdrawing hadn't avoided that. It turned out, I'd done something terrible and fallen in love with you, anyway."

Hannah could've flown home on her soaring feelings. "Why was that so bad?" She couldn't help smiling.

"I was a mess emotionally and mentally. I still am, to some extent. But the split with my mother brought a sense of freedom, and being around you, even as little as we were, helped push the echo of her voice away."

Hannah rose, drawing Vanessa up with her. She led them further down the patio away from the restaurant's windows. She linked their hands. "When do you put a flower in an arrangement?"

"What?"

Vanessa's amused expression was endearing.

"Do you put it in when it's looking its best?"

Vanessa studied her. "No, before. That way it reaches its peak when it's with the recipient."

"Exactly." Hannah pulled Vanessa to her. "That's how I want you, too. We're all works in progress. I don't believe for a second you're the definitive version of yourself."

Vanessa slowly smiled.

Hannah threaded her fingers into Vanessa's hair. "You are everything, the most incredible woman I've ever met. You deserve affection, loyalty, respect. Love. All of it." She lightly brushed their lips together. "You wound around me like those pea tendril things and didn't let go. I never stood a chance."

Vanessa laughed against her mouth. "You were right. We could be good together, have something special." She eased back. "Are you willing to forgive a woman madly in love with you?"

Hannah pulled her into a long, slow kiss. When her legs trembled, she leaned against the railing, Vanessa following. They kissed, slow and deep, under the starlight to the sound of the waves against the pilings.

At length, they settled into a tight embrace, Vanessa's head on Hannah's shoulder, holding on as if letting go wasn't an option.

Hannah knew then she wanted Vanessa. Not simply the feel and taste of her again—though that was true, too—but all of her. Tonight, tomorrow, and all the days and years ahead.

Knowingly, Vanessa kissed her cheek. "Let's go home," she whispered.

Hannah melted. Yes. A home with Vanessa was exactly what she wanted.

❖

In Hannah's living room, Vanessa didn't need to seduce her like she'd done in San Francisco. And there was no frantic sex up against a wall or on the floor like on Christmas. Instead, Hannah simply led Vanessa to her bedroom and quietly undressed her while they kissed. It was slow and sensuous and loving.

When Vanessa slid between the sheets, Hannah followed, settling the full length of her body on top of her.

Vanessa moaned. The arousal that'd been building all evening with the possibility and then the promise of what was to come flooded her. They kissed again until the rhythm of their hips matched that of their mouths. She explored Hannah's breasts, her back, her thighs, unable to get enough.

"I want you. I've wanted you since our road trip, maybe even before." She caressed Hannah's face. "And the one time since wasn't nearly enough." Vanessa gathered Hannah's hair and moved it aside. "It only made me want you more."

Hannah gazed at her, eyes smoldering. She ran her thumb over Vanessa's bottom lip. "This time's different, sweetheart. I told you what I plan to do."

Vanessa hadn't forgotten. *Make love to you.* "Yes." She trembled in anticipation and wrapped her legs around Hannah's waist. "Please touch me," she whispered.

Hannah hesitated. "You're shaking." She tightened the press of her arms against Vanessa's shoulders. "We've done this before."

"But like you said, this is different." Vanessa massaged the nape of Hannah's neck. "There's more involved this time."

"Trust me." Hannah softly smiled as she shifted and slid her hand between them. Vanessa closed her eyes as Hannah caressed her and kissed her throat. The gentle touches became firmer, and Vanessa pressed into them. The nip of Hannah's teeth grazing her nipple forced her eyes open, then almost immediately, she groaned at the balm of Hannah's hot mouth sucking the slight sting away. She thrust her hips against Hannah's thigh as she curled her fingers into Hannah's hair and moved to her other breast.

After lavishing it with the same attention, Hannah rested her forehead on Vanessa's chest, her fingers poised at her entrance. "May I?"

Vanessa tipped Hannah's face to her. "Darling, you never have to ask." She caught Hannah's bottom lip between her teeth.

Hannah slipped inside as she pressed her own wet center into Vanessa's hip. "Oh, God."

Vanessa's hungry kiss swallowed whatever came next.

She caressed Hannah's breast, brushed the soft skin of her stomach, and tried to reach lower. "I want to touch you."

Hannah moved so they could both lay on their sides, facing one another. When Vanessa reached for her, she rolled away. "Hold on." She turned over and opened a drawer. "Here. If you need it." She handed Vanessa a small vibrator as she rolled back. "It's mine. No one else has used it."

Vanessa blinked away tears. "How thoughtful. Come here." She captured Hannah's mouth in a heated kiss.

Hannah wasted no time sliding into her again, and Vanessa bent her leg to give her deeper access. *So good.*

She skimmed Hannah's hip, then her soft triangle of hair.

"Go ahead." Hannah pressed Vanessa's hand between her legs. "I'm ready for you."

Vanessa gasped at the wet heat of her.

Hannah's darkened eyes fluttered. "Vanessa."

They continued their leisurely exploration, and their strokes soon found a rhythm. While Hannah's touch made Vanessa's body respond, it was her intense gaze that captivated her.

"What do you need?" Vanessa searched her face.

"This. All of this. You. Just like this." Hannah brushed her mouth against hers. "I love you."

Vanessa smiled through her aching need. "I love you, too." With her chest bursting with awe for this newly realized thing between them, she nudged Hannah's lips apart with her own.

Leisurely transformed into passionate and hungry, and they moved together in search of the pinnacle. Hannah gasped and gave Vanessa's earlobe a gentle tug with her teeth.

At Hannah's low moan, Vanessa's need flamed, and she grabbed the vibrator. "I want to come with you."

Hannah nodded, her eyes hooded. "Yes." She coaxed Vanessa onto her back and straddled her thigh. She rocked gently. "Turn it on."

Vanessa did and thrust herself against Hannah's fingers as they brought themselves to the edge.

Hannah cupped Vanessa's breast, then kneaded her nipple. "Tell me when you're close." She studied her.

"I've been waiting for you." Vanessa thrust her hips harder. The sound of Hannah's laugh might've been the sweetest thing she'd ever heard.

"Now, then."

Vanessa pushed the button again, setting the vibration higher. "Oh, God."

"That's it." Hannah laced their fingers and pressed their hands into the mattress.

Vanessa held her gaze as they moved in tandem. "Curl your… oh…I'm—"

Above her, Hannah tensed, her head falling forward, her hair obscuring Vanessa's view of her face. Her muffled cry came right on the heels of Vanessa's orgasm. She rode Vanessa's leg for a few more long, languid strokes before dropping to the bed beside her.

Vanessa switched off the vibrator and luxuriated in the lingering pleasure of her muscles convulsing around Hannah's fingers until her climax was complete. She slipped Hannah's hand from between her legs and held it to her breasts as she snuggled against her. Vanessa struggled to wrap her mind around being here with Hannah with a future stretching out before them, the knowledge of what it meant, the fulfillment what they'd just done, and the unbearable desire to do it again.

Hannah kissed Vanessa's forehead, an obvious sign she was returning to the land of the functioning. "Rest up because that's just the beginning." She grazed her nails up Vanessa's back.

Vanessa shivered, then nuzzled her cheek against Hannah's breast. "I don't work tomorrow, so no quarrel here."

Hannah twisted, reaching toward her nightstand again.

Vanessa lifted her head to see her typing on her phone.

Hannah set it down with a thud. "Now neither do I. Come here." She brushed a few curls from Vanessa's face. "You're incredibly beautiful, especially when you smile like that. I thought I might have a heart attack when I saw you in that robe in San Francisco." She kissed her. After a moment, as if sensing something, she stopped. "What is it?"

"Do you ever worry that Bren will always be between us?" Vanessa hated to bring it up, but it'd been on her mind. "I don't want it to put a strain on what we have, but I'm not sure how to avoid it."

"Not if we're aware of it and focus on us. I learned things about myself because of my time with her." Hannah wrapped her arms around her. "Procrastination got me in trouble, so I need to live in the moment because the future is no guarantee. Look what happened when I delayed the breakup, then concealed the truth about it." She ran her fingers through Vanessa's hair, playing with a curl. "I've been too controlling as CEO, making unilateral decisions without trusting my employees to do their jobs. Thanks to you, I've discovered there's more to life than work, and I want to live each day with a newfound honesty, especially if you're going to be alongside me."

"You're amazing." Vanessa softly stroked Hannah's collarbone.

Hannah gazed at her. "Have you ever considered that neither one of us were meant to be with Bren? Maybe her role in our lives was to bring us together. So, maybe we should be grateful to her. I mean, without her, we might never have met."

Vanessa rested her head on Hannah's chest, the steady beating of Hannah's heart giving her unexpected comfort. "I like that. Being grateful. I'm thankful for anything and everything that brought us to this moment."

Hannah kissed her. "Perhaps there was always a grander plan."

Vanessa smiled against her lips. "Mmm. Perhaps." She eased on top of her. "Right now though, I'm interested in *our* plan for the rest of the night."

Epilogue

When Vanessa heard the front door close and footsteps in the hallway, she looked over her readers to find Hannah wearing a paint-splattered T-shirt and jeans and carrying an armful of mail. She took off her glasses. "Hi, darling."

Hannah set the stack on the table beside her and leaned down to kiss her. "Hello, beautiful." She massaged Vanessa's shoulders. "What are you working on?"

Vanessa gestured at her laptop. "I'm deciding how to spend the gift certificate Jeff and Sonja gave me for my fiftieth."

With her hand resting on Vanessa's back, Hannah bent to read her screen. "Drones?"

"Unmanned aerial systems. Sexist name, if you ask me."

"What would you do with one of those? Follow Sonja around her new fruit stand or find Duckie when the rabbit population booms?"

Vanessa put her arm around Hannah's waist. "No, agritech like these quadcopters help farmers' efficiency by cutting travel time to outlying fields for things like scouting for plant disease or checking for uneven crop growth."

"That's a camera there?" Hannah pointed to the model Vanessa had been researching.

"Two, actually. One forward and one downward-facing. It even has an option for a gimbal so the pilot can control the camera's direction."

Hannah squinted. "And you'd do that from here?"

"No, Sonja or Jeffrey would operate it, but having access to the photos and videos would mean I'd need to fly to Ashland less."

"Bringing your greenhouse total to eight wasn't enough for you, was it?" Hannah's playful teasing was just that. She'd been nothing but supportive. "Soon you'll be wanting to open a second Late Bloomer." Hannah put a finger to her chin and looked thoughtful. "What would we call it? The Late, Late Bloomer or the Super Late Bloomer?"

"Very funny." Vanessa lightly pinched Hannah's stomach, eliciting a squeal. "You're so ticklish." She scrabbled her fingertips into Hannah's side to the same effect.

Hannah caught her hands and pulled them behind her chair. She nosed her face into Vanessa's neck. "You're so bad."

It was Vanessa's turn to squirm.

"Watch yourself, or I won't be finishing the dining room floor for you today." Hannah kissed below her jaw.

"You promised you'd keep me company working on it while I stained the ceiling beams."

Hannah released her hands. "We both would've finished yesterday if you hadn't jumped me."

Heat washed over Vanessa. "That's a bit of an exaggeration. How was I supposed to resist you in that outfit on all fours?"

"You mean shorts?" Hannah raised an eyebrow. She grinned and kissed Vanessa's cheek. "Do you think we'll finish this house before *I* turn fifty?" Hannah raised her eyes to the leaded glass windows, and Vanessa followed her gaze.

"I hope so." The 1905 Dutch colonial they'd purchased last year had been renovated in 1990 but still needed work. Vanessa didn't mind. She'd enjoyed fixing up the Victorian five minutes away that they now rented to Zara, and working on this three-story beauty with the love of her life was no different. When she and Hannah toured the estate, the house captured her heart, but if it hadn't, the garden certainly would've. With its stunning architectural landscaping and central fountain, it offered more square footage of green space than most lots in Queen Anne. They'd put in an offer and signed papers within the week.

"Are you going into the office on Monday?" Hannah pulled the pile of mail closer.

"No, I'm working remotely. I need to pull some documents together for my accountant. You?"

"Same. Working from here." Hannah flipped through the letters and advertisements. "Oh! Look what arrived." She dropped everything except one glossy brochure. "Zara said she'd put it in the mail."

"That's right. You worked from home on Thursday and Friday, too."

"I have a stellar EA that allows me to do so."

Vanessa studied her. "Do you sometimes wish you had the control you used to have?"

"Only on the rare occasion. Overall, depending on those around me has been positive."

Vanessa leaned closer to see what Hannah held. "Is that the new marketing material for this year's Pride line?"

Hannah nodded and slid it toward her. "Didn't she do a fantastic job? Zara hired the same photographer we used last spring. She's so good at this marketing stuff."

Vanessa opened the brochure. Engagement and wedding rings glittering with rainbow-colored jewels adorned the pages. "I really like that there's nothing in here that says women's or men's rings."

"Zara's idea. She insisted on that from the beginning. We're catering to the queer community, and if there ever was a sector of the population to shirk binarism, we're it."

While most of the designs resembled the versions in Baros's first Pride collection, one stood out. "I really like this." Vanessa traced the delicate curves extending from either side of a center diamond. Within, smaller gems resided. "Was Priya or Johan the designer?" It didn't look like either of their styles, and the fact she could recognize that warmed her.

"Neither."

"Muriel? I thought rings weren't her thing."

"They're not."

Vanessa couldn't stop looking at it. "I didn't know you hired someone new. Well done finding them. It's gorgeous. That's the nicest ring in the collection, in my opinion." When Hannah said nothing, she looked up. "What?"

Tears filled Hannah's eyes. "That's my first attempt at a piece."

Vanessa pulled her close. "Why am I not surprised, my talented one?" She pulled Hannah down to kiss her and tenderly held her face. "You said you wanted to design, but your parents needed you to run the company. Yet somehow, you've done both. Will you ever cease to amaze me?"

"You really like it, even with all the colors?"

Vanessa returned to the page. "It's beautiful, but you know me. Maybe I'm old school, but I'd probably opt for traditional diamonds in it." She wasn't homophobic or in the closet, but she didn't feel the need to wear a rainbow on her finger.

"What do you think about the words inside the band?" Hannah tapped the image.

"Oh," Vanessa reached for her glasses, "I didn't even notice." She slid them on. "I don't see anything. Which ring, the one you designed?"

"Yes."

"Do you mean where an inscription would go?" She brought the brochure closer to her face.

"Maybe you can read it easier on this one." Hannah's voice no longer came from above Vanessa but beside her.

She turned.

Hannah had one knee on the carpet and a ring in her hand.

"What are you doing?" Vanessa whispered, peering over her glasses.

Hannah's beautiful, intelligent eyes held a hint of vulnerability.

Vanessa touched it. The ring was the same as the one in the photo, but sparkling diamonds filled each pronged placement. "How'd you know?"

"I make it my business to know everything I can about you." Hannah held it out to her. "Do you want to read what is says?"

Vanessa took it. Inside the band, $2 > 1$ was inscribed. She smiled and touched Hannah's cheek. "Two is greater than one. I remember when you first said that to me." She took off her glasses and placed them on the table.

"Would you like to try it on?"

"Absolutely not." Vanessa looked up to see disappointment on Hannah's face. "Only because you haven't asked me yet."

Hannah smiled and blushed. "I want to say something before I do." She took Vanessa's hand in hers. "I know you've been in this situation before, and," she looked down a moment, "I wasn't sure you'd want to be put in this position again."

Vanessa gripped her fingers, not wanting to interrupt whatever Hannah needed to say, but trying to impress upon Hannah her desire to be exactly where she was. She couldn't breathe, and her pulse pounded in her ears.

"I realize what happened before isn't something you want to experience again. No one would. And I know words and promises only go so far, and nothing I can say now will ease your fears. But if we do this, I'll prove to you every day through my actions how much I want to be your wife." Her eyes filled with tears. "Vanessa Holland, will you marry me?"

Vanessa slid from her chair. She threw her arms around Hannah's shoulders. "Yes, yes." Their lips met, the emotion of the moment spilling over into their kiss. "I love you."

"And I love you." Hannah pressed their foreheads together. "Try it on."

Vanessa slid it onto her finger. The diamonds sparkled as she lifted her hand. "It's perfect. It's positively gorgeous." She rested her palm on Hannah's cheek. "And my fiancée designed it." As she admired it again, she smiled, knowing she wouldn't have been prouder had Hannah been elected governor.

Hannah pulled something from her pocket and held it out. "Do you remember this?"

Vanessa picked up the tiny beer-label flower she'd folded for Hannah the day Zara called her to help Hannah pack. "You kept it."

"I'd like to work it into a design for my ring."

"What a wonderful idea." She handed Hannah the small piece of origami. "You haven't created it yet?"

Hannah stood and helped her up. "I wanted to make sure you accepted my proposal first."

Vanessa looped her arms over Hannah's shoulders. "Hannah Baros, did you really think my answer would be anything other than yes?"

Hannah's blush betrayed her uneasiness. "At times, this seems too good to be true."

Vanessa studied her a moment. "It's not. This is us. This is our life. We've worked hard for this, in our jobs and in the growth we needed to make. It took me a long time to find you. I'm not letting you go now." She kissed Hannah in a lingering way that made her think the dining room floor might have to wait another day.

"We could have the wedding on the farm." Hannah lightly held Vanessa's hips.

"And take photos with my new drone." Vanessa leaned in for another kiss.

"Unmanned aerial something. Patches could be the ring bearer."

Vanessa laughed. "Duckie would run off at the first sight of a squirrel."

Hannah's expression became serious. "I'll understand if you want to invite your mom."

"You're sweet, but absolutely not." Vanessa hadn't shared all the details of her mother's involvement in her last wedding day. Frankly,

Vanessa didn't need any more emotional setbacks that required months or years of therapy.

"Do you ever regret being estranged from her?" Hannah studied her.

"Do I wish I had a healthy relationship with a loving mother? Sure. But what we had didn't resemble anything like that. I'm content to support her financially but nothing more." This beautiful moment wasn't going to end on a sour note. "Have you thought about where you want to go for our honeymoon?"

Hannah beamed. "If you want to get married in the spring, we could go to Europe. See the Netherlands' famous tulip fields and France's lavender. And I had to research it, but the largest collection of roses is in a village in Germany called Sangerhausen. If you'd rather see orchids, apparently Singapo—are you laughing at me?"

Vanessa rocked her so they swayed side to side. "Are you sure you wouldn't rather see the Hope Diamond or the Crown Jewels?"

Hannah slid her hands beneath the hem of Vanessa's shirt and pressed their bodies together. "I don't care about those things. I want to see you happy. That's all I need in life."

"My engagement ring makes me very happy." Vanessa tilted her hand, and the jewels caught the light. "So, does my fiancée. I can't wait to tell Sonja. You know she's going to claim she's responsible."

"It was meddling to the extreme, and Zara's no better, but I'll admit Sonja and her sneaky ways put us in a forced proximity situation that allowed us to talk."

Vanessa grinned. "That was a memorable night."

"And next day." Hannah angled her head, their lips a breath apart. The open-mouthed kiss that resulted had them stumbling toward the stairs. "The floor's going to have to wait."

"So are the beams." Vanessa hooked her finger through Hannah's belt loop. "Thankfully, we finished the bedroom first."

About the Author

Alaina Erdell lives in Ohio with her partner and their crazy but adorable cats. She earned her degree in psychology from Gonzaga University, as well as her teaching credentials for K-8 and high school social sciences. She has either taught or been a substitute teacher for every grade from preschool through high school.

Prior to writing, Alaina worked as a chef in California. When she's not writing, she enjoys painting, experimenting with molecular gastronomy, reading, kayaking, traveling, and spoiling her four beloved nephews. Her favorite place is anywhere near the ocean.

Alaina has published four full-length contemporary romances and has a novella featured in the Bold Strokes Books anthology, *Hot Hires*.

Website: alainaerdell.com

Books Available from Bold Strokes Books

Flowers and Gemstones by Alaina Erdell. Caught between past loves and present secrets, Hannah and Vanessa must each decide if the other is worth making difficult changes for a shot at happiness. (978-1-63679-745-8)

Foul Play by Erin Kaste. Music librarian Kirsten Lindquist knows someone is stalking the symphony musicians, but can she prove that a string of murders and suspicious accidents are connected, all without becoming a victim herself? (978-1-63679-689-5)

Hollywood Hearts by Toni Logan. What happens when an A-list actress falls for a paparazzo, having no idea her love interest is the one responsible for the photos in a troublesome tabloid scandal targeting her? (978-1-63679-695-6)

Ride It Out by Jenna Jarvis. When the COVID-19 lockdown traps Mick and Katy in situations they'd convinced themselves were temporary, they're forced to face what they really want from their lives, and who they want to share them with. (978-1-63679-709-0)

Scarlet Love by Gun Brooke. Felicienne de Montagne is content with her hybrid flowers and greenhouses—until she finds adventurer Puck Aston on her doorstep and realizes nothing will ever be the same. (978-1-63679-721-2)

The Hard Stuff by Ana Hartnett. When Hannah, the sales manager for a big liquor brand, moves to Alexandra's hometown and rivals her local distillery, sparks of friction and attraction fly. It turns out the liquor is the least of the hard stuff. (978-1-63679-599-5)

The Hunter and Her Witch by Rachel Sullivan. When an ex-witch-hunter falls for a witch, buried pasts are unearthed, and love is placed on trial. (978-1-63679-830-1)

Trustfall by Patricia Evans. Devri and Shiv never expect their feelings for each other to linger, but sometimes what you've always wanted has a way of leading you to who you've always needed. (978-1-63679-705-2)

All For Her: Forbidden Romance Novellas by Gun Brooke, J.J. Hale, Aurora Rey. Explore the angst and excitement of forbidden love few would dare in this heart-stopping novella collection. (978-1-63679-713-7)

Finding Harmony by CF Frizzell. Rock star Harper Cushing has to rearrange her grandmother's future and sell the family store out from under her, but she reassesses everything because Gram's helper, Frankie, could be offering the harmony her heart has been missing. (978-1-63679-741-0)

Gaze by Kris Bryant. Love at first sight is for dreamers, but the more time Lucky and Brianna spend together, the more they realize the chemistry of a gaze can make anything possible. (978-1-63679-711-3)

Laying of Hands by Patricia Evans. The mysterious new writing instructor at camp makes Grace Waters brave enough to wonder what would happen if she dared to write her own story. (978-1-63679-782-3)

Seducing the Widow by Jane Walsh. Former rival debutantes have a second chance at love after fifteen years apart when a spinster persuades her ex-lover to help save her family business. (978-1-63679-747-2)

The Naked Truth by Sandy Lowe. How far are Rowan and Genevieve willing to go and how much will they risk to make their most captivating and forbidden fantasies a reality? (978-1-63679-426-6)

The Roommate by Claire Forsythe. Jess Black's boyfriend is handsome and successful. That's why it comes as a shock when she meets a woman on the train who makes her pulse race. (978-1-63679-757-1)

Close to Home by Allisa Bahney. Eli Thomas has to decide if avoiding her hometown forever is worth losing the people who used to mean the most to her, especially Aracely Hernandez, the girl who got away. (978-1-63679-661-1)

Golden Girl by Julie Tizard. In 1993, "Don't ask, don't tell" forces everyone to lie, but Air Force nurse Lt. Sofia Sanchez and injured instructor pilot Lt. Gillian Guthman have to risk telling each other the truth in order to fly and survive. (978-1-63679-751-9)

Innis Harbor by Patricia Evans. When Amir Farzaneh meets and falls in love with Loch, a dark secret lurking in her past reappears, threatening the happiness she'd just started to believe could be hers. (978-1-63679-781-6)

The Blessed by Anne Shade. Layla and Suri are brought together by fate to defeat the darkness threatening to tear their world apart. What they don't expect to discover is a love that might set them free. (978-1-63679-715-1)

The Guardians by Sheri Lewis Wohl. Dogs, devotion, and determination are all that stand between darkness and light. (978-1-63679-681-9)

The Mogul Meets Her Match by Julia Underwood. When CEO Claire Beauchamp goes undercover as a customer of Abby Pita's café to help seal a deal that will solidify her career, she doesn't expect to be so drawn to her. When the truth is revealed, will she break Abby's heart? (978-1-63679-784-7)

Trial Run by Carsen Taite. When Reggie Knoll and Brooke Dawson wind up serving on a jury together, their one task—reaching a unanimous verdict—is derailed by the fiery clash of their personalities, the intensity of their attraction, and a secret that could threaten Brooke's life. (978-1-63555-865-4)

Waterlogged by Nance Sparks. When conservation warden Jordan Pearce discovers a body floating in the flowage, the serenity of the Northwoods is rocked. (978-1-63679-699-4)